PRAISE FO

Jacqueline Winspear's MAIS

D1284703

"Compelling." —*People* (3½ out of 4 stars)

"Sometimes when you adore a series, you're terrified to crack open the next installment, fearing disappointment. Fortunately, Jacqueline Winspear's fans can rest easy. Her new Maisie Dobbs mystery, *The Mapping of Love and Death*, the seventh in the series, is excellent. . . . As Dobbs unravels the dead soldier's past, her creator brings the story to a satisfying conclusion. But the real pleasure is Winspear's insight into human beings and history." —Deirdre Donahue, *USA Today*

"Winspear surpasses herself in this absorbing novel."
—Marilyn Stasio, *New York Times Book Review*

"England between the wars is a milieu custom-made for fertile storytelling, and an excellent example is *The Mapping of Love and Death*. . . . Here, author Jacqueline Winspear invents a task worthy of the capable Dobbs's skills." —Adam Woog, *Seattle Times*

"Endearing. . . . As often in this winning series, the action builds to a somewhat sad if satisfying conclusion."
—*Publishers Weekly* (starred review)

"An engaging plot coupled with captivating characters makes this the best Dobbs novel to date." —*Library Journal*

"Maisie Dobbs, the brave, insightful, and compassionate heroine of Jacqueline Winspear's mystery series, has a lock on the hearts of readers." —Jim Higgins, *Milwaukee Journal Sentinel*

"The hunt gets the pulse racing, but the real draw is Maisie herself."
—Ellen Shapiro, *People*

"Well-crafted and well worth reading." —*Kirkus Reviews*

"The book's puzzle is challenging, but what charms most is Dobbs herself: a woman 'not as adept in her personal life as she was in her professional domain,' and all the more engaging for that."
—Tom Nolan, *Wall Street Journal*

"Maisie Dobbs is a revelation." —Alexander McCall Smith

"[Maisie Dobbs is] a smart, pragmatic private investigator and psychologist with extraordinary empathic sensitivity. . . . Every page of this novel is dense with affectionately rendered period detail. Winspear deftly intertwines multiple story lines. The tale becomes increasingly gripping as the novel progresses toward a truly moving ending."
—*Boston Globe*

"Winspear does her usual superb job of portraying London between the world wars." —*Publishers Weekly*

"Winspear's lively and graceful prose, strong sense of time and place, and her ability to create believable and sympathetic characters make the book a joy to read." —*Denver Post*

"An outstanding historical series." —Marilyn Stasio, *New York Times*

"Those unfamiliar with the Maisie Dobbs series are best advised to start here and work their way backward. . . . *An Incomplete Revenge* shows Maisie at the top of her detecting form." —*Newsday*

"When people ask me to recommend an author, one name consistently comes to mind: Jacqueline Winspear."

—Deirdre Donahue, *USA Today*

"What Jacqueline Winspear does to keep her series about the astonishing Maisie Dobbs alive and as fresh as new paint is impressive."

—*Chicago Tribune*

"Maisie Dobbs, Winspear's brilliant psychological investigator, returns for her fourth adventure. . . . Definitely more of apolitical and psychological read than a simple whodunit."

—*Daily News*

"Maisie's most assured outing to date."

—David Lazarus, *San Francisco Chronicle*

"A detective series to savor."

—Johanna McGeary, *Time*

"For readers yearning for the calm and insightful intelligence of a main character like P. D. James's Cordelia Gray, Maisie Dobbs is spot on."

—Hallie Ephron, *Boston Globe*

"A heroine to cherish."

—Marilyn Stasio, *New York Times Book Review*

"As with Winspear's first novel, *Maisie Dobbs*, much of the pleasure of being with Maisie lies in the underlying class conflict that permeates her world."

—David Lazarus, *San Francisco Chronicle*

"Succeeds both as a suspenseful mystery and as a picture of a time and place."

—Judith Maas, *Boston Globe*

"A quirky literary creation. If you cross-pollinated Vera Brittain's classic World War I memoir, *Testament of Youth*, with Dorothy Sayers's Harriet Vane mysteries and a dash of the old PBS series *Upstairs, Downstairs*, you'd approximate the peculiar range of topics and tones within this novel." —Maureen Corrigan, *Fresh Air*

"[Catches] the sorrow of a lost generation in the character of one exceptional woman." —*Chicago Tribune*

"A winning character about whom readers will want to read more."
—Associated Press

THE MAPPING OF LOVE AND DEATH

ALSO BY JACQUELINE WINSPEAR

Maisie Dobbs

Birds of a Feather

Pardonable Lies

Messenger of Truth

An Incomplete Revenge

Among the Mad

HARPER PERENNIAL

NEW YORK • LONDON • TORONTO • SYDNEY • NEW DELHI • AUCKLAND

THE MAPPING OF LOVE AND DEATH

A Maisie Dobbs Novel

JACQUELINE WINSPEAR

HARPER PERENNIAL

A hardcover edition of this book was published in 2010 by
HarperCollins Publishers.

P.S.™ is a trademark of HarperCollins Publishers.

THE MAPPING OF LOVE AND DEATH. Copyright © 2010 by Jacqueline Winspear. All rights reserved. Printed in the United States of America. No part of this book may be used or reproduced in any manner whatsoever without written permission except in the case of brief quotations embodied in critical articles and reviews. For information, address HarperCollins Publishers, 195 Broadway, New York, NY 10007.

HarperCollins books may be purchased for educational, business, or sales promotional use. For information, please e-mail the Special Markets Department at SPsales@harpercollins.com.

FIRST HARPER PERENNIAL EDITION PUBLISHED 2011.

Designed by Jennifer Ann Daddio / Bookmark Design & Media Inc.

The Library of Congress has catalogued the hardcover edition as follows:
Winspear, Jacqueline.
The mapping of love and death : a Maisie Dobbs novel / Jacqueline Winspear.—1st ed.
p. cm.
ISBN 978-0-06-172766-5
1. Dobbs, Maisie (Fictitious character)—Fiction. 2. Women private investigators—England—Fiction. 3. World War, 1914–1918—England—Fiction. 4. Cartographers—Fiction. 5. London (England)—Fiction. I. Title.
PR6123.I575 M37 2010
823'.92 22 2009049970

ISBN 978-0-06-172768-9 (pbk.)

19 ID/LSC 20 19 18 17

R0459376478

For John

"The Bluesman"

With my love

There is a great deal of unmapped country within us which would have to be taken into account in an explanation of our gusts and storms.

—GEORGE ELIOT, *DANIEL DERONDA*

War is like love; it always finds a way.

—BERTOLT BRECHT

PROLOGUE

The Santa Ynez Valley, California, August 1914

Michael Clifton stood on a hill burnished gold in the summer sun and, hands on hips, closed his eyes. The landscape before him had been scored into his mind's eye, and an onlooker might have noticed his chin move as he traced the pitch and curve of the hills, the lines of the valley, places where water ran in winter, gullies where the ground underfoot might become soft and rises where the rock would never yield to a pick. Michael could see only colored lines now, with swirls and circles close together where the peaks rose, and broad sweeps of fine ink where foothills gave way to flat land. Yes, this was the place. He had wired his mother a month earlier, asking her to cosign a document releasing the funds held in trust for him from his maternal grandfather's will. Each of the Clifton offspring had received a tidy sum. His two sisters had set money aside for their own children and together had indulged in a little investing in land, while his older brother had rolled the bequest into an impressive property. Now it was his turn and, following the example set by his siblings, he had taken his father's advice to heart: "Land is where to put your money. And if it's good land, you'll get your money back time and time again." Edward Clifton would be pleased when he saw the maps, would slap him on the back. *Well done, son. Well done. Didn't I always say you had the nose? Didn't I, Martha? Didn't I, Teddy?* And his brother would shake his hand, perhaps add a friendly punch to the shoulder. *Good for you, little brother.* And there would be no rancor, no slight because he had acted alone, only familial joy because he had succeeded.

Soon, perhaps early next year, a sign bearing the Clifton name would be set above the opening to a new trail into the valley, and travelers passing on the old stage road would assume that the famous company founded some forty years ago by Edward Clifton—a young Englishman who was still in his teens when he'd disembarked from a ship in New York in search of his fortune—was drilling for oil. But they would be wrong, for this Clifton was the youngest son, and this was his land, his oil.

Michael opened his eyes, gazed at the gold and green vista a few moments longer, and began packing away his equipment in a heavy canvas bag. One by one he took each piece and wrapped it carefully with linen and sackcloth: an octant, a graphometer, the surveyor's compass—a gift from his parents when he completed his studies—a waywiser, theodolite, and tripod. Using these tools attached him to the past, like a plumb line drawn across time connecting him to early mapmakers with that same curiosity. He'd always felt so young—the youngest son of a man who came to a young country in his youth. His roots were fresh, new, and in his love of the land—especially this very primitive land shaped by the power of nature—he felt those roots entrench into ancient soil.

He loaded the bag onto the back of a mule-drawn cart, the Mexican driver waiting patiently while he leapt up to sit on the floor and prepared to leave, his legs dangling down as he reached across for his stationery box. He opened the wooden box, checked that he had collected all his pens, sturdy German writing instruments each filled with a different colored ink. He liked the heft of the pens, the flow of ink, the narrow threads of color that issued from the pinlike point onto the heavy mapping paper. Michael Clifton might sometimes have been thought an impulsive young man anxious to make his mark, but he knew his business and he was nothing if not a diligent cartographer.

In Santa Ynez, Michael transferred his equipment and personal effects to a larger carriage for the journey into Santa Barbara. From there he could telegraph his father that he was on his way, but would save the good news for later, when he was home. He wanted to see the look on Edward Clifton's face when he told him of his discovery, he wanted to experience the joy and pride in person. For now he would check into The Arlington Hotel—the Clifton name alone meant a suite would be made available—bathe the dust from his skin, and then he would buy himself the biggest steak he could find in town. He might walk along the beach, smell that crisp Pacific air once more before boarding a California Pacific train bound for San Francisco tomorrow, and from there to the East Coast along the transcontinental railroad. Then, before you knew it, he would be home. But he would return soon to this place. Yes, he would be back—and this new Clifton Corporation would be his.

It was the newsboy outside the hotel who caught his attention.

"Read all about it. Read all about it. Britain goes to war! Kaiser to fight whole world. Read all about it."

Pulling a handful of coins from his pocket, Michael bought a newspaper and began reading as he made his way through the hotel foyer. He signed the guest register, only marginally aware of what he was writing, and where. He nodded upon receiving the key to his rooms, and continued reading as the bellhop struggled with his belongings. Once in the suite, he slumped down in a chair, looking up only to press a few cents into the boy's palm.

It had come as no surprise to his family that Michael Clifton chose to become a cartographer. He had loved maps since childhood, drawn to the mystery of lands far away, fascinated by the names of places and the promise he saw held within a map. "You always know where you are with a map," he had told his parents, while persuading them of his choice of profession. "And if you know where you are, why, you're more likely to be brave, to have an adventure, to search beyond where everyone else is looking. Think of what I could do for the company!" His father had laughed, seeing through the subtle entreaty. Yet Michael was right—it had been good for the company, to have a man in the family business who could read the land. You knew where you were with family, and as Edward had told his children time and again, you knew where your money was when it was in land. But what Michael never even tried to explain was the sense of wonder that came with a map, for each one told a story, and he, the surveyor and cartographer, was the storyteller, the translator, the guide to places a person might never otherwise see. He could tame a forest, prairie, or wilderness with a few strokes of his pen. And he had a knack for finding nature's buried treasures.

It had taken no time at all for Michael to make his decision. Before leaving his rooms he copied precise details from the maps and land documents into a small leather-bound notebook, adding sketches carefully marking those places where drilling should begin. That the valley held oil deposits was without question—William Orcutt, the surveyor for Union Oil, had the coast and much of the valley all but sewn up. Yet to know exactly where to tap into the riches took an expert eye. Some said you had to touch the land to know, that a man who knew where to sink his shovel could hear oil rumbling in the earth.

His task complete, and with the series of maps rolled and placed in a leather tube along with the original title documents to the land—his land—he went directly to the Central Bank of California on State Street, where he left the leather tube in a safe deposit box, withdrew a portion of the funds held in his name at the bank, and then made his way to the railroad station, where he purchased a ticket to Boston via San Francisco and New York. He left the office, then stopped short in the street before returning to the ticket counter, whereupon he informed the clerk that he had changed his mind, and would go only as far as New York. The clerk grumbled, but asked no questions as he made out the new ticket. From New York, Michael planned to sail to England as soon as he could secure a passage—and it was surprising the speed with which anything could be reserved, booked, obtained, and acquired when you were a Clifton.

It was only right that he go, because for his family, England was the old country. He'd read that other boys were going over, boys like him who had limey blood in their veins. Of course, he suspected they probably wouldn't let him bear arms, being an American by birth, but he had a profession, and he was only too aware that in wartime armies needed to know where they were going, needed to know the lie of the land. He would wire his family and let them know of his decision just before he sailed. His father might argue, but he would also be proud that his son was going to fight for the country he'd left a lifetime ago. And his maps of the valley and the deed to his land would be safe until he returned; after all, according to reports, the war in Europe would be over by Christmas. Thus, by the time a tall spruce tree was alive with baubles, tinsel, and lights in the window of the grand house on Boston's Beacon Hill, he'd be home.

ONE

Fitzroy Square, London, April 1932

"Would you believe it, Billy—three years and we're still in business!" Maisie Dobbs turned away from the floor-to-ceiling window, where she had been watching gray, rain-filled clouds lumbering across an otherwise springlike sky. She smiled and sat down at the table where she and her assistant, Billy Beale, had been working.

Billy ran his fingers through his hair. "And we've a few more clients on the books than we expected in January."

Maisie leaned back in her chair. "We've been lucky, there's no doubt about that. I just hope it continues throughout the year."

"Perhaps the Americans we're seeing this morning have a few friends over here who might need your services," said Billy. "I mean, that's how almost all the work comes in, isn't it? Through clients who were satisfied with what you did for them."

"Speaking of the Americans, I want to read that letter once more before they arrive." Maisie stood up and walked across the room to her desk. She took her seat and leaned forward, her forearms resting on the blotting pad. "Apparently they're very good people, quite down to earth, but they'll be expecting me to be completely prepared for the appointment, especially with such a strong personal reference from Dr. Hayden."

She reached for a manila folder with the words "Clifton, Edward and Martha" inscribed along one side, and took out a well-thumbed letter from Dr. Charles Hayden. Maisie had been introduced to the eminent American surgeon by Simon Lynch, a captain in the army medical corps, during the war. At the time Dr. Hayden was a volunteer with a medical contingent from the Massachusetts General Hospital. They had corresponded since the war, and now he wrote in response to a letter from Maisie.

Please do not apologize for the delay in letting me know that Simon has passed away. Though my first concern is always for my patients, in my dealings with families of the sick and dying, I know the passage of grief is a difficult one to navigate, so please do not concern yourself that you should have written sooner. You have been in Pauline's and my thoughts so often over the years, especially given Simon's medical circumstances. As a doctor, I confess, I was amazed at the man's continued physical resilience, when there was no obvious function in his mind.

He continued with reminiscences of times spent with Simon, and followed with news of his family. Then the letter took a different tack.

Maisie, I hope you don't mind, but I have taken the liberty of referring a friend to you. He and his wife are more than willing to pay for your professional services, and they are in any case planning to sail for France in late March, then will travel on to England in April. I know they will be in touch and you will want to hear the story straight from the horse's mouth. But let me fill you in on what I know so that you might be prepared for what's in store.

I met the Cliftons though their son-in-law, Bradley Marchant. He's married to their eldest daughter, Meg, and is one of my colleagues here at the hospital. We went to their wedding at the family vacation home on Cape Cod, and I'm a godfather to their eldest. I don't know if you need all this detail, but I thought I should let you know anyway.

Edward Clifton is an Englishman by birth. He came over here when he was about eighteen, nineteen, something like that. He wasn't exactly penniless, but he knew how to work—and to make something of himself, he had to work hard. He turned his hand to anything he could, then started putting money into land. Bradley said that acquiring land was an obsession with Edward when he was younger. I guess it's something about coming from over there and starting again in a new country—he needed to own a part of it, stake his claim. From land he moved into building and founded a construction company, then started investing in stocks; all tied to the land in some way. I'll cut to the chase here, and say that by the time he was thirty, Edward Clifton was very, very wealthy. Then he met Martha Stanbourne—she's from an important family, it's said their ancestors came to America on the Mayflower. *The Stanbournes are what we call "Boston Brahmins" over here. They married—there's no doubt it was a love match—and had four children. There's Edward Jr. (Teddy), then Margaret and Anna, and bringing up the rear, Michael. Couldn't have met a nicer family.*

Maisie paused. When she had first read the letter, as soon as she saw the word *Michael* the thought had crossed her mind: That's the one. It's Michael who has caused them pain. For there was no doubt in her mind, even in reading a few paragraphs, that the Cliftons were in some emotional turmoil. Why else would they need her services?

In August 1914, Michael was out in California—he was a mapmaker, surveyor of some sort. Apparently he'd bought a tract of land with money left to him by Martha's father. It would have been a lot of money, and according to Bradley, there's still plenty held in trust. He was very excited about the purchase, and was due to come back to Boston—couldn't wait to see his parents to tell them all about it. Then I guess you could say he crossed paths with fate when he saw the news about war in Belgium. He changed his plans at the last minute and sailed for Europe. Edward will fill you in on the details, but Michael enlisted in England and was attached to a military cartography unit—no doubt if it wasn't for his profession he would have been sent packing back to Boston.

"Cuppa, Miss, before they get here?"

Maisie glanced at the clock. "Oh yes, please. They're bound to be shocked if they see me drinking out of my old army mug. Americans always expect to see the English sipping tea from fine bone china." She went back to the letter.

Michael was listed as missing in early 1916. In January a farmer working the land (somewhere in the Somme Valley) put his plough into a gully, and when he and some other men were digging it out, the ground started to fall away and the bodies of several British soldiers were found. Michael was identified by his tags. By now you're probably wondering why the Cliftons need to see someone like you. Apparently the ground gave way to a dugout and a series of what you could only describe as rooms—so well made, the Brits might have been occupying an old German trench. It was there that the soldiers' belongings were found. They were members of a surveying team. Michael's journal was discovered, along with other personal effects. Don't ask me how the Cliftons managed to get their hands on the journal. You know the soldiers weren't allowed to keep any sort of diary, so it's a wonder it wasn't retained by the authorities. It's now with Edward and Martha, along with a collection of letters. His wallet was tucked in his jacket pocket, and apparently his surveying compass and other tools he'd taken with him were also returned to the family. Now, the reason they want to see you is this: the letters were from a woman, they think an English woman, and they want to find her. That's everything I know, but at least you'll be prepared when they arrive.

Please keep in touch, Maisie. Pauline sends her love—perhaps you girls will have a chance to meet one day.

It was signed with a flourish: "Charles."

"There you are, Miss. Nice cuppa the old char."

"Lovely—thank you, Billy." Maisie pushed back her chair, leaving the letter open on the table as she looked out upon the square again. She cupped her hands around the chipped enamel mug. "I thought we were in for a warm spring, but look at that rain."

"Coming down cats and dogs, ain't it?" Billy sipped his tea and reached for the letter. "You know what I reckon happened to this here Michael Clifton?" Billy continued without waiting for an answer. "I reckon he heard about the war starting and came over all patriotic for the half of him that was British. That and the fact that something gets into lads when a war starts. Makes them get all mannish, as if they can't wait to get on with getting old. Look at me and my brother—and him buried over there."

Maisie nodded. "I know—though it's true to say that you and your brother were also pushed by public opinion. I remember Charles—Dr. Hayden—saying that in America in 1914 it was different. There were a lot of people who had just emigrated from Germany, so there was a significant allegiance to the Kaiser at first. But thank heavens for the American doctors and nurses who volunteered when war broke out; they saved a great many lives."

"So, what do you think of this, Miss?" He held up the letter.

"Let's see what the Cliftons have to say—they'll be here in a minute. But I don't think it has anything to do with money. If they want to find that woman, it's because there's a link to Michael. The question is, what kind of link? It could be something as simple as wanting to speak to someone who knew their son at a time when he was at a great distance from them—it appears they were a close family. But my sense is that it's more than that." Maisie closed her eyes. "They want to unlock some door to the past, I would say. And they have reason to believe this woman holds the key."

The bell above the door began to ring.

"That must be them. Go on, Billy, go and let them in while I put these few things away."

Maisie turned up the jets on the gas fire and pulled four chairs closer, so that the room might be more welcoming when the new clients entered. She heard their footsteps on the stairs, and Billy asking how they were liking England and if they had had a good crossing from France. The door opened, and Maisie walked towards Edward and Martha Clifton, extending her hand to welcome them into the room.

"How lovely to meet you, Mr. and Mrs. Clifton. May I take your coats?"

Maisie judged Edward Clifton to be about seventy-seven or seventy-eight, probably a little older than her father. He was a man of average height, not stooped, but one who seemed ill at ease with the restricted movement that came with age. He wore a black woolen overcoat and black homburg, which he removed as he stepped into the office. His suit was of a deep slate gray fabric, a color matching the silk tie and the kerchief in his pocket. Martha Clifton—Maisie suspected she might be some ten years younger than her husband—removed a cashmere coat trimmed with fur. She was wearing a stylish ensemble of light tweed in which mauves were blended with earthen colors perhaps more suited to autumn than spring. Her cloche accentuated deep-set brown eyes, around which the skin was lined, gathering in gentle ripples when Maisie took her hand, and she smiled in return. Maisie could imagine that smile becoming broad upon greeting her children and grandchildren, and an image came to mind of her eyes filled with tears when she was reminded of her youngest son, Michael.

When her guests were settled, Maisie took the seat closest to her desk, while Billy handed cups of tea to Edward and Martha, and in those precious seconds without conversation, she was able to gauge their mood and feelings towards each other. They were, as might be imagined, somewhat tense, though Maisie could detect a connection between them that she found rare in a man and wife of their generation. They leaned towards each other in the way that a pair of ancient oaks might seem as one, their branches laced together as the years passed. Yet at the same time there was an independence and, Maisie thought, profound respect. She could see that there had been no secrets in the household, and decisions had never been made alone, until the day Michael left for England.

"Now, perhaps you could tell me what it is you would like to discuss with me, and how you think I might be able to help you." She was careful not to mention Charles Hayden's letter, as she wanted to hear the story from the couple.

"Well—" Edward Clifton looked at his wife, and reached for her hand, which she had already moved towards his. "Our son, who was an American citizen, came to England in '14 to join up." He cleared his throat. His voice was deep, and though one could not mistake the

Englishman in his accent, there was a slower rhythm to his speech, a cadence distinguishing him as one who had gone away and would never again be at ease in the country of his birth. "He decided not to tell us until just before he sailed." He glanced at his wife again. Martha Clifton nodded for him to continue. "Michael's mother and I, well, we thought he'd be turned away and shipped right back home, but that was not to be, given his profession."

"Which was?"

"Michael was a cartographer. He had been working for one of the family companies as a surveyor, assessing land prior to purchase."

"And is that what he was doing before he enlisted for service in England?"

"Yes—and no."

Maisie looked at Martha, who had leaned forward as she spoke. "Each of our children has money left in trust by my father. The trust stipulated that until they reached the age of thirty, I had to cosign transfer of funds from the trust. From the time he was in his teens, Michael had been fascinated by California. He said there was so much there for a young man, that he wanted to just go see what it was all about. Then, a month before he left to return to Boston, he wired me and asked for a significant sum to be transferred into an account in Santa Barbara—it's a little town along the coast."

"And you agreed?"

"It was his money. He was a man—twenty-three at the time. And both his father and I felt that if he lost the money, well, it represented an investment on a lesson that would stand him in good stead."

Maisie nodded. "And before I go on—may I ask how you felt about Michael making a decision that was not on behalf of the family business?"

"We were all for it," said Edward. He paused to clear his throat. "Let me explain. My great-grandfather was a shoemaker who built a successful business, which was in turn taken over by my grandfather, then my father. I was the only male in my generation, and from early childhood I was told that I was in line to take over the business. It was drummed into me time and time again." He smiled and looked at his wife. "And you know something, Miss Dobbs? I couldn't stand it. I hated the smell of the factories, the untreated leather, the whale oil when it was delivered, the tannery. I detested the shoe business and would have walked around in rubber boots to make my point. I had no mind to go into that company, and in the end, I suppose you could say I ran away. I had a bit of money of my own—we weren't poor, but I had to earn every penny—and America beckoned. Same thing happened in Martha's family, to her brothers; they were expected to join a family business without consideration of what they might have wanted. In my case, my father and mother disowned me, my letters were returned, and I never spoke to my family again—which grieves me to this day. So, with that in mind, my corporation is set up to be run independently. We never wanted our children to feel beholden to us. If they had it in them to join the company—fine. But if not, we still wanted them to sit at the table with us for Thanksgiving dinner without an argument about it. As it happens, Teddy—our eldest son—and our daughter Anna's husband both work for the corporation. Michael was just doing what I had done years before. He was breaking away, and we wanted to make it easy for him to come home again, always."

Maisie nodded. "Do you know why he wanted the money?"

"There's a tract of land in his name in an area known as Santa Ynez—that's with a *y*. It's a Spanish name. We haven't been there, but Teddy went out in '21, and said it was just the sort of place that Michael would have loved."

"What happened to the land?"

"There are legal and probate problems remaining. We have no proof of title, no bill of sale. Michael paid in cash—and of course, he was listed as missing." Clifton preempted Maisie's next question. "Yes, time has passed, and we should have had no difficulty in making the case that Michael died in the war, but gaining access to the land has been difficult. The area is awash with oil companies, and even though we've pressed the point that Michael was killed in the war, the court ruled that Michael's intentions were not known, and there might be other claimants—and believe me, there have been a few because it's valuable land, but we've managed so far to keep it all from being settled, pending the discovery of proof." He paused and shook his head. "And you have to remember, though we're here in 1932, when Michael first went out to California, there was still more than a hint of the Wild West about it. Well, that's how it seemed to East Coasters like Martha and me."

"I can see this must be very troublesome for you, on top of losing your son," said Maisie. "But how can I help you?"

Martha Clifton took her husband's hand in both her own. "We have a batch of quite a few letters. Given that they were buried for years, they are in fair condition due to the waxed paper and rubber cloth Michael had used to wrap them. They were clearly of some value to our son, yet we could not bring ourselves to read them." She looked down at her hands, then began to turn her wedding and engagement rings around and around, lifting them above the first bone in her slender finger, then pushing them back down again. She looked up. "I don't want to pry into my son's past, but to me the hand seems to be that of a woman, perhaps someone Michael loved, and I would like to know who she is. I—"

"I understand," said Maisie, her voice soft. She turned to Edward Clifton. "Do you have anything else?"

Clifton reached into the inside pocket of his overcoat. "I have a journal, a diary kept by Michael. Again, some of the pages are fused with damp, and foxed with age, but we have read a few paragraphs." He paused as he handed the brown-paper-wrapped book to Maisie, who reached forward to take the package from him.

"So, am I to take it that you would like me to read the letters and the diary, that you wish me to identify the letter writer, and—" She looked from Clifton to his wife. "Am I right to assume that you would like me to try to find the person?"

Martha Clifton smiled, though her eyes had filled with tears. "Yes, yes, please, Miss Dobbs. We can help a little, because we've already placed an advertisement in several British newspapers, and we've received a number of replies; you see, though we didn't read Michael's letters, we opened one or two to see if there was an address or full name—but there was nothing to identify the writer. In the advertisement, we said we would like to hear from a woman who had known Michael Clifton, of Boston in the United States, in the war."

Edward Clifton cleared his throat and began to speak again. "And I thought that, given your background, you might want to see this document, which we received from the French authorities." He held out a brown envelope towards Maisie. As she began to draw out the pages, Clifton continued. "It's a report from the doctor who examined our son's remains. A postmortem of sorts. Charles has seen the report, and we've talked about it."

"And I said I would rather not read it," Martha Clifton interjected.

"Yes, I understand." Maisie began to scan the page. She made no comment, but nodded as she reached the end of each paragraph. She could feel Edward Clifton's gaze upon her, and when she looked up she knew that in the brief meeting of their eyes there was an understanding. She knew why he had come to her, and that the truth of Michael Clifton's death had been kept from his mother. And she could understand how a French doctor—possibly tired, probably weary of another aging corpse brought from the battle-scarred land upon which so many had died—had missed what an eminent Boston surgeon, one who himself had served in that same war, had seen when he read the report.

"It all looks fairly straightforward, but I would like to keep it here, if I may."

"Of course." Clifton looked at his wife and smiled, as if to assure her that all would be well now and that they had made the right decision in seeking the help of this British investigator. "We'll have the letters sent over to you as soon as we get back to our hotel—we're staying at the Dorchester."

"And we'll send some photographs of Michael." Martha Clifton seemed to press back tears as she spoke. "I'd like you to know what he was like."

"Thank you, a photograph would be most useful, though I have a picture of Michael in my mind already. You must have been very proud of him."

"We were. And we loved him so very much, Miss Dobbs." Edward Clifton reached into his pocket once again and drew out another envelope. "Your advance, per our correspondence."

Billy escorted the couple downstairs to the front door, and helped them into the motor car waiting outside. Maisie looked down from the window and watched as they drove away, Billy waving them off as if bidding farewell to a respected uncle and aunt. She heard him slam the door, then make his way upstairs to the office.

"Brrr, still nippy out there, Miss." He sat down at the table and reached for the jar of colored pencils to begin work.

"Yes. Yes, it is." Maisie remained at the window, still clutching Michael Clifton's journal and the envelope containing the postmortem report.

"Should be an easy one, eh? We'll get the old letters, warm 'em up nice and slow, find out who the writer is, and Bob's your uncle. We'll find Michael Clifton's lady friend, and there we are. Job done."

Maisie turned and pulled back a chair to sit down opposite Billy. "Not quite."

"What do you mean?"

"Unless I am much mistaken, Michael Clifton was not killed by the shell that took the lives of his fellow men. He was murdered."

TWO

Why do you think Dr. Hayden didn't say something in his letter, about that postmortem report?" Billy stood in front of Maisie's desk, his arms folded. "I mean, it takes you by surprise, reading that sort of thing."

"In some ways I can see why he made no mention of it. He might not have wanted to influence me—he saw an anomaly and wanted me to spot it myself, without encouragement or direction." Maisie began to gather her belongings, checked a manila folder that she placed in her document case, and glanced at the clock on the mantelpiece before turning back to Billy. "Have you ever been on the street and seen someone looking up into the sky? Next thing you know, other people are looking up, and before long everyone reckons they've seen something. Well, independently, both Dr. Hayden and I spotted commentary regarding damage to the skull and concluded that it was not in keeping with other wounds. It was the sort of injury more likely to be found in a case of attack with a heavy, blunt object, and the notes suggest to me that there is room for investigation."

"I see what you mean, Miss."

Maisie picked up the telephone receiver, but did not dial. "The first thing I want to do is to show the report to Maurice. I want to hear what he has to say about it. Now, a parcel will probably arrive from the Cliftons in an hour or so—I am sure they will lose no time in sending a messenger with the letters and other items of interest. Would you stay until it arrives?"

"Of course, Miss." Billy fingered the edge of the case map, the offcut of plain wallpaper where all evidence, thoughts, hunches, and observations on any given case were noted using colored pencils. Some words were written in capital letters, others with a star next to them. Then clues were linked this way and that, as if the person creating the map were trying different pieces in a jigsaw puzzle to see if they might fit.

Maisie replaced the telephone receiver. "Is everything all right, Billy?"

"Y-yes, of course. Nothing wrong."

"Do you need to leave early?"

"No, no, it's not that."

Maisie stepped towards the table and sat down opposite her assistant. "Doreen's coming home soon, isn't she?"

Billy nodded and continued to rub the paper between thumb and forefinger.

"It's been a long time since she went away. But she's done well of late, during her weekend visits home, hasn't she?"

"Very well, all things considered."

"It's natural to be worried, Billy. You've all got to get used to living together again, and there isn't exactly a book to guide you."

Billy leaned forward and put his head in his hands. Maisie could see he was afraid.

"That doctor, the one you sent us to—Dr. Masters—said that once the anniversary of our Lizzie's passing had come and gone, she'd make better progress. And she has. It was as if there was a nasty old abscess full of memories in her head that had to open up. But that don't stop me feeling two things at once. On one hand, I'm pleased as punch that she'll be back with us, and on the other, I'm worried to the bone for our boys. They've done well, Miss. Her goings-on before she was taken away had made them like little ghosts around the house, never knowing what was going to happen next. They didn't know whether she'd be all sunshine and light, or whether she'd be ready to give them a stripe across the backs of their legs. They want their mum to come home, but I can see they're dreading it too."

Maisie did not respond at once, but allowed silence to follow Billy's confession. To speak with immediacy would suggest his words had no import, that such fears were unfounded. And he had good cause to be concerned.

"Those feelings are to be expected." When she spoke, it was with tenderness in her voice. "You and the boys have been on your own for four months, and they've become accustomed to a new rhythm to their days, and your mother is very good with them—solid as a rock, isn't she? Now you have to bring Doreen into your circle and welcome her home—which is so hard when you have such troubling memories of her before she was committed. Just take each day as it comes, Billy. Give Doreen time to negotiate her own path back into the fold—and remember, she's been in a place where she's found the healing she needed, so she must be scared too."

"It's not as if you can all talk about it, is it? I mean, you've just got to get on with it, like they say."

Maisie took a deep breath. "Don't be afraid to talk to each other. Talk to the boys before Doreen gets home, and talk to Doreen. After something like this happens, things rarely go back to the way they were before, but it doesn't mean it's all bad. Take it as it comes. Slowly. You're on fresh ground, Billy, so give yourself a chance to see the road ahead, and be ready to change course."

Billy scratched his head. "I reckon I can see what you mean, Miss. Canada was the only place I'd had my sights on for years. All I wanted to do was to get us all out and emigrate, just like my mate did with his family. But now Doreen's got to get back to her old self, and I've got to get more money put away before we can make a move anywhere." He sighed. "And London might be my home, and I might be Shoreditch born and bred, but now all I can see is a big ship going to Canada and all of us on it."

A bell ringing above the door indicated the arrival of a visitor.

"I bet that's the messenger from the Cliftons. Bring up the parcel, and then you go on home, Billy. You've got a lot to do before Friday, so you'd best be off."

Billy left the office and returned with a brown-paper-wrapped box. "Here it is, Miss." He placed the package on Maisie's desk. "I reckon you won't be in until tomorrow afternoon, if you're going down to see Dr. Blanche."

"Probably around two tomorrow. I just have to nip home to pack my case, and I'll be off down to Chelstone. The letters have to be warmed and opened very carefully. I know they may seem dry, having been out of the ground for a few months, but that kind of damp fuses the paper, and very hot air can cause the paper to crumble. I'll take them home and leave them near the radiator. Then we'll see what we can do. Oh, and in the meantime, could you start going through the list of respondents to the advertisement? Their letters should be in the parcel. We need to separate the wheat from the chaff."

"How do I know what's what?"

"Good question. Trust your instinct. Some stories will obviously take wide turns, and can be easily identified as the work of rogue claimants; others may be sob stories. Don't be taken in by the sad tales of lost love, but look for a ring of authenticity. I have a feeling that if Michael Clifton's girl saw and responded to the advertisement, she would have taken care to mention something personal to identify her knowledge of him—though we will need the Cliftons' help to confirm such a marker." Maisie gathered her belongings and paused at the door. "And I think that Michael's lady friend might offer more than solace to his parents. She might well hold the key to the identity of the person who took his life."

Maisie arrived at her flat in Pimlico and went straight to the radiator in the sitting room, where she pressed her hands to the thick iron pipes. They were lukewarm, a perfect temperature to dry the recently unearthed papers. The box sent from the Cliftons contained several items, including three smaller packages, each wrapped with brown paper and tied with string. One was marked "Letters from Claimants" and had been left with Billy to go through. The second was marked "Letters to Michael, found with his belongings," and it was this package that Maisie now began to unwrap, without first even removing her coat. She had planned to pack with haste and drive straight to Chelstone, but now wavered, the letters piquing her curiosity.

Maisie had read many letters during the course of her work. A client might bring a crumpled missive found in the pocket of a husband believed to be unfaithful, or a distraught caller might present her with a collection of letters from a relative, communication he hoped might prove wrongful omission from a will. Letters were submitted to prove innocence and guilt, to indicate intentions, whether untoward or kindly. And where letters were written over the course of some months or years, Maisie could follow the passage of a relationship between writer and recipient, could read between the lines and could intuit what the recipient might have penned in return. A collection of letters offered a glimpse across the landscape of human connection at a given time. But the letters written to Michael Clifton offered a seed of fascination for her even before she pulled the string and began to unwrap the paper, for they were written from the heart by a girl to her love—and Maisie had once been a girl in love, in wartime.

Sitting at the table, Maisie drew back the brown paper to reveal the collection of letters, still in their original envelopes, unopened since Michael Clifton himself had received each letter. In the third package, several photographs of Michael showed him to be a young man of some height, strong across the shoulders, a confidence to his stance. His hair was fair, short and combed back, though in one photograph it appeared as if the wind had caught him unawares, and a lock of hair had fallen into his eyes—in that image he reminded her of Andrew Dene, with whom she had walked out some eighteen months earlier. She had ended the relationship, but heard that he had since married the daughter of a local landowner.

Maisie brought her attention back to Michael Clifton. The photographs appeared to have been taken in the heat of summer, close to the sea. His eyes were narrow against the glare of the sun, and she could not help but return her attention to his smile. His was an open face, a face that bore no evidence of sorrow or past calamity; it seemed to reflect only a zest for life and spirit of adventure. It was the face of one who might be said to have lived a charmed life.

Though she had planned only to pack and leave for Chelstone, Maisie lingered over the letters, and slipped the pages from the first envelope.

Dear Lt. Clifton,

Thank you for your letter, which I received this morning. It is always exciting to receive a letter, but I had to wait until noon before I could rush to my tent to read it. . . .

Maisie pressed her lips together and looked away, remembering the casualty clearing station in France, and those times when a letter arrived from Simon, its pages seeming to burn through her pocket into her thigh until the moment she could run to the tent she shared with Iris, whereupon she would tear open the envelope to read: "My Darling Maisie . . ."

She turned back to the letter, lifted the page to the light, and continued.

I'm glad to hear that you enjoyed your leave in Paris as much as I. Who would believe that a war is on, when you can go from one place to another and have such a joyous time? You were very generous, and I will never forget that delicious hot cocoa the cafe owner made for us; I have never tasted anything quite like it. I'm so glad I bought a postcard with a picture of the Champs-Élysées. I felt as light as air walking along without mud and grime on my hem.

I've been thinking about your stories of America. I can't imagine living in a country that big. Until I came to France, I had never traveled more than ten miles from my father's house.

Well, I must go now—we are expecting more wounded this afternoon and there's much to prepare.

Yours sincerely,
The English Nurse

"The English Nurse?" Maisie said aloud. "The English Nurse? Don't you have a name? Why are you calling yourself 'The English Nurse'—and why no address?" Then she reminded herself that during the war she had never given an address at the top of the page; the official "Somewhere in France" had seemed both insipid and melodramatic at the same time. And in her chest she felt a tightening, imagining the tall

American with the broad smile on a sunny day laughing with this girl, perhaps teasing her . . . "*my English nurse*."

Maisie folded the letter and placed it in the envelope once again. She brought an old newspaper from the box room and laid it out on the floor, then took the letters and set them on the paper as if she were placing cards for a game of patience. They were close enough to the radiator to benefit from the shallow heat, yet away from any damp that might be leaching through the wall from outside. Each letter had enough space around it for air to flow freely, and when she returned, she would open the letters one by one, peel away the pages and set them to dry in the same way.

Though rain clouds threatened to slow the drive to Kent, the promise of better weather ahead was signaled by shafts of sunlight breaking through shimmering new leaves on the tree canopy overhead. Maisie began to feel more settled as she made her way through Sevenoaks, and down River Hill towards Tonbridge. Her recent visits to Chelstone had been brief, and she had visited Maurice only occasionally since the beginning of the year. She was anxious, as always, to see her father, who would be both pleased to see her and worried that she was visiting in the middle of the week. He was a man who liked the rhythm of routine, and any deviation gave him cause for concern.

At the sound of wheels crunching on the gravel lane leading from the manor house drive to his small cottage, Frankie Dobbs was quick to open the front door. "Maisie, love—" He walked towards the MG, his dog at his side.

"Hello, Dad—you're looking well! And so's Jook."

Frankie Dobbs leaned forward to kiss his daughter on the cheek, and carried her overnight case into the house while she made a fuss of the dog. Soon father and daughter were in the kitchen, the kettle on the stove to boil, and Frankie had opened the range door so that Maisie could feel the benefit of hot coals.

"This weather doesn't know what to do, does it? One minute you think it's spring, the next minute you're banking up the fire."

"That's exactly what Billy said only today."

Frankie nodded. "Here to see Maurice?" There was no resentment in his voice, for Maisie's father had long ago come to understand that the bond between Maisie and her former teacher and mentor was an enduring one, though tested at times.

"Yes, I want him to look at a report, just to see what he has to say."

"Must be urgent, if it couldn't wait until Friday."

Maisie nodded, reaching out to take the mug of tea offered by her father. "No, I didn't want to wait."

"He's been right poorly, you know."

"I thought he was getting better." Maisie set down her mug after one sip.

"To my mind, it was all that going over to France what did it. I told him, 'You can't be going over there when you still feel rough.' He said he had to go, had to get some affairs sorted out, and the next thing you know, Lady Rowan gets a message that he's staying there because he's gone down again—well, you know, don't you?"

"How is he now?"

"As soon as he came home, they brought a bed into the conservatory for him, so he could rest during the day—it's very warm in there when sun shines right through, plus there's that nice fireplace. I reckon the ailment's sitting on his chest and just won't be moved. Nasty cough he's got—and it's such a shock, because he's always been your busy sort, hasn't he? If he's not over there in France, or on business in London, he's out with his roses, or you can see him reading a book up there by the window. Always one to pass the time of day, he is. But this has knocked him for six, I can see that."

"I'll go up and see the housekeeper this evening, ask if it's all right to call tomorrow morning. I should have telephoned, but I thought—"

"I know—this isn't like him. And Lady Rowan is all beside herself. You know how she is, what with her 'I am beside myself.' "

Maisie laughed upon hearing her father's imitation of his employer, whom he held in high regard, a respect that was mutual.

"What's caught her attention now?"

"James is home from Canada?"

"James is home?" She reached for her mug again. "Well, that is a surprise, given that he hates sailing in what he calls the 'iceberg months.' I thought he wouldn't return until summer, and then perhaps not until next year."

"No, he's back, and they say—them downstairs—that he's back for good. There's talk of the London house being opened up for him, and Lady Rowan is said to be very happy because his lordship is going to retire."

"Well, I never." Maisie leaned back in her chair. "I don't visit for a few weeks, and look what happens. I wonder how things might change around here."

"We all wonder. It's like the changing of the guard—out goes one lot, and in comes another."

"I doubt it will be that bad. Lady Rowan loves Chelstone and hates going up to town now—even for the season."

"You watch. Next thing you know, James will be matched up, mark my words."

Maisie laughed. "He's about thirty-six now, Dad, and he's been engaged three times already. He won't be easily pressed into marriage."

"Another one who lost his heart nigh on twenty-odd years ago." Frankie shook his head and looked out of the window across the fields.

"Well, that's as may be." Maisie stood up, rinsed her mug under the cold tap, and set it on the draining board. "Now then, I think I'll nip up to see if I can have that word with Maurice's housekeeper."

Is that Maisie?" Maurice's voice could be heard calling from the conservatory as Maisie spoke with the housekeeper in the entrance hall.

"One minute, Dr. Blanche." Mrs. Bromley, the housekeeper, scurried away, returning a few minutes later. "He wants to see you now, Miss Dobbs. I was just about to bring him in from the conservatory—he does like to sit there until it's dark, and even though it's warm and we've plugged it up so there's no drafts, I do worry about him. The nurse comes in at about eight o'clock—she should be here any minute—and makes sure he's comfortable for the night, so you've time for a little chat. He's been waiting for you to come home."

Come home. Even though she had her own flat in London, even though she was London born and bred, when she came to her father's house, to all intents and purposes she was considered to be home. Maisie smiled. *He's been waiting for you to come home.* It was true, she always felt a sense of belonging at Chelstone, and particularly when she reflected upon the hours spent with Maurice at The Dower House.

Together with Mrs. Bromley, Maisie helped Maurice into a wheelchair, then to his favorite chair alongside the fireplace in his study. As he sat down, she noticed how frail he looked. His shoulder blades seemed sharp against the fabric of his dressing gown, and his eyes milky, sunken like those of an old dog.

"Maisie, I am so happy to see you."

"And you too, Maurice." She leaned towards him, and they kissed on both cheeks. "I wish I had known that you were so poorly—I thought you were getting well again."

He lifted a hand towards the chair on the opposite side of the fireplace, Maisie's usual seat; then he shook his head. "I did not want you to be worried, so I asked that you not be alerted to my ill health. I am sure that as soon as summer comes, I will be as fit as a fiddle." He coughed, reaching into the pocket of his woolen cardigan for a handkerchief, which he held to his mouth. Maisie could hear the rasping in his chest, the wheeze as he caught his breath. "I beg your pardon." He paused before continuing. "I saw the light from your torch as you came along the path. I'm glad you've come. Now then, Maisie, what is it you want to discuss? Give an old campaigner something to chew on; I'm fed up with being the resident invalid."

Maisie pulled an envelope from her pocket, slipped out Michael Clifton's postmortem report, and passed the pages to Maurice, who squinted to see the words even though he had set his spectacles on his nose. He read in silence, nodding on occasion, before speaking again.

"The body has been in the ground for some time—what, some sixteen years."

"Yes."

"But the body never lies, does it, Maisie? We may be pressed to see the message sometimes, and one person's eye is not as keen as another's, but the truth is always there."

"What truth do you see in that report, Maurice?"

Blanche smiled, a movement that caused him to cough once again. Maisie poured a glass of water, and held it out to him. When the coughing had subsided he replied to her question. "I see wounds consistent with the type of shellfire faced by the men—there's evidence of shrapnel infiltration to the bone from head to toe, and I would say that this man and those with him suffered vascular and arterial damage due to deep lacerations, though it's likely the deaths of the other men were ultimately caused not only by loss of blood, but by asphyxiation when the dugout caved in." He paused, and looked up at Maisie, the firelight flames reflected in his eyes as he tapped the page. "But this wound to the back of the head—that was not caused by shrapnel, or a gun. I would say it was a heavy object at very close range. This man was murdered by a more personal foe, not the enemy we call war. And you knew that already."

Maisie nodded. "Yes, I knew, Maurice. I wanted you to see the report and to have your opinion. I can see why a harried doctor might miss something; after all, the remains of soldiers are being discovered every week. Still, I thought a British military doctor checking the report might have seen what we have both seen, but this one seems to have slipped through."

"People often see only what they want to see. To draw attention to this particular anomaly would mean more paperwork, more time—and all for a truth that has remained buried for many years. Such truths can only cause pain for someone somewhere, so perhaps consideration was at the heart of the omission."

"Well, the father knows, and he is my client." Maisie leaned back in her chair.

"Tell me about the dead man."

"He was a cartographer and surveyor, an American whose father was British and who managed to worm his way into the army given his background—mapmaking is a valuable skill." She recounted Michael Clifton's history, as told by his father, and she outlined the nature of her client's brief.

Maurice was thoughtful. "Ah, a man who makes maps—an adventurer with his feet on the ground."

"An adventurer with his feet on the ground?"

Maurice coughed again as he laughed, then continued. "Who hasn't felt the stirring of wanderlust when looking at a globe? You see the names of far-flung places and want to see who lives there, and what paths they travel through life. Ah, but the mapmaker, he is one who looks at the land around him and interprets it for the rest of us, who gives us the path to our own adventure, if you like."

"I see what you mean," said Maisie. "But I wonder how someone like Michael Clifton truly felt about his role in the army. After all, his job was to interpret the land not for adventure, but for men to fight, for them to be wounded, and die."

"Indeed."

Maurice seemed to tire, and at that moment the housekeeper knocked and came into the room. She approached with hardly a sound, and spoke in an almost-whisper.

"The nurse is here, Dr. Blanche."

Maurice reached out to Maisie, and she took his hands in her own. "I must go now, Maisie. The only woman ever to frighten me has arrived to ensure I take to my bed. She is fraught because I know more about my medication than she, and because I am given to ingesting my own herbal tinctures—but they allow for a good night's sleep, which is a gift at my age."

"May I help you?"

"No, but please return tomorrow, have coffee with me before you leave for London."

"Of course."

Maisie turned to leave, and as she reached the door Maurice called after her.

"You might bump into James Compton tomorrow. He's home too."

"Yes, I suppose I might. See you tomorrow, Maurice."

Maisie planned to leave Chelstone at eleven o'clock, to be back at her office by one at the latest, so she was surprised when the telephone rang in her father's cottage at half past eight the following morning, and her father announced that Billy Beale wanted to speak to her.

"Billy, is everything all right?"

"Sorry, Miss. I know you're going to be back this afternoon, but I thought you'd want to know straightaway that we've had the police here this morning already."

"The police? Whatever's happened?"

"It's terrible, Miss—Mr. and Mrs. Clifton were attacked in their hotel room yesterday afternoon; left for dead, they were. They're in St. George's Hospital under police guard, and they're both very, very poorly. Mrs. Clifton's at death's door. And the police seem to think you might know who did it."

THREE

In haste Maisie gathered her belongings, packed her case, and loaded the MG. She ran up to The Dower House to see Maurice, who had not yet risen, so she penned a note to him:

My dear Maurice,

I must return to London immediately. Word came this morning that Mr. and Mrs. Clifton (parents of the young man whose postmortem we discussed yesterday) have been subjected to a most vicious attack at their hotel and both are seriously injured. I will return to Chelstone on Saturday, so expect me to call upon you in the afternoon.

Wishing you well, as always.

Maisie faltered when it came to closing the note; she felt her throat tighten at the thought of Maurice so compromised in health, and at the same time she was shocked by the news from Billy. She swallowed back a fearful anticipation of what she might have to face in the coming days and, holding the pen above the paper, wrote:

With fondest love,
Maisie

She folded the letter, placed it in an envelope, and passed it to Mrs. Bromley to give to Maurice on his breakfast tray.

Later, as she started the MG and waited for the engine to warm before driving away from her father's cottage, Maisie pondered the words she had chosen to sign off the message to Maurice. Her love and regard for him was without question, though neither had ever said as much. He was not her father, and her adoration of Frankie Dobbs was beyond measure, but she knew that Maurice, in his way, was parent to her intellect, to her understanding of the world she inhabited. Without Maurice she would not have become the person she was today, for better or for worse. He had guided her along the path of her growing, was witness to her successes and failures, and showed her the world that could be hers if she set out to stake her claim.

Reversing the motor car onto the driveway, she changed gear to drive out along the carriage sweep, but swung over to the left to allow another motor car to pass. Maisie was not familiar with the vehicle, and was surprised when the driver pulled up alongside and wound down the window, though the cloth top was already drawn back despite the cold morning.

"Maisie Dobbs—off so soon? When I saw your little motor parked here last night, I thought I might catch you this morning." James Compton was wearing a leather jacket over an Aran jersey, with a cream woolen scarf wrapped around his neck and reaching up almost to his nose. His fair hair had been rendered unruly in the wind, his nose was red, and his eyes—the gray-blue of a winter sky—watered from the chill air. He pulled down the scarf to speak. "I wanted to see if you were up for a spin in the old girl here."

Maisie was anxious to leave, but at the same time, she had known James for years and had also accepted investigative work from his company in the past, so thought it best to exchange at least a few words. "Sorry, James, but I have to return to London as a matter of some urgency." She looked along the lines of the motor car. "And the old girl in question doesn't look so old to me."

James grinned as if he were a boy. "She's only on loan—extended loan—from a company called Aston Martin. They're in a bit of a financial bind, actually, so I may buy this one. It's for racing, thought I might take it to Brooklands."

"Oh. . . ." Maisie was not sure what the appropriate response might be to a prospective racing driver, but another thought occurred to her. "Might that not be a bit risky for someone who has responsibility for the smooth running of a large company?"

"Oh, the jungle drums, they are a-beating."

" 'Fraid so, James." Maisie slipped the MG into gear, the change in engine sound signaling that she was ready to leave.

"Back soon?"

"Saturday afternoon, I would imagine."

"Good—I'll take you for a spin."

Maisie smiled and waved. "I'll think about it. 'Bye, James." And before James Compton could reply in kind, Maisie was on her way.

Detective *Inspector* Caldwell?" Maisie was sitting at her desk, with Billy seated opposite. "Caldwell has been promoted?"

"Yes, and full of himself, he is."

"Oh, why did Stratton have to move to Special Branch?"

"I thought the same thing. And Caldwell isn't any nicer for moving up, either. Throwing his weight around even when he's asking a few questions. He's what my old mum would call a bombastic little nit of a man."

"I'll remember that every time I see him now."

"Anyway, he wants the contents of the parcel sent by the Cliftons." Billy looked up at the mantelpiece clock. "And he'll be here in a minute."

"Well, let's see what we've got for him to take away." Maisie scraped back her chair and stepped across to the table by the window where the Clifton case map was laid out. "We'll fold this and put it away for a start—don't want him snooping. Have you worked through the letters from the claimants?"

"Yes. Every name noted, and I've put them in batches, just like you said. They're listed from the believable to the downright loony."

"Then let's give him the letters. Shame I have the correspondence sent to Michael Clifton by his ladylove safe at home, isn't it?"

Billy grinned. "I didn't hear that, Miss."

"I'd like to keep the photographs, but Caldwell will probably want them. Luckily, I brought them with me. There are some other odds and ends here, but nothing of note as far as I can see." Maisie reached into the box and took out an oblong leather case which, when opened, revealed a collection of pens. She lifted the red pen from the case and removed the cap. Where there might have been a nib, had this been a fountain pen, there was instead a point rather like that of a needle, and when she drew the pen back and forth across the paper case map, the ink ran in a hair-thin red line that reminded her of blood. "These must have cost a pretty penny—and I cannot believe they still work, after all this time!"

"Being underground, buried, kept in the dark, that's what must have stopped the ink from evaporating. Amazing, really, but that's what you get when you spend good money on something," said Billy.

Maisie nodded, replaced the top on the pen, and put the pen in the case, which she slipped into the drawer on the underside of the table. "Right, let's put this box aside ready for Caldwell. He should be content with his find."

The doorbell rang, announcing a caller.

"Better go and let them in, Billy. I'll fold and file the case map."

And the purpose of Mr. and Mrs. Clifton's visit to you, Miss Dobbs?"

"They wanted to find a woman they believed their deceased son to have had a liaison with in the war. An advertisement had been placed in several newspapers and they were overwhelmed with inquiries, so they came to me to wade through them, investigate each individual, and try to find the one authentic claimant."

"Is there money involved?"

"They will of course pay my usual fee."

"I meant, is there family money, Miss Dobbs—will the woman receive any money, as far as you know?"

"I do not know what plans they might have once the woman is located, though you must know that the Cliftons are a family of some considerable wealth, with their deceased son favored by a trust that has been accumulating interest for some time and which was not adversely affected by the Wall Street crash."

"What do you know about the Cliftons?"

"They are among America's aristocracy, so to speak."

"Cliftons?" Caldwell shrugged. "Clifton—the shoemaker's son? An aristocrat?"

"I'm given to understand that moving up the social ladder can be achieved by hard work alone on the other side of the Atlantic Ocean." Maisie smiled at Caldwell.

"And there's some who make it look easy here—but I suppose that depends who you know."

Maisie knew the comment was spoken in an attempt to undermine her, but she did not wish to rise to the bait. "Yes, I suppose it does, Detective Inspector. But at least you and I are both familiar with the meaning of hard work, aren't we?" She smiled to accentuate a willingness to assist the police. "Now then, we've collected the items you requested. I hope they help you in your investigation. In the meantime, I wonder if you could give me an account of Mr. and Mrs. Clifton's progress. They were a close couple who seemed to have good intentions, so we were shocked to hear of the attack."

Caldwell appeared to relax, leaning back and shaking his head. "It was a nasty business—there was blood all over the place. And talk about ransacked! Fortunately Mrs. Clifton used the hotel safe for her jewels and valuables, but that didn't stop the perpetrator turning over the whole room. We think they disturbed him when they returned after tea."

"What kind of weapon was used?"

"He didn't need to bring a weapon, there was one already there."

"What do you mean?" Maisie leaned forward.

"An interesting piece of equipment—they call it a theodolite. Heavy it is, made of solid brass. This one was engraved with their son's name. Apparently it was retrieved from the dugout after his remains were found—and they found other tools that belonged to him, all with his name engraved. According to communication I've had with the eldest son, each member of his family bought him an item of equipment when he first became a cartographer, so their names were also on the tools of his trade."

"I see. . . ." Maisie was thoughtful.

"Right then, this will never get the eggs cooked, will it, Miss Dobbs?" Caldwell stood up, buttoned his coat, and picked up his hat. A detective sergeant who had accompanied him put away the notebook into which he had inscribed details of the conversation, and the two walked to the door.

"Oh, before you leave, Inspector—do you have a description of the assailant? Did anyone see an interloper make his way to the room?"

Caldwell shook his head. "The hotel's a busy place—don't know how people can afford that sort of money, myself—so we've little to go on. We've been interviewing the staff, but it seems that any suspicious characters, when described, could be just about anyone on the street. Now then, Miss Dobbs, I really do have to leave. I trust you'll be in contact should you come across any information that will assist us in our inquiries."

"Of course, be assured you'll be the first to know. Oh, and Detective Inspector, when do you think Mr. Clifton might be well enough to receive a visitor?"

"Not yet, Miss Dobbs, but . . ." Caldwell faltered. "But I'll see what I can do in a day or so."

"Thank you. I appreciate your consideration." Maisie paused for a second. "Might we expect return of the letters when you have had an opportunity to go through them? Mr. and Mrs. Clifton were anxious for work to begin on the investigation as soon as possible."

Caldwell shook his head. "We'll need them for a while. You'll have to start work with whatever you have at the moment." He placed his hat on his head and made one last comment before turning to leave. "Oh, and I should tell you that Mr. Edward Clifton *Junior* is on his way, expected to arrive in Southampton at the end of next week. He'll be joining his sister's husband, who's been in England on company business."

A theodolite? Sounds like something you'd find in a church." Billy came back into the room after escorting the policemen to the door.

"And it actually looks a bit like something you'd see in a church, too, because it's a hefty piece of equipment—and could do a lot of damage if used to clout someone over the head."

"What's it used for?"

"I know it's used in surveying and engineering work, and obviously by cartographers. I think it's for measuring the angles—up and down, and across—of a given landscape, and I think it's particularly useful when assessing ground that is not easily negotiated. A battlefield, for instance."

"So it was buried with him all this time, and now they've got it?"

"Yes, seems like it."

"Bet a tool like that could tell a few stories if it could talk." Billy was looking out of the window, as if pondering the life of the object under discussion.

"You've been reading the penny dreadfuls again, haven't you, Billy?" Maisie's tone was light as she teased her assistant, though the same thought had occurred to her.

"Funny that the Cliftons never told us about the son-in-law being over here too, don't you think, Miss?"

"Yes and no. There was no need for them to tell us, and I think that perhaps they were more concerned with meeting us and knowing that someone had taken the load of seeking out the source of the wartime letters to Michael."

Soon the case map was situated on the table once more. Maisie had begun to read through the list of names from the letters weeded out by Billy as most promising. He had made notes on each letter.

"I didn't have time to put down more about the others, just the ones with a bit of a ring of truth to them. Mind you, can't all be the one, can they? And that means there are some good storytellers out there."

"The whiff of wealth can make even the most dull eloquent."

"It's certainly made me learn a new word or two, make no mistake!"

Billy smiled, then appeared more serious. "Miss, what happens if the lady in question didn't even see the advertisement? Or what if she saw it and didn't want to be found? How will we find her then?"

Maisie tapped a pencil against the palm of her left hand. "To tell you the truth, I think that's a distinct possibility. But there's more to consider here. I don't think the attack on the Cliftons was as simple as their encountering a burglar who happened to choose their room to break into. And though the letters are important, the search that Mr. Clifton really wanted me to take on was not for a woman, but for a murderer—the man who killed his son. So, first of all, I have to educate myself in the practices of the surveying party. I need to find out who they were, how they worked, and anything anyone can tell me about them."

"That's going to be nigh on impossible. It was a long time ago, and it sounds like they're probably all dead."

"We'll see. . . ."

"You know, Miss, I've been thinking about maps, what with Michael Clifton being a cartographer and him being fascinated with maps since he was a nipper. I've always wondered why you call this a case map, where you got the idea from." He tapped the edge of the paper. "After all, it don't look much like a map."

She looked up from her work. "It was what we did when I worked for Maurice. The idea was to lay out all your suspicions, facts, clues, ideas, and you look for patterns. In this way you can see everything before you, rather than simply a notebook filled with scribble. It's the difference between seeing the land laid out on paper like a picture, and someone describing it in words."

"And then trying to make sense of it all." Billy sighed. "I can't get that Michael Clifton out of my mind. I mean, he seems to have been a good sort of bloke, someone you'd want as a mucker. So who would want to kill him? It was bad enough when the enemy had it in for you, let alone the men you shared the dugout with."

Maisie nodded. "And that's exactly what we have to find out." She stood up and moved to her desk, where she picked up the telephone. "There's a few people I need to talk to—and with a bit of luck, someone in the army who knows something about cartographers in the war would be a good start."

"You going to have a word with Lord Julian?"

"He's my source for all things military. He can usually help me out, though I am sure he'll begin charging me soon."

"I always thought they were brave, them blokes who went out there surveying. Sappers, they were, like me, though they did a lot of work with the artillery—because without them, who would have known where to fire a gun? And then there was all that work with trench maps and what have you."

"Do you know anyone I could talk to?"

Billy shook his head and looked down at the list of names before him. "Nah, Miss. Them I've kept up with were like me, the ones out there laying wire, telephone lines and the like. I reckon I did most of my work underground—like a rat I was, tunneling away down there."

Maisie placed a call to Lord Julian Compton. Ten minutes after she replaced the receiver, the telephone rang and Lord Julian suggested Colonel John Bartley as the man who might be able to assist her in her inquiries.

"Shame about Maurice, isn't it?" Lord Julian added, having given her the information she sought.

"Yes, I hadn't realized he'd been so ill."

"He likes to keep himself to himself, as you know, but we're making sure he's kept an eye on. Will you be at Chelstone this Saturday or Sunday?"

"I hope so, Lord Julian. I'll see Maurice again then."

"Good. Yes, that's very good. Now then, I must be off."

"Of course." Maisie replaced the receiver and sighed deeply. Though she had become used to her position at Chelstone—years ago she had been an employee in a lowly position, her education sponsored by Lady Rowan Compton, and now she was a professional woman of some standing who was as welcome in the servants' quarters as she was in the drawing room—she was never completely comfortable when speaking to Lord Julian. He had always accorded her respect, and had even recommended her services to both business and personal associates, yet she remained in some awe of him. Due to his position at the War Office during the years of the Great War, however, he was often the only person who could assist her when it came to making military contacts crucial to a case.

"Got someone for you, has he?" Billy looked up from his notes.

"A Colonel John Bartley."

"Oh, I remember hearing about him," said Billy. "A soldier's soldier, that one. He was spoken of very highly, if I'm remembering right."

"That's the sort of man I need to see—and I hope he can help me understand the cartographer's job. I'll telephone him now."

Maisie placed a call to Bartley, who came to the telephone with little delay.

"Bartley here. I understand Julian has sent you to me."

Maisie introduced herself and explained the reason for her call, though she gave only sufficient details to describe her need to speak to someone who might have known Michael Clifton.

"Well, m'dear, let me see. I don't think I can be of any help myself—I remember the faces, but not the names, even if the young man was an officer. Now, I'll have to think." There was silence on the line for a few seconds; then Bartley cleared his throat and began speaking once more. "I could name a few, but to get to the nub of the matter sooner rather than later, I suggest you speak to Lieutenant Colonel Archibald Davidson. Mind you, you'll have to jump to it because he's off to India any day now. In any case, he was in the artillery at the time—very young for the job, made a bit of a hash of it, I'm afraid, though he learned from his errors—anyway, you know what my chaps used to call the cartographers, don't you?" He did not wait for Maisie to guess. "They called them the artillery's astrologers. Not sure it was particularly complimentary, but a good mapmaker had to be something of an expert in divination, as well as the more formal aspects of his profession. In any case, I'll get in touch with Archie Davidson and make the introduction for you; collar him before he shoves off to endless gin and tonics on a hot veranda."

"Thank you, Colonel Bartley."

"Not at all. Here's the number you can reach him on; temporary, you know. He's at a relative's house while he winds things up here. Heaven knows where he's packed his wife off to. Anyway—" Bartley gave a number in Chelsea, then repeated it for good measure, though Maisie had transcribed it the first time. "You know, I must owe Julian more than a favor or two—everyone else seems to owe him something." The man seemed ready to go on, but Maisie nipped further conversation in the bud.

"You've been most kind, Colonel Bartley. As you said, time is of the essence. I'll ring off so that you can speak to Lieutenant Colonel Davidson on my behalf."

FOUR

The address Archibald Davidson had given Maisie over the phone led her to a well-presented mews house five minutes from the Sloane Square underground station. A housekeeper showed Maisie into the first-floor drawing room, where Davidson joined her almost immediately. He was a wiry man, tall, with long limbs, an angular face, and high cheekbones dusted with freckles, which made him seem boyish for his years; Maisie thought he might be in his early forties. Davidson held out his right hand towards Maisie, while pressing down the collar of his tweed jacket with his left.

"Miss Dobbs, delighted to meet you. I'll apologize now for the fact that I can only spare about ten minutes. As I said on the telephone, I'm due to leave for India tomorrow, and even though my wife dealt with most of the packing before she took our children back to school, I am rather snowed under. We've had months to prepare for this posting, and now all hell seems to have broken loose—this is my sister's house, and we've made a thorough mess of the whole place."

"I appreciate your time, Lieutenant Colonel. Thank you."

"Please, do sit down." He looked at his watch as he sat down at one end of a deep red sofa, while Maisie took a seat in the armchair opposite. In brief, she explained the purpose of her visit.

"So, as you can see, I'm not only trying to find someone who might remember this young man, but I would like to know more about cartographers in the war."

"Well, first off," said Davidson, "I can't remember any Americans, either in the ranks or among the officers I knew personally. You'd remember someone like that, someone different." He paused. "But it's true to say that, though the cartography units were part of the Royal Engineers, they were chiefly in the service of the artillery, and of course the infantry. Without them we would not have known where to fire which guns, and without maps we would have been lost; our success depended upon the integrity of the maps and the precision of the mapmakers."

"To say nothing of the lives of thousands of men."

"Yes, of course." Davidson checked his watch once again, and glanced at the clock on the wall for good measure.

"And you personally liaised with one or more cartographers?"

"Yes, but now that I know more about your line of inquiry, I can tell you that I was not in the geographical area you're interested in." He sighed. "Look, I'll give you a quick rundown of the way the cartography boys worked, then I'm afraid I really have to dash."

Maisie opened her mouth to thank him, but he had already launched into an explanation that was brisk, filled with military jargon, and included terms such as *flash spotters* and *sound rangers*. She did not want to interrupt to ask questions, but it occurred to her that if he had been writing instead of speaking, she would be looking at little more than scribble. When he appeared to have ended his soliloquy, Maisie spoke again.

"That's very interesting, Lieutenant Colonel, but I wonder if there's anyone you can think of who might have crossed paths with the American. Is there anyone else you would suggest I speak to, someone who can throw a little more light on the subject for me, or who was in the region at the time?"

Davidson shrugged. "I can't think of anyone, sorry, but . . . well, off the top of my head, there are a couple of people you could speak to. First off, there's Duncan Higginbotham. He was at Sandhurst with me, and he might be able to assist you—but I think he's just been posted to Aden. The other man is Peter Whitting. I believe he might have been in the region. I know that he had a training job and then requested a posting to the front, which surprised anyone who knew about it. I mean, we all did our duty, but there again, you didn't want to shove yourself into the wasps' nest if you could possibly help it. I remember being told about him going over voluntarily, and we all thought he should be looked at; it seemed he'd taken leave of his senses." He shrugged. "In any case, I've seen him at a couple of dinners and so on. He left the army after the war, but still hangs on to the title—I think he's still got a finger in the defense pie, but I couldn't say what it might be." Davidson consulted his watch. "I'll just get you the addresses and telephone numbers; then I really have to get on."

He left the room, returning a few moments later with a piece of paper, which he handed to Maisie.

"There you are. Now, is there anything else I can do for you?"

Maisie thanked Davidson for the addresses, adding, "Just one thing—I thought I might pay a visit to the School of Military Engineering in Chatham. Do you know anyone there I could speak to?"

Davidson scratched his head. "There is one person, but I don't know him that well; however, if you telephoned out of the blue, he's probably the person you'd be referred to. His name's Ian Temple—Major Ian Temple. He's the person who seems to be responsible for any liaison with civvy street, and there's a fair bit of that sort of thing in Chatham, as far as I know." He rubbed his chin. "I think he might have crossed paths with Whitting during the war. Can't for the life of me remember how I know that, but perhaps Whitting could tell you more. Oh, and that reminds me, before you go—a word of warning about Whitting. He really knows his stuff and is something of a map buff, so he'll probably be able to give you quite a bit of background—but he could do with a lesson in manners. Not a terribly likable chap, a bit gruff. Lives alone in Hampstead, but with the usual help—a butler and cook. I understand he has three cats. They've probably lasted because a cat will just walk off when it gets a bit fed up with you."

Maisie smiled. "Thank you, you've been most kind, and I've outstayed my welcome. I wish you and your wife well in India."

He nodded. "Give us a month, and we'll be begging to come home."

As Davidson closed the door behind her, Maisie heard him bellow: "Mrs. Bolton? Mrs. Bolton, have you seen my best brown shoes? They were here yesterday and now I can't find the bloody things!"

Maisie was glad to see an empty telephone kiosk on the way to the station. With the first call she ascertained that Duncan Higginbotham had already sailed for the port of Aden; and with the second call she managed to secure an appointment to see Peter Whitting—*Major* Peter Whitting—at four o'clock. She would have time to return to her office and collect her motor car for the journey to Hampstead.

Architecturally, Peter Whitting's home was like so many in Hampstead: an imposing four-story Georgian terraced mansion, the white exterior grayed by the elements and London's smoke-filled air. Parking the MG outside the property, Maisie looked up and thought the major probably rattled around like a pea in a pod, with his two servants and three cats. However, on the other hand, it was entirely likely that the retired officer was not quite as retired as he might seem, given that Davidson had suggested that Whitting was still in the employ of the government.

Maisie walked up the damp stone steps and pulled the bell handle at the side of the door, which was answered after a short wait by a manservant dressed in a black suit, white shirt, black tie, and black shoes and socks. His beaked nose gave him an austere appearance, and Maisie thought he resembled a crow, yet his smile was broad as he stood aside to welcome her into the entrance hall.

"You must be Miss Dobbs. Major Whitting is waiting for you in his workroom. I'll show you right in and bring tea—one's always gasping for a cup at this time in the afternoon, isn't one? Your coat and hat, Miss Dobbs?"

"You know, I *am* gasping for a cup of tea. I've hardly had time to stop all day." Maisie slipped off her coat and hat, patted down her hair, and smiled as they were taken from her. She was unused to such familiarity among the domestic staff of those she visited in connection with a case, and found the man's light manner refreshing. "Mr.—?"

"Dawson. Follow me, Miss Dobbs."

Dawson walked towards the broad staircase that led to the upper floors, and bade Maisie follow him along a corridor filled with paintings of past battles, from Hastings to Verdun. He stopped outside a door that seemed almost wedged between landscapes depicting Trafalgar and Marston Moor, knocked, and waited.

"I may have to knock again. He could be in the midst of battle." He turned to Maisie. "Do not be misled by the major's eccentricities, he is an extraordinarily acute man."

Dawson rapped on the door, this time with more force. A loud "Come!" was bellowed in return. Maisie was shown into the room, and could not hide her surprise at the interior. A window at the far end of the room, not unlike the floor-to-ceiling windows in her office, was flanked by bookcases that extended to cover walls to both left and right. On the wall behind her, a map had been pulled down from a roller. A special case had been built alongside to house rolls of maps, the extent of which indicated that Major Whitting was a serious collector. But the focal point was the large square table in the center of the room. Maisie thought *tableau* would be the only word to describe the scene in front of her. There, on the table, was a model battlefield complete with miniature armies, and at first glance, she could see that the major battles of the Western Front during the years 1914 to 1918 were represented there. It was an extensive relief map, with hills, towns, and farms, though many of those had been lost to battle.

"Miss Dobbs. Do come in."

"It's good of you to see me, Major Whitting."

The man before her was as much a surprise as Dawson and the "workroom" itself. Despite the fact that she had been told Whitting might still have some military connections, she had envisaged meeting a portly man in his sixties, retired with his cats and with little interest in the world outside his club, his old officer friends, and a hearty snifter of brandy at the end of the day. In reality, he was probably much younger, and was also what her friend Priscilla might have called "a bit of a dish, for his age," but at the same time he did not smile, and in his manner did not welcome his guest with an air of warmth.

Whitting was not overly tall—perhaps only a couple of inches taller than Maisie herself—but was far from portly and moved with a quick ease that suggested he engaged in some exercise each day. His dress was casual: beige woolen trousers, a fawn check Viyella shirt, with the top button open at the neck, and a V-neck pullover. A gold watch with several dials adorned his wrist, as if it were crucial for him to know not only the hour, but the very second at which he consulted the timepiece. He wore nut-brown brogues, polished to a shine, and his graying hair was combed back in the fashion of the day, but it seemed he used only the smallest amount of oil to keep it in place.

"You seem rather surprised by my workroom." Whitting's tone was abrupt, almost curt, as if to challenge his guest.

"It's quite awe-inspiring, I must say." Maisie moved closer and looked down at the model landscape laid out on the table. "It's more than a map, isn't it? It's as if you've laid out the whole of Belgium and France in miniature." She looked up at Whitting, who came to her side.

"And you're wondering what I do with this, aren't you?"

"It crossed my mind." She smiled, suspecting that her host might be one who looked for an argument where none might otherwise exist. A composed demeanor on her part would do much to calm Whitting's agitation.

"It comes down to the fact that I'm still trying to learn—what we did right, what went wrong, and, of greater importance, what might happen in the future. This hasn't been finished long, and I can change it to reflect the way in which the region has altered with the regrowth of forests, the reestablishment of agriculture, and the new buildings that have been going up."

"I see."

Whitting paused. Maisie was aware he was looking at her as she stared at the map. She reached out and laid her finger close to a small French village, not far from the Belgian border. "I was right there, in the war."

"Nurse?"

Maisie nodded.

"Bit young, weren't you?"

"I lied. I wasn't the only one."

"No, and you won't be the last. War does that—until people realize that it isn't a game to be played"—he held out his hand towards the map—"like draughts or chess. It's a matter of life and death. Chiefly death."

"I know."

At that moment, Dawson arrived with a tray set for tea. He brought it to a low table between two armchairs situated on one side of the room, close to the fireplace.

"Miss Dobbs, do take a seat. We'll have tea, and you can tell me in more detail why you're here to see me."

Whitting showed Maisie to one of the armchairs, which were covered in a woven tapestry-like fabric; comfortable enough for a lady, but with a masculine austerity about them. Coals were smoldering in the fireplace, and as Whitting was about to sit down, she noticed a large calico cat asleep on his chair. He swept up the cat, placed her on the arm of the chair, and waited while Dawson handed a cup of tea to Maisie before accepting a cup himself. After they were each handed a slice of cake on a fine china plate, Dawson left them alone to their conversation.

"Lieutenant Colonel Davidson thought you would be the best person to tell me more about the role of cartographers during the war."

When Whitting smirked, the right side of his mouth tweaked upward. "'Lieutenant Colonal Davidson'—that's one for the books. Promoted to keep him out of trouble, if his record's anything to go by, then sent out to the far reaches of the Empire." He shook his head. "But with the way things are going over there in India, heaven only knows what trouble he'll cause. And no wonder he sent you to me; he probably wouldn't know where to begin to describe the work of the cartographers. In any case, why do you want to know?"

Maisie remained calm in the face of her host's attack on a fellow officer, placing her cup on the table before she reached into her document case, which she had laid at her feet. "I beg your pardon, I should have given you this when we were introduced. I am an inquiry agent, among other things, and I am working on behalf of a client." She went on to tell Whitting about the Cliftons' search for the woman with whom their son had formed some sort of liaison.

"He was an American, you say?"

"Yes, that's right."

He shook his head. "I wonder why we accepted him."

"I thought you might be able to tell me."

"Our cartographers and surveyors are, in general, trained at the School of Military Engineering, in Chatham. It could have been that your chappie, though an American, satisfied the enlistment officers regarding his British connections, and of course, it sounds as if he was quite highly qualified in his field, so he would have been snapped up. In a time of war, we can't be picky when it comes to keeping the clever ones."

Maisie had heard Maurice say as much, though perhaps not in such blunt terms.

"He sailed to Southampton in August 1914. Apparently, he'd heard about the declaration of war whilst working in California and booked passage straightaway. Then in 1916 his parents received a telegram with news that he was missing. His remains, and those of other members of the survey party, were discovered by a farmer at the beginning of the year."

Whitting set down his cup and stood up, his back to the fire, whereupon the cat slipped into the warm seat vacated by her owner.

"We had our work cut out for us from the Battle of Loos onward—and that was a debacle. On the face of it our cartographers seemed to be doing a brilliant job. They were printing maps over there, distributing them, developing special sheets for commanders and top-secret sheets for the intelligence boys. As fast as our cartographers could work, we were pushing the fruits of their labors into the hands of the people who needed them."

"So what went wrong?"

"Too much to tell, but suffice it to say that it started when we took over significant stretches of the line from the French, and began basing our maps on those we'd been bequeathed by our predecessors. In a nutshell, our armies were fighting a battle for which the commanders were using incompatible maps, with different scales. In hindsight, the distortions were dramatic." Whitting paused. "But you don't want to know all that, do you, Miss Dobbs? You want to know how a cartographer works."

"If you have time, Major Whitting."

"You're here now, might as well get the job done. Let's start with the equipment."

Whitting's desk was neat, clear except for a pile of three books, several pages of an unfinished letter laid out on the blotting pad, and various items of equipment set on the edge of the desk, almost like ornaments. He picked up the sheets of paper and placed them in a drawer, then pulled a brass object towards him.

"This is an octant . . ."

One by one, Whitting took each piece and described its purpose to Maisie, explaining as he went how a cartographer was trained, and how a military mapmaker worked. He pointed out the challenges that a land surveyor or cartographer working in a civilian role would have encountered when required to do things differently in a battle situation. Maisie took notes as he spoke, taking account of his tone, which revealed more of the authoritarian military official than the man who had first welcomed her into the room.

"And I think that's all I can tell you, Miss Dobbs, without going so far as to begin actually training you in the art of mapmaking."

"Art? Not science?"

"The mapmaker is not only a mathematician, but an artist. He has to look at the earth and see what needs to be seen, then represent it in a way that means something—to a class, a sailor, a walker on the hills, the driver of a motor car, or those who orchestrate a battle. They have to look at that map and see a range of possibilities, not just one. Enormously important decisions hang on precise representations of what is before the commander—and as you know, most of the important decisions are made many miles away, by men in warm offices and with dry clothing. Everything rests on the fallibility of the map—and it takes more than science to do the job well."

"I see." Maisie paused. "Thank you for your time, Major Whitting. You have been most helpful."

He said nothing in response, and reached to the side of the window to ring the bell that would summon Dawson. As he pulled the curtain aside, another cat, as black as jet, walked from behind the fabric into the room.

"This one will always retreat to a hiding place when there's company."

Maisie and her host watched the cat brush up against the chairs before clambering up onto a shelf and crawling into the dark space above a row of books.

"I was thinking of contacting the School of Military Engineering in Chatham, to see if I can find out anything about Michael Clifton there."

"Might be worth your while," said Whitting. He folded his arms. "But I should advise you that they're very busy down there, and given the strategic importance of Chatham to both the army and the navy, an inquiry agent probably wouldn't be the most welcome visitor."

At that point, Dawson knocked and entered the room, holding open the door for Maisie to leave.

"May I telephone if I have any more questions, Major Whitting?"

"As long as you call in the morning."

Maisie had just stepped across the threshold when she looked back. "You know, there's one thing that rather surprises me: given that the cartographers and survey teams worked closely together, and were a small group in comparison with the battalions, for example, I rather hoped you might have a recollection of an American among their number. I understand you were responsible for men across the area where this particular cartographer was working. I would have thought with the accent . . . and by all accounts, he was a tall man, as so many Americans are, and—"

"It would be like you trying to remember another nurse, Miss Dobbs. At first blush, it might seem as if you should know every young woman who served, but on the other hand, how could you possibly? If you did, you would know exactly where to go to find the young man's lover."

Maisie looked away, determined that Whitting not see how his choice of words had unsettled her. Turning back, she held out her hand, thanked him once more, and bid him farewell.

FIVE

Maisie was leaving Hampstead when she turned off the High Street towards Belsize Park, stopping outside a mansion similar in style to Whitting's. Yet whereas the major's home was flanked by other houses, this four-story property was at the end of a terrace, and partially hidden by surrounding lush green gardens. She breathed deeply, knowing that the sudden decision to come to this place had been welling up inside her for some time.

It was the home of Basil Khan, Maurice's old friend and mentor. Years before, in Maisie's girlhood, Khan had taught her that in silence, with body and mind still, a depth of understanding may be achieved that is not available to one who languishes at the mercy of life's relentless chatter. At first Maisie found such lessons embarrassing, and wondered how she could ever remain motionless for hours without the itch to move. But Khan's quiet expectation that she sit in silence and stillness until he touched the brass bowl with a piece of wood and a mellow ringing sound echoed around the room, together with the kindness in his eyes when he took both her hands in his and said she had done well, inspired her to continue. She had drawn upon those lessons in the war when she was a nurse in France, when the screams of men dying did not end with the working day, but echoed back and forth in her head and were not silenced until she saw Khan in her mind's eye and heard his words: "Be still, until there is nothing . . ."

Though an old man—indeed, Maisie could not guess Khan's age, for he had always seemed old, yet had not appeared to age since their first meeting when she was but fourteen—Khan was much in demand. Among visitors to the mansion, where Khan's students also lived, were political leaders, men of commerce and the cloth, academics, artists, and writers. Many had known Khan for years, many came to hear him speak, but only a few gained a personal audience. Maisie was shown into the same room where he had first greeted her so long ago, and there, alongside the window, Khan sat cross-legged with his eyes to the light, as if he were not blind. It was from Khan that Maisie learned that seeing was not something that necessarily required the faculty of ocular vision.

"You have not come for so long, Maisie." He patted a large square cushion set on the floor close to him. "Come, let us talk."

Maisie bowed before Khan, then took her place on the cushion.

"Have you seen Maurice of late?"

"You know he has been unwell, a bronchial affliction." Maisie looked into the pale eyes and felt her own brim with tears.

Khan nodded. "Yes. He is not a young man, and he has given much in the service of peace, and of those who do not have a voice because it has been silenced."

"Will he get better?"

Khan smiled, and as he turned to her, Maisie saw the wide blind eyes filled with grief. Instead of answering her question, he responded to her thoughts.

"Extremes live within us all. The joy of association resides alongside the anticipation of loss. What is given will be taken, what we have is often only of value to us when it is gone." He paused, his face now held to the light once more. "Maurice knows this. Whatever is to be, Maurice is at peace."

Maisie shook her head. "I am sure he will be all right. As soon as the weather gets better and he can sit outside, that will clear his chest."

Khan's voice was soft. "Yes."

"Shall I bring Maurice to you? I am sure he would like to speak to you."

"Oh, but we do speak, Maisie. We may not be in the same room, but we speak."

Maisie looked at the light as it began to diminish. "I'd better go now, Khan." She moved as if to stand, but Khan reached out and placed a hand on her arm.

"No, stay. Sit with me as I taught you when you were a girl. Sit with me here. Tell me about your work. It is such hard work, though I know Maurice instructed you well."

"Yes, he did. Very well." Maisie sighed. "My work at the moment involves a young man—a mapmaker—who was killed in the war. He was very skilled, apparently, and had loved maps from the time he was a boy. There is evidence to suggest he had been murdered, and not by the circumstance of war."

Khan nodded, his head now lowered.

"A map is a conduit for wonder, a tool for adventure. But it is also an instrument of power—and like all things, power has two faces."

Maisie sat with Khan for some time, and was so deep in thought—or not-thought, as he might say—that when she opened her eyes he was gone and the empty room was illuminated by just one candle. She slipped her shoes on, then made her way to the hexagonal entrance hall, where she stopped to say good-bye to one of Khan's helpers. As she turned to walk towards the front door, it opened. The visitor was James Compton. His color rose when he saw Maisie, whose surprise was marked by a half-smile, and she herself blushed.

"James, what are you doing—"

"Oh, hello, Maisie. Didn't expect to see you here."

"But—"

"Sorry, I'm a bit late for an appointment. Business. Lovely to see you, Maisie." He nodded towards Khan's helper, who inclined his head in return, and walked towards the door that Maisie knew led to Khan's inner sanctum.

Maisie could not disguise her fluster, and engaged in dialogue with herself all the way to collect her MG. What on earth was he doing there? He was nothing but a dilettante, a light, party-bound . . . She opened the door of the motor car and sat down in the driver's seat, slamming the door behind her. It occurred to her that she didn't know James Compton very well at all; though she had accepted an assignment from him of late, her understanding of his character was based on her memory of a young man referred to as "Master James" in his parents' household. He was the happy-go-lucky wartime aviator who some eighteen years earlier had been in love with her friend Enid. He had seemed to lose his way after the war, as a result of both his wounds and the loss of Enid, who was killed in a munitions factory explosion. A round of parties would often be followed by self-imposed exile, as if James were trying to find a place where he might belong in a changed world. In sending him to work for the family corporation in Canada, his parents had hoped he would regain some sense of himself and his responsibilities—or as his father was heard to say, "He's got to get a grip!"

No, Maisie clearly did not know James Compton as well as she thought, and found herself a little unsettled to learn that he, too, was a visitor to Khan. She started the engine, and as she drove away, her thoughts moved to her conversation with Khan, and she reflected upon his words.

A map is a conduit for wonder, a tool for adventure. But it is also an instrument of power—and like all things, power has two faces.

Billy had gone home by the time Maisie returned to the office in Fitzroy Square. The thick smog of winter, encroaching to envelop the square and barely lifting all day, had given way to a thin fog with just a tinge of yellow as town dwellers began to do without coal fires with the onset of spring. Maisie looked out at the cloudy swirls and thought about the Beale family, about the challenges they had faced, and those still before them with Doreen's homecoming from the psychiatric hospital. She had heard the tension in Billy's voice as he spoke of his concern, especially for young Billy and Bobby, who had borne the slings and arrows of their mother's distress. And Maisie knew that now, with Doreen at home, and with the family used to a new rhythm to their days, every moment, every word spoken, would represent a step into the unknown through a blanket of fog, with Billy and the boys haunted by the specter of Doreen's damaged mind. She wondered how she might help the family, but realized that this part of their journey was theirs alone, that they had to come together to regain the ground lost—only then could Billy lead them forward into his dream of a new life in Canada.

She sat down in a chair set alongside the fireplace, and leaned forward to turn on the gas jets, but as she sat back in the chair once again, she became restless, and moved instead to her desk, where she picked up the telephone and dialed Scotland Yard.

"Detective Inspector Caldwell, please."

There was crackling on the telephone line, and soon a voice boomed into the receiver.

"Caldwell!"

"Maisie Dobbs here, Detective Inspector Caldwell." The words felt like glue in her throat. *Detective Inspector Caldwell.* She needed an ally at Scotland Yard, and her interactions with Caldwell had always been far from cordial.

"Miss Dobbs—to what do I owe the pleasure?"

"I was wondering—how are Mr. and Mrs. Clifton?"

"Mr. Clifton is much improved. Sadly, Mrs. Clifton has not made progress and is still in a very poor state. It would not be over-egging the pudding to say that she might not last the night, though I am told that each hour she's alive gives the doctors some level of hope."

"I see."

"Anything else, Miss Dobbs? I am a very busy man, as you must know."

"Yes, there is—when may I visit Mr. Clifton?"

Maisie heard Caldwell sigh. "Leave it with me. I'll try to get you in tomorrow."

"That's most kind of you, Detective Inspector."

"I'll be in touch."

"Oh, and one more thing—do you have any information about the Cliftons' son-in-law that you would be willing to divulge?"

Caldwell sighed again. "If I refuse, I know you'll find out anyway. We've been talking to him, and there's nothing he can add to the statements from staff. He's upset, obviously—they're a close family—so tread carefully."

"I won't get in your way."

"The name is Thomas Libbert—they call him Tommy—and as you already know, he's at the Dorchester."

"Thank you, Detective Inspector."

Caldwell offered no words to close the conversation. Maisie replaced the telephone receiver, and shook her head. Despite his sharpness of tone and Billy's summation of his manner, it occurred to her that Caldwell had changed somewhat since his promotion, now that the struggle to move beyond Stratton's shadow had ended with the latter's move to Special Branch. He might yet prove the ally she needed.

Before leaving for home, Maisie made one more telephone call.

"Priscilla."

"Maisie, darling—how are you?" Maisie heard the clink of ice against glass, and as she was about to speak, Priscilla was quick off the mark. "And I know what you're thinking—'Pris is at the sauce again.' Do not fear, my friend, I have kept to my resolution, and having partaken of my *one* evening cocktail, I am now drinking soda water with angostura bitters—monumentally disgusting, but it's a jolly-looking little beverage. I'm told that grenadine might be better, or lime cordial, but that's a children's drink."

Maisie laughed, glad that her friend seemed to have a semblance of control over the drinking that had dulled the fear of losing her sons. Though they were young and far from an age at which young men are sent into battle, Priscilla had lost three beloved brothers to the war, and a concern for the well-being of her sons had grown unchecked into an obsession with keeping them safe at all costs.

"I must say, I do love it when you laugh, Maisie, and I'm glad to have been of service. When will you come to see us again? The boys have been asking for Tante Maisie, though I believe it may have something to do with that delicious homemade toffee you brought last time. It certainly helped to bring out an errant baby tooth from the mouth of my youngest."

"I'm driving down to Chelstone tomorrow, so how about Sunday evening? I could detour on the journey back to Pimlico."

"Excellent. Come for supper. Douglas will doubtless scurry away to his study afterwards—he's composing an essay for the *New Statesman*, in fact, it might well turn out to be a book—so once Elinor has the toads tucked up in bed, we can retire to my sitting room for a good old chat."

"That sounds just what I need. Oh, and Priscilla, I think I'm going to have to pick your brains."

"Me? The intrepid Maisie Dobbs wants Priscilla Partridge, drinker of silly pink joyless cocktails, to help her on a case?"

"Yes, I do. In fact, you can start putting the gray matter to work if you like. I want to compile a list of all the nursing units in France in 1915. It's a bit tricky, as there were not only the government-sanctioned units but privately sponsored ones, and some of our nurses went to work for the French and Belgian medical corps—and of course, there was your lot, the First Aid Nursing Yeomanry."

"Not so much of the 'your lot.' " Priscilla lifted her glass to take a sip, and Maisie heard the ice clink again. "That's not as easy a job as it first sounds, is it? I mean, as you've said, there were groups of women who just went out and set up shop, so to speak—and God bless 'em, eh?"

"Put your mind to it, Priscilla, and use your old contacts—but be circumspect."

"Oh, you know me, 'circumspect' is my middle name." Priscilla laughed before continuing. "Who are you looking for?"

"I don't know, not yet."

"That's a good start."

"I said 'yet'—I'll have a name soon."

"Sunday—come when you like. Supper at half past six—inhumanely early, but as you know, we eat with the children in this house, unless they've been really, really naughty."

"See you then, Pris—and thank you."

"Gives me something to do—I might even get to use my fluent-and-without-an-accent French. Au revoir!"

Maisie arrived home at seven o'clock. Her flat was cold and dark when she entered, so before taking off her coat, she turned up the radiator and ignited the gas fire. Over the winter months, Maisie had taken to walking soon after arriving home in the evening. The exercise warmed her, and when she opened the door to her flat upon her return, it was as if she were returning to a snug cocoon.

There were those who might have cautioned her against leaving her home in darkness, pointing out that there were too many people cold and with empty bellies who would attack a young woman for the coat off her back, if only to sell it again. And in walking alongside the river, one could catch one's death—why, the stench alone would lead to consumption. But Maisie was drawn to walk the streets, in part, by Maurice's teaching that problems were best solved when one was moving, because if one is trying to find the key to a troubling case, moving the body will move the mind. In the early days of her learning, she was confused by the apparent contradiction of teachings from Maurice and Khan, but it was Maurice who explained: "When you are sitting in silence, you open the door to a deeper wisdom—the knowing of the ages. When you are walking, with the path to that wisdom already carved anew by your daily practice, you find that an idea, a thought, a notion, comes to you, and you have the solution to a problem that seemed insoluble."

But Maisie was also drawn to walk because she sought out the warmth of companionship, if only by proxy. She might stroll past a house where the family were gathered in the drawing room, perhaps talking by the fire, the scene illuminated by soft oil lamps. She passed another house where people were sitting at table, the spirited conversation audible from the street. And in the next house, the children, in nightclothes and dressing gowns, sat on their father's lap as he read a story. In each house, a fire, a family, and the blanket of companionship drawn close. She pulled up her collar, turned, and walked home. The flat would be warm by now.

Maisie prepared a supper of thick oxtail soup and bread, then with care gathered the letters she had placed close to the radiator and set them on the small table adjacent to her armchair by the fire. She had already turned down the radiator for the sake of household economy, and pulled a shawl around her shoulders as she sat down. She reread the first letter, and picked up the second.

Dear Lt. Clifton,

How lovely to receive another letter from you. I am pleased you are well. The farmhouse where you are billeted sounds quite lovely, and you are most fortunate to have fresh butter on your bread. We are lucky if we get drippings.

I fear I may bore you, as my days are not as exciting as yours. We are always busy, always at work, but, if I may be candid with you (and if it is a liberty, as I hardly know you, please forgive me), there is not much to tell in matters of life and death, and that which I could recount, I would rather not, because each day I want to forget.

Please tell me more about America. I am sure Boston is quite thrilling, and I cannot imagine three thousand miles on a train, and that one side of the country is so different from the other. Your letters bring a ray of sunshine to the day. I hope it is not forward to tell you that I read them more than once.

I must close this letter now, as I want to catch our messenger before he leaves.

Yours sincerely,
"T.E.N"

Maisie rubbed her forehead and whispered: "What's your name? Tell me who you are." She sat back and closed her eyes, remembering the letters she had written to Simon. Where were they now? Had they been destroyed? Sent back to his mother with his personal effects? It occurred to her that she had never wondered about them, yet they were so very personal. And she recalled how she became more careful with her signature when Simon was working at the base hospital and she was at the casualty clearing station—their letters were passed along the line, from ambulance driver to supply wagon, and at any time could have been confiscated because they were avoiding the censor. Yes! Michael Clifton and his nurse were doing the same thing! But where was she?

Maisie reached under the pile of letters and brought out Michael Clifton's journal. She turned to the beginning to read, then flicked through the pages, searching for a name, a clue, a hook. She would stop, read a line or two, her eyes scanning each line written in Michael Clifton's distinctive hand—for the most part he wrote in capital letters, and with one of his fine-nib pens. He interspersed words with drawings, sometimes a diagram, or perhaps a sketch of a flower not usually seen in the land of his birth. Maisie could feel herself becoming impatient, so she turned back the pages. She would have to start at his arrival in England.

August 31st. Well, here I am, olde England. Albion, I've arrived!

She read on, the journal revealing Michael's path from an enlistment office in Southampton to London, where he was interviewed by an officer in the Royal Engineers, a cartographer himself. He spoke of his excitement upon being accepted. "You're British enough, boy," he was told, "might even be enough for the officers' mess—and if I were you, I'd try to sound a bit more like one of us, if you don't mind." Michael wrote of how much he had laughed, later, when he thought about his interviewer's comment—he couldn't wait to tell his family in a letter. Then there was more:

> *It didn't take long for TL to find me! Received a cable this morning—he's probably worried that the Hun have a bullet with my name on it, and then who will he go to? I only give in because our dear Anna's heart will be broken, and if Teddy finds out . . .*

SIX

Maisie arrived at the office with the intention of clearing a few items of correspondence before she embarked upon the drive down to Chelstone. Spring showers had blown across London earlier in the morning, and now gray-tinged cumulus clouds moved heavily across the sky in such a way that the odd patch of blue allowed the sun to filter through, though such moments were fleeting. She turned on the gas fire low, then set to work, but had been reading through some notes for only a few moments when the telephone rang.

"Fitzroy—"

"Miss Dobbs, Detective Inspector Caldwell. I said I would be in touch about the Cliftons."

"Oh, Detective Inspector, how kind of you to remember." Maisie's eyes widened, registering her surprise that Caldwell had kept his word. "May I visit Mr. Clifton?"

"This morning at ten—I'll meet you outside the main entrance to the hospital, it's as good a place as any. By the time you get to his ward, you'll have about ten minutes with him."

"Do you have word on Mrs. Clifton's progress?"

"Or lack thereof, Miss Dobbs—she's not changed since we last spoke. Still in a deep coma. The doctors are hoping that her son's presence, when he arrives, might give her the jolt she needs to regain consciousness. Now then, see you at ten."

"Right you are, Inspector."

Caldwell ended the conversation without a formal "Good-bye," just "See you at ten." Instead Maisie heard only a blunt click as the receiver was hung up, and a long monotonous tone signifying the line was clear for another call. She replaced the black telephone receiver and checked the hour on the mantelpiece clock. There would be little time to finish odds and ends in the office if she were to be at St. George's Hospital at the specified hour.

Maisie had been to St. George's Hospital at Hyde Park Corner on several occasions. The main hospital had been built on the site of Lanesborough House—itself constructed in the early 1700s, when it would have been situated among fields instead of a burgeoning metropolis—and was also home to what was considered to be the best medical school in the country. Until recently, Maurice had been an occasional lecturer on the subject of medical jurisprudence, and in her younger days Maisie had attended lectures there. Though she was not a student of the school, a word from Maurice gained entry to selected lectures for the bright Cambridge graduate.

There was a certain austerity about the building, as if the stone itself would have no truck with nonsense, and the only important thing was to advance medical knowledge of the human body and how to make it well when sick. As Maisie paced back and forth at the allotted meeting place, an Invicta police vehicle swung round and came to a halt, at which point the passenger door opened, and Caldwell stepped out onto the curb.

"Good, you're on time."

"I do not think I have ever been late for an appointment with Scotland Yard."

"Hmmph!" Caldwell paused to touch the brim of his hat and lost no time in instructing Maisie to follow him.

With a brisk walk, he led Maisie along the street and in through an entrance she was not familiar with, then down freshly mopped corridors, up stairs and more corridors, until they reached the room where Edward Clifton was recovering from his injuries. A solitary police constable was on duty outside, and as they arrived, a nurse left the room holding a kidney bowl filled with soiled bandages.

"Ugh," uttered Caldwell. "Doesn't that make you want to heave?"

Maisie registered her surprise; Caldwell must have seen his fair share of deceased persons while working for what the press termed the "Murder Squad." "No, not really," she said. "I was once a nurse. There's not much I have to turn away from."

"It's not that I mind them dead. I just can't stand the mess when they're alive and bloody." Caldwell shook his head and approached the constable. "Ten minutes for this lady. And make sure it's ten, all right?"

"Yes, sir." The constable stood to attention when Maisie entered the room, and nodded as she passed him.

"You'll not be in the room with me, Inspector?"

"No, I'll wait. I've already spoken to the doctor, but I want to be here if the nurses need to come in or if the doctor returns. I trust you'll apprise me of any facts you manage to extract from the victim."

Maisie nodded. It seemed that, like her assistant, Detective Inspector Caldwell did not care to risk feeling queasy if he could possibly help it, though it also occurred to her that he assumed she would come out empty-handed. She entered the room, walked to the bed where Edward Clifton lay back on several pillows positioned to keep his head stable, and stood at his side. Slowly he opened his eyes and focused on her face. His head was bound with bandages, as were his palms. The skin under his eyes was black and smudged, and seemed almost blistered as the wounds on his head drained. And though Maisie had seen many much more serious wounds in the war and had stood for hours on floors thick with the blood of the dying, her eyes smarted when she thought of someone inflicting such injuries upon an elderly man who had come to London to discover the truth about the death of his beloved son.

"The police said I could see you for a moment or two, Mr. Clifton."

He nodded, licked his lips, and then spoke in a cracked voice. "Do you think the police will find out who did this?"

"I know they are working on it—and so am I."

"Thank you. I suppose—" He coughed, and winced as the pain reverberated through his body. "I suppose you want to ask me a few questions, or however the saying goes."

"If you don't mind."

Clifton nodded again.

"And I know you've probably been asked these same questions before, so forgive my repetition," said Maisie. "Can you tell me if you recollect anything about the person who attacked you?"

He paused before answering the question. "That's an interesting thought—the police asked me if I remembered anything about the *man*."

"We need to cast the net wide before dragging it back to the boat to inspect the catch."

He sighed. "I've tried to remember, but it's a blur—I just remember the movement, the struggle, hearing Martha scream, as if she were trying to stop someone attacking me. Then everything went black."

"Yes, I see." She looked at Clifton and wanted to lay her hand on his, as she would with Maurice or her father. Instead she went on. "I know this is terribly difficult for you, Mr. Clifton. I can see you are weary and in pain, and I would not ask you to press on if it were not important. Do you think you can cast your mind back a bit?"

"I know it's important. I'll try."

"I'll be quick. Now, what do you remember before you returned to your room? Let's start with when you left to go out."

"Oh, I don't know, I can't—"

She reached out and touched his arm. "Mr. Clifton, close your eyes for a moment—not tight, but just allow your eyelids to touch." Maisie paused as Clifton followed her instructions. "Now, imagine you and Mrs. Clifton are leaving your room, see it as if you were at the picture house—what happened next?"

"I—I locked the door. Yes, and I can remember Martha asking if I was warm enough because I looked cold—always worrying, my Martha."

"Go on."

"We went downstairs, through the lobby."

"Let's linger there for a while. Look around, who was there?"

Clifton nodded. "Well, there was a darker gentleman—looked like a Spaniard—signing the register. Martha said she thought he must feel the cold, if he came from somewhere warm." He coughed and winced as the pain reverberated from his chest to his head, but struggled to continue. "She remarked on the flowers in a vase. Lovely flowers, with big blooms. She thought they must have been brought in from your Channel Islands."

Maisie said nothing, though she found herself closing her eyes as if she, too, could conjure the scene being brought forth from Edward Clifton's deepest memory.

"There's a boy struggling with a woman's luggage, and she's talking in a loud accent—reckon she was from New York. Martha whispered that it was embarrassing to come from the same country." He laughed.

"And I said, 'It's *your* country, my love!' " He wiped his eyes with the backs of his fingers, and flinched at the feel of bandages.

"Do you want to stop, Mr. Clifton?"

"No, no." He paused and took a deep breath. "Now, where was I? Yes, there was the man to the left. I remember him. Very correct. Very English, as if he was in the Guards. Wore an open-neck shirt and a—" He held his hand to his neck. "I've forgotten what you call them here? Cravat. Yes, he was wearing a cravat. At his neck. Shoes polished. I remember him because of the way he looked at Martha, and I thought to myself, Look at her, sixty-eight and she can still draw a guy's attention."

"Can you tell me about his hair, his eyes—can you remember?"

"Darkish graying hair, silver at the sides. Then I heard the couple arguing, near the door, so I looked away."

"Arguing?"

"Don't know what about. They didn't look as if they belonged, if you know what I mean. And it wasn't so much the woman as the man. I remember thinking he looked like someone you wouldn't want to meet on a dark night with those broad shoulders, but he looked as if he could do with a good meal all the same. She didn't want him to come into the hotel, and was trying to pull him away; then one of the hotel clerks took care of it, told them to leave, I reckon. It was all done very quietly. Can't say as I remember much after that." He opened his eyes. "Except, when they'd gone, Tommy—he's our son-in-law—called out to us. He'd just come down to the lobby. He wanted to know when we'd be back." Clifton touched his head.

"Do you have a headache?"

"Starting to." He closed his eyes again.

"Then let's stop, Mr. Clifton. You've been very kind to see me, and I cannot thank you enough for trying so hard to remember. Perhaps when you feel well enough—"

Maisie leaned forward to check Clifton's pulse. He was already asleep. She stood up and lifted the chair to one side so as not to scrape the legs against the floor, then tiptoed towards the door. It was Clifton's voice, speaking low but with a forced strength, that stopped her.

"Find whoever did this to Martha, Miss Dobbs. And find the man who murdered my son."

"I will, Mr. Clifton. Don't worry, I'll find them."

On the drive down to Chelstone, Maisie barely noticed the landscape around her, and at times realized that she could not remember driving past some of the usual landmarks on the journey. In her mind she was playing and replaying the scene described by Edward Clifton. Of course, each of the people he described seeing—the man with the cravat, the man with a dark complexion, the arguing couple, and Thomas Libbert—could be completely innocent. But someone had gained entrance to the Cliftons' room, and had been so intent that his or her identity remain secret that he or she had left the couple for dead before escaping. It was clear that the person was looking for something specific, and it was possible that the very item being sought was in the hands of either the police or Maisie. Could the letters from women who had responded to the Cliftons' advertisement have inspired the attack? Or perhaps Michael Clifton's personal effects? Somewhere there was something of great value to another person—what was it, and where was it? And who wanted it so much that they would kill to have it?

Stalled in her quest until Monday, Maisie planned to spend time with her father, and Maurice. As her thoughts transferred to her ailing mentor, Maisie's eyes filled with tears. She had known him for so long, and had it not been for Maurice Blanche, she might never have walked through the doors that had been opened for her time and time again. It was as if, the moment they were introduced when she was still only thirteen years of age, he had led her to a table heaped with knowledge—

only there never seemed to be a point at which her hunger to learn was sated. He had shown her a path that, in her wildest imaginings, she might never have found alone, had offered her counsel when she returned from war wounded in both body and spirit; and he had chosen her to become his trusted assistant, and taught her so much.

A recent estrangement in their relationship had been healed, and though she felt strength in her independence, she was also glad that he was still there to offer advice, to hold up the looking glass to her innermost thoughts so that she could see that what was already within her had merit and worth. If her father was her rock, then Maurice Blanche was the witness to her journey, and for that she accorded him great affection.

Maisie's thoughts came back to the present as she reduced speed to turn in to the entrance to Chelstone Manor. To her left was The Dower House, Maurice's residence, which he had bought years before when the old Dowager Lady Compton, Lord Julian's mother, died. Once she had passed The Dower House, Maisie would turn off the carriage sweep that led to the manor and into a downward-sloping lane to the left, at the end of which was her father's cottage. The gardens of the two houses bordered each other, and Maisie would often take the path from her father's garden up to The Dower House. The conservatory where Maurice spent warm days overlooked the gardens, and Maisie knew her old mentor would be aware of her arrival at Chelstone, and would be awaiting her visit.

As she passed The Dower House, Maisie saw James Compton's Aston Martin move from its place at the front of the mansion and begin to make its way towards the gates. She sped up enough to turn into the lane before she had to pull over to make way for his motor car, which would likely necessitate a conversation. She still hadn't worked out what she might say to him. "Funny seeing you at Khan's house" did not seem quite right, though her curiosity regarding his visit had not diminished in any way. No, it was best not to linger.

Maisie sat with her father at the kitchen table, and breathed an audible sigh.

"All right, love?"

"Yes, Dad. Just a bit weary, to tell you the truth. I had to visit a very poorly man at St. George's Hospital this morning." She was aware that she rarely spoke of her work with her father, conscious that he would worry about her safety and well-being.

"What was wrong with him?"

Maisie paused before answering the question. She was sorry she had mentioned the visit to see Edward Clifton. The lie came easily. "He'd suffered a fall, and he is an important witness."

Frankie Dobbs was not easily fooled, but took his daughter at her word. "Nasty that, a fall. I remember when I came a cropper in the stables a couple of years ago, I felt more sorry for you than meself. It's always the ones who are left waiting who suffer the most, the people anxious for news. Terrible thing, having to wait to find out if they're all right."

Maisie knew her father spoke from the heart, from his memories of waiting, of hoping her mother would get well again, then watching her die. He waited once more, years later in the war, when Maisie sailed for France with a contingent of nurses, and he waited for her to regain her strength and health when she came home wounded.

"Which reminds me," added Frankie. "I saw Mrs. Bromley today, and she said Maurice was very much looking forward to your visit. You could pop over now, before they put him to bed."

Before they put him to bed. Maisie felt the swell of ache press down on her chest, her heart beat faster, and she thought she might not be able to breathe. *Before they put him to bed.* Maurice was failing, and she could no more bear to think of life without his presence than she could imagine being without her father's love and companionship, both always waiting for her at Chelstone.

"Yes, you're right. I'll go up now and see if he's well enough for me to sit with him for a while."

Maisie kissed her father on the cheek. "I'll put that pheasant in the oven before I go—we'll have a tasty supper tonight, Dad."

Mrs. Bromley opened the door before Maisie could set her hand upon the bellpull. "Miss Dobbs, how lovely to see you. Dr. Blanche saw you coming up the path and sent me to the door—he might be weary, but he still doesn't miss a trick! Come along into the conservatory. It's still quite warm in there."

The housekeeper spoke to Maurice as she entered the conservatory. "She's here, Dr. Blanche. Shall I bring a pot of tea?"

Maurice waved his hand. "No, I think a schooner of cream sherry would be more to Miss Dobbs' liking—and a malt whiskey for me, if you would be so kind."

"But the doctor said—"

"I *am* the doctor. Some dry biscuits would go down very well too, I think, and perhaps a little Stilton. Thank you very much!"

Maisie smiled, but did not speak until Mrs. Bromley left the room. "I think you just pulled rank on the doctor—and he wasn't even here!"

"So be it. I have earned all the rank I want to pull, so let that be a lesson to you when you are in your dotage." He began to laugh, but the breath caught in his chest and he started to cough. Maisie reached for a glass and filled it with water from a jug, but Maurice raised a hand. "It will pass. Please. It will pass."

The housekeeper returned, pushing a wooden trolley set with two decanters, crystal glasses, a plate of plain water biscuits, and a wedge of the pungent blue-veined cheese Maurice favored. With a reminder to Maurice to have no more than one glass, she left the room.

"A decent pour for us both, if you would be so kind, Maisie."

Maurice took a sip of the single-malt whiskey and closed his eyes. "I have always believed in the medicinal properties of this particular eighteen-year-old distillation."

"I won't argue with you, Maurice, even though I am inclined to agree with your doctor."

"So am I, Maisie, but that this stage of my life it does me a power of good to flout rules." He paused, lifted the amber liquid towards the setting sun, and turned to Maisie. "And what about you?"

"About me? Well, this morning I went to see Edward—"

"I'm not talking about work, Maisie. It's your life I'm interested in."

"My life? But my work—"

"Your work is not your life."

"But . . ." Maisie faltered. "But your work was most of your life."

"Granted, it might have seemed like that, but there was more. My life here, my life in Paris, my garden, my friends, associations. How about you?"

"Well, I . . . there's my friend Priscilla, and her children." Maisie took a sip from the schooner she had half filled with cream sherry. "What do you want to know, Maurice?"

Maurice Blanche rested his glass on the trolley, then looked at his hands, turning them over, frowning and smiling in equal measure. "They say the face tells all there is to know about a life, but I personally believe much can be deduced from the hands. There are lines and scars, bumps and calluses; indeed, the hands are both the sketch and the final work of art."

Maisie looked at her hands. She had always been somewhat embarrassed by them. They were hands that told a story of hard manual labor when she was a child, hands that had scrubbed floors, had polished heavy oaken furniture. Later, they had soothed the sick, and had rested on the foreheads of the dying. She realized that she had no recollection of her hands as a schoolgirl, and she was uncomfortable with the conversation's direction.

"I saw Khan this week."

Maurice smiled, aware of the change in topic. "How is my dear friend?"

"We sat together for a while. He seems old, yet at the same time, he seems not to have aged since I was a girl." Maisie paused for just a few seconds to take a sip of sherry. "And you will never guess who I saw there."

"I think I can."

"This one might stump you, Maurice."

"Might it have been James Compton?'

Maisie's widened eyes underlined her surprise. "How did you know?"

Maurice again waited before speaking, as if gauging his words with care. "Now, Maisie, you know better. I have to observe that, in personal matters, you do not have the breadth of vision that is at your disposal in your work. You have made a decision about James, that he is a certain kind of person, and that—given his character, as you have interpreted it—he is not worthy, perhaps, of an audience with someone you hold in the highest regard."

"I just didn't think he was the type." Maisie felt her neck grow hot, and knew how her words sounded.

"Again, you know better."

"You're right, I do. I'm sorry. But James Compton—"

"Is a lonely man in crisis, and if I were to commend anyone to your good graces, it would be him."

"I feel as if I had just been reprimanded by my teacher."

"You have."

Maisie looked at Maurice, and they both began to laugh, though Maurice soon held up his hand as the unforgiving cough claimed him. She poured a glass of water and helped steady him as he held the glass to his lips.

"I asked for that, didn't I?" said Maisie. "I am guilty of allowing my past memories of James to color my view of him, which I concede is wrong."

"James has floundered for some time, though as we know he has always found a certain peace of mind in Canada. But now he is back here, and to be once again—and likely forever—in a place where you never quite fit is like experiencing the worst of times once more."

"Never quite fit?"

"No. James Compton is his mother's son, his father's heir, and a man of his generation of young men. On the one hand, his mother has always enjoyed flying in the face of what was expected of her, and on the other, his father is a businessman with barely an equal, a man who has served his country without question when called to do so. Julian is a man of compassion, but he does not suffer fools gladly. And then there was the England that James came home to—and a young man who has been wounded in body and spirit, one who was seeking both solace and joy, found easy consolation in the antics of his peers. But that behavior gnawed at him, Maisie. He grew to hate himself before he went back to Canada. And now he is here again, and though he is a man of some accomplishment, showing every sign of being his father's worthy successor now that he has taken over the highest position in the everyday running of the Compton Corporation, his is not an easy journey."

"I can see your point, Maurice, but there are starving people in lines for food in London—and theirs is not an easy journey either."

Maurice took another sip of the whiskey, wincing as he swallowed. "A little compassion for James, Maisie, might not go amiss."

Maisie nodded, but said nothing in return.

"Have you made progress with your case?"

She was thoughtful before replying. "Yes, yes, I think I have. Lord Julian gave me the name of a man to contact, and he in turn suggested others, one of whom I went to visit. Usually any connections initially effected by Lord Julian are without question, yet this time I . . . I can't say—there's just something about him."

"Remember, Julian does not know all contacts personally—he just has an extraordinary roster of names at his disposal, not only through his commercial interests but also through his work for the government during the war. I am sure he could find out more about this man, if you wished to inquire."

"Yes, yes, of course."

A knock on the door, followed by Mrs. Bromley and the nurse entering the room, brought the conversation to an end.

"Here come the Furies!" Maurice shook his head and reached for Maisie's hands with his own. His eyes met hers, and she was pained to see the milky patina of age and sickness. "Remember your childhood, Maisie. Remember being at Ebury Place, and here at Chelstone. Remember being different and having to make your way in a world for which there was no set of directions. Remember that next time you try to avoid conversation with James Compton."

"But—"

"I've always loved sitting in this conservatory, Maisie. Have you never looked out across the estate from here? You can see the gardens, the carriage sweep. I can see down the slope to your father's house, across the lawns, right up to the entrance to the mansion. Indeed, if I am situated in a certain place, I can even view the stableyard and the paddocks—I take great joy in seeing your father with the young horses, or instructing the grooms when they exercise the hunters. I miss nothing, so the sound of an MG's engine accelerating when James Compton is leaving the manor would attract my attention."

Maisie smiled. "Guilty as charged." She took his right hand, kissed the liver-marked skin, and felt the web of veins touch her lips. "Good night, Maurice."

"Good night, my dear."

SEVEN

As if it had been orchestrated by Maurice, while Maisie was leaving Chelstone for London, James Compton was walking his mother's dogs, a Labrador and a springer spaniel, across the lawns. It would have been an obvious omission had she not stopped to greet him and ask after his mother, so instead of driving on towards the gates, she pulled over. James waved and came towards her.

"Hello, Maisie. Leaving the fold so soon?"

"I have to get back to London, James—busy as usual."

"You're never here long enough for us to have a chat." James turned away to whistle the dogs to him. "Those dogs are tearaways. My mother has let them get away with murder."

Maisie nodded. "I've noticed."

"I suppose that isn't the sort of thing I should say to you, is it? You'll be taking each of them by the scruff of the neck and marching them over to Scotland Yard." He paused. "Look, I was going to ask if . . . well, do you like motor cars?"

"Me?" Maisie was unsure of how she might answer the question, wondering where it might lead. "Well, yes, I do—I mean, I love my MG, which as you know, I bought from Lady Rowan."

"Um, would you like to come with me to Brooklands next weekend? There's a meet there. I thought it might be rather fun to watch. We could leave from London, take a picnic." James reddened. "I—I just thought it would be something—"

"Yes, that would be lovely, James. Saturday, is it?"

"Pick you up at eight, if that's all right?"

Maisie nodded. "Now I must go, James." Maisie slipped the motor car into gear, then paused as a thought occurred to her. "James, just a minute—I wonder if I might ask a quick question?"

"Fire away."

"Do you know a family, very big in building and land in America? They come from Boston—the Cliftons."

"Yes, of course I know of them. In fact, I've had a few dealings with Teddy Clifton—he's the eldest son. A few years ago the Compton Corporation was engaged in several consortium projects in which they were also involved, mainly in Chicago. We've also been on a couple of advisory boards together, nothing too formal, just meetings of interested parties gathered by local dignitaries. Lots of blah-blah-blah. Teddy was always a good, solid person to talk to. Rather do business with him than with that brother-in-law of his."

"Which one?"

"Tom Libbert. I believe he's married to the second daughter. Can't remember her name now." He paused, frowning as he recalled details. "I think it was Anna. Yes, that's right: Anna. And the eldest daughter, Meg, is married to a doctor, though I understand both sisters are not above a bit of speculation on land themselves. It seems to run in the family blood."

"Why don't you care for Libbert?"

James shrugged. "He's managed to garner a bit of a reputation for himself as playing a bit too hard with the family money. He's had a few land deals go bad—and apparently he was warned to be careful by Teddy, but on the other hand, Teddy doesn't want to upset his sister. Mind you, I had my misgivings about Libbert before I'd garnered those nuggets of information. Can't put my finger on it, but as the saying goes, if it doesn't feel right, then it probably isn't, and even though I like a lot of background to any deal—as you know after the purchase last summer, when you played such an important part—I tend to depend on good old instinct."

"Goodness, James, you seem to know a lot about them."

James shrugged. "Same business, same continent. Hardly surprising. Mind you, I'm half surprised myself." He paused. "They're a close family, Maisie, so despite anything I might have said, the fact remains that they are tight, and they treat Libbert as any other member of the inner circle; he's Anna's husband, therefore he's family."

"Thank you, James."

"I know I daren't ask why you inquired—but can I help with any more details? I have employees in Toronto whose sole remit is to uncover information on land, markets, and people—I call them my intelligence squad."

"I think you should be doing my job, James." Maisie sighed. "You've probably not read the papers—mind you, the press were asked not to release the news immediately—but Edward and Martha Clifton were attacked in their hotel room earlier this week. Between us, I had just taken on an assignment for them and received my usual advance on expenses and my fee, and I consider both finding their attacker and fulfilling the terms of our agreement to be paramount."

"Dear Lord, Maisie, are they all right? Where are they? I must get in touch with Teddy to see if there's anything I can do to help."

"They're at St. George's Hospital—but don't count on seeing them yet. Mrs. Clifton is in a critical condition, and her prognosis isn't good.

Teddy is arriving in a few days." Maisie sighed, then smiled. "James, I had better be going. See you on Saturday, then."

James Compton smiled in return and patted the roof of the MG. "Drive carefully. Oh, and remember to dress for the cold and mud—Brooklands is hardly the place for one's finery, not if you really want to see the action." As Maisie pulled away, she looked back to see him watching her motor car drive off, the dogs now sitting at his feet. She put her hand out the window and waved once. He returned her wave, and when she looked back upon reaching the Chelstone road, she saw him wave once more, then begin to walk back across the lawns. She began to accelerate and reflected upon Maurice's words—"*a lonely man in crisis*."

As soon as Maisie arrived at her flat in Pimlico, she knew she wanted to speak to Thomas Libbert at the earliest opportunity. She needed to see him for herself, to gauge the measure of the man. She unpacked her small case and went out once more, this time walking along the road to the telephone kiosk, where she placed a call to the Dorchester. Thomas Libbert was not available, so she left a message, asking him to telephone her on Monday morning. With luck they would meet that day. She was just about to leave when she changed her mind and dialed Priscilla's number. The housekeeper answered, and soon Priscilla came to the telephone.

"Darling, you can't let me down. If you leave now, you can join us for supper. Slight change of plan. The boys have had theirs—they are eating us out of house and home—so it's only the grown-ups." She lowered her voice. "And Douglas has a visitor, a charming man. Bit of a writer, but frankly, it looks as if money is no object—you know how some of them always look as if they could do with a meal, well, this one appears to be rather well-heeled for a change. Do come, I think you should meet him."

"Oh, Pris, please stop playing with Cupid's bow, I'm sure he has a much better aim than you."

"Not if you read your Shakespeare, he doesn't."

Maisie changed the subject. "I thought I would see if you'd made any progress with the little task I put your way."

"Little task, my eye! If I tell you what I've found out, will you come?"

"Blackmailer."

"Call your detective friends and shop me. Do I hear a yes?"

Maisie sighed, but smiled at her friend's subterfuge. "Yes, I will. Against my better judgment."

"Where men are concerned, Maisie, you haven't the experience to have garnered judgment. Anyway—" She paused. "I just happen to have my little dossier by the telephone, and here's what I have for you—and I will be brief, because I can tell you more later and give you my notes. Makes up for all the times I filched your essays at Girton." Maisie heard the rustle of paper, then Priscilla continued speaking. "Now, as you know, not all nursing contingents would have been able to go to Paris for the odd day or two off. You went to Rouen, if my memory serves me well, and if you had longer, then you went on leave back to Blighty. The American and Canadian nurses tended to have more time in Paris—and remember, even though the Yankee boys weren't at the front until the tag end of 1917, they sent out medical contingents right from the outset. Having said that, by hook or by crook, I have made a list—by no means complete—of the British units that allowed leave in Paris for their nurses. This gets very confusing, because 'British' means from the Empire."

"Oh, dear." Maisie sighed, not for the first time realizing the enormity of the task.

"And you have to consider something else, Maisie."

"Go on."

"This nurse may have been English, originally, but she might have been an immigrant to Canada, or Australia, or America. After all, so many young men went out to the lands of opportunity before the war, but enlisted to help the old country as soon as war was declared—many of the Canadians were born in Britain. Might be the same with the nurses. Your English nurse could have been with a Canadian contingent, or Australian." Priscilla paused again, and Maisie heard the raspy breath as she inhaled from her cigarette, doubtless affixed to the long holder she favored. "If she wasn't with a private nursing contingent, one of those sponsored by Lady This or the Duchess of That, I bet she was a Canadian. Australia is a bloody long way to go, after all."

"Thank you, Pris. I'll look at your notes later."

"Oh, and there was this one unit, quite a few nurses, paid for by a very wealthy woman, Lady—can't find her name, where is that piece of paper?"

Maisie felt the skin at the base of her skull tingle. "What about the unit, Pris?"

"Well, it was called, simply, 'The English Nursing Unit.' Bit of a cheek, if you ask me, I mean, what did it matter where you came from, as long as you were there? Anyway, the nurses wore these badges with the coat of arms of Lady Whatever-her-name-was, and the name of the unit. All a bit elitist, in my opinion."

Maisie nodded. "I'll just go home and dress for dinner, and I'll be over as soon as I can."

"Changed your mind about the writer?"

As was so often her wont, Maisie stood in front of the open doors of her wardrobe and regarded the contents. Knowing Priscilla and

Douglas, dining would not be a formal affair if only one other guest was to join them, and one of Douglas' writer friends at that. But on the other hand, Priscilla might want to bring a level of sophistication to the proceedings if she were in a matchmaking mood, so evening dress might be appropriate—she could just imagine Priscilla wearing a pair of her signature wide silk trousers and a loose silk top with a broad sash drawn around her hips. On her feet would be a pair of satin mules embellished with an oriental design, and her thick hair would be drawn back into a chignon with a crystal-studded clip. Though Maisie had been the grateful recipient of several of Priscilla's cast-off gowns, she did not feel that such a choice would be appropriate for her this evening, so instead took out her black day dress, which could be given something of a flourish by adding the fine cashmere wrap that Priscilla had given her in France almost two years earlier. It wasn't quite warm enough yet to wear the matching silk trousers—Priscilla might dress as if she were still living on the Riviera, but it would not feel right to Maisie.

Maisie, dear, if it weren't for the fact that I would be sending you home naked, I have a good mind to confiscate that dress. Even I'm getting sick to death of it, and I'm not the one wearing it."

Priscilla had brought Maisie to her upstairs sitting room while Douglas and their guest were in the library putting the finishing touches on a joint literary endeavor.

"Just as well my enemies don't comment on my attire, with friends like you to set me right!"

"Oh, come on, you know what I mean. Where's that lovely red dress, the one you dyed yourself? And what happened to that vibrant color phase you were going through, when you'd taken up those arty classes with that Polish woman—Magda, or whatever her name was."

"Marta." Maisie sighed as she corrected the name. Priscilla was right, and she knew it. After a flirtation with color and texture, she had slowly retreated to the comfort of the more familiar items in her wardrobe.

"Well, I know when I'm right, because you don't argue with me," said Priscilla. "I can tell what's happened—you've been buried in your work, and you've forgotten about yourself again. Here, let me look at you." Priscilla stood up and pulled Maisie to her feet. "That dress is very well cut, I'll give you that, but let's cheer it up a bit, shall we? Oh, and before you say that work should come first, we can talk about my little investigative endeavor after supper—we'll leave the men to their port and engage in our own important business. In the meantime, I think we'll brighten up that dress with a splash of gold—though perhaps we should choose a wrap that really brings out those eyes of yours, something sort of deep violety midnight blue."

Maisie, how lovely to see you again—looking radiant as usual." Douglas leaned forward to kiss Maisie on both cheeks, before drawing back and introducing her to his friend. "Maisie, may I introduce Benedict Sutton—all-round good chap!"

"Miss Dobbs, a pleasure to meet you—Priscilla has told me a lot about you."

"That's a frightening thought!" Maisie smiled. Sutton was a good six feet tall and, she thought, better looking than she had expected. Though his swept-back hair was somewhat mousy, deep brown eyes and clear, pale skin gave him a more interesting countenance.

"All good, Miss Dobbs, it was all good."

"Oh, dear, do let's get over the 'Miss Dobbs' and 'Mr. Sutton'—otherwise supper will drag on like a turgid opera." Priscilla claimed the group's attention. "Maisie—Ben; Ben—Maisie. Now, let's have a glass or two of bubbly, shall we?"

The butler stepped forward holding a silver tray topped with four glasses filled to the brim with champagne.

"Who needs room to let the champers breathe, when it won't be that long in the glass?" Priscilla took two flutes of champagne and passed one to Maisie.

Benedict Sutton reached towards Maisie with his champagne, and allowed their glasses to touch with a *clink* that was so resonant, she feared they might shatter.

Soon supper was announced, and Priscilla put her arm around her husband's waist as they led their guests into the dining room. Douglas Partridge had suffered an amputation to his arm in the war, and used his remaining hand to wield a walking stick. His wife never considered the protocols of society matrons when accompanying her husband and thought nothing of putting an arm around his shoulder or waist.

Conversation was light while the first course—a spinach mousse—was served; then as more wine was poured, Sutton began to quiz Maisie.

"I understand you engage in rather interesting work, Maisie. Are you allowed to tell me about it?"

Maisie lifted her glass and took a sip of wine before responding. "Yes, it is interesting—to me, in any case. I don't generally discuss my work, though, given that my clients expect a certain high level of confidentiality."

"I see—and you liaise with Scotland Yard?"

"On occasion. There are times when I am asked to provide assistance on a given case—and it works both ways, because I have contacts there who have provided me with valuable help in the past."

"Bit dangerous, isn't it?"

Maisie twisted her wineglass, and then looked up at Sutton. "And which newspaper do you work for, Ben? Or are you paid according to the value of the scoops you uncover?"

Sutton laughed, joined by Priscilla and Douglas.

"Not so clever now, are you, Ben?" Priscilla shook her head and put her hand over her glass as the butler stepped forward to pour more wine. Maisie smiled in acknowledgment—Priscilla had been struggling to control an excessive drinking habit, and now took only one or two glasses of wine on occasion.

"No, I suppose not—but who can blame me for trying to sniff out a story when in the company of a charming inquiry agent?"

"Psychologist and investigator, so mind your p's and q's," said Priscilla.

"Priscilla—" Maisie blushed at Priscilla's correction.

"Don't try to stop her, Maisie—she's incredibly proud of you, though I doubt she'd tell you that." Douglas laughed and raised a glass to his wife and, as intended, the laughter defused Maisie's embarrassment.

Again conversation changed direction, with politics, books, and current theater offerings all coming up for discussion. Sutton demonstrated an interest in moving pictures, and soon the group was engaged in talk of improvements in cinema.

"When I think how far it's all come—it's amazing." Sutton had picked up a spoon and was holding it above the syllabub served for the pudding course. "A great friend of mine was working with cine film during the war—for the government, as you might imagine. He always said to me, 'It's just as well we didn't have sound. The punters could see their heroes at the front, but if they could hear them, they'd have known it wasn't all beer and skittles, and there would have been an outcry.' " He paused to sink the spoon into the smooth, pale yellow syllabub, then continued talking. "In fact, he's kept a lot of film. I was over there watching just the other day. We went through reels of film—it was incredible, what he had managed to record." Sutton shook his head. "There was film of some wounded horses being cared for by the army veterinary service—you never think of that sort of job, do you? And that's what was interesting, he filmed soldiers doing the things you never think about; it wasn't all guns, trenches, and 'Over the top, boys.' He even filmed a cartography unit. Now there's a job you wouldn't want to do, but you should see the maps they produced in terribly difficult circumstances—some of them are like works of art. Henry filmed them and he's exceptionally good with a camera, brought the lens in very close so you could see the details. But one wonders what he could have done with sound to accompany the cine film."

Having delivered his soliloquy, Sutton tucked into his pudding. Maisie had put down her spoon and leaned forward.

"Mr. Sutton—Ben—do you think you might be able to introduce me to your friend? I would love to see his cine film."

"Aha—has it to do with a case?" Sutton lifted his table napkin and drew it across his lips.

Maisie shook her head. "No, not at all." She paused. "I've just always been interested in cine film, and I would imagine your friend's work is incredibly interesting." She avoided meeting Priscilla's eyes, knowing her friend would comment on her subterfuge later.

"All right, I'll have a word with Henry—I am sure he'll jump at the chance, though you'll probably need a chaperone, knowing him."

"I can look after—"

"I think it's time we left the men to their port, Maisie," said Priscilla. "And gentlemen, we have some business of our own to attend to, so we'll join you for coffee in the drawing room."

"What a load of tosh, Maisie—when did you garner an interest in moving pictures?"

"When I learned that someone called Henry had been in France in the war and accompanied a cartography unit. There weren't many of those units, Pris—and I have a feeling that this meeting with Mr. Ben Sutton might just be a serendipitous gift."

"I was right, he is dishy, isn't he?"

"That's not exactly what I was thinking." Maisie pointed to a collection of papers set to one side with "For Maisie" printed on top. "Now then, let's look at your notes—I can't thank you enough."

"Yes, you can."

"What do you mean?"

"If he asks, do go out with him."

"Who?"

"Ben bloody Sutton, for goodness' sake!"

"Oh, Pris . . ."

By the time Maisie returned home, she was feeling more positive about the direction of her inquiries. She had once described her work to her father as "finding my way along the Embankment in a thick pea-souper." There were times when she imagined she was reaching out in the dark, her fingers moving to touch something firm, anything solid to give her a landmark. Sound was distorted in the ocher blend of smoke and fog. Sometimes a noise that might have come from the river echoed as if between buildings, or vision was compromised and one strained the senses to find a path that led somewhere. With the Clifton case, though there were pages of information and snippets of knowledge, she hadn't thus far felt the tug in her gut. But now, after the discussion with Priscilla, she could feel a familiar excitement welling, as if, now that she'd uncovered that one thread of possibility, a vein was not too far away, even though it was still out there in the thick, swirling mist of unknowing.

Priscilla had discovered that The English Nursing Unit had been founded by Lady Petronella Casterman, a former suffragist who had been disgusted when so many of her fellow agitators had supported the war as a means to greater freedom for women—they had foreseen that women would take on the jobs vacated by men and boys, and in the process assume a measure of the independence enjoyed by men. Casterman had ploughed much of her not-inconsiderable wealth into founding a medical unit staffed entirely by women, which she sent to France in early 1915. Her husband, whom she married in 1898, when she was eighteen and he was thirty-five, had died in 1919 of a heart attack. Throughout their marriage he had, apparently, supported his wife's endeavors, partly out of guilt, given his predilection for long hours spent in his library, with friends at his club, or riding to hounds in the hunting season. According to Priscilla's notes, penned in her large eccentric script, having nursed her husband following a serious fall from his horse, Petronella Casterman had felt qualified to help in the unit herself, though she never donned the distinctive uniform supplied to her nurses. It was said that many a wounded soldier had regained consciousness as a bejeweled hand was laid on his forehead, and a woman of about thirty-five, dressed as if she were going to lunch at Fortnum and Mason, leaned over and said, "Lovely to have you with us again, Private. Now, let's see if we can knock you out for an hour or two more." The morphine would be administered and sleep would claim the soldier once again.

Maisie sat alongside the gas fire and smiled as she read Priscilla's notes, often with snippets of opinion scribbled alongside. "I think you ought to try to see her. Would you like me to telephone? I am sure Julia Maynard knows her." Another read: "Can you imagine waking up to that?" And, "I bet that soldier dined out on that story for years."

The nurses were sent to Paris for rest, and their employer-benefactor saw to it that they were lodged in comfortable hotels and that no expense was spared in ensuring they rested in some style. According to the account, it was not unusual for Petronella (" 'Ella' to her friends") to drop in on her nurses at any point and push a few coins into their hands with the instruction, "Do something with your hair while you're in Paris."

"Very nice, I must say," Maisie spoke aloud to the empty room. "That's where I should have enlisted."

The most interesting point about Petronella Casterman was not her eccentricity, but her early life. She was the daughter of a shopkeeper who had premises in the village close to the Casterman ancestral seat. Her parents had been anxious to see their children transcend their lot in life and had encouraged education. They had hoped that Petronella might become a governess. Instead their daughter became the object of Giles Casterman's affection when he saw her in the village. Furthermore, it was clear that the subsequent marriage was a good one; the couple became parents to two daughters and later on a son, all of whom were known for being somewhat outrageous and often opinionated, if undeniably likable—especially the youngest, who was barely two years old when his father died.

Maisie was anxious to meet Lady Casterman, and made a note to telephone Priscilla to see if she could facilitate an introduction. She hoped the former shopkeeper's daughter would have kept complete records of her staff.

Putting Priscilla's notes to one side, Maisie picked up the collection of letters found close to the body of Michael Clifton. She had intended to read through them at speed, noting points that might help her discover the identity of his lover, as well as clues to what had happened in the dugout where he died. But she found that when it came to unfolding the letters, she was not drawn to such swift analysis, and instead she approached each communiqué as if she were turning the pages of a much-admired book, indulging in the slow revealing of the love affair as if the writing itself had come from the pen of a favorite author.

My dear Lt. Clifton,

Perhaps I should call you "The American Mapmaker." Or do you call yourself a Yankee? Your letter arrived today, and I was very pleased to be in receipt of good news and am delighted to hear that you will be in Paris at the same time as I—what a coincidence.

Maisie bit her lip to control the welter of emotion rising in her chest. It was not just the journey back in time, but a sense that she was something of an interloper, a person who might linger outside an open window at nighttime, and who would watch, hand on heart, while a young couple professed their love for each other. As she read the letter sent to a man who was now dead, she could feel the excitement that the English nurse must have felt, the sudden joy of knowing that she would soon see the one who had caused such butterflies in her stomach; who had teased and delighted her, and who had, perhaps before they had declared themselves to each other, caused her to fall in love with him—because Maisie could feel, even as she touched the still damp, brown-edged pages, that Michael Clifton's English nurse loved him dearly.

As you know, I will be spending my leave at the usual hotel, and with the usual chaperone. My employer is quite good to us, though we all work very hard. Our chaperone said to me, "What I do not see, I shall not harbor concern about." So I think we will be able to stay out at that lovely cafe until closing. . . .

EIGHT

The following morning, Maisie had only just closed the front door behind her when she heard the telephone ringing in her office above. She ran up the stairs, unlocked the door, and reached for the telephone before it fell silent.

"This is Maisie Dobbs." It was not the usual greeting: in general, the accepted manner of answering the telephone was to announce the telephone number first.

"Ah, yes, Miss Dobbs, I have a message here saying that you called and wanted to talk to me." The accent was unmistakably American. "Thomas Libbert."

"Mr. Libbert, how kind of you to return my call, I—"

"Are you from the press?" Libbert's tone was curt, sharp to the ear, his words cutting into the silence with a bladelike edge.

"No, I am not from the press." Maisie tempered her voice, keeping it low and steady. "I telephoned because I know your parents-in-law, and I wanted to ask if there was anything I could do for them at the present time. They are both lucky to be alive, I know, and I wondered how I might best help, in the circumstances."

"You know them?" Libbert cleared his throat, and Maisie was relieved when he went on in a manner that suggested he had relaxed. "Yes, it's been a terrible time. Their son, my brother-in-law, Edward, is en route from Boston to Southampton."

"According to the reports I've read, it was a terrible business." Maisie made her move. "Look, Mr. Libbert, I wonder if you might be able to assist me. I am actually working for your parents-in-law, a small matter of helping to locate an item of some value to them, and I thought—"

"An item of some value? What do you mean?"

"I think I would rather we met in person, Mr. Libbert—might I see you at your hotel later this morning?"

"I'm at the Dorchester, but—are you some sort of dealer?"

"Yes, I suppose that's a good description. Shall we say eleven?"

Libbert cleared his throat. "Eleven it is. I'll meet you in the foyer."

"Very good."

"How will I know you?"

"I think I'll know you, so don't worry—I'll find you."

Billy Beale walked into the office as Maisie replaced the receiver.

"Morning, Miss." He stopped before removing his cap. "Bad news?"

"No, not bad news. That was Thomas Libbert. I've just arranged to see him this morning."

"What was he like?

Maisie shrugged and began removing her raincoat. "I'm not sure."

"I know that look, Miss. You think he's up to something." Billy reached out to take Maisie's coat as he spoke.

"I don't want to jump to conclusions, Billy." She passed her coat to him, took two manila folders from her document case, set them on the desk, then sat down, placing the case alongside her chair. She looked up at her assistant. "How have you been getting on? How's Doreen?"

"As well as can be expected, Miss." Billy turned away. "We went for a nice bus ride with the boys yesterday, got out of Shoreditch for a bit, you know. It's early days yet, eh?" He placed their coats on hooks behind the door and went to his desk. "I did some more work on that list, and I think I've whittled down them names again for you—you know, the women who wrote to Mr. and Mrs. Clifton."

Maisie nodded, noting the quick change of subject. "I should call Caldwell and find out how they are, but first I must telephone Mrs. Partridge." She lifted the receiver and proceeded to make two quick calls, first to leave a message at Scotland Yard for Detective Inspector Caldwell, then a brief conversation with Priscilla, asking if she could use her connections to put her in touch with Lady Petronella Casterman.

"Should be a piece of cake, darling. Ella loves new people, according to Julia. I'm amazed I haven't met her myself, though we Partridges do tend to scramble out of London on Friday evenings, so we miss quite a few social goings-on, and while I'm at it, you must come out to the country with us again."

"That's lovely of you, Pris, and I will, soon. Look, I must go now, lots to do. I'll talk to you later."

"Has Ben telephoned you?"

"Oh, Pris, I doubt very much if he will."

"Don't be too surprised."

Maisie promised to telephone again later in the day, and had just reached out to take Billy's list from his hands when the telephone rang. This time she gave only the number.

"Maisie, it's Ben Sutton here. How are you?"

"Mr. Sutton, good morning." Maisie smiled and nodded at Billy, who returned to his desk to continue working. "What can I do for you?"

"I think it's what I can do for you that's of the essence here. I've been talking to my friend Henry Gilbert this morning."

"Oh yes, the man with the cine film." Maisie looked at the clock on the mantelpiece. Sutton had been in touch with his friend at an early hour.

"That's right. He's busy throughout most of the week, unfortunately. He's out at the Twickenham Film Studios until Friday, when he said we could come to his house to view the old cine films you were interested in."

"Oh, that is excellent news. Thank you very much, Mr. Sutton."

"Please, let's not stand on ceremony again, Maisie—do call me Ben."

"Of course, Ben—and I am most grateful to you for talking to your friend."

"I thought we could meet at eleven at his home in Notting Hill—and, um, how about a bite to eat afterward?"

Maisie's reply was not immediate. "Yes, a lovely idea—though I am afraid I might not be able to stay long."

Sutton replied as if he had heard only her acceptance, rather than the limitation of time. He gave her the address and then said. "Excellent, see you at eleven on Friday."

"Eleven it is."

As Maisie set down the telephone receiver once again, Billy pulled two chairs up to the table by the window, ready to go through the list of names and make notations on the case map, as was their practice when they worked together on a given assignment.

Maisie joined him and reached for his notes, at first trying to avoid eye contact. Then she gave a half-smile and shrugged. "Oh well, sometimes you have to meet with eligible men just to get on in a case." She felt almost like Priscilla.

Soon Maisie and Billy had eliminated more names from the list of respondents to the Cliftons' advertisement.

"So, we've arrived at ten women who might be telling the truth." Maisie set the notes on the table and looked at Billy.

"Yes."

"All right, as our friends at Scotland Yard might say, it's down to shoe-leather detective work. Fortunately, apart from one in Harrogate and one in Chester, these women are all from London and the immediate home counties, so at least we won't be incurring great travel expenses. Let's start close to home first and concentrate on the ones either in or within striking distance of London, then move out. You take the first five, and I'll take the rest. And if I am to see Lady Petronella Casterman—"

"Lady who?"

"Casterman."

"I mean the first bit."

"Petronella?"

"I know her."

"You know her?"

"Certainly do," said Billy. "I did a bit of private work for her, few years ago now, not long after I came home from the war. She'd had a telephone put in and wanted it all wired so she had one in her bedroom and one somewhere else, and what with one thing and another, she wanted it done on the quick and a mate of mine knew the butler. Next thing you know, I was asked to see him, and I put a dog and bone in about three rooms for her. Took me a couple of days, it did, what with all that old plaster to look after, and them high ceilings, and of course, the rooms she wanted rigged up weren't exactly next to each other. Not that I saw her, mind, but she came into the library while I was working one day. Had what they call the common touch. Her youngest, the boy, must have been only about three years old at the time—they had two older girls, if I remember rightly. And while I was there, reckon it must've been the second day, a couple of young women came to visit. They'd worked with her during the war. Apparently she took care of them who worked for her." Billy's eyes widened. "Now I see what you're getting at—she had something to do with nurses in the war, didn't she? Here, you don't reckon—"

"No, I don't reckon, not definitely," said Maisie. "But it's a pretty strong lead, given that she sponsored a nursing unit in the war." Maisie went on to recount her conversation with Priscilla, and what she had gleaned thus far from reading the letters from the young woman for whom Michael Clifton had great affection.

By the time she left the office to meet with Thomas Libbert at the Dorchester, Billy's list was divided, and she was in possession of the names of five women, now in their early thirties: Ivy Acton, Sybil Bates, Anne Callan, Harriet Evans, and Barbara Harte. Billy took those whose surnames beginning with letters from the second half of the alphabet: Ethel Jempson, Sylvia Lance, Elizabeth Peterson, Rose Stephens, and Theresa Tolliver.

A top-hatted and uniformed doorman welcomed Maisie to the Dorchester with a smile and "Good morning, madam," as he drew back the doors to allow her to enter. Though there were a few men in the foyer, she knew straightaway which one was Thomas Libbert, but did not approach him—she wanted to observe him first, to judge his mood and gather information about his frame of mind before they met. She stood to one side behind a flower arrangement. Libbert was dressed in a suit of light brown wool, with an open-collared shirt and a cravat at his neck. His brown hair was combed back and oiled in place, and his otherwise polished shoes were scuffed with mud at the heel and sides—she surmised he had likely taken a walk in Hyde Park before returning to meet her at the assigned hour. The American paced back and forth, his eyes on the ground in front of him, then looking towards the entrance. His left hand was pushed into his trouser pocket, and in his right he held a cigarette, which he smoked not as a man relaxed and enjoying his tobacco, but as if it were vital that he inhale as much smoke as possible. He looks like a train, thought Maisie. But more than the smoking or his pacing, Maisie could feel his nervousness, as if his composure were hanging by a thread—which was to be understood, considering the attack on his wife's parents, and the fact that his brother-in-law had not yet arrived in the country to share the burden of concern. At that moment Libbert, who was now looking at the floor as he paced, collided with a young clerk who was walking at speed to deliver an envelope set on a silver tray.

"Hey, watch out, pal!" Libbert admonished the clerk, who was offering profuse apologies while kneeling down to pick up the tray and envelope, which he had dropped in the collision. "Just look where you're going—I'll have you fired, you idiot."

Maisie stepped forward, smiling as she approached and speaking his name so that he looked towards her. "Mr. Libbert? Good morning—Maisie Dobbs." She held out her hand, then turned to the clerk. "Are you all right? You almost came a cropper there."

The young man nodded, apologized once more, and walked on, clutching the silver tray and letter.

"I could have his job for that."

"But it's good of you not to complain—he might be the sole supporter of his family in these times, so I am sure he's grateful to you for just letting him off with a reprimand." She looked around. "You must be under tremendous strain—shall we talk over a cup of coffee?"

Libbert rubbed a hand across his forehead. "I—I'm sorry. I shouldn't have been so rough on the kid—too much on my mind." He nodded. "I could use a cup of coffee."

"So, you're working for my father-in-law, but you can't tell me what he's asked of you?"

"Only that it is in connection with his son, Michael. There are some outstanding questions regarding his estate, and Mr. and Mrs. Clifton wanted to be in touch with anyone who might have known him in his final days." Maisie smiled in acknowledgment as a waiter poured two cups of coffee, and cast her eyes around the opulent surroundings, at the swags of fabric decorating the walls and the marbled pillars. She turned to Libbert again. "I suppose you could say they are trying to close the book on his life in a manner that allows them, and their son, to rest in peace."

"The only big outstanding question is that land. There have been probate problems over the years, given his status. I've been out there with Teddy, and as far as I can see, it's all desert and a bit of scrubby forest—nothing like the East Coast. That's what you call forest."

"I thought it might be an area rich with possibility."

Libbert shook his head. "Union Oil has the most valuable land tied up with its mineral rights and it's snapped up anything of worth. And I can't see Michael knowing more than these people, so heaven only knows why he bought the land. Not that we can sell it anyway, not until the legals are all sorted out."

"We?"

Libbert shrugged. "It's a pretty safe bet that, in his will, Michael would have left the land to my wife—after all, she was his favorite sister. We'll sell as soon as we can."

"Was there a will?"

"Yes and no."

"What do you mean?"

"When Michael enlisted—the fool that he was—like all soldiers, he was asked to make a will. After his death, Edward discovered that Michael had simply written, 'Done.' Now that his remains have been found, we hope this can all be sorted out—but let me tell you, the banks don't give up anything without every single last document in place."

"It's clear that Mr. and Mrs. Clifton would want to honor Michael's will, rather than jump to conclusions about his wishes regarding distribution of his wealth."

Libbert shook his head. "Like I said, everyone knows that we—I mean, my wife—would have been the number-one beneficiary."

A waiter approached and poured more coffee, and as Libbert picked up his cup once more, she put another question to him.

"Were you aware that Michael had a very strong association with a young woman while overseas?"

He rolled his eyes. "Oh, great! If anyone was going to fall in love with a penniless girl in wartime, it would have been our romantic Michael, wouldn't it?" Libbert sipped his coffee, then reached forward and placed both cup and saucer back on the tray. "No doubt there's some money-hungry woman out there right now trying to get her hands on her deceased lover's wealth."

"I think if the woman in question was going to do such a thing, she might not be so hard to find. And in any case, if she is not specifically mentioned in Michael's will, surely she would have no claim."

"Oh, trust me, Miss Dobbs, as far as the Clifton money is concerned, you would not believe the people who might come out of the woodwork. And even though Edward's family shoe company over here closed down years ago, people still remember Clifton's Shoes—heck, there are people out there still wearing them. Of course, that was half their trouble, they made shoes to last. They didn't seem to understand that if shoes don't wear out, then people don't buy more shoes."

"They did very well for over a century, Mr. Libbert, and certainly I have never heard of making shoes that do not last—after all, what do we have a cobbler for, if not to repair a good pair of shoes?"

Libbert shook his head. "That's not how it's going to work if people want to make money—you wait and see." He looked at his watch. "Now, is this all you wanted to see me about? To talk about Michael?"

Maisie set down her cup and saucer and picked up her gloves, shoulder bag, and document case. "Yes, that's more or less it." They stood up together, and as they walked towards the foyer, Maisie asked another question.

"I understand you were here at the Dorchester when Mr. and Mrs. Clifton were attacked."

Libbert cleared his throat, and Maisie thought his color heightened a little. "I was staying here, but not here at the time. I'd gone out earlier for a walk across the park—can't just sit in business meetings all day, can I? I was planning to join them for dinner later, but had yet to see them on the day it happened." He shook his head. "I just wish I'd seen them earlier, gone out with them . . . anything to stop them going back to their room when they did. It's a tragedy, a family tragedy."

Maisie nodded. "They are in excellent hands, Mr. Libbert."

"So I've been told, but Teddy is bringing a family friend across with him—man called Charles Hayden. Brain surgeon and one of the best."

"Charles Hayden?"

"Heard of him?"

Maisie smiled. "I met him in France, when I was a nurse. He was a friend of a friend."

Libbert shrugged. "Small world, Miss Dobbs. Very small world. Now, I've got work to do."

"Thank you for your time, Mr. Libbert."

"You're welcome," said Libbert. Then he turned and walked away.

Maisie pulled on her gloves and stepped out into spring sunshine breaking through the clouds. She thanked the doorman and they exchanged a few words about the weather, and that spring seemed to have sprung at last. And when she looked across towards the park and saw the last of the daffodils, she thought she would walk and consider the conversation with Libbert. But instead, the words that came to her were those of Edward Clifton, when she visited him at St. George's Hospital and asked him to recollect the day's events leading up to the attack in their hotel room: "*. . . when they'd gone, Tommy—he's our son-in-law—called out to us. He'd just come down to the lobby. He wanted to know when we'd be back.*"

As she walked in Hyde Park, Maisie's thoughts were on Edward Clifton and his wife, and she thought she would make her way to Hyde Park Corner and St. George's Hospital, where she might be able to learn more of their progress, and—if luck favored her—even see Edward again. The image of the hospital and the elderly man she hoped to see reminded her of Maurice. She confessed to herself that she had been pushing all consideration of his ill health to the back of her mind—she did not want to entertain the implications of his not getting well again. She felt as if she were on a trapeze at the circus, flying through the air, but with no net below to catch her. She stopped on the path, and as she closed her eyes, she felt the tears well up once more. Who would be there if she fell? Maurice had picked her up from the cold, wet ground when she collapsed at the site of the casualty clearing station where, in the eyes of the dead and dying, she had seen a terror she could never have imagined, and where an already compromised youthful innocence was lost to her forever. He had remained with her, had ministered to her when she needed him most—was she failing him now by not being at his side?

Maisie tried to shake off the chill that had enveloped her, and walked on along the path, so consumed by her powerlessness against the march of time and sickness that she did not hear the steps behind her, nor had she considered that the earlier sensation had been anything more than a physical manifestation of her fear. The attack was sudden, the shove between her shoulder blades sending her lurching forward and crashing to the ground. She felt her cheek strike the path, and as she fell forward, she released her grip on her document case to break the impact of her fall.

Maisie gathered her thoughts within seconds, pushed down on the ground with her hands, and came to her feet. The document case was gone, and in the distance she could see a man running towards the gate. She gave chase, shouting, "Stop! Thief! Stop that man—stop that thief!"

As she ran, Maisie felt the air scratch her throat and her chest began to burn, but she did not relinquish speed to discomfort. She ran out through the gate in time to see the man dodge through Marble Arch traffic; then he was gone.

"Damn!" She looked down at her hands, the deep grazes and scrapes along the base of her palms, and as a policeman came towards her, she brushed the back of her hand against her cheek and felt the wetness of blood where gravel had torn at her skin. "Oh, that's just lovely!" she said to herself.

"Are you all right, Miss?"

"I think so. Did you see him, the man who attacked me? He took my document case—black, leather—and ran off towards the tube."

"I'll take the particulars, Miss. We'll see if we can nab him along the line. Tricky, though—these thieves are light on their feet, you know. And there's more of it now, what with people being out of work."

"Yes, I know, Constable." She reached into her pocket for a clean handkerchief and wiped blood from her cheek and hands.

"I'll just put out the call," said the policeman after noting Maisie's description of the man. He ran to a nearby police telephone kiosk, and returned after a few minutes.

"There, they'll do what they can along the line, though I think you might have seen the last of your case, miss. Just as well he didn't take your handbag, though it would have been hard to get it off your shoulder—it's easier to just grab the case."

"I don't think he was after my bag," said Maisie.

"Oh, I don't know, miss, what with your money in there."

Maisie shook her head. "No. He was after the case. I'm fairly sure of that." She paused, touching her face again. "Now, if you would be so kind as to call me a taxi-cab, Constable, I think I might go to get this cheek sorted out."

The constable hailed a taxi-cab, and soon Maisie was on her way to St. George's Hospital. She'd had worse scrapes as a child, playing in the streets of Lambeth, and the attack had signaled that she had no time to lose, no time to read Michael Clifton's journal and letters as if they were a novel, no time to indulge herself in grief over events that might not yet come to pass. She knew her assailant had been waiting for her, had in all likelihood seen her enter, then leave The Dorchester Hotel. It was good fortune that the document case contained only a folder with a few sheets of notes unrelated to the Clifton case, along with her Victorinox knife, a pair of rubber gloves, a surgical mask, and a very small set of tools in a drawstring bag. She suspected that the thief might well be disappointed with his haul.

NINE

At the hospital, Maisie went straight to the ladies' lavatory and filled a washbasin with hot water. The cuts on her hands began to sting again as soon as she steeped them in the steaming water, and she winced as she leaned forward, rested her forearms on the basin, and closed her eyes for a few seconds while she absorbed the pain. She rubbed her palms together to loosen the dirt and grit embedded in her skin, then pulled the plug to release the bloodstained water, refilling the basin again to rinse away more debris before shaking her hands and pulling a clean white handkerchief from her shoulder bag. Maisie moistened the cloth and began to dab around the deep abrasion to her right cheek, then inspected the wound in a mirror above the basin.

"That's a picture," she said aloud, before continuing to apply pressure around the outside of the graze. She knew she should have added disinfectant to the water, but at the same time, she wouldn't think of bothering nurses in a busy hospital, and they would likely point her in the direction of the casualty department. No, she had been a nurse, she could take care of her own medical problems.

Having done the best she could to diminish bruising and inflammation with a final few splashes of cold water, Maisie made her way up to the floor where Edward Clifton was recovering. As she walked along the corridor, she noticed that the same policeman was on duty, and there were no medical staff in the immediate vicinity of Clifton's private ward. She lost no time in taking advantage of the situation.

"Good afternoon, Constable. Having a good day?"

"Afternoon, madam. I wasn't told to expect you."

"Oh, I expect that because we've met before, Detective Inspector Caldwell probably thought it unnecessary. Do you know how Mr. Clifton's progressing?"

"The doctors are pleased, that's all I know really. It'll be better when his son gets here, I would imagine. Not very nice when no one comes to see you of a visiting hour."

"No visitors? Not even his son-in-law?"

"Son-in-law?"

"What news of Mrs. Clifton?" asked Maisie, without responding to the constable's question.

"According to the nurses, there's been some improvement—her breathing's stronger, though they think that if she comes around, she might not be all there." He tapped the side of his head. "Upstairs."

"Oh, dear—they are such a close couple, it would be devastating for Mr. Clifton to lose her."

Maisie knew the policeman was warming to the conversation. His present task was, at best, boring, so Maisie's presence was a welcome interlude in an otherwise tedious shift—unless of course he was called upon to protect his charge from an interloper.

"What did you walk into this morning, madam? That's a nasty scrape you've got there."

Maisie smiled. "To tell you the truth, I fell over my own feet while rushing across the park. I should have known better than to run. Serves me right for waiting until the last minute to leave for work. By the way, speaking of being in a bit of a hurry—it is visiting time, so I wonder if I might just pop in and see Mr. Clifton?"

"I should have prior permission, but—" He looked to the left and right along the corridor. "Go on. I'll knock in ten minutes, earlier if someone comes along."

Maisie smiled as the policeman opened the door. "Thank you, Constable. Very kind of you." She slipped into Edward Clifton's private ward.

Edward Clifton was lying back on his pillows, awake, yet gazing out of the window to his left. He turned as Maisie entered, and gave a brief nod in her direction by way of greeting.

"How are you, Mr. Clifton?" Maisie came to his bedside, pulled up a chair, and sat down.

Clifton regarded Maisie in a way that reminded her of Frankie. It was the look of a father of children now grown. "I think I might be doing better than you today, Miss Dobbs."

Maisie laughed and touched her cheek. "Oh, this? No, it's nothing. Your wounds are much deeper and more worrisome for the doctors." She quickly changed the subject to make the most of the next few minutes. "I understand that Mrs. Clifton has shown some improvement."

Clifton nodded. "That's what they say." He shrugged. "I'll clutch at any straws out there, but to me progress would be my dear wife recognizing me, talking to me."

"There is cause for optimism, Mr. Clifton."

He nodded in a sage manner, staring out of the window once more, but said nothing.

"Mr. Clifton, may I ask one or two more questions?" she went on, without waiting for a response. "Has your son-in-law been in to see you yet?"

Clifton turned to her. "I think he came before I regained consciousness—I remember the nurse saying he'd been to see me. And I know he's telephoned the ward staff, so he's keeping up with our progress—he's probably calling back to Boston every day so that Meg and Anna know how their mother and I are doing. Tom's dealing with a lot at the moment—company business in London on top of what's happened to us—so I'm sure he's busy." He paused for a moment. "To tell you the truth, we've never had too much to say to each other, Thomas and I. Not that he's not a good fellow—he's a fine husband and father—but we simply don't have much in common. If he was sitting here now, we'd both be stumped for conversation."

"So I expect the last time you actually saw him to talk to was in the foyer of the hotel, prior to the attack in your room."

Clifton frowned. "Yes. Yes, I suppose it was."

Maisie nodded. "When we last spoke, you said something about a couple close to the entrance. They were arguing, there was a row or something. Do you remember anything more about them?"

After a pause, Clifton responded, and shrugged, as if what he was about to say was unimportant. "You know, this is going to sound strange, but I remember thinking that the woman reminded me of Anna, our daughter. Something about the eyes, and of course the hair—Anna's the only one who took after me with my dark hair. Yes, she reminded me of Anna. I remember thinking that if anyone ever treated one of our girls like that, I would have had to interfere, do something about it. You see, Martha and I, we always agreed that no matter what happens, our children have their own lives. They choose their mates, and we can't do a thing about it. But I might have had to step in if I was that woman's father." He sighed, then added, "Sad. It made me very sad, thinking about it."

Maisie did not respond immediately, allowing the moment of reflection to linger. To have interjected at once with another question would have been thoughtless after Clifton had revealed his feelings in such a way. She picked up her bag just as a light knock at the door signaled that her ten minutes had come to an end.

"Thank you for your time, Mr. Clifton. I am glad your wife is making progress." Without thinking, she reached out and held his hand, and he nodded acknowledgment. He may not have been her own father, but he was father to grown children he loved, and he missed them. Releasing his hand, Maisie stood up and walked towards the door. It was only as she reached for the handle that a thought occurred to her.

"Mr. Clifton, may I ask another question?"

"Of course."

"I know your old family firm, Clifton's Shoes, closed down some years ago. What happened to the company?"

Clifton sighed. "It was all my fault, I suppose—or my father's for establishing a company based upon male inheritance of responsibility. I heard not a word from my family after I left home for America—that's probably why family means so much to me now, why it's important to be on good terms with my children. They didn't communicate with me again, and I was shut out of any decisions regarding the business; though of course I was not surprised by the latter. I had made my bed, and I was expected to lie in it, come what may, and I was many miles away in any case. As far as I know my sister married, and it was she and her husband who kept the business going after my father passed away. Then her husband died and she sold out to the first bidder at a knockdown price. They weren't businesspeople, and she was also hampered by the company's bylaws, so it had run into the ground—trying to keep that quality at a good price. I believe she married again, but I have no idea what happened after that, except that she was still quite young when she died. And she probably went to her grave having given her life to maintain the claim that not one pair of Clifton's shoes went on sale that would not last a good ten years of solid daily wear." He looked at Maisie, his head to one side, his eyes now half closed as fatigue claimed him once again. "Is it important?"

Maisie shrugged. "I don't know, Mr. Clifton. But I thought I'd ask."

Maisie sat at the dining table in her flat, with one hand dabbing the wound to her cheek with a cloth soaked in salted water, the other turning the pages of Michael Clifton's journal.

I'm trying to remember her face. I could recognize her in a crowd, such a pretty girl could not be missed. But sitting here on my bunk in this French barn, waiting to go out with my guys again, I just can't picture her. I can imagine the dark hair—thick and glorious hair, like silk down her back when she pulls out the pins and lets it fall. I can barely believe I'll see her in less than a week—four days' leave in Paris. They were going to ship me back to Blighty, but I said it was no good me going back, because I don't have people there. A couple of the guys (the lads, as they say), Mullen and Perry, each invited me home with them, but I said no, I would go to Paris. Pretended I knew someone there. And I do. I do know someone there.

Several ink dots speckled the page, as if the writer was thinking of how to express in words the feelings in his heart.

I am a bit more scared each time I have to go out into the field. I play brave. I'm taller than a lot of the men, and for some reason, because I'm an American (they call me the Yank), they expect me to be the most fearless of all. So I just get on with it. We all just get on with it, but we're all scared, standing out there setting up our equipment. We're like sitting targets, like ducks in hunting season, the ones that just land in front of the guy with the gun. But we just work away as if no one was there, as if it was only us and the land. I'm glad I did this. I'm not sorry I enlisted when I did; after all, they need good mapmakers. But I'll be happy to go home again, as soon as the war is over. . . .

Maisie stood up, went into the kitchen, and disposed of the soiled cloth. She allowed the graze on her cheeks to dry, but had wrapped the base of each palm so the cuts would not break open when she used her hands. She returned to the journal, and the letters, trying to reconcile events from one to the other.

Dear Michael,

The days in Paris were lovely. How we were blessed with the weather, only one day of rain. I am sorry about the Wednesday, but our chaperone insisted I remain with the other nurses, so I could not meet you at the arranged time. I'm glad you received my note and did not think that I had stood you up. Our chaperones have been instructed not to breathe down our necks, but at the same time, we are expected to conduct ourselves according to the rules. It seems as if we were not meant to meet on that final day in any case. You must have been so surprised when your brother-in-law turned up in Paris. I wonder how he managed to get there, with so many travel restrictions in place. But it must have been lovely for you to see a member of your family. I know how much you miss them.

I'm not due for more leave for some time, but at least we can write. . . .

Maisie leaned back in her chair. Which brother-in-law met with Michael Clifton in Paris? She could not jump to conclusions and assume that it was Thomas Libbert; after all, the older sister, Meg, was married to a doctor—a doctor who knew Charles Hayden, who was himself in France in the war. Perhaps Meg's husband was also a doctor with an American medical contingent and had sought out his wife's younger brother while they were both serving overseas. Maisie could imagine the family pressing him to locate Michael, to seek him out, perhaps to send their love and to bid him Godspeed.

I will never forget her again. I am the luckiest guy in the world, to have found such a wonderful girl. They'll love her back home, really love her, I'm sure. Teddy always said that I could fall in love at the drop of a hat, but this is for real, forever, I just know it. Now all we've got to do is make it out of this war. I guess the only cloud over our days together was when we bumped into old stiff breeches himself. Mullen thought up that name, and it suits him well—stiff upper lip and all that. In all of Paris, how did that happen, how did our paths cross? He hates me, really hates me. Every time I come in with a new map, he finds fault. He thinks I've done nothing but swan around stateside on my father's dime—but I did my time at Chatham, they just didn't have to teach me from scratch. I know MORE than him, because I've done more and trained harder, and I've said as much—not that they've ever heard of Berkeley here, these Oxford and Cambridge types. I know I said too much, could have been put on a charge for insubordination. Mullen said I ought to watch my mouth, but I've never been pushed like that, never. Told him that when that clown can find oil just by looking at the land, then perhaps he could correct me—I'm not just a cartographer, I'm a surveyor, and I'm done with being kicked around by some busybody stiff-upper-lipped limey who did his best to needle me about a darn shoe company that I know almost nothing about. I never thought I would want to be called something other than Clifton, but in that last week before my leave, I wished I was plain old Smith or Jones. Mullen asked me what he was talking about, so I told him about Dad leaving England, and he said he knew of Clifton's Shoes. Then he asked about the oil, and I told him about my land there. Kind of wish I'd kept my mouth shut—again. I wanted to keep the land a secret until I went home and brought Dad and Teddy out to see it. Even showed Mullen my maps of the valley, and my little piece of it. I beat the Union Oil guys to that piece of land, and they can set up their drills and derricks all around me and I bet they won't get my oil. You should have seen Mullen's eyes. In all his days with maps, he said he would never have a chance to survey land and then buy it. Guess I'm a very lucky guy—got the land and I've got the girl.

"Mullen?" Maisie said the name aloud, then wrote it out on an index card. She pulled out another card and wrote, "Stiff breeches." If Michael Clifton had risked being put on a charge for answering back in such a manner, he must have been referring to an officer of greater rank. Was it his commanding officer? And if so, why wasn't he put on a charge? Soldiers had been court-martialed for less. On a piece of paper she made a list of inquiries to be made, and it was clear that a visit to Chatham, to the place where the artillery's mapmakers were trained, would have to be a priority. It was the second time in one sitting that she cautioned herself not to jump in with the first thought that came to mind.

Maisie continued reading, though now the events of the day were catching up with her, and her eyes were gritty and dry with fatigue. She checked the time; just half past eight in the evening, and she was exhausted. But she did not want to rest yet, so she picked up another letter and slipped the paper from the envelope, carefully unfolding the foxed and fused pages. At that moment the bell in the hallway sounded, alerting her to a visitor at the front door.

Maisie disliked the fact that as soon as she opened the door to her ground-floor flat, anyone waiting outside could see her. She had asked about having frosted glass installed, but other owners didn't appreciate the need for such expenditure. She wondered who might be calling without being in touch with her first. On the other hand, she did not have a telephone, so an uninvited guest could be expected, though it was rare. Maisie pushed back her chair and began to walk towards the hallway, but then turned around and came back to the table, where she gathered the letters and journal and put them away in a kitchen cupboard. Now she was ready to greet her caller.

As she opened the door to the foyer, she could see Detective Inspector Caldwell, together with his new detective sergeant, waiting on the step outside the main entrance. Caldwell was just about to press the bell again, so she waved to attract his attention and stepped towards the door.

"Detective Inspector Caldwell, to what do I owe a visit to my home—and at such an hour?"

"I think you know very well why I am here, Miss Dobbs—two reasons, in fact."

"Would you care to come in?"

Caldwell and his assistant removed their hats and followed Maisie into the flat. She saw Caldwell look at the painting over the mantelpiece—of a woman standing on the beach, looking out to sea—and the collection of photos, some framed, some simply pinned, that surrounded the painting. He cast his eyes around the room.

"Do take a seat, please," offered Maisie. "Would you care for some tea?"

Caldwell shook his head, though Maisie saw the detective sergeant begin to smile as if he was about to accept the offer. He looked away when he heard Caldwell's quick reply.

"No time to sit here drinking tea, Miss Dobbs, but thank you for offering all the same." He didn't miss a beat before launching into his reason for the visit. "First of all, I want to know—from you—the circumstances of the attack on your person in Hyde Park. Then I want to know why you went to St. George's Hospital and talked my policeman into letting you into Mr. Clifton's private ward."

"Well, one event led to the other, as is so often the case. I was the victim of a robbery in Hyde Park, and because I had hurt my hands and cheek, as you can see"—she held up her hands with her bandaged palms facing the detective—"I went to the hospital to receive treatment. The last thing I want is a case of lockjaw, so I thought I should have the wounds attended to straightaway. While I was there, I decided to go up to Mr. Clifton's ward and ask after his progress. The patient was awake, so I thought I would pop in and see him—after all, it happened to be visiting hour, and I understand he has had no visitors since he regained consciousness. He's an old man far from home, and I thought he might welcome a bit of company."

"Did you talk about the attack?"

"Yes, of course. I inquired about his health."

"Is there anything you'd like to share with us, Miss Dobbs?'

"There is nothing else that I believe is of any great significance to you. It was a rather pedestrian conversation. To tell you the truth, I was rather curious as to why his son-in-law had not visited since he regained consciousness, but Mr. Clifton informed me that he has received messages from him, but they have never really had much in common—those were his words."

Caldwell nodded. "Why didn't you inform us about the robbery attempt in Hyde Park as soon as it happened?"

"I summoned a constable to help me, and though he had tried to give chase—as had I—the robber escaped on foot, probably down into Marble Arch underground station. He took my document case, but there was nothing of value inside. The case is old, a bit tattered, but it holds great sentimental value for me—I would love to have it back."

"Present from a suitor, Miss Dobbs?"

Maisie shook her head, not rising to the bait. "No, from the staff I worked with when I was in service. They bought me the case when I left to go up to Girton College in 1914. It was such a big event, not just for me but for all of us—one of their own going away to college. So they had a whip-round and bought me the very best document case they could afford, and it has lasted all this time."

Caldwell heard the catch in her throat as she spoke, and responded in a softer tone. "We'll see if we can get it back for you, then. If we can do that, we'll likely catch the thief—and you never know how valuable he might be to us."

"Thank you. Now, if you don't mind . . ."

"Yes, of course. Much obliged to you, Miss Dobbs. Please try to remember to request a visit to Mr. Clifton until further notice. And I'd appreciate being kept informed of any leads you might uncover in this case. It was a violent attack on two prominent visitors to our country. I'm expected to get to the bottom of it in short order."

"I'll keep you posted."

Maisie saw the men to the door and bid them good night. She returned to her chair by the fire, which she had not ignited earlier, but because she felt chilled, she knelt down and turned on the gas jets, lowering the flame for the sake of economy. Instead of sitting on one of the two armchairs, Maisie pulled a cushion towards her and made herself comfortable seated on the floor in front of the fire. She found the combination of heat and flame almost hypnotic, and allowed her mind to wander.

It was not until she spoke of the loss of the document case that she had realized how much it meant to her. She was but seventeen years old when a special "below stairs" supper had been organized for her at Chelstone Manor, where most of the household staff were located over the summer months. War had been declared on August 4, and in September, the staff were happy to send one of their own on her way to better things. The document case earned a few scratches at Girton, then was put away when she enlisted for nursing service after just two terms. It was brought out again when she returned to complete her studies in 1919—after she had already been wounded, had recovered, and then worked in a hospital for the shell-shocked. The fine leather became even more scuffed when she became assistant to Dr. Maurice Blanche, as she filled it daily with papers and files and the accoutrements of her trade. The bag had been repaired where stitching had loosened, and had required a new clasp some years earlier, but she had never been without it since the end of the war.

Now it was gone, and in her mind's eye she saw the staff gathered around the table on the day it was presented to her. There was Enid cracking a joke, always a bit sarcastic, always sharp. Dear Enid, who had died in a munitions factory explosion. Mrs. Crawford was still there, not yet retired, and Carter, the butler, before the years began to tell. She had no idea, then, what she would make of her life. No thoughts of love had entered her mind, her drive to educate herself usurping all other measures of happiness, contentment. Priscilla, Simon, the girls who had served alongside her in France—they were all yet to come, on the day she opened the box and drew back the fine tissue to reveal the aroma of good leather, soft to the touch. The path from there to here had been far from straight, had looped back and forth, yet always with an imagined place ahead—that she would be a woman of independent means and would rise above her circumstances.

As she sat by the fire in her own flat, the retreat and refuge she'd imagined in those dreams, she thought about other places where she had laid her head. There was the room in Lambeth—why had she lived there at all? She came from Girton, straight to London to interview with Maurice. Then when he'd sent word that the job was hers, she found lodgings in the only area she could afford and knew at all, the place where she'd grown up: Lambeth. Her room was clean, tidy, and there was a meal in the evening when she arrived home, but she walked through the slums each day, through streets of depression and want. She had realized, even then, that her choice to live in a place so compromised, among people so wretched, was due to the fact that she was still numb. Living in such troubled quarters was tantamount to touching her skin with a hot needle—it reminded her that she was still alive, that she was not dead, that the war might have taken so much, but it had not taken her life.

It was later, after Maurice retired and she set up her business on her own, that at the behest of Lady Rowan she came back to live at the Comptons' Ebury Place mansion. Her rooms were more than comfortable and clean, they were light and cozy, and her every need was catered for—yet she had still not found her place, had never quite felt at home. She was neither this nor that, not one class or the other. Now, as she reflected upon her journey and the years past, she realized she had come this far and had no idea what might come next, or what there might be for her to aspire to. She understood that she knew only how to climb mountains; having reached a certain place of elevation, she was unaccustomed to the view of the road already taken, and where her next steps might lead. Losing the document case had been akin to losing a suitcase of clothes on a very long journey. She knew neither the next destination, nor how she might prepare to travel.

TEN

The following day, after a brief meeting with Billy at their office in Fitzroy Square, Maisie embarked upon the drive down to Chatham, where the army's cartographers were trained at the School of Military Engineering. As Davidson predicted, Maisie's telephone call to the school was shunted along to Major Ian Temple, who had been described to her by the young man who answered the telephone as "the one who looks after outside people, and that sort of thing." She suspected it was not a welcome task, but one delegated to an officer who seemed to have time on his hands.

A long journey in her motor car, a two-seater MG 14/40, always gave Maisie an opportunity to engage in uninterrupted thought. There was something about the rhythm of the road, the tires against tarmacadam that allowed her to delve deeply into whatever challenge was engaging her attention. She would change gears, slow down, speed up, as the journey required, and at no point was she anything but attentive to the task of driving, but at the same time, it was as if in the act of travel, her immediate concerns were lulled, and in her contemplation she seemed to plumb a greater depth of understanding.

She had put a folder and some index cards into a plain carrier bag with string handles, instead of her document case, and she found that once again the loss of her case took on a deeper meaning during the course of her day. Each morning she donned clothing suited to her work, sensible garb that suggested she should be taken seriously as a professional woman with her own business. She dressed as if she were putting on a suit of armor for battle, and when she finally picked up the document case as she left the flat, it became as important to her as a scabbard might be to a warrior. Now, on the passenger seat, her belongings were held in a bag of paper and string. The significance of such a development occupied her for most of the journey.

The School of Military Engineering was another forces establishment in a town that was also home to the Chatham Dockyard, and as she made her way to Brompton Barracks, where Major Ian Temple had agreed to meet her at noon, she thought of the thousands of young men across the centuries who had come to the town in service of their country. What might Michael Clifton have thought of this place? He came from an historic part of America, a city that had no form in Maisie's imagination because she could not comprehend a country of such expanse and difference; but growing up in such an environment, he must have developed a keen respect for the past and, as a cartographer, a sharper sense of the events and experiences that frame a place and define its people. How would he have felt as he made his way up to the barracks? Chatham had been the focus of military operations since the Middle Ages, and had earned its reputation as a naval base in the Napoleonic Wars. What might his first impressions have been, and how might he have made friends? Had he been teased about his accent by his fellow men? Or had they looked up to him, curious as to why he had enlisted in a war that was not of his country's making?

More than anything, she hoped she could find someone who might remember him.

Maisie parked and, before leaving the motor car, placed several index cards in her shoulder bag. She set off towards the main entrance to a series of boxlike buildings built in the early 1800s, and was surprised to be greeted at the door by Major Temple, a man of distinct military bearing but with an approachability that had eluded Peter Whitting. Temple led Maisie along a corridor where white walls were half paneled with English oak, towards a wooden staircase, where they made their way up to the first floor. It seemed that nothing was out of place in Temple's office. Equipment similar to that which she had seen at Whitting's house was positioned on a series of shelves alongside the door, and behind the desk more shelves held books on military strategy.

Temple was businesslike in his approach, and had made an effort to accommodate Maisie's inquiry. "I'm sorry I didn't have much time when you telephoned, Miss Dobbs; however, I have managed to locate some information on Michael Clifton. Of course, you understand that your request is somewhat out of the ordinary. We are not used to the bereaved contacting us, especially via a third party."

"Yes, I do understand; yet by the same token, the circumstances of Lieutenant Clifton's enlistment and service are unusual—he was an American citizen, so I would have thought he might have been turned down for service."

Temple shrugged and leaned back in his chair. "I wish it were as simple as that, Miss Dobbs. It's so easy, after the event, to look at what procedure should have been employed, but in a time of war people do what they feel is right to get the job done." He picked up a folder on his desk and untied a short length of twine securing the pages inside. "I have here Clifton's enlistment details, and the notes of the officer on duty at the time. Clifton had evidence of an impressive background in a field in which we had to improve—that of cartography. He had an engineer's university education and had worked as both a surveyor and a cartographer, and he was familiar with developments in measuring the land. He was young, clever, and inquisitive, and we were trying to get new tools and practices out into the field, using sound and aerial photography. In short, he was exactly the sort of chap we were hoping to recruit. Clifton was just what we wanted."

"Major Temple, you sound as if you knew him personally."

Temple shook his head and looked down at his notes. "No, I didn't. I was an artilleryman in the war. But I know what our priorities were, and I know that Michael Clifton would not have been turned away. The fact that his father was a British citizen was in his favor—if the infantry were turning a blind eye to age in a bid to recruit, then we could let a matter of citizenship go through without comment."

"Yes, so I understand."

"I don't know if you are aware of the problems we faced in the early months of the war," said Temple.

"It has been explained to me."

Temple went on as if he had not heard. "The French were the world's best mapmakers, yet the maps of their own country were pitiful, and we were working to different scales—it was a nightmare."

Maisie nodded, but her interest was more immediate. "I'd like to know more about Lieutenant Clifton's record vis-à-vis personal interaction with his peers and superiors. Was he liked? What did his commanding officer say about him?"

Temple shrugged. "I get the impression he was well liked, an affable chap." He opened the folder again. "Typical of those Americans, eh? Says here that he was always one to keep the spirits up, would help out, and was exceptionally brave—he and his men had been targeted by a sniper in the weeks before he was listed among the missing, and he had carried a badly wounded soldier back to the dugout with him, then went out again to bring back the body of another. He apparently did not want to leave the man to the rats of no-man's-land."

"Major, I wonder, do you have the names of the other men who died alongside Lieutenant Clifton? I'm particularly interested in a man named Mullen."

Again Temple consulted the notes and flicked through the pages. "Hmmm, yes."

Maisie leaned forward. "You have him listed?"

"As you probably know, we received notification that the bodies of Clifton and others in the unit were recently discovered, but Mullen isn't listed here. However—" He turned the pages to one he had looked at earlier. "Yes, here it is, thought I'd seen that name before. The wounded man, the one who Clifton brought back, was named Mullen. Seems he owes his life to Clifton, but I obviously have no record of his whereabouts after his medical discharge."

"Of course, yes." She paused. "And who was Lieutenant Clifton's commanding officer?"

"His immediate superior was a Captain Jeremy Lockwood, and according to the file, Lockwood was killed several weeks before Clifton was listed as missing. Single sniper bullet to the head."

"That's all in Clifton's notes?"

"Not all held as part of his military record, but I thought I'd try to dig further, in anticipation of your questions."

"That was good of you to go to the trouble. Thank you."

Temple looked at his watch, at which point Maisie stood up and held out her hand. "Thank you for your time, Major. You have been most helpful."

"Doesn't seem much, really. Mind you, his father must be well-heeled—if you excuse the pun—being from Clifton's Shoes."

"Is that sort of information held as part of his military service record?"

Maisie thought for a moment. "It's not an uncommon name, though I suppose Michael might have mentioned the connection to support his claim of British ancestry."

Temple looked down at his notes once again and closed the file. "Well, it must have been written up somewhere." He cleared his throat, then looked up. "Let me escort you to your motor car. The weather looks as if it will hold for a clear journey back to London. Are you a Londoner by birth, Miss Dobbs, or . . ." Temple continued the conversation as they made their way downstairs, along the paneled corridor, and out into the afternoon light. Maisie barely said a word, aware that the very correct army officer was allowing her little opportunity to interject, or put another question to him. He had given her sufficient information, then a little bit more to keep her happy, though she thought the comment regarding Clifton's Shoes was a slip he regretted. It was, she thought, an interview with a man quite used to dealing with questions from outside the establishment, and his responses—just enough here, a snippet more than requested there—were designed to ensure there would be no more inquiries forthcoming.

Where do we look for Mullen? Maisie knew that such a search could be lengthy and lead to a dead end, but she thought it was important to find the man who owed his life to Michael Clifton, and who—she hoped—would be able to identify the officer with whom Clifton had experienced some antagonism. The journal entries might offer a clue to Mullen's origins, some mention of where he came from, any loose thread of information that could be unpicked.

As Temple predicted, the weather was kind for the rest of the day, and Maisie enjoyed the drive, which at one point commanded a view across the North Downs before she went on to London. The way in which the light moved across the hills caused Maisie to pull onto the side of the road for a few moments. As clouds crossed the sun, each beam slanted down on the earth's folds and inclines, giving an impression of movement, as if searchlights were in pursuit of a vanishing day. She wondered if this was how a cartographer might begin his work, simply by standing at a vantage point and regarding the land he must interpret for others to find their way. It occurred to Maisie that, just as Whitting had described, the cartographer must be both the artist and the technician. He must be the storyteller and the editor, seeing the curves and movement of the land with a practiced eye, and then bringing a mathematical precision to the page. If he was wrong, then people would become lost on their journey. And if the mapmaker had been charged with interpreting a field of battle, then his errors would cause men—many, many men—to die.

Maisie resumed her journey, and soon, with the country behind her, she drove first through the ever-growing suburbia, then into London and along the Old Kent Road towards the West End. She arrived at four o'clock, in time to see Billy walking across the square.

"Hello, Billy!" Maisie called out and waved as she entered the square from Fitzroy Street.

"Afternoon, Miss." He smiled as she approached. "How did you get on this morning?"

"It was interesting, I'll say that for my day so far. Let's get up to the office, and I'll fill you in on what I've found out. Any luck with those names?"

They continued talking as they went up the staircase to the first floor.

"I managed to find to three of them who were in London, but it didn't take an awful lot for their stories to crumble, I can tell you. Two of them were alone, one living in a bed-sit and one at a ladies' boardinghouse. One was looking for a way out of her circumstances, and the other one said her friend put her up to it, and she didn't want to get into any trouble. The third was a nanny to two nippers. She looked a bit pale, I must say—they were a right pair of tearaways. Little villains who could talk proper. I tell you, Miss, my boys might not sound upper-crust, but they know their manners and would put those two to shame. Anyway, she was another one looking for the golden path to another life."

Maisie unlocked the door and pushed it open, walked to her desk and took off her hat.

"Blimey, Miss, what've you done to your face? You look like you'd stopped at one of them boxing clubs down the Old Kent Road for a few rounds with a heavyweight. Ow, I bet that hurts."

Maisie touched her cheek. "You know, it's funny you mention it, but it stopped stinging today, so I forgot about it for a while—yet the officer I saw at the School of Military Engineering didn't blink an eye, didn't say a word. He could have been trying not to embarrass me, though."

"Nah, Miss. That's a nasty old scrape, is that. You'd have to mention it to stop yourself looking at it. What happened? Did you fall?"

"Actually, Billy—I was pushed. And robbed."

While they sat alongside the case map, Maisie recounted the events of the past two days to Billy.

"I reckon we should be looking out for this Mullen. Want me to see what I can find out? I can ask around some of my old mates, you never know, someone might know something, 'specially with all of us being sappers. I can do a bit of snooping to see if I can locate his medical details. And then there's that other bloke, Jeremy Whatsisname. I know them mapping blokes were sitting ducks, so it don't surprise me that he was caught by a sniper. But you never know, he might've been the one that Michael Clifton had words with—unless he wrote it in his journal when it first happened, when he had a head of steam, and it wasn't much more than a storm in a teacup."

Maisie nodded. "Yes, do what you can to find Mullen, and more on Jeremy Lockwood." She picked up a wax crayon and made some notations on the case map, linking two names with a red line. "Be on the lookout for anything that doesn't seem right regarding Lockwood's death. I don't know what you might find, but I think you'll know it when you see it—pay attention to your gut."

"My gut?"

"Yes. Most people don't realize that they feel something is wrong before they think something is wrong, but by the time they've finished trying to ignore the physical sensation, they've pushed that particular nudge from their mind."

"I know what you mean, Miss. I did that with my Doreen. I could feel it here." He touched his belt buckle. "I knew she wasn't right in the head. Felt it before I ever admitted it to myself, and by then it'd got a lot worse. I just kept saying to myself that it was all normal, that she would get over it and be as right as rain the next day."

"She's getting better now, that's the main thing. How is she faring at home?"

"She has her bad days, but nothing like before," replied Billy. "Mind you, I wish I had a little book with instructions in it. Whenever I get worried, if I see her doing something that looks dodgy, like folding only half the laundry, then leaving the rest while she sits by the fire or something—I wish I had something to go back to, you know, a manual that could answer my questions: 'Is this all right?' 'Is she going backward?' Or, 'Is this normal?' "

Maisie nodded, thinking of the searchlight sunbeams across Kent's undulating terrain. She nodded. "Wayfinding . . . ," she said, her voice almost a whisper.

"I beg your pardon, Miss?"

"Oh, just thinking out loud. I was reading about maps, when we first took on the Clifton case, and it said that the primary role of the map is in wayfinding." She looked at Billy. "It seemed such an interesting word: *wayfinding.* Not 'to find our way' but 'wayfinding.' It occurred to me that that's exactly what you need—a wayfinder of sorts, to negotiate the journey ahead with Doreen. But you don't have such a thing to fall back on. There's no map, just the doctors' knowledge of previous similar cases, so they can only advise you to a certain point along this road. You have to depend upon your sense of what is right and what is wrong—and as I said, you'll feel that before you think it."

"I reckon I see what you mean, Miss." Billy scratched his head.

"It's what we're trying to do with this map, isn't it?" Maisie tapped the case map with the red crayon. "Wayfinding." She paused. "I wish I had one for life," she whispered to herself.

"Sorry, Miss?"

"Oh, nothing, Billy. Nothing at all. Let me know if I can be of any help with Doreen." She looked down at the map and circled Priscilla's name. "And in the meantime, I'll see if Mrs. Partridge has managed to wheedle an introduction to Lady Petronella!"

Billy stood up and stepped towards his desk. "You shouldn't have any trouble getting her on the dog and bone. I did the job over at her house to last a lifetime, and she can hear the ring from any room in that house."

Maisie smiled as she moved from the case map table to her desk in the corner. "You're a good man, Billy. Now then, let's see if we can cover more ground in this case—I want to know who attacked me and why, and I want to know why half the people I've spoken to seem to be lying to me. Call that a gut feeling."

As she was about to take her seat, the telephone on her desk rang.

"Miss Dobbs—Detective Inspector Caldwell here. Have you a moment?"

"Of course, Inspector. Do you have some news for me?"

"Some good and some not quite so good."

Maisie sat down, curious regarding possible developments in the case, while at the same time pleased that relations with Caldwell seemed to be moving in a positive direction. Even on the telephone she felt his manner was more conducive to collaboration than it had been in the past.

"I'm not sure which I'd like to hear first."

"Let's start with the good: We've found your case."

Maisie shivered. Her senses heightened to the darker side of Caldwell's purpose for calling.

"And now you have to tell me about the circumstances in which it was recovered."

"I'm afraid so."

"Go on."

"The police were called to a flat just off the Edgware Road where a disturbance had been reported. I'll be frank, it was a miserable cold-water flat, a right slum—and I've seen a few glory holes in my time, I can tell you. Anyway, the men had to force entry—the door was locked—and when they broke in they found the body of a man, close to which was your case."

"Have you identified him yet? And what was the cause of death?"

"Multiple wounds to the skull, your usual blunt object wound—might have been a cosh, a poker, you name it. Something heavy, no doubt about it. Dr. Barrow—the examiner—will be able to give more information, though I can tell you now, he's no Maurice Blanche, so we don't expect the same sort of breadth of speculation in the report that we were used to when your former employer was advising us. I can tell you there was extreme loss of blood, and most of it seems to have washed across your nice leather case, I'm afraid."

"Oh—"

"And the deceased goes by the name of—" Maisie heard Caldwell turn pages as he looked for the name. "Sydney Mullen."

"Mullen?" She looked across the room at Billy, whose eyes were wide.

"Small-time market trader and even smaller-time crook. More of a tea boy to certain higher-up villains over in the East End that we'd like to have longer let's-get-to-know-you conversations with, if only we had something to pin on them. Know him?"

"Not personally. But he knew Michael Clifton in the war. He owed his life to Clifton."

"That's all I need, a bloody maze to get lost in."

"I know how you feel, Inspector." Demonstrating a willingness to collaborate might not be such a bad thing, thought Maisie. "I'll do my best to find a way through at this end. Has a motive been established?"

"Could have been someone he was working for, come to see what he'd brought in from his day's work. He could have owed money to the sort of person you should never owe money to. Who knows, with a fellow like that? Our men are talking to the neighbors, and they're looking for anyone he associated with. Seems he'd been seen with a woman lately. Bit of a nice-looking woman, according to a report. Apparently she was nicely turned out, even if her clothes weren't brand spanking new."

"Did she have dark hair?"

"Yes, she did. Know anything?"

"It might be nothing, but Mr. Clifton said he saw a man and woman arguing in the hotel foyer on the day of the attack. He remembered her dark hair."

"The hotel should have their names."

"I don't think they were guests. But they were there for a reason—you don't just wander into the Dorchester unless you are staying there or meeting someone. In any case, they were asked to leave, I understand. That sort of racket isn't appreciated by guests at the Dorchester."

"I could have done with a different sort of crime to launch my promotion." Caldwell sighed. "What would you like me to do with this document case, when we're finished with it?"

"Was it empty?'

"There's a Victorinox knife—a good one, I can see. And a small bag of tools. I won't ask what you might use these for. No papers, but a couple of those medical masks."

"A pair of rubber gloves?"

"No, but now I know why we didn't find any dabs other than those of the deceased."

"And the case is badly stained."

"Put it this way, Miss Dobbs. My wife accuses me of being a hoarder, of keeping things that are old, don't work, or are beyond repair—and I would throw this in the dustbin without looking back, particularly with that man's blood all over it."

"Then please dispose of it when it has served its purpose as far as Scotland Yard is concerned."

"Sorry about that. After all, it meant a lot to you."

Maisie nodded. "Yes. It held a lot of memories, but at least they can't be stolen or destroyed. I'd like the other items back, though—the knife was a gift from my father."

"Right you are. In the meantime, I'll keep you apprised of the Cliftons' progress. I know you're working in their best interests. The elder son will be here soon; however, one more thing—don't be surprised if you receive a visit from an American embassy official. The fact that two American citizens were attacked has given rise to their own internal investigation, and I've already had representatives from the embassy under my feet."

"Forewarned is forearmed, Inspector. Thank you."

"Now then, I've got work to do here."

"Thank you for your telephone call, your consideration is much appreciated."

Maisie replaced the receiver and turned to Billy.

"Mullen copped it then?"

"Yes. Blunt object to the head, significant loss of blood, and most of it drenched my document case."

"Aw, that's rotten, Miss."

"Mind you, I have the examiner's name. We might need to see him at some point. In the meantime, Billy, I'd like you to see what you can turn up on Mullen. I know Caldwell is being very accommodating, very friendly, but that's not to say he'll share and share alike with the most pertinent information. And you think you can see those other women on your list by the end of tomorrow?"

"Yes, Miss."

"Good. I suppose you'll start with the watering holes in the search for more on Mullen."

"I keep it to a half a pint for me, and as much for the other blokes as it takes for them to totter down memory lane and reveal all." Billy tapped the side of his nose and winked in a conspiratorial fashion. "That's one thing about us East Enders, Miss, we've got the gift of the gab, and we're good at telling stories. I just have to find the blokes who are good at the telling—as long as it's the truth. Being a Londoner, I can always tell. Might even be a gut feeling."

"And you'll let me know if there's anything I can do for Doreen?"

Billy pulled his coat from the hook behind the door and turned to Maisie as he placed his cap on his head. "I'm sure she'd like to see you, Miss, if you can spare the time. It always meant a lot to her, that you came over to Shoreditch for our Lizzie, and that you did so much for her." He looked down at the floor. "And it meant a lot to me, that you sorted it all out for Doreen, that you got her out of that terrible asylum and into a decent hospital with a doctor who could really help her. So, if you can come over, I'd—"

"Of course I can, Billy. How about Friday afternoon, as soon as I've finished with the man with the cine film?"

Billy smiled. "Thanks, Miss. I'll see you tomorrow morning, then."

"Bright and early."

ELEVEN

Mullen's been good to me. They're all pretty good to me. There's a bit of teasing here and here, but I get along fine with everyone—well, almost everyone. I don't know that Mullen and I would ever have become friends in civvy street, but here in France, and out there when we're working, Mullen has become my friend, and it's good to have a buddy—or a mate. As Mullen said, "You and me's mates." I told him that, when all this is over and I go out to California again, I'll need good men to work with me, and he said he'd come like a shot ("Couldn't keep me back, guv'nor," he said). The fact is that I've talked about my land so much now, I am sure Mullen knows every last inch of it, almost as if he'd been there himself. He's a good worker, a man to depend on. This war might have created soldiers of some and officers of others, but it also mixes people up, blends them together. I think Mullen might have been in a bit of trouble before the war, which is probably why he enlisted, and I reckon it's why he would like to hightail it out of Blighty when this whole thing is done. He's palled up to some

of the officers, which is okay, whatever he wants to do, but some of the other lads don't seem to like it. They tell him off for sucking up. It doesn't hurt me—so long as we all do our jobs and get out of here, I don't mind what people do. I'm okay when there's no one around to get at me because he's got more pips on his shoulder.

Maisie turned the pages of Clifton's journal, once again cocooned within the quiet evening solitude of her flat. In the distance she could hear foghorns drone their song of warning along the river, their call like that of fairy-tale mermaids to boatmen navigating the sometimes treacherous waterway.

She wondered about Mullen and thought he was, perhaps, a man easily led, and probably by a yearning for a better life—after all, wasn't something better what most of a certain station wanted, if not for themselves, then for their children? But would Mullen have betrayed Michael Clifton's trust? If Mullen was the man who had attacked her—and without doubt evidence pointed in that direction—she did not sense that he could kill. The incident in the park seemed to have been an error; playing the memory back in her mind, as if it were a moving picture, she recalled the man turning to look back as she fell, a certain shock registered on his face, his eyes wide, as if in other circumstances he might be the first to come to her aid. And then he was gone, running away with his catch: her document case. What was he after? Indeed, if he was working for someone else, what did they think they would find? She had just left the hotel and her meeting with Thomas Libbert, so it was fair to assume that she had been observed entering and later exiting the hotel. Could Libbert be involved, perhaps informing a waiting Mullen that their quarry was on her way out? Had he instructed him to the effect that the old black case she carried must be obtained at all costs? Or was Mullen—a "tea boy" to more powerful men, according to Caldwell—working for someone else altogether? All in all, as she leafed through the journal, she thought Mullen might have been a likable rogue but a weak man, a man who would follow the scent of a quick shilling earned by dishonorable means.

There were times when Maisie wished she could simply pick up a telephone from her home and place a call to Maurice. He had always kept late hours, before this more recent illness, and there was a time when she knew he would have been sitting by the fire in his study, a glass of single-malt whiskey in his hand, a book or some papers in the other. When she had lived at Ebury Place, using the telephone at a late hour did not present a problem. Now to do such a thing necessitated a walk along the road to the kiosk—and Maurice would be in bed anyway. She wished it were otherwise, that she could lift the receiver and in a minute be talking to her mentor, telling him the story of her case and waiting for his advice, which always came in the shape of a question. *How might it be if you look at the problem from this vantage point, Maisie?* And even though she was not with him, at the end of the conversation she knew he would be smiling. That knowing smile would not be due to the fact that he had given her clues, but because he was aware that his questions had helped break down a wall so that she could see a door—and they both knew the knowledge she had in the palm of her hand had been there all the time; it had just taken a conversation with Maurice to enable her to recognize it.

Over the past two years, since the time of discord in their relationship, those telephone calls placed late at night had been few and far between, and more often because Maisie knew that Maurice missed his work to some degree, and—as he often said—could live vicariously through his former assistant as she journeyed thought the twists and turns of her cases. But now she would have been grateful for his counsel.

Maisie read on for a while, then made ready for bed. Before slipping between the bedclothes, she sat on a cushion already placed on the floor in her bedroom. She crossed her legs and closed her eyes in meditation.

Though she tried to keep up with her practice, in recent weeks she had worked late and fallen asleep without first quieting the mind so the soul could be heard. But tonight, as she felt the day slip away and her consciousness descend to a place beyond her own immediate existence, she saw an image of Maurice standing before her. Her eyes were closed, yet she was aware of his presence, and felt his smile as he spoke. "You know the truth, Maisie. You know the truth, but you need the proof. The facts are there, Maisie, between the lines. The evidence is always between the lines, whether it is written or not. Look between the lines."

She remained sitting for a while, clearing her mind so that any nuggets of insight tucked away in her subconscious could come to the fore; then she opened her eyes, stood up, and returned to the dining table where Michael Clifton's journal and his lover's letters had been stacked. Many of the letters were difficult to read, so she had set them aside in favor of those whose pages had come apart with only the slightest slip of the finger along an adhesion. Now she went to the kitchen for a table knife and began to work on those letters where the paper was fused and the ink faint, despite her earlier attempts at careful drying. With a steady hand she divided pages joined by the years since Michael Clifton wrapped them in paper and waxed cloth, as if they were jewels to be cherished.

Priscilla, good morning to you!" Maisie twisted the telephone cord between her fingers as she greeted her friend.

"Heavens above, what on earth is the time? My toads are on their way to school, and I had just settled down to a quiet cup of coffee while I read this morning's dire warnings of the demise of the world, and there you are, bright and early and far too chipper." Priscilla paused. "I know, I bet Ben telephoned and you are over the moon."

"No. Well, Ben has telephoned, but that's not why I'm calling."

"You sound very bright."

"Am I usually so dour?"

"Not dour, just, well, let's say *thoughtful.* A bit less thinking and more having a bit of fun might not do you any harm."

"That's what you always say. In any case, I'm going to Brooklands on Saturday, for a motor racing meet."

"I never took Ben for the racing type."

"He probably isn't. I'm going with James Compton. He invited me last weekend."

"James Compton? Good lord, Maisie, that's not half bad."

"Just a friend, Pris. And probably not even that."

"Then why did he ask you?"

"I think he's lonely."

"Hmmmm." Priscilla paused, and Maisie heard her lift her cup to her lips to sip her coffee, which was always brewed strong, with hot milk added. She continued. "I've managed to pave the way for your introduction to Lady Petronella. Of course, you could have just picked up the telephone yourself, but as we both know, the path is often easier when trodden down earlier by those who are close to the subject."

"You sound like an old hand."

"I feel like one. Let me just grab my notebook—I have a 'Maisie' notebook now. Right, here we are: call her at this number—Mayfair five-three-two-oh—and make the arrangements with her butler, though I am told she often answers the telephone herself. Has them all over the house. She's very approachable, but at the same time no-nonsense, as you can imagine—you don't get things done in the way that she gets things done if you are wishy-washy."

"Anything else you can tell me about her?"

"Very active socially, as Julia said. She's quite the philanthropist and supports several mother-and-baby homes for wayward girls. Hmmm, wonder why no one ever mentions the wayward boys who put them there? Her two adored daughters are grown up, as you know, and she has the much younger son, to whom she is devoted. While not exactly the merry widow, she hasn't let the grass grow under her feet either."

"Thank you, Pris."

"Anything else?"

"Can I come round later, for tea perhaps?"

"Darling, you know you don't have to ask—you're family! I would love to see you—part of the joy of being back in London is having you in the same town, though frankly I never know where you are, with all your gallivanting around."

"See you this afternoon, then."

"Au revoir, Maisie."

Maisie had arrived at her desk early, and when Billy walked into the office, she was sitting at the table where the case map was pinned out, jotting notes on the length of paper. She stood back to see if any links or associations could be established where she might not have seen a connection before.

"Morning, Miss. I'm not late, am I?" He pulled up his sleeve to check the hour, always pleased with an opportunity to demonstrate that the timepiece she had bought for him was being used.

"No, I'm early, that's all."

"Cuppa the old char for you?"

"That would be nice, Billy. Then let's talk about Edward Clifton—and the shoe business he left behind."

Soon they were both seated alongside the table, mugs of tea in hand, and Maisie was ready to begin with a recap of information already gathered.

"I've found out a bit more about that Sydney Mullen." Billy flicked through several pages in his notebook until he found the entry he was looking for. "There we are. Right then, it turns out our Sydney might have got himself in over his head, as they say. As far as I can make out, he went about his business more or less like Caldwell told it; a bit of knowledge here, pass it on there, money changes hands with a contact; putting this person in touch with that one, being the middleman between people who would never have come across each other in the normal course of things."

"Something of an ambassador crook then."

"Ah," said Billy, "but no one plays fast and loose with Alfie Mantle."

"Mantle? From the Old Nichol?" Maisie raised her eyebrows. The conversation had taken an unexpected turn.

"Yes, him. Born in the Old Nichol at the Shoreditch end. They tore down the slum to build the Boundary Estate, but not before Alfie had stepped on the first rung of the ne'er-do-well ladder. You had to be light-fingered to survive in that terrible place, and Alfie was a right Artful Dodger; he moved up to running some rackets, careful all the time not to tread on anyone else's turf. If you know anything about Mantle, Miss, you'll know he was sharp. There'd be a slap on the back for everyone and lots of making nice conversation with the hounds doing business across the water and them others who had the West End by the tail. After the war, when a lot of blokes he wanted out of the way were a few feet underground, he went for bigger fish—and that's where Caldwell would know more from his Flying Squad mates."

"And Mullen was mixed up with him?"

"Here's how I reckon it happened: Mantle was once a bit of a loan shark, and he decided to spread his wings. Now, knowing he couldn't take on new business by working another man's manor, if you know what I mean, he decided to move up in the world, scout around for marks that were a bit better off—if someone wants money that bad, they don't care where it came from. So his blokes start watching the clubs and the hotels, they see who's spending money and who looks like they need a bit extra, and they make their move. Alfie Mantle had an in with more than a few of the more posh establishments, and as he moved up, so he looked more the part; he dresses in Savile Row suits, has his shirts and shoes handmade, and is loved by all who came from the Old Nichol. You'll hear people say, 'He's so good to his old mum.' Mantle looks after his own, but I wouldn't want to be on the wrong side of him."

"So Mullen was one of his runners." Maisie paused. "But he didn't work exclusively for Mantle, did he?"

"Probably not—and that could have been where he went wrong. I reckon he was a go-between, like I said. Someone who puts this person in touch with that person, the sort of fella who's always got another train of thought going on, you know, wondering what he can make out of knowing you."

Maisie tapped her fingers on the desk, then looked up at her assistant. "I wonder—"

"What, Miss?"

Maisie shook her head. "Nothing. Just thinking. Thank you, Billy. This information has stirred up the river, no two ways about it. That was good work." She penned a series of dots on the edge of the case map, first an inward spiral, then outward. She sighed, then spoke again. "Now then, let's get back to Edward Clifton."

Billy picked up a colored crayon as Maisie began.

"So, Edward Clifton left home at, what, nineteen? He could see only more shoes and whale oil to soften the leather in his future, and fled to the promise of America."

"Lucky fella."

"It would seem so," said Maisie. "And while he didn't exactly land on his feet, it didn't take him long to establish a life for himself, though I imagine he had to conquer more than a few mountains before he could rest on his laurels."

"He married well," said Billy.

"Of that there's no doubt. But what about the family in England? They must have been shocked at the loss of a son and brother—if someone emigrates, it's tantamount to having them taken from you in death. You assume you'll never see them again. People cannot conceive of the distance—I know I can't. And when I think of James Compton sailing back and forth once or twice a year to and from Canada—it's a long way."

Billy sighed. "I wish me and Doreen and the boys could sail *to* Canada. I've never wished for anything more in my life—except in the war, when I didn't want to die over there in France, and when I've wished for Doreen to get better. Then there was wishing for Lizzie to live."

Maisie understood Billy's anxiety regarding his dream of emigrating to Canada, and realized the extent to which the story of Edward Clifton's journey as a young man must have added fuel to his desire to start anew in a land that held the promise of opportunity. It was as if Doreen's full recovery, together with accumulating enough money to gain a foothold on the other side of the Atlantic Ocean, was his guiding light.

"I know how much you want to go, Billy. Doreen will get well in her own time, and while she's on the mend, you can make up the money you spent on the doctors." She smiled, hoping to inspire some optimism on his part, a sense that all would be well. "But in the meantime, we've got to get to the bottom of this case, so let's put our heads together. Now, where were we? Yes, the family Clifton left behind. Did you manage to find anything out about them?"

"I was talking to an old bloke who works in that big shoe shop down Regent Street," said Billy. "He remembered that when he was an errand boy for the shop, there was talk about young Edward Clifton, as he was then, leaving the country and the business behind him. There was a lot of wondering about what would happen to the company, being as he was the only heir. Apparently, his grandfather and father cut him off, and the family were forbidden to reply to any letters or telegrams; they said that nothing good would come of him, and good riddance."

"That's more or less what he told me. No wonder he sets a lot of stock in keeping his family together and happy."

"His sister—who was about twenty-one—stepped forward and began working with her father, and then she took over the business. Name of Veronica Clifton."

"Did you find out anything about her marriage?"

Billy nodded. "Yes. It was a bit unusual; she kept her maiden name, never became a missus until after her husband died—quite young he was, apparently. By that time the business was not doing very well, so she sold it and got herself hitched to a Mr. John Paynton. They say the strain of her brother leaving and then her having to step up in his place sent her to an early grave."

"Did she have any children, do you know?"

Billy shook his head. "I asked the old boy, and he didn't know. He said that even if she did, according to them who knew more about her, she wouldn't have publicized the fact, being as she had a company to run, and she didn't want anyone trying to take advantage of her just because she was a woman."

"Yes. Yes, I can see why she would make that decision."

"Do you, Miss? I can't say as I can see anything normal about their goings-on—'cept of course old Edward running off on a ship. Funny old world, ain't it?"

Maisie sighed. "Could you dig a bit deeper for me, find out about other family members, cousins, aunts and uncles by marriage? There might have been stepchildren, for example. Oh, and if you could plough through a bit more of your list of those women who wrote letters to the

Cliftons, it would help. I'll attack mine this afternoon, though I may have an appointment with your Lady Petronella of the telephones. I should call her now."

As Maisie stood up to walk to her desk, the telephone began to ring.

"Funny how that always happens, ain't it, Miss? You mention the word *call*, and off it goes." Billy went back to his notes.

Maisie picked up the black Bakelite telephone receiver, but did not have a chance to greet the caller with either the number or her name before Frankie Dobbs began speaking.

"Maisie, love, can you hear me?" Frankie shouted in his usual manner, never quite believing that the miracle of modern telephony could connect him to his daughter, who was in an office over eighty miles away.

"Dad! Dad, is everything all right?" Maisie felt the skin at the base of her neck grow cold, along the still-livid scar that remained from wounds she'd suffered in the war. "Are you unwell? What's happened?"

"I just thought you would want to know—" She could hear her father breathing as if he had been running, and there was a rawness to his voice.

"Dad . . . Dad—take a deep breath, and sit down on that chair by the telephone. Have you been running?"

"I came back here as soon as I heard. As I said, I knew you'd want to know."

"As soon as you heard what, Dad?" Maisie felt her heart beat faster, and a pressure on her chest. She took a deep breath in an effort to radiate calm from the center of her body.

"Dr. Blanche has been taken into hospital. A clinic in Tunbridge Wells. For observation. Apparently his lungs are just filling up."

"I'll come straightaway—"

"No, you can't do that. No visitors. No one's allowed to see him, from what I've heard."

"I'll talk to Lady Rowan. And I'm coming down to Kent as soon as I can."

"He wouldn't want you to come rushing—"

"It wouldn't be the first time I've done something he wouldn't like. I'm on my way."

"You drive careful, Maisie. And—"

"Dad—rest. I don't want two of you in hospital. I'm hanging up the telephone now, Dad. All right? I'll be in touch again later. Have a cup of tea, sit down, and put your feet up. Everything will be all right."

"I'd better be off then. Take good care, my Maisie."

Maisie held on to the receiver, and pressed down the bar to disconnect the call. She began dialing again.

"That's bad news, Miss, ain't it? Is your dad all right?"

Maisie nodded. "It's Maurice."

The color drained from Billy's face.

The call was answered on the second ring, and Maisie did not wait for a greeting. "May I speak to Lady Rowan, please, Mr. Carter."

"I thought it would be you, Maisie," said the Comptons' butler.

"Do you know how he is?"

"Her Ladyship is more informed than I. I'll tell her you're on the line."

Maisie heard a series of clicks, then another before Lady Rowan picked up the receiver.

"Maisie. I was just about to telephone you, counter to instructions from dear Maurice. He didn't want to worry you."

"Didn't want to worry me? Oh, dear . . . how is he?"

"The nurse summoned the doctor early this morning, and he arranged for Maurice to be transferred into the clinic. According to Maurice's specific instructions in such an eventuality, Dr. Dene has been asked to attend him. The news I've heard so far is that, all being well, he should be out in a few days. He's had some difficulty breathing, as you know, and his health simply continued to get worse."

"He seems to have gone downhill so quickly, Lady Rowan." Maisie heard the catch in her voice, the fear revealed with each word. "I—I will be on my way to Tunbridge Wells as soon as I hang up this call."

"I knew you would insist upon coming, despite Maurice's entreaty that you not be informed of his condition. He said you were very busy and that you should not be concerned about an old gentleman. I took it upon myself to inform him that he had just spoken a load of codswallop, probably for the first time in his life."

Maisie smiled and shook her head, trying to fight back the tears.

"In any case, you won't need to drive. I would imagine James will be knocking at your office door within minutes, he—"

"James?"

"Yes. James. The James who is my son." Lady Rowan's sense of humor could verge on the sarcastic in the best of circumstances. "I telephoned him with the news and suggested he escort you to the clinic as soon as possible."

"*You* told James?"

"Yes. Haven't given him an order in years that he actually chose to act upon, so there was a certain pleasure attached to it."

Maisie said nothing, her thoughts too confused to second-guess the situation.

"Don't worry, Maisie. Maurice is a tough old sort. He's clearly in difficulty, but I am assured by the doctor that he will get over this setback."

At that moment the bell sounded, and Billy went to answer the front door.

"I think that's James now, Lady Rowan. Thank you."

"Not at all. Just hold on. I'm told he drives like me, but frankly, he's far too sensible."

Maisie grabbed her shoulder bag, and automatically reached for her case files. Then she stopped. Her case was important, without doubt, but it paled when set against the ill health of one so cherished. She left the files behind, collected her coat and hat, and ran to the door just as Billy was showing James into the office. Even in a hurry, Maisie noticed that he seemed every inch the successful businessman, and in that moment he reminded her of his father. His hair was combed with a side parting, and he wore a well-cut charcoal suit of fine wool with the ease of one who is used to working at the highest levels of commerce. He had one hand in his pocket as he walked into the room, and he smiled when he saw Maisie.

"So this is where you—Maisie, what on earth have you done to your face?"

"Not now, James. I want to see just how fast that Aston Whatever-it-is of yours can go."

"Right you are." He stepped aside, nodded to Billy, and followed Maisie downstairs, then to his motor car, which was parked in Fitzroy Street.

"I should get you there in about three-quarters of an hour, all being well with the traffic." James held the door for Maisie to take the passenger seat. He ran around to the driver's side, slipped into his seat, and started the engine, setting off towards Tottenham Court Road. For just a moment he looked sideways as a single tear slid across her cheekbone. She wiped it away with her fingers. James reached across and took her hand in his. "It'll be all right, Maisie. We'll get the best doctors, the best care. We'll do everything we can for him."

She nodded and, looking out at the London traffic, squeezed his hand in return.

The Mount Pleasant Clinic was situated on a hill just behind The Pantiles, where in days gone by travelers were drawn to the healing spa waters of Tunbridge Wells. As soon as James parked the motor car, Maisie opened the door and dashed into the clinic, almost colliding with Andrew Dene, who had also once been a protégé of Maurice Blanche. Though not as close to their mentor as Maisie, Dene was still involved in the running of clinics for the poor that had been set up by Maurice over thirty years before, and he was now directing his medical care.

"Good Lord, Maisie, slow down. I really don't want to have to admit you with a broken skull—and what have you been doing to your face?"

"A fall. Andrew, I'm so glad you're here with him. How is he?"

"He'll be kept in for observation for a couple of days, just to make sure." He brushed back his unruly fringe, a habit that at once touched Maisie. Though she knew he was not one she wanted to spend her life with, she had great affection for Dene, and had missed his easygoing personality and ready humor. "I've given him a sedative, so he's asleep at the moment."

"Can I see him?"

At that moment, James Compton stepped forward, held out his hand, and introduced himself.

"Ah, Chelstone's son and heir. Weren't you in Canada?"

James nodded. "Back here now, and doubt I will be returning in the foreseeable future."

Maisie was aware that James had become tense. She suspected that Dene's comment was meant to lighten the atmosphere, but at the same time, it could be misinterpreted as a goad—and she wasn't entirely sure that it wasn't. She changed the subject.

"I understand congratulations are in order, Andrew?"

Dene blushed and grinned. "Yes. Abigail is expecting a baby—not long to go now, end of May, all being well."

"That's wonderful—I'm happy for you."

"Thank you. Yes, thank you." Dene cleared his throat and turned towards the door that led to the corridor of patients' private rooms. "Come this way." He continued walking, and addressed James as he opened the door for the visitors. "I expect you know Maurice quite well yourself, James. He's a great friend of your parents, isn't he?"

James stepped past Dene, responding as he walked alongside Maisie. "I've known him all my life. He's been an enormous help to me. I don't know what I might have done without him."

Maisie looked at James, her curiosity piqued by his candor.

The conversation continued, this time with James questioning Dene about Maurice's care, and whether a specialist should be called. Dene was an orthopedic surgeon now, and though it was known that he was trusted by Blanche—his mentor since boyhood—James did not show any reticence when querying whether a consultant in respiratory illnesses might attend Maurice.

"If you wish to bring someone in, I would be more than willing to make my notes and Maurice's medical history available," said Dene.

As they reached Maurice's room, Maisie looked through the glass window. Maurice was asleep, his head to one side. He seemed rested, though she also noticed equipment at the ready should breathing become difficult once more.

"What do you think, Maisie?" said James. "Shall I bring in someone from Harley Street? It would take only minutes and I could have a man on his way to Tunbridge Wells."

Maisie looked at Dene, then at James Compton, and shook her head before placing her hand on James' arm. "Andrew loves Maurice as much as I, and as much as you, James. Let's leave things as they are for now." She turned to Andrew. "You'll let us know if you think otherwise, Andrew?"

Dene nodded. "Of course." He reached for the door handle. "In you go, Maisie. I know I have no need to give you instructions."

She nodded, and entered the room. She heard the door close behind her as she walked towards the bed where Maurice was resting. His breath at first seemed easy, but she could hear the occasional rasping in his chest, a sound that reminded her of two pieces of wood being rubbed together. She leaned across the bed and rested her hand on Maurice's forehead. He did not stir, but continued to breathe with some difficulty, as if with each inward breath he was searching for more air to sustain him. In that moment, Maisie reflected on the time when he had cared for her in France.

Upon revisiting the site of the casualty clearing station where she had worked, now a cemetery for those who died when the unit came under enemy fire, Maisie had suffered a breakdown. It was Maurice who had looked after her until she regained consciousness, and Maurice who had brought much-needed healing when he directed her to face her past so she could move beyond the memories and the years of suffering. "Wound agape," he had said, "is when we find healing in the blood of the wound itself." And she understood, then, that to rise above the pain that still inflamed her heart, she had to face the dragons of her war, or she would forever be at their mercy. Now, in this clinic where Maurice was clinging to life, it was as if every lesson, every memory of him, was being brought back to her to see again in her mind's eye. He had offered balm for so many of her wounds, and for that she loved him as if she were his own.

Maisie rose from the chair, leaned across the bed, and kissed Maurice's forehead. She waited only a few seconds more before leaving the room and joining Andrew Dene and James Compton.

"Thank you, Andrew. I'm glad you're here. I'm relieved to know you're in charge of his care."

"It was in his instructions, actually. His doctor told me that he has everything planned for the future, right down to who should be summoned at whatever stage of his illness. And I was to be brought in if he was transferred to the clinic."

"Just like Maurice. Always one step ahead of everyone else." James took a calling card from his pocket and handed it to Dene, then shook hands with him. "I meant no offense when I asked about the consultant, and I hope you don't take it as such. We all love him so very much, don't we? Anyway, if you need anything—and I mean anything—with regard to his well-being, be in touch with me straightaway at this number."

Dene nodded. "Will do—thank you." He turned to Maisie, leaned forward, and kissed her on the cheek. "I'll see you again soon, Maisie. And don't worry, I will keep you posted. He should be going home on Saturday or Sunday, and if there's any change, I will telephone you."

Maisie nodded her thanks, at once unable to speak.

"And before you go, let me give you some ointment for that graze. It'll heal faster, and you don't want a scar, do you?'

Dene led the way to the consulting room, and as they walked along the corridor, James Compton put his arm around Maisie's shoulder, as if to protect her. Later, she would try to give words to the effect that the gesture had upon her, and had to admit that it made her feel as if she was protected, and safe.

TWELVE

Maisie placed telephone calls to her father and Priscilla prior to leaving the clinic, and when she informed her friend of the reason she was unable to come to tea, Priscilla insisted that she and James drive from the clinic straight to the house in Kensington for an early supper. "We'll be sitting down with those toads, but as I always warn you, that's how we do things in this house in all but the most illustrious company. In any case, as soon as they know that James was an aviator in the war, they will be all over him like a sprawling vine—your eldest godson has aeroplanes on the brain, and is already saying that he wants to be a fearless flier when he grows up. I swear that one of them, and probably my budding airman, will send me back to daytime drink!"

Having had her cheek tended by Andrew Dene, Maisie left the clinic with a heavy heart, and for a time she and James Compton sat in silence on the drive back to London. Yet it was a comfortable silence, soothing her as much as the journey itself.

They were close to Sevenoaks when Maisie spoke. "It was good of you to take me to the clinic, James. I do hope it doesn't seem like too much of a wasted journey because Maurice was asleep."

"Absolutely not. And remember, I was under my mother's orders to chauffeur you to Tunbridge Wells, so there's no blame on your part. It was important that we went—for me as much as you, Maisie." James slid the motor into a higher gear as they went up River Hill. "Dene reckons Maurice will be able to go home on Saturday afternoon, so I imagine you'll want to come straight to Chelstone after we've been to Brooklands—and if you don't want to go to the racing, do say. You won't be letting me down." He turned and half smiled. "But perhaps the day out might help take your mind off things."

Maisie felt unsure at first, for she could not imagine her mind being on anything but Maurice. Yet on the other hand, the thought of hours filled with mounting concern at home was not an attractive proposition. She turned to James. "Yes, let's go. You're right—if I'm at Brooklands, I won't have time to worry. But I would very much like to return to Chelstone as soon as the meet is over, to see Maurice as soon as he's settled. Andrew said he'd telephone tomorrow and Friday to keep me apprised of his progress."

James nodded, and for a moment Maisie thought he might ask about her courtship with Andrew Dene.

"We're making good time. We'll be in Kensington before you know it—and Maisie, I know that your friend Priscilla has extended the invitation for me to come to supper, but if it's awkward for you—"

"Oh, please—do come. Priscilla loves meeting new people, and her boys will be thrilled to come face-to-face with a man who flew aeroplanes in the war. You'll be grilled about your exploits, and by the time they go to school tomorrow morning, they will have elevated you to being personally responsible for taking down the Red Baron."

"Oh yes, James Compton, aviator extraordinaire, who sustained his war wounds while on the ground."

"You came under enemy attack."

"I would have felt better about it if I'd have been up in the air at the time."

"Well, your mother was delighted that you came home wounded, and not at death's door, doubly so when you were transferred to a desk job. She thought she would lose you."

"It's a bit hard to face someone like Douglas Partridge, a man who was felled by his wounds, who cannot walk without a cane, and who has had an arm amputated. And whose writing—his pacifism—makes him a force to be reckoned with."

Maisie turned to face James. "You've read his articles?"

"Of course. The man is brilliant. To tell you the truth, I am looking forward to meeting him. Why?"

"Nothing. I suppose I was just a little surprised, James."

They were silent again, and in that time, Maisie felt James' discomfort, as if there were more he wanted to say. On her part, there was also a lack of ease, as she considered that she had held on to impressions of James gained in earlier days, when she was a girl and he was the young man for whom Enid—the outspoken housemaid who had taken Maisie under her wing when she first came to work at the Ebury Place mansion—had set her hat. Enid, who would forever be twenty years of age.

Maisie was so wrapped in her thoughts that she was startled when James spoke again.

"Look, about that day at Khan's house."

She raised her hand. "You don't need to say anything, James. I have known Khan for a long time. Whatever the purpose of your visit, it's no business of mine. Your reasons for being there are your own, so there is no need to explain anything to me."

"Thank you. Yes—yes, you're right. Perhaps another time."

"Another time. Of course."

Maisie could see that Priscilla's sons had been coiled like springs, the three of them waiting on the staircase for the much-anticipated guests to arrive. After running to Maisie to welcome her, they turned their attention to James and, she thought, all but saluted him.

Priscilla came out to meet her guests, and was introduced to James. Maisie could see that he had merited her friend's broadest smile.

"I hope you don't mind, but they have been champing at the bit, lurking on that staircase to get a bird's-eye view of you as soon as you crossed the threshold. I know this is not how young English boys should behave, but, well, they've been used to a different kind of life. Now then, let's repair to the drawing room for a glass of something interesting, eh." Priscilla led the way and gestured her guests to follow. "Douglas, they're here!" she called out to her husband, then leaned towards Maisie. "By the way, your assistant called at the house earlier. I have a message for you." She took a folded envelope from the slanted pocket set at the side of her wide palazzo pants. "Let's get settled, then you can huddle by yourself in the corner for a moment or two to read. If you need to use the telephone, nip up to use the one in my sitting room, for some privacy." She turned back to James and, taking his arm, introduced him to her husband. "Darling, here's Maisie's friend, James Compton. Do engage him while you can before your sons drag him off to their lair."

As soon as she was furnished with a drink—Priscilla had ensured that a bottle of champagne was chilled ready for their arrival—Maisie made her way to the French windows overlooking the courtyard and garden beyond and took out Billy's note, written in his distinctive primary-school hand.

Dear Miss,

I telephoned Mrs. Partridge to see if she was still expecting you, so I thought that if I brought a note round, it would be the best way to get in touch. We had a visitor today, from the American embassy. He came in to ask some questions about Mr. and Mrs. Clifton. Seemed more like a copper to me, to tell you the truth. I said that you were the person to speak to, so he left his card and said he'd be in touch as he'd like to ask a few questions for his report, being as American citizens were attacked in London. Then when he was gone, old Caldwell turned up, and what with the notes and names all over the case map on the table, I had to cover things up a bit sharpish because that man has eyes in the back of his head. He said he wanted to see you, and asked if you would be so kind as to telephone him—apparently there have been developments. And he also said to tell you that Mrs. Clifton is improving, and that the doctors have said they're a bit happier with her progress, but not to get all over the moon because she could go on the turn again. Then there was a telephone call from Lady Petronella Casterman. She said she had received word that you had reason to talk to her and that she could see you on Thursday—that's tomorrow—at half past two in the afternoon. I felt like reminding her of who I was, but thought better of it.

I will tell you everything else in the office tomorrow morning.

Yours sincerely,
Wm. Beale (Billy)

The usually boisterous Partridge boys were on their best behavior throughout the meal, though Maisie suspected the show of exemplary manners was mainly to ingratiate themselves with the much-anticipated guest, and to persuade him to look at their aeroplane drawings and models. The youngest, Tarquin, soon began to give in to tiredness, and rubbed his eyes as he became rather grumpy with his older brothers.

"All right, that's it. Time for grown-ups to talk now, boys." Priscilla called for Elinor, who came to take the children upstairs to bathe. James promised to come to their room as soon as they were in bed, and the boys seemed mollified by his offer as they followed their nanny.

"You've done it now, James—they will never let you out!" Douglas Partridge reached across to pour more wine for his guests.

"You have a lovely family." James raised a glass to Douglas and Priscilla. "My boyhood was rather unconventional for the day—mainly due to my mother, who did not subscribe to the notion that children should be seen and not heard—but I still had to endure the rigors of boarding school."

Priscilla laughed, and Maisie joined her, having been present at the boys' former school when Priscilla decided that such an institution was not the best place for her sons.

"We tried, James, but our boys didn't quite fit," explained Douglas. "Now they are day pupils at a school that draws from the more international families. It seems to suit them a bit better."

"Very much so," added Priscilla. "And they have each other. Both you and Maisie are only children, aren't you? I had three smashing brothers, and Douglas has a sister and brother, so we both wanted a houseful."

James cleared his throat. "Actually, I did have a sibling. A sister." He swirled the wine in his glass and seemed to concentrate on the whirlpool plume created by the liquid as it moved.

Maisie and Priscilla exchanged glances. It was Maisie who spoke first. "You had a sister, James? I didn't know."

He shrugged. "No, I daresay you wouldn't know. It wasn't really spoken about after she . . . after the loss. My mother and father were so distraught—I don't know how they managed. If it hadn't been for Maurice . . ." He raised his glass to his lips and finished his wine.

Maisie nodded to Priscilla, sensing that, having begun to speak, James might either want to change the subject immediately, or continue his story. If he were relaxed enough in their company, he might go on.

"What was her name, James?" asked Maisie.

"Emily. Emily Grace Compton. She was eleven years old when she died." He did not look up, but remained staring at the dregs of white wine in the glass. Douglas reached forward with the bottle again, and James smiled, but Maisie could see that it was a smile with no immediate feeling, as if his face were subjected to some mild paralysis. "Thank you—just half a glass."

Maisie, Priscilla, and Douglas allowed silence to punctuate James' slow telling of the story. At the same time, Maisie recalled Lady Rowan's anxious inquiries about the Beales, her interest in Doreen's progress, and the way she brushed off the fact that the bereaved mother had fallen behind in work—alterations and needlework—for Lady Rowan. *"It's the last thing she should worry about, the clothes on my back. Oh, the poor, poor woman. She won't know where to put that terrible grief."*

"What happened, James?"

He looked at Maisie, and brushed the fingers of his left hand through blond hair threaded with barely distinguishable gray. "We'd gone down to the woods—you know, at the bottom of the field just beyond the Dower House garden. It's a grand place for children. We used to climb trees and make camps out of fallen branches as if we were medieval bandits living in the woods. It was all very wild, but we were allowed a fairly free rein. My parents believed that too much oversight would deprive us of spirit, and already Emily was a very energetic girl. She rode her horse like the wind and was fearless when it came to jumping a hedge or fence—you should have seen her keeping up with my mother, who was a bold horsewoman in her day."

James paused, breathing in deeply.

"I was about nine at the time, just a couple of years younger than

Emily. There used to be a place where a sort of dam had been built across the stream that runs through the wood. I think children from the village dragged some logs into position so that a makeshift swimming pool formed. There was a rope hanging from the old beech tree, so we would swing from the bank across the pool—and the water was always fresh and cool on a summer's day. The idea was to let go and splash down into the pool, which went down at least six feet in depth. So you fell in and then had to swim to the side in short order. That was the game." He took another sip of wine, his voice cracking as he spoke.

"On this day, we'd gone down to the wood—I can still remember the smell of wild garlic underfoot wafting up around our ankles as we ran to the pool. I went first, then Emily. Time and again we ran to the swing and jumped in—we were soaking wet, but it was such fun." He paused and placed his hand on his chest. "The trouble is, I still can't quite say what happened next. I have gone over it again and again and again in my mind, and I just don't know. I can only say what I think happened." He closed his eyes. "It was my turn, but Emily was out of the water just after me and we raced each other to the bank and grabbed the rope at the same time, both of us hurtling across. We were flying through the air, giggling and whooping . . . then I heard a crack that seemed to ricochet through the trees, and before we knew what was happening, we were falling into the water, and the giant limb from which the swing had been hanging came down upon us." He seemed to wince as if in pain, and as his chest rose and fell against his hand, Maisie could see that the memory of being unable to breathe was still imprisoned within each cell of his body.

"I was pressed down into the water, and I remember Emily's hand at my neck, grasping for my collar. When I tried to turn, to pull her with me, I could see she was trapped. I was coughing, trying to get out of the water, trying to get some purchase on the river mud underfoot, but the branches were clutching at me, as if the tree were alive. I could hear screaming, and realized it was me. Then I must have passed out, because the next thing I knew my father's voice came into my consciousness. Mrs. Crawford was holding me, and there were a couple of grooms from the stables on the bank trying to pull the limb out. I looked up and saw my father in the water, lifting the tree, and my mother had launched herself in to help him. I watched them try to move the branches while my mother went down into the water in a bid to free Emily. They dragged her to the bank together, and they tried so hard to save her, to no avail. I was helpless. Utterly helpless. My sister had saved my life, and I could do nothing for her. I was no better than useless."

Maisie remembered Maurice's counsel that when a person has made a confession, it is important to accord that person the gift of silence, if only for a moment. After a suitable hiatus, Maisie leaned forward. "You loved your sister, James, and you did your utmost to help her. You did all that you could. And you were a child."

Douglas laid a hand on James' shoulder, allowing him to feel the weight of support, then reached for his cane and pushed back from the table. "We need something a little stronger than that bottle of Montrachet, I think."

"I say, I must apologize, going on like that."

"James, we're friends here," said Priscilla. "I've known Maisie since Girton, and we have seen each other through thick and thin—with rather more of the thin, I must say. The circumstance of your sister's death is the stuff of nightmares in every family, and clearly it is something that will never be banished from your memory. So, even if we weren't before, we are now friends, James, because you have trusted us." She looked at Maisie as if for approval, and Maisie, her eyes red-rimmed with unshed tears, nodded at Priscilla.

It seemed that as soon as Douglas had set a snifter of brandy in front of James, Elinor came to inform the company that the boys wanted to show James their drawings and model aeroplanes. Priscilla waited until he left the room before turning to Maisie.

"Did you know any of that?"

She shook her head. "It must be the best-kept secret at Chelstone—no one has ever mentioned it to me, and certainly Lady Rowan has never spoken of it. It explains a lot, though."

"Such as?"

Maisie tapped the side of her coffee cup with a silver spoon. "Maurice always said that carrying a heavy burden will cause a person to stoop and stagger, even though their bearing might suggest otherwise."

"I think I see what you mean." Priscilla paused, taking a breath as if to ask a question. "Mais—oh, nothing, really."

"What were you going to say?"

"She wants to know whether you and James Compton are courting," interjected Douglas, who reached across to ruffle his wife's hair in an affectionate manner. "But she thought she might have gone too far with her inquisitiveness."

"Fine ally you are in a time of need!" joked Priscilla, taking Douglas' hand.

"And the answer is no—he's just a friend, and anyway, I don't think the likes of James Compton would be seriously considering me for courtship."

"Could you be languishing in your sackcloth and ashes, Maisie?"

"No, Pris. It's just how I view the situation."

"The view from your mountain might be wrong."

At that moment James Compton returned to the room, and smiled at Maisie before turning to Priscilla. "I'm not sure how much your toads will sleep tonight. I left them planning acts of airborne derring-do."

"As long as it doesn't involve a chandelier," said Priscilla, rolling her eyes.

"I think I'm ready, James," said Maisie.

The four bid their farewells, with gratitude expressed for a welcome supper and good company, and as Maisie and James walked down the steps towards his motor car, Priscilla called out, "Do try to avoid the ground, Maisie. That thing on your cheek is hardly something you can cover up with a puff of powder."

As they walked to the motor car, Maisie thought that Priscilla was wrong. The wounds of the past could always be camouflaged. Erasing them to extinguish all trace was the greater challenge.

When they arrived in Pimlico, James parked the motor car and escorted her to the door.

"So, this is where you live. Quite modern, isn't it?"

"Yes, I was lucky. The builder went out of business, so the bank decided to sell the flats individually. And property seemed as good a place as any for my nest egg."

"Very wise. And a good time to buy." James smiled at Maisie. An onlooker might have thought that neither of them knew quite what to say next, but after a lapse of a few seconds, James continued. "I'll see you on Saturday, then. At least I know where to come to pick you up now."

Maisie nodded. "I'm looking forward to the day, though I know I'll be worrying about Maurice."

"Yes, I think we all will. Anyway, I'd better be getting back to the club. And do let me know if you change your mind."

"Of course. And thank you so much for taking me to see him. I just hope he gets over this spell of ill health." She looked down at her door keys and turned them in her hand. "I—I just can't imagine what I'd do if—"

James reached towards her and pulled her to him. He said nothing at first, allowing her to weep into his shoulder. As her tears abated, he reached into his pocket for a clean white handkerchief, then lifted her face and dried her tears.

"Everything will be all right, Maisie. I'm aware you've been through a lot in the past few years, but Maurice is a resilient chap, he bounces back. You know that."

"I think this is different."

"Wait and see. There." He pressed the handkerchief into her hand. "Will you be all right?"

She nodded and smiled as she looked up at him. James kissed her on each cheek; then, just at the point when she thought he would turn to leave, he took her in his arms once again and kissed her on the lips. She did not draw back.

"So, like I said, the American bloke, from the embassy, name of John Langley, said he'd be in touch with you before the end of the week, which I suppose means by Friday for the likes of these diplomatic types."

"What? Sorry, Billy, what did you say?"

"Is everything all right, Miss?"

"Yes. Yes, of course. Why?"

Billy shrugged. "Nothing, really. You just seemed miles away, that's all, and I wondered if you were all right. You had that nasty fall, and a rotten time of it yesterday, what with having to rush down to Tunbridge Wells with that James Compton—and I bet he drives like a madman as well."

Maisie shook her head. "No, not at all. He was quite, well, careful."

"Hmmm. Always thought of him as a bit of a fast one. A bit of a jack-the-lad."

Maisie said nothing, but remained deep in thought. Had Billy known of the romantic encounter with James Compton, he might have attributed her distraction to the fledgling courtship. He would not have known that, after James had left her flat, Maisie had once again turned to the letters from the English nurse to Michael Clifton. It was when she read the penultimate letter that she drew back to absorb its meaning.

Dearest Michael,

I have never been terribly good with my good-byes, so forgive the stilted nature of this letter. I think it's best that I come straight to the point, rather than linger with explanations or fumble with my words.

For various reasons that do not bear recounting, I have decided that our courtship, or whatever you might call it when you hardly see a person, must come to an end. This war has made all thoughts of the future almost worthless. Neither of us knows what might happen tomorrow, next week, or next month, so it's probably best if we cease all communication. If you like, I can have those items you gave to me for safekeeping sent back to you. Please let me know what you would like me to do. Rest assured, I will take good care of them until I receive word from you.

I hope you understand, dear Michael. I see nothing but the wounded and dying each day. Perhaps that's why I cannot see a future for us.

Yours, fondly,
"Tennie"

THIRTEEN

Having left her motor car parked outside her flat in Pimlico that morning, Maisie traveled by trolley bus and the underground for most of the journey to the Mayfair mansion where Lady Petronella Casterman lived with her son, Christopher. Priscilla had informed her—with information from her friend Julia Maynard—that the son was about sixteen years of age, and was known as "Tuffie" to members of the family. The two daughters were now married, with the eldest due to give birth to Lady Petronella's first grandchild in the not-too-distant future, to the delight of the grandmother-to-be.

Though on the outside the mansion seemed much like any other in the area—an imposing white stucco exterior; large windows on each of three floors, with smaller top-floor windows for the servants' accommodation; and a grand entrance with Grecian-inspired columns on either side of the front door—as soon as she stepped into the light-filled entrance hall, it was clear that Lady Petronella had indulged in extensive alterations to the interior of the house. Upon entry the home inspired good cheer and optimism, its walls painted the shade of a bride's satin wedding gown, and the doors a lighter but complementary hue. It seemed that even on a bleak day, light would filter past the swags of golden fabric that adorned the windows, to be transmuted so that one might believe the sun to be shining. There was no grand collection of paintings of now-dead ancestors, though in the drawing room Maisie's attention was drawn to a family portrait of Lady Petronella and her daughters, with Tuffie sitting on his mother's knee, a toy train in one hand and the thumb of his other hand in his mouth. Another large yet simple charcoal sketch revealed Giles Casterman to have been a man of fine features, with slightly hooded eyes and a wry smile that suggested he and the artist had just shared a joke.

As Maisie was looking at a series of silver-framed family photographs set on the grand piano by the window, the door opened and Lady Petronella entered the room.

"Miss Dobbs. How lovely to meet you."

Maisie turned at the woman's entrance and stepped in her direction. Not all women, especially those of a certain age, expected to shake hands in greeting with another female, especially one they presumed to be of a lower station—and a working woman was often thought of as such—but the aristocratic widow showed no such sensibility and held out her hand to take Maisie's in a firm grasp.

"Thank you so much for agreeing to see me, Lady Petronella, and for taking the time to place a telephone call to my office."

"Not at all. If someone wants to see you, you might as well get it over and done with and help them if you can." She held out her hand towards a chintz-covered sofa, and as they were seated, Maisie took stock of her hostess.

Lady Petronella was of average height, perhaps a couple of inches shorter than Maisie, but in the way she held herself, she seemed taller. She had retained the leanness of girlhood, her clothes were fashionable without revealing a woman loath to give up her youth, and her rich black hair—the color possibly enhanced with a tint—was cut in a soft, wavy bob. She wore little makeup, which drew attention to still-flawless skin, and had a ready smile and eyes that seemed to sparkle upon meeting her guest for the first time. Maisie thought she was the kind of woman that one could not help but like upon meeting.

"Would you care for some tea, Miss Dobbs? Our cook has just made delicious macaroons—they're my son's favorite, and she spoils him terribly."

Maisie smiled. She remembered Mrs. Crawford making ginger biscuits for James when he returned to Ebury Place, and the playful teasing between the two when he sneaked into her domain to steal the hot-from-the-oven treat.

"Yes, a cup of tea and a macaroon would be lovely—thank you."

Lady Petronella summoned the butler and asked for tea and macaroons to be brought to the drawing room, and then turned to Maisie. "Now then, Miss Dobbs, perhaps you could tell me why you've been anxious to see me. I understand you're interested in my work during the war."

Maisie nodded. "Yes, that's right. I'm trying to locate an English nurse who became . . . let us say, she became romantically involved with an American man. I should add that he enlisted in 1914, and was a military cartographer with the Royal Engineers. He was able to enlist in our army because his father was born a British subject, and of course his expertise in his field made him a valuable recruit."

"Yes, yes, I can imagine." Lady Petronella looked up as the butler returned with tea, and did not continue speaking until the table in front of their chairs was set for the repast. "Milk and sugar?" asked Maisie's hostess, before she poured tea.

"Just a dash of milk," said Maisie.

When they were both equipped with tea and a small plate bearing a single macaroon, Maisie offered more information. "The young man,

Michael Clifton, was killed, though his remains have only been discovered quite recently. His parents are in possession of a collection of letters from the young woman in question, and would like to trace her."

"Don't they have her name and address?"

"She used a pseudonym throughout the letters—it seemed to be an affectionate nickname used by her lover. He called her 'The English Nurse,' which then became 'Tennie.' It appears they used methods other than the available postal services to exchange letters. The censor was avoided, so that was another reason for her to keep her name private."

"Ah, I see," said Lady Petronella. "And because my unit was known as The English Nursing Unit, with the initials T-E-N, which might then become 'Tennie,' you thought I might know the girl in question."

"That's the measure of it." Maisie paused. "I realize it's a long time ago now, and rather a leap, but I was hoping you might recall if one of your nurses was involved in such a liaison. I was informed that you took a personal interest in all of those who worked for you."

Lady Petronella sighed. "I wish the whole thing didn't seem so immediate sometimes—do you know what I mean?" She looked at Maisie directly. It was not a rhetorical question.

Maisie nodded. "Yes, I do. I know exactly what you mean. You'll be going about your daily round, and then, for one reason or another—" She shrugged. "I don't know—possibly an aroma in the air, or the way the wind is blowing, or even something someone said—you feel as if you're back there, in the midst of it all, and that it will never end." Her cheeks became flushed as she recognized her own candor.

"It's so refreshing to speak to someone who knows. Sometimes one really needs to have a good chat with someone else who has gone through a similar experience and is willing to talk about it." She stared out towards the piano, as if she could see into the gardens beyond, then turned back to Maisie. "I sometimes think that we—the whole country—would have benefited from just talking, all of us having a good old chat about it all and what we all lost instead of simply wading on through. I'm rather fed up with this 'buck up and put your best foot forward' approach to the terrors that face one in life." She reached forward to pour more tea. "Mind you, I am probably not a good example. People always say I am rather accomplished at just getting on with things."

Maisie smiled, for the woman's honest account of her feelings had given substance to her first impressions.

"Lady Petronella, I—"

"Do call me 'Ella.' Petronella is such a mouthful. I rue the day my mother picked up that book she was reading prior to going into labor on the day I was born. The heroine was a Petronella, and I have always wished someone had given her a copy of *Jane Eyre*. It would have made life so much simpler."

Maisie edged forward. "Lady Ella—"

"Ella. I insist."

"Ella, then—and thank you for according me the privilege, Ella. Your attitude to memories of the war would be a source of some optimism among a few doctors I know who work with the damaged psyche. Not all, mind, but those who are at the forefront of new research." She took a sip from the just-poured second cup of tea. "As I said, I understand you had something of a matriarchal approach to the care of the doctors and nurses who were retained to work in your unit, so I thought you might recall hearing about a courtship between one of the nurses and an American. After all, the fact that he was an American was one thing, but he came from a very good family."

"Did he?" Ella frowned. "How extraordinary."

"What's so extraordinary?"

"No, nothing." She shrugged. "There were chaperones, you know, so that when the nurses went away for some well-earned rest, they didn't get into any troubling situations, if you know what I mean."

"Yes, I think I do," said Maisie.

"You see, that's one of the things people never talk about afterward—or even when it's all happening—that these events lead people to do things, take chances that they might never take if they didn't think they were going to die, or were afraid that they might lose someone they loved. There's always that last good-bye, that final kiss, that promise of a future spoken in the heat of the moment and in the fear of dying, that leads to all manner of problems later. The girl who is left with a broken heart when her sweetheart returns to his fiancée in Australia, the young man who discovers that the woman who pledged to wait for him cannot face him when he returns with terrible wounds—and after those earlier fervent protestations of never-ending love. Then there are the children, the innocent fatherless children."

"I understand." Maisie spoke quietly, aware that her voice was barely more than a whisper. Too many of her own memories converged into the present, along with a more recent encounter that gave weight to the opinions of the woman before her. "Eighteen months ago, my best friend met her niece for the first time. The child was born in the war, in France. My friend's brother had been killed, and the child's mother was shot by the occupying German army. The girl is the image of her aunt, my friend. Fortunately, they now enjoy summers together, and are close."

"Ah, a story with a happy ending. Not all are so fortunate."

"Is that why you came back and set up the homes for unwed mothers?"

"More or less. I saw no reason why such women had to be branded as wanton. There had to be a means by which they could be with child without disapproving eyes upon them, and we also provided additional care when the children were adopted. There is so much to account for here." She laid a hand on her chest. "One cannot abandon a girl in that situation, one can only look after her and then set her on the path of life again—a good path, a path that might lead her forward to a reasonable future, and not the gutter."

"Did you start the first home during the war?"

She shook her head. "Before the war, actually. But with all those soldiers flooding into the country from all over the world, I asked my husband if he would help me support another two homes for girls in trouble." She looked up at the charcoal drawing. "He was a wonderful, most generous man. One in a million."

Maisie cleared her throat. "So, going back to the issue of our English nurse, you don't think she was one of your employees?"

Lady Ella shook her head again. "They were a fine group of young women, all of them, and I am sure they were pursued by many a soldier, but I am equally sure I would have heard through the grapevine if an American was involved. I worked in the unit too, you know. Of course, I wasn't there all the time—otherwise my husband and I would not have had our darling Tuffie! But I did my bit. I don't believe in asking someone to do something you couldn't or wouldn't be willing to do yourself." She smiled. "The staff here know I would be quite capable of turning my hand to any job in this household, if it came to it. And there's a certain strength in that, my dear."

"Lady—Ella, I understand you kept very precise records of your staff. Would it be an imposition for me to peruse them? I don't doubt your conclusion that 'Tennie' was not one of your nurses, but I would like to see the files, if possible. Just in case anything resonates with other evidence I've gathered."

Lady Ella smiled, put her hands on her knees, and stood up. "Let me take you to the library, where I have a cabinet containing a dossier on each of the women—both doctors and nurses. We can go through them together."

"Thank you, I appreciate your help."

"Not at all." She waved a hand as if to brush away any concern regarding the intrusion. "As I said, it's good to be in the company of someone who was there—and you were there, weren't you, my dear? I have spent a considerable amount of time with nurses. I can tell one a mile off, even if she is doing something quite different now." She beckoned Maisie to follow her. "Let's go to the library."

The women spent another hour together, with Maisie seated alongside as Ella passed the records to her one by one, supplementing the notes with her own recollections: "She was a lovely girl, Cornish farming stock, and this one—so committed to her work, she's a matron now, you know. . . . Ah, this girl married her sweetheart. He's in a wheelchair, but that hasn't stopped them having three children, and this one has really done well for herself, she's a secretary to someone terribly important. . . ."

Maisie made notes on index cards, and tried to commit to memory the images set in front of her. A photograph of each employee was attached to the top right-hand corner of a dossier containing her personal information and employment history, and it seemed that Ella Casterman remembered every single one of her nurses.

When they had gone through the files, the two women remained seated at the table exchanging stories of the war, and their thoughts about life since the Armistice. Maisie had just pushed her chair back to stand up when the door to the library opened with a thump that caused it to bounce back against the wall.

"Mama, you will never guess—oh, I am terribly sorry, I didn't know you had a visitor." The boy-man who had just entered was still dressed as if for an afternoon's rowing. His brownish blond hair looked as if it would benefit from an appointment with a barber, and his ungainly long arms and legs were an indication of his age. Maisie knew without being informed that this was Christopher.

"Tuffie, how many times do I have to tell you—"

He turned to Maisie, his smile wide and with no trace of embarrassment. "Do forgive me, madam. That entrance did nothing to support my claim to be the gentleman my mother always hoped I would be."

Maisie laughed. "You're forgiven, young man, though I suspect your ear might be in for a chewing when I depart."

Ella nodded. "It will indeed. Do run along, darling, and change out of those clothes—you reek of river."

Christopher Casterman nodded, with a grin and a mischievous twinkle in his eye. He bowed to Maisie, kissed his mother on the cheek, and was gone, slamming the door behind him.

"If you ever have a son, be advised, that age represents the best of times and the worst of times. I am sure we will all come through it in one piece, though I am not sure about every door in the house, or indeed the bathroom floor."

Maisie smiled. "I think I'm getting on a bit to worry about that."

"Nonsense! I was thirty-seven when Tuffie was born. Elizabeth Barrett Browning was forty-three when she had her first child, and she was not only far from being a picture of health, but also rather fond of opiates."

"Well, anyway . . ." Maisie held out her hand. "You were most kind to allow me so much of your time. With your family and your charitable work, you are a busy woman."

"And about to be busier—we have a new baby due soon, my first grandchild."

"Many congratulations, Ella."

"Do let me know if I can be of further assistance."

"I will. Most certainly."

As Maisie walked towards the bus stop, in her mind she replayed different stages of her conversation with Lady Petronella Casterman as if she were reading chapters in a book. She would go back over a sentence, a look, a gesture in response to a question, a comment. And when she saw a bench, she sat down and took out her index cards to make notes while the memory was still fresh in her mind. She liked Petronella—*Ella, to her friends*—and found herself drawn to the woman's honesty when questions were put to her. She was sure she had a solid family life, with children she loved and who loved her. When she recalled the photographs atop the piano, it was clear that they all resembled their mother more than their father. Yes, Ella had responded with straight answers throughout their meeting. But then, it was also true that Maisie had drawn back from asking two or three questions that occurred to her, because she thought she already had the answers.

"*You know the truth, Maisie. You know the truth, but you need the proof.*"

Maurice's words echoed again in her mind. She put the index cards and pencil in her shoulder bag, and began to run when she saw the bus coming along. And even as she clambered on board and the conductor rang the bell for the bus to be on its way, it was as if Maurice were with her. "*The evidence is always between the lines, whether it is written or not. Look between the lines.*"

Maisie checked the time on a clock above a shop window as the bus passed along the street, and decided that it would be a good idea to detour via The Dorchester Hotel, to see if she could meet with Thomas Libbert again. At this time of day many men of commerce were returning to their hotels, perhaps to rest before venturing out for supper with colleagues. She stepped off the bus at the next stop and walked to the underground station, from which she traveled to Marble Arch by tube, then made her way down Park Lane to the hotel. She found that she rather missed the very grand Dorchester House that had been demolished to make way for the new hotel. It had spoken of the limitless ambition of old wealth, and though it might have looked more at home in Venice, she had rather liked the building, which looked out over

Hyde Park as if it were an elderly lady surveying her garden from the comfort of a soft old chair while feeling very pleased with herself as she regarded each tree, shrub, and flower bed planted over the years.

Maisie entered the hotel and asked a clerk if a guest by the name of Mr. Thomas Libbert might be available.

"Ah, yes, madam, I believe you will find him in the bar. He's been expecting you."

"He—" Maisie almost revealed her surprise, but instead thanked the clerk and began to walk towards the bar. Libbert had obviously informed the clerk that he was in the bar, should his expected guest arrive soon. She was not the anticipated arrival, but she was curious to see who it might be. Should she approach Libbert? Or should she seclude herself in a corner with a vantage point from which to observe the comings and going of the clientele? She did not want the clerk to question her if he returned, so she decided to continue with her plan.

"Mr. Libbert?"

Libbert turned, and frowned when he saw Maisie.

"Oh, Miss Dobbs."

"I beg your pardon, Mr. Libbert—were you expecting someone? I was passing the hotel and thought I might drop in and take my chances as to whether you might be here. If you've a moment or two, I have a couple more questions—but only if you've time."

Libbert glanced at his glass, which was full, signifying that he was not in a hurry. "Yes, of course. Drink?"

"Thank you. A ginger ale would be lovely, please. I have been rather busy today, and I'm parched." The lie came with ease, though Maisie was far from thirsty, having had two cups of tea with Ella Casterman.

Libbert raised a hand to the barman, ordered the ginger ale, and turned to Maisie, who was now seated alongside him. "So, are you making progress, Miss Dobbs?" He took a sip of Scotch and let it linger in his mouth before swallowing the liquid.

"Yes, there's been some progress." She thanked the barman, who placed a glass with one cube of ice and the effervescent ginger ale in front of her. "I am curious, though, Mr. Libbert—I know you've spent a lot of time in Europe on business, and I'm wondering if you ever visited Michael while he was in Paris on leave."

Libbert rubbed his forehead, and Maisie thought he might be considering whether she knew of a visit, or whether she was engaging in investigative brinkmanship. "Paris. Lovely city. My wife and I went there for our honeymoon. Idyllic."

"Were you there during the war?"

He shook his head. "Not that I can remember. So much traveling, you see, on behalf of the company."

"Yes, I see. I must say, though, I don't think I will ever forget a moment spent in Paris. Especially had I been there in wartime. And especially if my brother-in-law was on leave there."

"Sorry, Miss Dobbs, you've rather caught me at a bad time. I've a lot on my mind—Anna's parents are still fighting for their lives, and my brother-in-law is due here tomorrow."

"I'd heard that Mr. and Mrs. Clifton were improving—much to the relief of the doctors."

"Y-yes, yes, they are, but there's no guarantee you know, with blows to the head. They could go like that." He snapped his fingers.

Maisie nodded and reached for her ginger ale. She took another sip, set down the glass, and had just drawn breath to ask another question when Libbert looked past her, distracted.

"I must go, Miss Dobbs. My business associate has just arrived, and I do want to get this deal sewn up before Teddy arrives tomorrow—it's rather important for our company."

"Of course, Mr. Libbert." Maisie smiled, and held out her hand. "And thank you for accommodating my unexpected arrival, and for the refreshment."

"You're welcome." He shook her hand, nodded good-bye, and hurried from the bar.

Maisie thanked the barman as he came to collect the glasses, then walked back towards the foyer. As she came out into the low spring sunshine of late afternoon, she saw Libbert clamber aboard a taxi-cab, and though she could not be sure, it seemed the man with him, at that moment caught in a ray of sunshine that lightened the otherwise shadowed interior of the vehicle's passenger compartment, was wearing a cravat at his neck, a white shirt, and a blazer. He was a man one might have described as distinguished, and Maisie thought that if she saw him walking along the street, he would strike her as a man who knew how to hold back his shoulders and step forward with some purpose. And in that shaft of light, she saw a man who was probably used to giving orders. Orders that were always carried out to the letter.

FOURTEEN

Maisie prepared a simple evening meal of soused mackerel and vegetables, with a slice of bread and jam for pudding. In general, she did not mind a solitary repast, often taken on a tray while she sat in one of the armchairs, a fork in one hand and a book in the other. And she was under no illusions regarding the significance of the book, whether a novel or some work of reference. As she turned the pages, the characters or the subject matter became her company, a distraction so that the absence of a dining companion—someone with whom to share the ups and downs of her day, from the surprising to the mundane—was not so immediate. Guests to her home were few, and after such a visit, during which a linen cloth would be laid on the dining table and cutlery and glasses set for two, the vacuum left by the departing visitor seemed to echo along the hallway and into the walls. It was at those times, when her aloneness took on a darker hue, that she almost wished there would be no more guests, for then there would be no chasm of emptiness for her to negotiate when they were gone.

This evening, though, as soon as she had finished supper and the glass, plate, and cutlery were washed, dried, and put away, Maisie sat at the dining table in front of Michael Clifton's letters and journal, which she had opened at the beginning and was reading once more. She found herself smiling at certain excerpts—his mimicry of his soldiers' accents, which, when written out phonetically, were certainly humorous. A listing of new words learned along the way had led him to observe, "And I thought they'd be speaking the same language. I might as well have joined up with the French."

I don't know where the idea came from that the English are subdued. The boys—the mates—I've met aren't afraid to let you know exactly what they're thinking. Mind you, they all keep quiet when the inspecting officer makes the rounds of the billets and says, "Any complaints?" That's a stupid question, when you've got "cooties" running along the seams of your shirt and driving you crazy. If you say, "Well, sir, I do have a complaint," you're likely to find yourself up on some kind of disciplinary action. And as for cooties, they're the nasty little bugs that get into everything. I'd never heard that word before. I think Dad must have lost his native language by the time I was born.

Here are a few words I've learned. The Tommy calls his rifle his "barndook," I think because it's harder to say than "rifle"—that's a limey thing too. And I've started liking the thick sludge they call "char." It's tea, but the way they brew it! "Go on, mate, it'll put 'airs on your chest!" they'll say. It's more likely to cut off the blood supply to your throat! I really don't mind Oxo, a sort of beef cube that when dissolved in hot water makes a fortifying drink—the boys' mothers send them out because the advertising says that Oxo is "British to the Backbone."

Another one: gum boots—rubber boots to keep your feet dry in the trenches, should you be one of the lucky lads to get a pair (the rest of us just get wrinkled feet that you have to rub with rum, otherwise they'll drop off when you most need them). And the lads have all sorts of nicknames for the different bombs—the hairbrush (looks like one), the Minnie (Minnewerfer, a German trench mortar, you don't hear it until it hits you), a fifteen-pounder (one of ours, thank God!), five nine (one of theirs), and the one the Germans hate—the four-point-five. There are so many of them, I could write a dictionary of British warfare! But here's a name I like—the "housewife"—Tommy calls it a "hussif." It's a little needlework kit, so you can fix your own uniform, otherwise that guy with the pips will be all over you like a rash of cooties if you're so much as missing a button—and it doesn't matter if you lost it while narrowly avoiding being hit by a Minnie!

Maisie smiled as she read more of Michael Clifton's impressions of the men who were serving alongside him, and could see that these early entries had been made before he had received his promotion to junior officer. But although she was drawn in by the young American's observations of life among the Tommies, she was more interested in the unfolding of his love affair with the woman known as Tennie. She went over paragraphs she'd read before, then came to a place where the pages had fused and she had not attempted to pry them loose earlier because she thought they might tear. It seemed that only layers of mold were holding them together. Once again, she used her Victorinox knife—Caldwell had sent a man over to the office to return the gift from her father—to work on the pages, taking care to protect the handwriting as far as she could. Soon the task was accomplished, with only a few words here and there missing.

I don't know how I managed to swing another short leave in Paris, but here I am, and it is perfect. Even more perfect than it was before, and I thought I came here to walk down memory lane with my head low, but instead . . . who would have known the outcome. I don't know how this will end, but I know that right now, in this place, I am a man who is on top of the world, yet on the edge of the precipice.

Maisie frowned. She picked up the letters and identified the point at which, according to letters from "Tennie," the courtship had ended. Then why was Michael Clifton so happy at what she thought must be a later date? Had there been further correspondence from the unknown woman that had since been mislaid? Were they reunited in Paris? Perhaps there was another letter he'd kept close to heart and that had been lost in battle, or mulched down into the earth along with skin and bone? After so many years, when human remains were discovered, she knew they really were *remains*. Had Michael's lover changed her mind? Was there news from her that elated him? Here was a man experiencing a joyous hiatus away from war, and at the same time he could see ahead, down into an event he called "the precipice," which she took to be his return to the battlefield. Indeed, as she turned the pages, she realized that this was Michael Clifton's last journal entry—what she had assumed would be the next page of writing was a combination of mold and ink that had soaked through the paper.

I am a man who is on top of the world.

But why?

Maisie looked back and forth through the journal and letters, scanning over excerpts again and again. She ached each time she read of the affection between Michael and his English nurse, and recognized that feeling of joy juxtaposed with a sense of despair waiting in the wings. Had she not felt the same when she was with Simon on leave? It was as if the thrill of the moment, that being together, was intensified, framed by the knowledge that their emotions were distilled in an almost make-believe hiatus from the war. Soon they would be there again, among the dead and dying, and the intimacy so dearly cherished would be like a dream gone before morning.

She rubbed her forehead, closed the journal, and set it down on the table, but as she did so, she noticed a loose page opposite the back cover that had slipped free. She reached forward, opened the book, and saw that it was not a page, but a folded sheet of paper. Using her knife, she teased the sheet apart and set it down to reveal a single curl of black hair. She picked up the hair to examine it, then placed it on top of the journal while she read the note, which had faded into invisibility in several places. It was a poem fragment.

What's the best thing in the world?
June-rose,

Truth, not cruel to a friend;
Pleasure, not in haste to end;
Beauty,

Love, when, so, you're loved again.

—Something out of it, I think.

Though Maisie enjoyed verse, so many other aspects of her studies had demanded attention that she immersed herself in poetry only to the extent necessary to pass an exam or gain a respectable mark on a paper. She knew that to discover any significance in the curl's wrapping, she would have to take the fragment of verse to someone who knew poetry and see if knowledge of its author might help her in some way. She had no idea who might assist her, but there was something about the words that remained with her, that nagged at her to take notice. *Pleasure, not in haste to end.* She picked up the lock of hair, turning it between thumb and finger. *Love, when, so, you're loved again.*

Later, after she'd put away the letters and journal, first taking care to replace the poem and single black curl, she turned off the lights and made ready for bed. And try as she might to banish all thoughts of the day so that she could meditate before sleeping, the words echoed in her mind so that, eventually, when she at last went to bed, she drifted to sleep knowing that this was one poem, or fragment thereof, that she would not forget:

Love, when, so, you're loved again.

When Maisie first bought her MG, she had taken the opportunity to drive everywhere. She loved the freedom to go where she wanted, when she wanted, and when she traveled outside London the open road ahead beckoned, along with the promise held in the journey itself. But now, often frustrated by slow-moving London traffic, she drove to work only when her day demanded an excursion outside the metropolitan area, or she had to visit a place not reached by the transport services. For the most part, within the capital the bus, tram, and tube served her well, and in particular, she had always enjoyed traveling by bus. She would step aboard, make her way up the winding stairs to the top deck, and from that vantage point look down upon the world as it went about its business. The bus passed houses where people were getting ready for their day: a husband kissed his wife on the cheek as he stepped out on his way to work, briefcase in hand and bowler hat in place; a woman opened the door of her ground floor flat clutching a worn kimono around her as she let the cat in from a night on the prowl and collected the milk from the doorstep; and in another house, she saw children being made ready for school by a uniformed nanny. As the bus drew nearer the shops of Oxford Street, already clerks and assistants were walking and running purposefully towards their day's toil. And she could see the moving throng as it formed into tributaries and streams, running ever onward towards the ocean of commerce, a day's work and a day's pay. Each of the people had a life and, if they were fortunate, family who loved them and who they loved in return—perhaps a wife at home, a babe in the nursery, an aging parent who needed help, brothers and sisters. It was as if she had been looking down upon a landscape of human activity, a charting of everyday endeavor. As she considered, not for the first time, the part she played in the grand scheme, a question came to mind, almost as if Maurice had prompted her. Was she forging ahead in a stream of her own making, or was she allowing herself to be carried out by a riptide, ever onward towards . . . what?

Mornin', Miss!" Billy was already at his desk when Maisie arrived at the office. "You've been a bit busy, haven't you? How was Dr. Blanche? Any improvement?" He stood up, ready to take her raincoat.

"I have been rather busy, Billy—and I am afraid I haven't yet made a dent in my list of female letter writers."

"Want me to crack it open?"

Maisie nodded. "Yes, I do. In the meantime, Dr. Blanche is not at all well, but I am assured by Dr. Dene that—"

"Dr. Dene?"

"Yes, Billy. Dr. Dene is close to Maurice, as you know, and Maurice gave instructions that he should attend him should a deterioration in his health lead to him being admitted into hospital care." She paused. "It was all right, Billy. It was nice to see him—his wife is expecting a child, so they are very happy."

Billy nodded. He was not one to pry, nor would it have been proper to do so, but he knew that once upon a time Maisie and Dene had been close.

"So, what did Dr. Dene say? Will Dr. Blanche be better soon?"

"He thought Maurice would be home by Saturday afternoon. I'll go down to Chelstone in the evening, and hopefully see him on Sunday." Maisie flicked through the post as she was speaking, but looked up as Billy sat down again. "Oh, and I'm still planning to drop in to see Doreen this afternoon—is that all right?"

"She's looking forward to it, Miss." Billy began placing mugs on a tray, ready to make tea. "And I'd like to know what you think, Miss. Whether you reckon she's getting better."

"She's going back for her outpatient appointments, isn't she?"

He nodded. "Never misses, so far. But I . . . I still worry."

"I'm sure you do, Billy. Remember, you've all been through so much, and recovery is a long road to travel. You can expect some stumbles while she—and you and the boys—feel your feet. Everything's changed now, but you'll see that, at some point, her progress should speed up. She'll gain ground, and you'll realize you can't remember the last bad day."

Billy shrugged. "From your lips to God's ears, as the saying goes."

Maisie smiled. "Think how far you've all come. Now then, let's have a cup of tea and see where we are before I have to go off to see Ben Sutton and his friend with the cine film."

They discussed the Clifton case while sitting in front of the case map.

"So, what you're saying, Miss, is that when Mr. and Mrs. Clifton came down into the hotel foyer, before they went back upstairs to their rooms and were attacked, there were six people there who stood out, and two of them might've been acquainted, but the Cliftons didn't know that?" Billy tapped the map with his pencil.

"Yes. It's rather a leap, but yesterday I saw Thomas Libbert, who was in the foyer on the day of the attack. He got into a taxi-cab with a man who—even though I didn't get the best view of him—appeared to be wearing a cravat and had the look of a military type. If you remember, when I asked Mr. Clifton to try to envision coming down to the foyer, he said he recalled a man with a cravat. And then there was the man and woman who were having an argument—could that man have been Mullen? Or was it someone else? And if it was Mullen, who was the woman? And did Mullen know Libbert?"

"There's a lot of ifs in there, Miss. And I hate to say this, but a lot of blokes wear them cravats when they're not wearing ties, and as for having that military bearing, well, look how many men were in the army in the war. All that 'chin up, chest out' lark gets trained into you."

"What we do is peppered with 'ifs' all the time. If it wasn't for the 'ifs' we would take more steps backward than forward." Maisie sighed. "And this case is beginning to feel a bit like that." She stood up, walked around the table, leaned against the window frame, and looked out at the square. "Then there's this fragment of verse—at least, that's what I think it is. I'll stop at the library to see if someone can tell me whether it's from a well-known poet, or perhaps it was something Michael Clifton's ladylove penned while on night duty in a freezing cold ward."

"That's definitely more up your alley, Miss. Never been one for your verse, unless it's rhyming slang, of course."

Maisie laughed, and shook her head. "Billy, you're a diamond. Now then, I had better be on my way. You'll look into the rest of our list?"

"It's as good as done. I'll stick to the ones in London today."

Maisie arrived early for her appointment with Ben Sutton at his friend's house in Notting Hill, which gave her an opportunity to look around the area. Priscilla had informed her that as far as she knew, Henry Gilbert had inherited the red-brick terrace house, and now rented out the upper two floors to students, which seemed to fit Maisie's brief observation of the comings and goings of several people who might have been described as "bohemian" in certain circles—a man wearing a coat of Edwardian vintage with a bright yellow scarf, and a woman with very short hair and equally short skirt, even though, as far as Maisie knew, the very fashionable women had allowed their skirt lengths to fall once more.

She watched Ben Sutton arrive in a taxi-cab. He ran up the steps and knocked at the door, which was opened some moments later by a young man with an open-necked shirt, his sleeves rolled up. He was wiping his hands with a cloth, and smiled at Sutton as if they had met before.

Maisie suspected that it was time to cross the road and knock at the door.

"There you are, on the dot! Just as I expected you would be." Ben Sutton stepped back so that Maisie could cross the threshold, then leaned down and kissed her on the cheek as if he had known her for more than one evening. "Henry's waiting for us in his studio. He has a sort of complex of rooms downstairs in what used to be cellars—completely purpose-built for his work. Perfect for running cine film. Follow me."

Sutton led her down a staircase, then along a dark corridor and into what was a surprisingly large room. She looked around and, when she became accustomed to the light, could see that there had been reconstruction to provide a spacious studio, and behind her a smaller room with what she took to be a film library and a glass window with a hatch through which the lens of a projector extended. There was another door at the opposite end of the room, which was closed. A dozen quite comfortable-looking chairs were positioned in two semicircular rows; the experience would be somewhat more pleasing than a visit to the cinema—at least one would be able to view the cine film with a few friends, rather than half of London, most of whom always seemed to be sneezing.

"The door leads out into another couple of rooms, one where Henry and his assistants do their editing and such like, though of course, they do a lot of this sort of thing at the studios in Twickenham."

"I see," replied Maisie, though she really did not see at all. "I should confess, my knowledge of film stops at the odd trip to the cinema, and in viewing X-rays."

Sutton laughed at the same time as the door opened and two men entered, one carrying a series of large round canisters. "Ah, Henry, here's Miss Dobbs."

"Delighted to meet you, Miss Dobbs—Maisie, isn't it?"

"Thank you for agreeing to show me your cine film, Henry—and yes, it's Maisie."

"This is my assistant, Roland Marshall." He turned to introduce the young man who had opened the door for Sutton. He nodded his head, his burden too heavy to allow him to extend his hand.

Henry Gilbert was not quite six feet tall and wore his hair short, Maisie suspected, so as not to draw attention to a growing bald patch. His movements were precise and quick, and she had no trouble envisioning him working on the front line, filming soldiers going about the business of war.

"Now then, let's get the show running. I have a lot of film, Miss Dobbs, so I wondered, do you have any specific interests? The veterinary corps, for example."

"Well, yes—do you have anything on cartographers in the war? Or mapmaking? I know it's a bit obscure, but I thought you might have something—especially as, from what I've been given to understand, you may have been in France at the same time as my friend's son. He was a cartographer."

"You may be in luck—I spent quite some time filming cartographers," said Gilbert. "I didn't want to come back with hours of film of basically the same thing, so I chose several different areas of work: the men who operated the big guns, the veterinary corps, and the cartographers. Of course, I have some film with soldiers in the trenches, the wounded being brought back, but for the most part I wanted to draw attention to the fact that there is more to war than Tommies with guns. And the cartographers took extraordinary risks, all for information—as we all know, a war is never won without information."

Maisie held her breath, hardly able to believe her good fortune. "Henry, do you remember the soldiers you met? I mean, did you spend sufficient time with them to have made some sort of acquaintance?"

"Yes and no. Of course there was a lot of joshing, the lads beaming into the camera, pulling faces—after all, many of them weren't much more than boys. And we took our meals with them, slept alongside the men while we were filming them, so of course, there are those that one remembers. But I am sure you will appreciate that, in my job, there has to be a level of dispassionate observation—the cinematographer's protection—otherwise it would be impossible. You see, very often the men on the other side of my lens were dead within days of their images being immortalized on cine film. But you can always try me—do you have a name?"

"This cartographer might stand out—he was an American, and—"

"An American, you say?" Gilbert interrupted Maisie and, without looking at his assistant, motioned for him to put the metal containers down on a table set against the side wall. "You're right, that is unusual. There couldn't have been two of them in the British army—could there?"

Maisie shook her head. "I doubt it."

"Good, then we can cut out a lot of time, because I know exactly where to look for that film." He went over to the canisters, but continued talking. "We were out in the field for some time and, as I said, I filmed several cartography units in northern France through into Belgium."

Maisie continued talking while he searched through the canisters.

"What was the cine film used for, and what will you do with it all?" she asked.

"Some of it was used for newsreels in the war—you know, the 'Jolly old Britain's winning the war' sort of propaganda. Helped everyone to buck up when things were looking bad." He picked out two canisters and passed them to his assistant. "Load these, start with this one, and call when you're ready." He turned his attention back to Maisie. "The business of filming is changing rapidly, you know, and in Britain we're at the forefront of a new genre in the craft. It's called the documentary; a sort of hybrid between documenting an event or moment in time, and then blending it with a story, so it's a bit more entertaining. That's what I want to do with this film"—he waved his hand across the canisters—"though I've a few other things on my plate at the moment, and one has to earn one's money."

"So, may I ask, is there anything you remember about the American cartographer?" asked Maisie.

Gilbert rubbed his chin. "Martin—Michael—Mitch? Somebody-or-other beginning with M, wasn't it? Anyway, I just remember he was a very approachable chap, very mannerly, always answered a question with 'sir,' and not because he was in the army. You had the sense that he was brought up to be respectful. Not that the others weren't, but he was a young man of his type—I've been to the east coast of America, you know, and he was a real Bostonian, though he was interested when I told him I'd been to California." He smiled. "I'd forgotten all that, to tell you the truth. Now that I come to talk about it, the details are coming back. I met so many young men, you see—of course, I was not so old myself, but I wasn't able to join up. Given my profession, you'd be surprised to note that the reason was my shortsightedness. I told you about the cinematographer's protection—well, I remember being told that the entire unit, which would include your American, was listed as missing not long after we shot the film. The thing is that I couldn't help but remember him, and not just because of his accent. He was a happy-go-lucky sort, one of those who have a perennial hail-fellow-well-met approach to everyone they meet."

The assistant raised his voice to let them know the film was ready to run. Gilbert held out his hand to seats close to the middle of the room, and when Sutton had taken a place beside Maisie, the wall lights were extinguished. The screen in front of them seemed to splutter into life, and a series of numbers counted down until a rough board was shown. It read: "France, cartographers," along with a date that Maisie could not discern. The screen became black for a moment, until a grainy image flickered into life, of men carrying equipment across the mud and through barbed wire. The film rendered their movements jerky, unstable, and as they set up their tools, Maisie thought they looked rather like doomed marionettes, and though she could not tell whether it was a fair day or foul, the gray cloudless background gave the impression of cold, a day when the wet damp of France in wartime could bore into the bone. She shivered.

The camera came closer, and the men looked up and were brought into greater focus. There was a moment of camaraderie, when they stood with arms about each other's shoulders, like a rugby team preparing for the season's photograph. Then the cameraman must have drawn back, because they continued with their work again, squinting through an eyeglass, one man making notes while another took measurements. Again the camera moved in closer, then seemed to sweep across the landscape. In the background, the projector whirled and chattered as the film continued. Maisie half closed her eyes in a squint, searching for a face she knew.

The camera came back to the unit, and once again moved closer to the men. At that moment, one of the men began laughing, and it seemed he elbowed his comrade in a playful gesture. The other soldier laughed, and gave him a shove, and the first soldier, who Maisie could now see was an officer, pushed back his helmet to rub his forehead.

"Can you stop there?" Maisie called out.

"Stop!" Gilbert's voice carried well, and the film stopped mid-frame. "Run it back to the soldier moving his helmet."

The stick figures moved backward at speed, then the frame was frozen for a moment and began running again.

"There!"

"Stop!"

"Is that the American you remember, Henry?"

Gilbert nodded. "Yes, that's him."

Maisie waited a moment, trying to match the image on the screen with the photograph she had already seen.

"Shall we continue?"

She nodded. "Yes, thank you. Go on."

Henry called out to his assistant, and the cine film began rolling again, and soon it was clear that during the filming, shellfire was coming closer, as the earth seemed to explode in the background. The camera had caught the men hurrying to pack up their equipment before running for cover, and as their movements became faster, so the images became almost unwatchable; in that moment, the men seemed like clowns at the circus, running back and forth in an attempt to protect their equipment and themselves. The screen changed to black, and the countdown of numbers signaled the end of the reel.

"There's another with that same unit, Maisie. Want to watch it?"

"Of course, yes."

Ben, Maisie, and Henry Gilbert were silent while they waited, and soon the assistant called out once more that the film was about to start. A series of numbers filled the screen, then nothing but black, then a board with the date and location. This time the men of the unit were outside what seemed to be a farmhouse or a barn. With stilted movements, they were checking kit and preparing their packs for another expedition onto the battlefield. Maisie wished she could lip-read so that she might know what they were saying to each other, and she wondered whether their conversation was about the job at hand, a night out in the village, or their last leave. There was another second of black screen, and when it cleared, the camera had been brought in closer, and this time Maisie could see Michael Clifton clearly. He was laughing with the man next to him. The camera pulled back, and another man, an officer, came into view. The man was carrying a baton under his arm, and seemed to walk in that same matchstick-man manner, but he was evidently a more senior officer. He appeared to be taking the men to task, then looked around and came towards the camera, waving his baton. The screen went black, followed by a series of numbers.

"Do you remember that last incident?" Maisie turned in her chair as Gilbert stepped towards the light switch.

"I do indeed. Can't remember the man's name, but he was a bit of a killjoy. Waved his stick at me and threatened to put my camera into the mud. He should have tried it! Anyway, you don't forget those incidents. Mind you, they're not that unusual in my line of work, but rather unsettling when it's a man in a uniform threatening you."

She stood up and smiled, holding out her hand. "Thank you so much for your valuable time, Henry. It was kind of you to do this."

"I owe Ben a favor or two," said Gilbert, as he shook her hand. "So this helped me pay down my debt."

They turned to leave, and as the trio made their way to the front door, Maisie turned to Gilbert. "I know you said that you don't remember everyone, but you must have become somewhat familiar with that unit; you mentioned that for a short time you lived alongside some of the soldiers you filmed."

"As I said, you try not to get too close, for the sake of objectivity. But yes, I sort of took to that little group, though the American is the one who sticks out most."

"Do you recall any conversations between the men?"

"That would be a tall order, Maisie," Sutton interjected.

"I know, but—"

"The boys teased the American, but he could give it back to them, and it was all in good heart, from what I can recall. There was one sapper who mentioned that he—the American—was a man of some extensive property, out in California. And he teased him about his girl—she'd broken it off, but he was convinced the American wasn't wanting for female company when he was on leave. He'd not long returned from a few days away. Mind you, a handsome young fellow like that—can't imagine him spending much time alone when he was off duty." He laughed. "Anyway, as I said, it was all a long time ago now. I might have it wrong, and it could have been the other way around—you know, the other fellow on leave, that sort of thing. I'm really interested in the image in front of the camera, not the subject's private life."

Maisie nodded.

After more good-byes, and some final conversation, Maisie and Sutton left and stood outside the house.

"Ready for a bite to eat?"

"Ben." Maisie smiled. "Would you forgive me if I decline your offer of lunch? It's a bit early for me in any case—that didn't take as long as I thought, and I have so much to do today. Watching your friend's films has given me a lot of food for thought."

Sutton nodded. "I'll hold you to our lunch another time—or perhaps you'd come with me to the theater, and supper afterward?"

"What a lovely idea, thank you. And I do appreciate your understanding, especially as it was so good of you to cash in a favor on my behalf. Oh, and Ben, may I trust you to keep what we have seen today to yourself—just for a while."

"I'll not tell a soul, and I'll make sure Henry knows too. And cashing in the favor was my pleasure, Maisie." He smiled. "There weren't that many men doing what Henry was doing out in France, so I had an idea you might be in luck with his film. Serendipity, eh?" He smiled. "Anyway, I hope I'll see you again soon. May I walk you to the tube, madam?"

They said good-bye at the underground station, and Maisie waved as she made her way down the steps and around a corner out of view. She waited a few moments until she was sure Sutton had left, then retraced her steps to Henry Gilbert's house and knocked on the door. When his assistant opened the door, Maisie asked if she could see Mr. Gilbert for just a moment.

"Maisie, back so soon! What can I do for you—did you leave something behind?" Gilbert took off a pair of spectacles as he walked towards her.

"I am sorry to bother you, but I have one quick question—do you mind?"

"Of course not. Fire away!"

"Is it possible to make a photograph of part of your cine film? I am sure there are appropriate words to describe this, but what I'd like is a picture from the last few seconds on that final piece we watched; something I can hold in my hand to study."

"You mean the nasty ogre rushing at my camera?"

"Yes, that's it."

"It's not a simple task, but it can be done."

"I would be most willing to pay for your time."

"First things first. I'll have the frame printed and sent to you. Roland here can take down the details."

Maisie smiled. "Thank you very much." She paused. "And if we could keep this between ourselves, I would appreciate it."

Gilbert smiled. "Absolutely. We don't want Ben to know you want a picture of another man, do we?"

Maisie blushed. "No, we don't."

Later, as she left the house for the second time, Maisie could not recall any part of the conversation with Ben Sutton either before they viewed the film, or on the way to the underground station. In fact, she could barely remember any interaction with him at all. But an image continued to flash into her mind's eye, of a man brandishing a baton as he reached towards the camera that was filming his every move.

FIFTEEN

Maisie stopped at a pie and mash shop on her way to Shoreditch, and had a large helping of meat pie with mashed potato and gravy, followed by a cup of strong tea. It was the sort of place she rather liked to frequent; the service was quick and the repast plain yet hearty, better described as fodder than as food. Though she never stayed long, she liked to watch the customers coming and going, an assortment of men and women, all of whom were working class and valued a good meal. And as Maisie would not bother to cook a meat pie just for herself, and she rarely stopped for a proper lunch, the break was a welcome one—even though the Clifton case remained uppermost in her mind.

She was thinking about lies. About the many times in the course of her work she had been lied to. It was a hazard of her occupation. She rarely missed a lie, seldom overlooked the sense of doubt that assailed her when she had been offered less than the truth. Indeed, she thought it was the presence of doubt—rather than certainty, perhaps—that led to cracking open many a case. *Doubt.* Was it an emotion? A sense? Or was it just a short, stubby word to describe a response that could diminish a person in a finger snap? When she felt doubt, she asked more questions of herself, though she also knew those questions were no guarantee that her attention would be pointed in the right direction. *There's a lot of ifs.* Yes, Billy had it right, there were a lot of ifs. *What if.* Without that question, she would not have decided to make a detour back towards the British Library. What if a librarian could identify the verse she'd found tucked into Michael Clifton's journal? And would such information have any meaning, any relevance to her search for the truth about Michael Clifton's death and the attack on his parents? As she walked along, she planned to spend only a short time in the reading room, which might allow her the opportunity to drop into Bourne and Hollingsworth on Oxford Street before dashing over to Shoreditch. She wanted to go to the shoe department to see if someone there remembered something of the Clifton story. It was an important London shop, so the buyer might have more detailed knowledge about the company in its final years than Billy had managed to uncover, or he might have remembered something after being questioned. She thought she could accomplish those two things and still be in Shoreditch at a reasonable hour.

The reading room of the British Library was pin-drop quiet. A librarian might tiptoe across the floor to replace a book on the shelves, or a reader might begin to cough, then look around and mouth "Sorry" to the person alongside who had looked up, scowling at the interruption. Patrons moved deliberately—whether turning pages or taking notes—as if in a manner of respect, reminding Maisie of churchgoers at evensong. She slipped into a vacant seat, took out an index card and pencil, and closed her eyes, trying to envisage the words written on the notepaper tucked inside Michael Clifton's journal. She crossed out a line, then another word, and when she was satisfied, wrote the partial verse without error on another index card, then approached the librarian's desk.

"I wonder if you could help me," she whispered.

The librarian nodded, and leaned towards her.

"I have a fragment of verse, which I think is part of a longer poem. I know this is rather a shot in the dark, but do you recognize it?"

The man took the card, looked at the words, and shook his head. "No, I'm afraid not." He looked around.

"Do you have a librarian who is more of a poetry buff?" She hoped she had not insulted him, but he seemed to have taken no offense.

"I'm more of a history man, myself." He turned both ways. "I was looking for old Mrs. Hancock. She comes in almost every day—she's had a reader's ticket for years and generally settles down with the newspaper before taking up a book of poetry. She's getting on, but can still remember many, many poetical works off by heart." He picked up the index card. "Let me see if she's over there. She sometimes drops off for the odd forty winks, poor dear. Do you mind waiting?"

Maisie shook her head. "Not at all." She stepped back as the librarian turned and walked out into the room, then circled the desks searching for Mrs. Hancock. She lost sight of him; then a moment or two later, he was walking towards the stacks with an elderly woman who was using her walking stick to point up to one of the shelves. Maisie smiled, for the woman seemed to enjoy giving orders to the man in charge. She watched as he reached for a book, then handed it to the woman, who sat down at the closest vacant seat and turned the pages, squinting as she brought the book so close to her eyes, it was touching her nose. A moment or two elapsed before she discovered what she was looking for and lifted up the open book for the librarian to read. Her smile was that of one well satisfied with herself, and Maisie was glad she had made the inquiry, for the woman seemed to stand straighter, as if in being asked to share her expertise, she had received a validation of worth.

The librarian returned with the book held open.

"Mrs. Hancock to the rescue!" The librarian kept his voice low, despite his enthusiasm for a task successfully completed. "It's a poem called 'The Best Thing in the World.' " He passed the book to Maisie.

"Thank you very much." She took the open book and walked to a desk, careful to make as little noise as possible. She took out another index card and her pencil, and sat down ready to transcribe the poem.

What's the best thing in the world?
June-rose, by May-dew impearled;
Sweet south-wind, that means no rain;
Truth, not cruel to a friend;
Pleasure, not in haste to end;
Beauty, not self-decked and curled
Till its pride is over-plain;
Love, when, so, you're loved again.
What's the best thing in the world?
— Something out of it, I think.

Maisie read the words over twice and sat back in her chair, still engaged by the poem and what it might have meant to Michael Clifton. Sighing, she flipped the book over to look at the spine. It was from a collection of poems by Elizabeth Barrett Browning. She sat for a moment longer, then closed the book, collected her bag from alongside her chair, and returned to the librarian.

"Thank you," she whispered, as she set the book down in front of him.

He nodded in response, and as Maisie walked out of the reading room, she glanced back to see Mrs. Hancock watching her. She raised her hand and nodded acknowledgment, and the woman waved in return, her smile puffed with importance.

Maisie checked the time on the way out of the library. Much as she wanted to try to find someone, somewhere, who could tell her more about the demise of Clifton's Shoes, she had promised to visit Doreen Beale, and knew she should be on her way to Shoreditch. In any case, if she was to be honest with herself, what she truly wanted was not so much new information, but to see if one of her what-ifs might be true.

To an outsider, the journey from the west end of London to the east end might have seemed like leaving a full buffet dinner with the finest china, for bread and water at a rough-hewn table. The houses on many streets were still without running water, so women gathered at the communal pump to fill their buckets and kettles, then huffed and puffed their way home carrying their burden. But despite such inequities, and a level of poverty that threatened to grind the soul to dust, there was a spirit here that Maisie understood, a language in which she was fluent, and a camaraderie among the likes of the women at the pump that underlined a certain resilience borne of want. And though the communities encompassed within London's boroughs still retained something of their respective tribal forefathers, there were common threads of experience between the people of Lambeth, where Maisie was born and brought up, and Shoreditch, with the most distinct being poverty.

The people who lived on Billy's street had done their best to rise above the grayness of life in the East End. Most of the children playing in the street had no shoes and were clad in hand-me-down clothes that were ill fitting and worn. Though the Beales made ends meet and ensured their children wore clean, if not new, clothes, they were among those who just couldn't make the leap to a better standard of living somewhere else. For Billy there was a comfort to be had from living in the surroundings of his childhood, with his elderly mother nearby, yet Maisie knew that such comfort could not be confused with contentment. The desire to get away burned within Billy Beale, so the plans had to be grand plans, and the destination not to a better borough in London, but to a land some three thousand miles away.

Having drawn long looks as she walked from the bus stop—a well-turned-out woman such as Maisie was rare on the streets of Shoreditch—she arrived at Billy's house and made her way to the front door. Looking in, she saw Doreen sitting in a chair by the window. She appeared to have fallen asleep while keeping vigil, her deceased daughter's ragged toy lamb held close to her chest, as if she had been breathing in the scent of a childhood gone. Maisie knocked lightly at the door. Standing alongside the window, she could see Doreen waken, rub her eyes, and rest her head on the back of the armchair as she regained full consciousness. Maisie knocked again, and this time Billy's wife pushed the toy behind her chair, stood up, came to the window, and waved to her before leaving the room to come to the door.

"I'm sorry, Miss Dobbs, I must have dozed off when the boys went round to their nan's for tea." She stood aside for Maisie to enter the narrow passageway.

"You deserve a nap, Doreen, what with Billy and Bobby keeping you busy."

Doreen smiled as she stepped aside for Maisie to enter the narrow passageway. "Please go on into the parlor, Miss Dobbs, and I'll put the kettle on."

The Beales' house was typical of many small terraced houses in their area, but atypical in that only one family lived there, though Doreen's sister and her family had resided for some time in the house while her husband looked for work in London. The parlor was a small, square room with a fireplace, a picture rail about a foot from the ceiling, and two armchairs that had seen better days. It was a room hardly used by the family, who made the kitchen the center of their home life, keeping the parlor for Sundays, Christmas, and the odd special occasion. Maisie's visit was a special occasion.

"Here we are, Miss Dobbs. Nice cup of tea does you good, doesn't it?"

"It certainly does—and I am gasping."

Maisie regarded Doreen as she set the tray on a table positioned along the back wall and proceeded to pour two cups. Just before Doreen was sent away to a psychiatric hospital, some four months earlier, she had lost a good deal of weight and was run down in mind, body, and spirit. The usually meticulous woman had relinquished care of both herself and her children, and had demonstrated a temper never before revealed. The grief at losing her youngest child, a daughter who was dear to everyone whose life she touched, had dragged Doreen into a cavern of darkness that she had neither the strength nor the will to escape. Now she seemed as if she was on her way back to being her old self. She'd regained some weight, and her skirt and blouse were plain, but laundered and pressed.

"How are you keeping?"

"I'm doing much better, Miss Dobbs. Dr. Masters helped me with, you know, how to get on without Lizzie. And now I'm back on the mend, so we'll be all right, me and Billy and the boys. Yes, we'll be all right." She passed a cup of tea to Maisie with two hands, but still managed to spill some in the saucer. "Oh, I am sorry, here—"

"Not to worry. I'm always doing the very same thing. That's why I get Billy to serve tea to our clients when they visit!" The lie came easily. "Pour yourself a cup and sit down with me, Doreen."

Doreen Beale brought a second cup of tea, again held with two hands, and sat in the chair in which Maisie had seen her sleeping.

"Are you managing, Doreen?" Maisie thought there was no point in any conversational subterfuge, for she had visited Doreen when she was in hospital, and had seen her after she had been subjected to a violent procedure. Maisie had subsquently pulled strings to have the woman transferred to another, more humane psychiatric institution.

Doreen nodded. "Like I said, Miss Dobbs, I'm doing better. I'm taking in some needlework again, and I'm managing to finish a dress or alteration without forgetting about it. Billy's mother comes around every morning after the children go to school, and we have a chat and she helps me. I know it's not right, a woman of that age helping the likes of me, but she's very good. She makes sure I eat some of her broth. I don't always feel like eating, you see, so I forget, and she reminds me. Yes. I'm getting better."

The neat hair pulled back in a bun and a trace of color in her cheeks, were further evidence of a slow recovery. Maisie remembered her visit at Christmas, when the usually meticulous Doreen—the want of money had never stopped her caring for her appearance—wore clothes in need of repair and laundering; her complexion had been rough and gaunt, and her hair ill-kempt.

"Are you getting out, Doreen? You could do with some fresh air, you know."

"That's hard to find here in Shoreditch, Miss Dobbs. I'm a Sussex girl, you know, I didn't come up to London until I married Billy. I don't know that the air ever feels fresh to me."

The conversation went on for another fifteen minutes or so, and when Maisie announced it was time to go, she carried the two teacups into the kitchen while Doreen took the tray with teapot and milk. The kitchen, though small, was spotless, and while they continued talking, Maisie picked up a tea towel and dried the crockery as Doreen placed each washed item on the draining board. She put the things away in a cupboard, and while she was still talking to Maisie—about the boys, about Billy's dream of going to live in Canada—Maisie noticed her wiping down every surface in the kitchen time and again. Then she washed her already clean hands once more, shook them dry, and wiped the draining boards for the umpteenth time to absorb droplets of water.

"That was a lovely cup of tea, Doreen. It's a treat to see you looking so well."

"Thank you, Miss Dobbs."

"Let Billy know when you're up to taking on more work. I'm fed up with the blinds in my flat and would like some curtains. I don't think I'd trust anyone else to make them for me, so when you're ready—"

"I've got a few things to finish, but in about a fortnight I reckon I could take them on."

The two women exchanged pleasantries at the door, and soon Maisie was on a bus traveling away from Shoreditch. Throughout the journey, which took her along the narrow streets of the City and then in the direction of Fitzroy Square, her deliberations were firmly on the Beales and their future. Doreen's behavior had revealed a tendency towards obsession, which was not unusual in a case such as hers. It gave her a sense of control over her environment and what happened in her life. Maisie wondered if she should say something, or whether certain fixations might diminish as Doreen grew stronger. Billy's fierce pride had recently been put aside so many times to accept help from Maisie, and there was only so much more she could do. She had not the resources to offer more money, but she felt it incumbent upon herself to provide support where she could, so that at the very least, Billy knew that someone cared enough to help them find a way through their barren desert of despair to something approaching a better way of life.

The shank of the afternoon was giving way to dusk as Maisie ran from the bus stop on Tottenham Court Road, and when she entered the square from Fitzroy Street, she could see a light on in the first-floor office. The business week extended until Saturday afternoon, and in their line of endeavor, it was not unusual to work on a Sunday, but she was still surprised to see that Billy had not left for home at this time on a Friday. It was as she walked closer to the front door that she saw the reason—a chauffeured motor car was parked outside, indicating that visitors had arrived and were waiting for her.

As she reached the top of the staircase, the door to the office opened, and Billy stepped out onto the landing.

"I heard the front door go, Miss."

"Who do we have the pleasure of seeing so late in the day?"

"It's Mr. Clifton—the son, that is. And his friend, Dr. Charles Hayden."

"Oh, Charles—" She opened the door and entered the room.

Billy had offered the men chairs in front of Maisie's desk, and as she walked in, her cheeks flushed, they came to their feet.

"Charles, how lovely to see you again."

"Maisie!" He took her hands in his own and kissed her on the cheek in greeting.

Charles Hayden was tall, with broad shoulders, and if he carried any extra weight, it served only to make him seem more of a contented man, happy in his family and a success in his profession. His ready smile made Maisie feel as if she were part of an inner circle. While still holding her hands, he turned to Teddy Clifton.

"Teddy, I met this young lady when she was just—what was it, Maisie? Eighteen years of age?"

Maisie smiled and gently pulled her hands away so that she could welcome her guest.

"Mr. Clifton, it is such a pleasure to meet you, though I wish with all my heart that the circumstances were less tragic."

"Thank you, ma'am. Charles has told me a lot about you."

"What news of your parents?"

"My father is much better. Charles examined him today and went through some tests—the doctors accommodated us—so we are pleased with his progress. My mother has regained consciousness, but it will be a few more days before we know what sort of lasting damage there might be."

"I'm optimistic, though," added Hayden.

"And I feel better knowing Charles is over here now—not that there's anything wrong with your doctors."

"I understand, Mr. Clifton." Maisie pulled her chair from behind her desk so that the coming conversation might be more open, less businesslike. Maurice had often cautioned her that the desk could be seen as barrier to honest dialogue, and if she had control of the situation, and if the circumstances warranted it, she should never let the desk come between herself and her clients, or anyone she was interviewing. It was one of many nuggets of advice she had taken to heart.

"Have you had tea?"

"Mr. Beale has filled us with tea and—what do you call those things? Biscuits?" Charles Hayden laughed as he asked the question.

" 'No better than hardtack.' That's what you said once, when we were all in France." She took her seat and invited Billy to bring his chair over to join them. "My assistant has been actively helping me with this case," she explained to the men.

Maisie did not know how much Charles Hayden had brought Teddy Clifton into his confidence regarding his suspicions upon reading the postmortem report on Michael Clifton's remains. She looked at Hayden and nodded, a signal that she wanted him to begin their meeting.

"Maisie, I have talked to Teddy about my thoughts on the postmortem report. I didn't say much in my letter but I suspect you might have come to a few conclusions yourself—Edward intended to show you the report."

"Yes, he brought it to my attention." She looked at Clifton, then Hayden. "And though you did not color my assessment of what was indicated there, I believe we can set our cards on the table and see a match."

"Go on, Maisie." Charles Hayden nodded to her to continue.

She concentrated her attention on Clifton. "It is my belief that your brother's life was taken deliberately prior to the shelling that killed other members of the cartography unit and led to further wounds to his body. They were in a former German dugout, and it was quite sophisticated, with separate rooms, if you will; there were bunks and so on. This was no ordinary tunnel or hole in the ground—the Germans were excellent engineers. The men could all have been at rest when Michael's life was taken, and it would not be a stretch to suggest that they might not have discovered his body prior to the shelling. It is a question that cannot be readily answered."

Maisie could see that Teddy was familiar with the story, for he showed no shock at the news, but brought his hand to his mouth for a few seconds.

"Do you think the killer perished in the shelling?" The weariness brought on by travel across the Atlantic and arrival in Southampton, along with the shock of seeing his parents in hospital, was evident in Clifton's demeanor; his shoulders were rounded, and his voice cracked with tiredness.

Maisie shook her head. "I couldn't say, Mr. Clifton, but if I were to hazard a guess, I would say no. No, I don't believe he was killed. I can think of several circumstances wherein the killer could have taken your brother's life and then been on his way. Of course, he may himself have lost his life to war at a later date—but no, I don't think so." She paused. "There's the distinct possibility of a connection between Michael's death and the attack on your parents. I do not think they are isolated events."

Clifton blew out his cheeks as he nodded. "I know what Charles here thinks, but how do *you* think Michael was killed?" He put the question to Maisie.

"I believe his life was taken by a single blow to the back of his head. The weapon was likely one of his own pieces of equipment—a theodolite, for example. And I think your parents were attacked in the same way. They had your brother's tools with them in their room—I can imagine your mother, for example, putting certain items out, to remind her of your brother."

"Yes. Yes, that's just the sort of thing she would do. How do you know?"

Maisie shrugged. "She struck me as the sort of woman who decorates her home with pictures of family, with the trophies of childhood accomplishment, and probably went as far as to frame a school tie, or whatever would have the same significance in America."

Clifton's eyes widened, and he looked at Hayden again. "Can you believe this, Charles?" He turned back to Maisie. "Mother actually had our football jerseys put into frames. We laughed like crazy, but she said we'd appreciate it one day." He paused, then became serious once more. "So you think the killer is on the loose. Are my folks still at risk? We've seen Detective Inspector Caldwell and he is keeping a guard on their rooms."

"In my estimation, the risk to your parents is minimal, but at the same time, it would be foolhardy to discontinue guarding them."

"Why?"

"I believe the man who attacked your parents is himself dead. But in my line of work, Mr. Clifton, one soon realizes that the true killer is sometimes not the person who takes the life of the victim."

"What do you mean?"

"While there are similarities between the murder of your brother and the attack on your parents, I have a feeling that your brother died following one single blow. Your parents' attack seemed more frenzied, one borne of fear. I think the perpetrator was disturbed while searching for something he wanted—or that someone else wanted—and picked up the first thing that came to hand when he was disturbed by your parents' return to their room. He might not have wanted to kill anyone."

Teddy Clifton nodded. He was about to ask another question, when Charles Hayden interjected.

"Maisie." He leaned forward and touched her cheek. "How the heck did you get this?"

"I thought I'd managed to cover it up."

"Come on, I'm a doctor. It's my job to see these things. How did that happen?"

"A man pushed me onto the ground. He had just stolen my document case."

"Did they catch him?"

"His body was discovered later, in the rooms he rented."

"Was he important to the case?" asked Clifton.

"Yes, I believe he was. Of course, I could be wrong, but I think he was the man who almost killed your parents. And I don't think he intended to do anything of the sort."

SIXTEEN

"James, I think I ought to confess to you that I know precious little about motor racing. Nothing, in fact." Maisie smiled as she spoke, relaxed in James Compton's company as he drove them out of London towards Surrey.

"Well, first of all, Brooklands is famous for being the first motor racing track in the world. Absolutely purpose-built for the business in 1907." He grinned, ready to tease. "And I must say, I'm glad to have found something that you don't know and I do, Maisie Dobbs!"

"You're right. The only racing I have any familiarity with is horse racing."

James changed gear to negotiate a bend, then increased speed as the road straightened. "Then you're more than halfway there. Almost everything about racing motor cars has been based on horse racing, so the language will be familiar—the grandstand, the track, the paddock where the drivers assemble. It's all a bit like a day at Newmarket—but faster."

"How fast?" Maisie realized that James was increasing speed as he spoke. "As fast as you?"

"Oh, dear—point taken." He slowed down. "But to be perfectly honest, I couldn't drive anywhere near as fast as the racers at Brooklands, even though I might dream about it. At the end of March, Tim Birkin—rather famous driver, was in the Flying Corps in the war; his real name is Henry, but he's been known as Tim since he was a boy—anyway, he was putting his Bentley through its paces, doing practice laps, and was clocked at 137.9 miles per hour. That's a new record over the distance. Mind you, one of the other chaps—Malcolm Campbell—recently secured a new land speed record in the USA, at Daytona. He was just three seconds shy of 254 miles per hour. Beggars belief, doesn't it?"

"It's terrifying." Maisie held on to her seat.

"At the very least you'd put your neck out trying to follow him." He looked out at the countryside as he spoke. "Actually, I learned to fly at Brooklands."

"At the speeds you've just mentioned, I would have thought staying on the ground presented quite a problem."

"Oh, very funny!" said James, and they both laughed again. Then James explained. "There was already a flying school at Brooklands, and then before the war, Tommy Sopwith came in with his own flying school and aircraft manufacturing concern. So it came as no surprise when the owner, Hugh Locke-King, offered Brooklands to the War Office for whatever purpose they saw fit—and the Royal Flying Corps moved in on August 5, 1914. They took it over lock, stock, and barrel." He sighed. "And from the time I arrived, I had six weeks to become a qualified Royal Flying Corps pilot."

"Six weeks?" Maisie was thoughtful. "And if I remember correctly, the average life of an aviator after arriving in France was three weeks—

it wasn't exactly a secret statistic. So you knew that from the time you arrived at Brooklands to begin training, you had nine weeks of life, unless you were one of the lucky ones."

"But you've forgotten something." James slowed as they approached the entrance to Brooklands. "We were all no more than boys—eighteen, nineteen, twenty, for the most part—and we only thought of this big game in the sky and getting back at the Hun. It was a very serious game, though. You don't have any real conception of the possibility of your own death, not at that age. If I look at myself, all I cared about was flying. Bit like Priscilla's boys, only older. Then of course, you come down to earth with a bump if you're hit." He paused. "No, that bump comes when you fly over your own chaps in the trenches, and you see them going over the top straight into the machine guns. Not a scrap of innocence remains after that."

They were silent as James negotiated his way to park the motor car. He switched off the engine and turned to Maisie.

"Do you know what's so comfortable, talking about the war with you? I mean, it's not as if one wants to talk about it much, but when I mention it to you, I know that you *know.* We had very different wars, Maisie, but I—I don't have to explain anything."

Maisie nodded. Yes, she had experienced the same feeling, a sense of comfort that someone else understood. And as an image of Ella Casterman came into her mind's eye, she realized she'd had almost the same conversation earlier in the week.

It's so refreshing to speak to someone who knows.

James cleared his throat. "We should get going."

"What are we going to see today? Is there a special race—something like the motoring equivalent of the Derby, or the Grand National? You haven't told me."

"Maisie Dobbs, on this, your inaugural visit to a motor racing track—and I promise, there will be more—you'll be seeing some of the very best drivers in the world competing for the British Empire Trophy. There are fifty-mile heats for each engine capacity, and of course, for my money the big motor heat is the one to watch. John Cobb will be driving the Delage, then there's Birkin of course, and Jack Dunfee, and George Eyston in his Panhard. Very exciting stuff!"

James stepped out of the motor car, then came around to open the passenger door for Maisie. He held her hand as she alighted from the vehicle and did not let go. As they walked towards the bank where they would stand to watch the races, he crooked his elbow so that she could put her arm through his. They wove their way past parked vehicles, some surrounded by friends having a picnic, their collars drawn up against a chill breeze while they helped themselves to treats from a hamper set in an open boot. There seemed to be plenty of flasks of hot tea to hand, possibly laced with brandy to bolster their stamina for watching the day's events.

"I'm glad you wore those stout shoes, Maisie. It can get a bit muddy up on the bank there, but it really is the best place from which to watch a race. Oh, I should have asked—do you want to place a bet? It's all part of the fun, if you want to."

"I have no idea what—or who—I would bet upon. I'm just happy to watch, James."

"But we should go down to the enclosure for a while, just to soak up the atmosphere; we can come back to the bank before the races. You'll find it's just like a horse race down there."

The day was lifting her spirits. James seemed to be having a good time, and though they had exchanged affections, neither had referred in conversation to the increasing closeness between them. For her part, Maisie realized that she had no immediate wish to embark upon a dialogue about yesterday, tomorrow, or the future. She simply wanted to enjoy today. But she could not avoid thinking about what he had said earlier—"*and I promise, there will be more.*" She blushed when she thought of more todays with James Compton.

The tic-tac men were already busy taking bets, and James had been accurate in his description of the atmosphere. Excitement grew as the race times drew nearer, with spectators lining up to place their bets. James stopped to talk to people he knew, introducing Maisie to each person in turn, most of whom seemed to be in groups. And each time they moved on, it was as if she could feel the hot breath of speculation at her neck as they left a mumble of conversation behind them. She wondered what they might be saying to each other, these acquaintances of James Compton, son and heir of Lord Julian Compton.

"Who do you think she is, that woman with James?"

"Haven't heard of her before, have you?"

"Wasn't she at that party . . . ?"

"Didn't he break off an engagement . . . ?"

"It could be one of his little maids—don't you remember, there was that rumor, in the war . . ."

She shook her head.

"Is everything all right?" James stopped and looked at Maisie.

"Oh, nothing, I just thought I had something in my eye and rubbed it—it's gone now, though."

James put his arm around her shoulder and laughed. "Come on, let's get a drink, then go back up to the bank."

Soon James and Maisie were standing at the top of a steep banked incline that would challenge the drivers as they came around one of the most testing bends at the Brooklands motor racing track. Spectators were huddled several rows deep, and all were straining to claim a good view. Maisie could not see the track very well, but found herself carried along with the growing excitement. The cheers, ooohs, and ahhhs of the crowd, along with the smell of motor oil and petrol, infused the Surrey air with mounting expectation, and it was the big car heat that crowned the race card.

"John Cobb's leading," said James, giving Maisie a second-by-second account. "Oh, now it's Eyston—that's something, the Panhard he's driving." He gasped. "Birkin's dropped back—looks like a tire—and Eyston's still in the lead. It's bound to be Eyston—look at that man drive! Cobb's coming in second, and yes, it looks like Birkin's third. What a race, what a race, Maisie." He laughed and kissed her on the cheek.

Following an aerobatic display organized to excite the spectators, a race of the finishers in each of the separate heats brought an end to the day's events, and the infectious thrill of the crowd had left Maisie feeling as if she had run each of the races herself in her bare feet.

As they walked back down to the enclosure, James suggested a hot beverage before they left Surrey for Chelstone. The crowd was dispersing in different directions, and as they entered the enclosure, James again nodded or waved to people he knew, but did not stop to talk. As the crowd began to thin, Maisie overheard a conversation between two men, one of whom, she thought, had not realized that the noise in the enclosure had lessened, so his words were louder than he might have expected.

"Bad luck, old chap. Lost rather a bit there, didn't you? Never mind. At least the pater-in-law has more where that came from." The voice seemed somewhat affected to Maisie, reminding her of a music hall performer emulating someone of a higher station.

She looked around, wondering how the other party to the conversation might reply, and then quickly turned back, so that she was not recognized.

"I'd better be on my way back to London now. My brother-in-law will be waiting for me at the Dorchester."

It was Thomas Libbert. And he had just lost "rather a bit."

Following a back-and-forth recounting of the day's racing, and a series of questions from James regarding Maisie's enjoyment of her first visit to Brooklands, they did not speak for a while during the drive down to Chelstone. Maisie once again felt a comfort in the silence, as she reflected upon the chance sighting of Libbert and the conversation she had overheard, which served to confirm her suspicion that he had been reckless with the family's company finances for some time. She planned to read sections of Michael Clifton's journal again, for she was sure Libbert had visited Michael in Paris to ask for financial help. It was clear that Libbert's wife, Anna, was the sister to whom Michael was closest, and from what she had read already, it seemed that Michael was intent upon protecting Anna and her children at all costs. She wondered about a will. Had Michael left his estate to Anna, as Thomas Libbert assumed? Could that be at the root of his interest, or was there something else? She was sure of one thing: Libbert was very interested in discovering the whereabouts of a final will and testament.

James cleared his throat. "About Khan."

"Yes, about Khan." Maisie turned to James. Dusk dimmed the light in the motor car as James drove, and she knew he had chosen this moment to talk about their chance meeting at Khan's home because she could see only his silhouette.

"I wanted you to know why I was there, seeing him."

"You don't have to, you know. It really is all right if you don't tell me."

"But I want to. I want you to know why I was there." James cleared his throat again, as if the words were stuck and could barely be spoken. "I haven't been well, not really, for a long time. I—I mean, I am well in my body—very fit, actually. But I knew I had to sort myself out. The truth is, at first I didn't realize I knew that, but I was talking to Maurice one day and I began telling him all sorts of things, and—you know, there's something about Maurice that makes you want to just tell him everything as soon as you sit down."

"I know," said Maisie. "It's his way."

"That must be where you got it from." James sighed, then continued. "I know this sounds mad, but I felt as if I was shedding a skin, a bit like a snake, and I told Maurice that very thing. He agreed with me and pointed out that when a snake sheds its skin, it's in fact very vulnerable, not least due to the fact that it can't see. So he suggested I spend time with Khan."

"Because Khan could teach you that seeing is not something you necessarily do with your eyes."

James slowed the motor car and pulled onto a grass verge. There were no other vehicles on the road, and they were in silence until James continued. "You see, you know. You've spent so much time with him."

"Since I was about fourteen."

James nodded. "Seeing Khan has helped me to . . . I don't know how to explain it. He's helped me to feel as if I'm . . . I'm . . . as if I'm all there again. After the war, after all that happened, I felt as if parts of me were missing, and I now know that it wasn't all the war, because part of me had been missing since Emily died. I'm not very good at all this, talking about these things, but it's as if I now know more about who I am and what I want in my life, rather than just being swept back and forth."

"I understand, James, really I do."

"I know you do."

They were silent for a few moments before James reached across and took Maisie's hand.

"And I know that I want to spend more time with you, Maisie. If that's all right with you."

Maisie nodded, though James could not see her gesture. "Yes, James. I'd like that too."

"And I don't want to do it in secret either. I will not hide my affection or my regard for you from my mother and father, or from anyone else, for that matter."

Maisie did not reply. Was she prepared for such a thing? That Lady Rowan, Carter, her father—Maurice—might know of the fondness between James and herself? She had never set out to be an example of social climbing, nor would she want her feelings for James to be interpreted as such. Perhaps she should nip this liaison in the bud, before it had time to bloom in full view of all who might judge if it began to fade.

"I know we've both loved before, Maisie. I am not a monk, nor have I wanted for the company of women. But will you take a chance on me? And please, be honest with me."

Maisie knew she must be honest, for in opening his soul to her, James had touched her heart.

"James, I want to be by myself to think things over. Let's go for a walk tomorrow morning—you can call for me at my father's house after breakfast, if that's all right. I want to really think about what you're saying, and what it will mean for me. You see . . ." She faltered, not sure of her ground. "You see, I am not as brave as Enid, you know. I never was. And I do care what people think, what they say, when it's about me. I've worked hard, James, and I don't want there to be any misunderstanding, especially—and I have to say this—with your mother, who has been one of my most ardent supporters over the years."

"Enid was a long time ago, Maisie. I was no more than a boy when we fell in love, and I am now a man in middle age. I have come to terms with all that happened between us, and the others since then. But I understand your reticence. I'm just glad it's not on account of me, of everything I've just told you."

Maisie shook her head. "Oh, no, James. Far, far from it."

"And don't worry about my mother. I think she would be delighted to know that we were seeing more of each other. She is enormously proud of you."

"That's not the same as seeing us walking out together."

"I know, but—"

Maisie rested her hand on his. "Let's talk again in the morning, James. It's been a lovely day, hasn't it? Now I want to go back to Chelstone to see Maurice."

Maisie could hear the dog barking as she walked along the path leading to her father's cottage, and before she could reach for the handle, the door opened and she was greeted by both Frankie Dobbs and Jook, the gypsy dog Maisie had brought home the previous year.

"There you are! I knew James Compton was bringing you home, so I've been worried. They say he drives like a madman."

Maisie kissed her father on the cheek and bent down to make a fuss of Jook.

"Don't believe everything you hear, Dad. He was the perfect gentleman and a capable driver—probably doesn't drive as fast as me, and definitely not as fast as Lady Rowan."

"That's all right, then. Come on, I've got a nice soup going in the kitchen."

Later, Maisie and her father sat at the kitchen table, soup plates filled with piping hot broth in front of them, along with slices of fresh crusty bread cut into deep "doorstep" slices. They talked of the estate's news, then of Maurice, who had returned in an ambulance just a few hours earlier.

"I'll go up to see him tomorrow morning," said Maisie, buttering a slice of bread.

"I wouldn't go too early, being as he's only just come home," said Frankie.

Maisie shook her head. "No, it won't be. I'm going for a walk with James." She looked up at her father.

Frankie sighed, rested his spoon in the bowl, and sat back in his chair. "I've never been one to interfere, Maisie, you know that. You're as old now as your mother, God rest her soul, when she was going back and forth to the hospital. And you're a grown woman, not a girl. But—"

"But?"

"Hear me out, Maisie." He leaned forward. "But are you sure walking out with that James Compton is the right thing to do? I mean, there's been talk, you know."

Maisie felt color rush to her cheeks. "Dad, if I had listened to talk, I might still be shoveling coal in the morning in a grand house in London."

"Now then—everyone in that house was proud of you, of what you've made of yourself."

"So why are they talking now?"

"Because no one wants to see you hurt. Not with Simon gone last year."

Neither spoke for some moments, then Maisie broke the silence.

"Simon had been gone for years, Dad. Years. And I will be all right—I won't make an idiot of myself. But I enjoy his company, Dad. He's a good man."

"I hope he is, Maisie."

Later, in her small bedroom with the low beams and diamond-paned casement windows, Maisie lay in bed and considered James Compton. She was no expert in love, and she knew she had floundered when it came to personal relationships with men. After Simon was wounded in 1917, returning home to live in a hospital for men whose minds had been sacrificed to war, she had not even looked at a man until she returned to Girton College to complete her education. Then there had been occasional evenings out, the odd accepted invitation to lunch or even a party. There had been a time when she'd had what Priscilla might have called a "fling," but she had neither confided in her friend nor considered the matter again. There was nothing to touch her heart anyway, just a passing comfort; and such moments of warmth, even if temporary, were balm for the wounds in her heart. But she was different now. She had grown up, and she knew she was, as James had said, "all there again." And she liked being with someone who knew how that felt.

It was late morning by the time Maisie left the cottage by the back door and walked up to The Dower House to see Maurice. Mrs. Bromley had brought a note earlier, suggesting that before lunch would be the best time to visit.

"Maurice." Maisie went to her old mentor's bedside, took his hand, and kissed his forehead. "You have worried us all."

She tried not to reveal how his pallor concerned her still, how the hollowed cheeks and sunken eyes told all she needed to know about his state of health. But he seemed to have more energy than during their last visit, though she knew he would tire soon.

"Andrew told me that you came to the clinic—such a long way to see an old man not at all present with the world."

"You were ill, Maurice, and your respiration was compromised by fluid in your lungs. How are you feeling now?"

"Well enough. Andrew would not have allowed me to return to my home had he not been satisfied regarding my condition."

"Oh yes he would—if you'd bullied him."

"You underestimate Andrew Dene."

"No, I don't—but he was your pupil too, and would let you have the last word."

"I am well enough, Maisie. Now, come on, sit down next to me. First, tell me about your work, about progress on the case of the young mapmaker."

She shook her head. "I'm waiting, Maurice."

"Waiting?"

"For some of the dust to clear." She recounted the events of the past week, taking care to give as much detail as possible.

Maurice was silent, nodding his head, and then closed his eyes for a moment before speaking again.

"So what are you waiting for, my dear, if you know who must be brought to book for the death of Michael Clifton, and for the attack on his parents?"

"I'm not quite ready. I have a feeling we will locate the woman with whom Michael was involved very soon. And I'm waiting for more proof. I have to be sure."

"And then?"

Maisie looked down at her hands, and rubbed the back of one hand with the palm of the other. "I don't know . . . there are people to consider, people whose lives will be changed. I'd like to see if I can avoid too much damage."

"I suspected that might be the case." Maurice sighed, then went on. "Of course, such an impact might be the best thing. The truth always finds a way, Maisie, in some manner or form. You cannot deliberately change the course of the river without causing a flood or drought somewhere else."

"But everything changes when you unearth the past," said Maisie.

"That's not necessarily a bad thing, is it? You bring old events and choices to the surface, and you change the vista—but spring will come, the soil will seed itself, that flood or drought will abate, and life goes on in that new landscape."

Maisie nodded, but said nothing, so Maurice continued.

"The past was unearthed when Michael Clifton's remains were brought up from the battlefield where his life was taken."

"And you don't mean the battlefields of France, do you, Maurice."

Maurice smiled and began to cough, allowing Maisie to lean him forward and rub his back. When the coughing had diminished, she poured water for him and held it to his lips. Soon he was settled and answered her question.

"No, I don't. Life's battlefields are just as violent. Michael was caught in another offensive, wasn't he?"

Maisie nodded.

"Then it is your job to be an advocate for truth, Maisie."

"I've kept quiet about a few things in my time."

"So have I. But never a killer."

"No. Never a killer."

Maisie had decided earlier in the day that she would travel back to London by train on Sunday evening. James did not have to be at his office early on Monday, and in any case wanted to spend the evening with his parents.

As the train rocked from side to side, Maisie looked out into the darkness and thought about the chain of events since she left the house on Saturday morning. On the one hand, she deliberated about the case of Michael Clifton and his family, and on the other, there was her relationship with James Compton. He had called for her on Sunday morning, as they had planned, and after a brief conversation with her father about the horses, they walked to the gate at the bottom of Frankie Dobbs' garden, then across the fields to the woodlands below.

With primroses, shiny egg-yolk-yellow celandines, and delicate white wood anemones underfoot, they followed an old path down to the stream that ran through a woodland of hazel, hornbeam, oak, and beech, and soon the pungent aroma of the wild garlic that grew alongside Kentish streams was released with every step taken. The place where James stopped, a benign meander in the rushing water overlooked by the lichen-covered remains of a broken beech tree, was marked by a chill in the air that caused Maisie to pull her woolen cardigan close around her body.

"This is where it happened," said Maisie.

James nodded. "Yes. It's not like it was then." He pointed to the high side of the meander. "There were logs across there, which created a large swimming hole here. I mean, it wasn't much of a swim, but that's what we called it." He indicated the beech tree. "And that's where the limb came down. As you can see, we're not that far from the house, and on the day it happened, my parents were taking a walk together. It was their habit to walk alone sometimes, just the two of them. They heard my screams."

Maisie sat down on an old moss-covered log. "Do you come back to this place often, James?"

He shook his head. "No. Never, in fact. But I knew I would find it with no trouble."

She nodded. "Yes. The tragedy seems to have lingered in the air."

He sat down beside her. "I don't know what to feel, actually. It all seems so innocent here, in its way."

"There is healing for you in this place, James. The kind of healing that is to be found in the wound itself."

"I'm not sure I know what you mean. I'll think about it though."

They both laughed, and James cleared his throat.

"I wonder, have you thought about what I said yesterday, about . . . you and me?"

Maisie nodded. "Yes, I have." She looked at him. "Yes, I have, James. I've enjoyed your company. I'd like to . . . to spend more time with you."

James nodded, gazed at the old beech tree, and took her hand in his. Then he turned and kissed her. "We'll have good times, Maisie. We've both got some catching up to do, haven't we?"

She reached towards him and touched his face. "Let's just enjoy today, James. Tomorrow's ground is a bit too soft for me yet."

James Compton stood up, took her hand, and pulled her to him. "Shall we go back now?"

"Yes, let's. Maurice will be ready to see me soon."

James turned and stepped back onto the path, and just before she joined him, Maisie reached down to pick a single primrose, and threw it onto the water at the base of the beech tree. She watched the bubbling current catch the solitary bloom and carry it along until she could see it no more.

"Coming?" James called back to her.

She turned and smiled, feeling the color rush to her cheeks and a swell of anticipation. "Yes, I'm coming! Wait for me, James."

SEVENTEEN

Detective Inspector Caldwell was waiting in a parked Invicta motor car when Maisie arrived at the office on Monday morning.

"Having a bit of trouble getting up in the morning, Miss Dobbs?" asked Caldwell, pushing back his sleeve to look at his watch with something of a dramatic flourish.

"I don't think that's any of your business, Detective Inspector." She unlocked the front door and held it open as the policeman and his sergeant followed her up the stairs and into her office.

"And it looks like your trusty assistant is just as tardy on this fine Monday morning."

Maisie rolled her eyes. "Just as you were beginning to grow on me, Inspector." She smiled as she removed her mackintosh and placed it on the hook behind the door. "Now then, what can I do for you?"

"I thought I wouldn't let too much time go by without receiving some sort of report on your activities on behalf of Mr. and Mrs. Clifton. I allowed your personal investigation to continue, and I keep wondering whether you've uncovered information that might be of interest to us as we put the final touches to our report regarding the attack on our American visitors." He sighed, and again Maisie thought it rather theatrical. "Did you hear from our friends at the embassy, by the way?"

She shook her head. "We heard from a man named John Langley, but nothing since. Seeing as Mr. Clifton's son and a family friend—Dr. Charles Hayden—are now here in London, I thought perhaps they had smoothed the way with the consular officials."

Caldwell seemed to smirk. "Personally, I think it's a bit of a cheek, him coming over here with his fancy doctor. As if our doctors aren't good enough. Who do they think they are, these Americans?"

Maisie was guarded in her response. "I can see what you mean, Inspector. Mind you, I know Dr. Hayden. We met in the war. And no one objected to him or his fellow doctors from the Massachusetts General Hospital being one of the first medical units in France, before our medical corps was properly established. And he's no ordinary doctor now—he's an eminent brain surgeon. I think if it was your parents in hospital with head wounds, and you had such a friend, you would have enlisted his services without so much as second thought."

Caldwell nodded. "Point taken, Miss Dobbs. Now, to my reason for calling—anything you want to tell me?"

Maisie leaned forward. "Well, actually—"

At that moment the door opened, and Billy entered the room.

"Sorry I'm late, Miss, but—oh, Detective Inspector. I beg your pardon." He took off his cap, rolled it, and placed it in his jacket pocket as he went to his desk.

"Good morning, Billy." Maisie noted that her assistant seemed tired before she turned back to Caldwell.

"May I telephone this afternoon? I do not want to waste your time; however, I might well have something to discuss with you later—I want to be sure my information is sound."

Caldwell said nothing at first, looking at her with some intensity, as if to gauge her intentions. He stood up, buttoning his coat. "Right you are, Miss Dobbs. I'll trust you on this. Mind you, if you've been keeping anything from us, I will have you in court for obstruction and your feet won't touch the ground on the way there."

"Detective Inspector, you seem more than a little agitated," countered Maisie. "I thought we had come to an understanding."

Caldwell shrugged and sighed. "I've got some higher-ups breathing down my neck on this, being as Mrs. Clifton is from a powerful family over there in the colonies, just as you said, and the son is making his presence felt. I probably shouldn't tell you this, but he said that he'd be hiring you himself if the police didn't get a move on and get to the bottom of what happened to his mother and father—he reckons there's more to it than just a bloke who decided to break into a hotel room at random. On the one hand, he's got a point, and on the other—let's face it, it's only the moneyed who stay in a gaff like that, so if you were looking to come away with some valuables, you could probably find them in any room you choose. Trouble is, he said it to the embassy fellow, who told it to the foreign secretary, who belongs to the same club as the commissioner, and before you know it, I'm being strangled by the old school tie."

Maisie smiled. "Ah. I see. Don't worry, Inspector—as I said, I think I may have something for you soon. Just give me time—and by the same token, this is a share-and-share-alike business."

Caldwell ignored Maisie's final comment, placed his hat on his head, touched the brim, and motioned to his sergeant to follow him. When the door closed behind them, Billy looked up at Maisie.

"He's gone on the turn again, eh? I thought we were all getting along."

"We were, but he's being leaned on, and I don't think he's as good at bearing the brunt of the higher-ups as Stratton was." She sighed. "There are times I miss Stratton."

Billy nodded. "Better than that miserable whatsit, eh?" He walked across to Maisie's desk. "Don't mind me saying so, Miss, but I reckon you've sorted it all out, you know, in your mind. I know that look."

"There's a missing link or two, but I'm almost there. Come over here." She took the case map from the filing cabinet, unfurled the roll of paper, pinned it out on the table by the window, and pointed to two names she had linked in red. "See?" she asked, and turned to Billy.

"That's a turnup for the books, ain't it? I mean, I don't know what will come of this."

"Neither do I." She turned to Billy. "But I do want to ask *you* a question, Billy—has something happened at home? Has Doreen relapsed? I know she coped very well with the odd overnight visit, but now she's at home full-time—are you all managing?"

Billy shrugged. "We're all right, Miss. Yes, nothing to worry about. Just the boys were a bit hard to settle last night—it was that wind howling over the rooftops, I think. Young Billy was scaring his brother with ghost stories, and that set him off. They are a pair at times." He turned away towards his desk, but not before Maisie had seen the color rise in his cheeks.

When Billy had left for the morning—he was planning to visit three of the women on Maisie's list—she picked up the telephone and dialed the home of Ella Casterman, but replaced the receiver before the call was answered, and leaned back in her chair. Was it really necessary to see her again? Could she close the case without involving the widow and her family? She decided to wait. Maurice had cautioned her, in the days of her apprenticeship, that if the way ahead is not clear, time is often the best editor of one's intentions. She reached for the telephone again, this time to place a call to Lord Julian Compton, and again she began to dial, only to replace the receiver when she realized that James might well have talked to his parents about his affection for her, and his intention to see more of her. What would she say to Lord Julian? How would she negotiate the new footing in what had, in recent years, been a pleasant professional relationship? It was one thing for a peer of the realm to have regard for her as a working woman with her own business, but quite another for him to accept his son's wish to enter into courtship with someone who had once been a maid in his house.

"Blast!" Maisie pushed back her chair and paced back and forth, then sat down at her desk again and aired her frustration to the empty room. "I've got a job to do, whether Lord Julian likes me or not!" She reached forward to grasp the telephone receiver, but was startled when it began to ring.

"This is—"

"The quite lovely Maisie Dobbs."

"James!"

"You sound surprised to hear my voice."

"Where are you?" She glanced at the clock on the mantelpiece. "Did you drive up to town this morning?"

"No, not yet, but I'm leaving Chelstone soon," replied James. "I thought I would telephone to see if I could stake a claim on your company for supper this evening."

"I'm a bit busy, and—"

"Bertorelli's? I happen to know you love Italian cooking."

Maisie laughed. "All right. I'll come."

"And let's dine early."

"About six o'clock, then?"

"Perfect. I'll collect you from your office."

"All right." Maisie chewed the inside of her lip.

"Maisie?"

"I—I was just wondering—do you think it's a good idea for me to telephone your father on a business matter?"

"Yes, of course it is. You've never worried about it before, have you?"

"No. Not at all. But—oh, never mind."

"See you at six."

"See you, James."

Maisie felt foolish. Lord Julian spent only two or three days each week in his London office now that James was more established at the helm of the Compton Corporation, so he would still have been at Chelstone anyway. She would wait to place her call until James had left to return to London. In the meantime, she wanted to see the Cliftons again.

She arrived at St. George's Hospital at eleven o'clock and made her way up to the private ward where Edward Clifton was resting. There was no longer a policeman at the door, but when she walked in, Charles Hayden was sitting with Michael Clifton's father.

"Good morning, Maisie." Hayden came to his feet and held out his hand to the vacated chair. "We were just talking about you."

"You were? I do hope it was all good." She stood at Clifton's bedside. "How are you feeling, Mr. Clifton?"

"Much better, my dear. Charles here says I can return to the hotel in a day or so, but they're moving Martha to the next room, so I'll stay here for now. It'll be easier to see her."

"How is she?" Maisie looked to Hayden for an answer.

"She's still bandaged, but she's conscious, though very tired. I've asked for more X-rays, and I'll be looking at them later today. She remains slow to respond verbally and cannot construct sentences—she can only give one- or two-word answers to questions. It will be some weeks before she can leave the hospital, however; the doctor there suggested she should be sent to the Atkinson-Morley convalescent hospital, and then perhaps to the country for a short while, but of course, Edward wants to be as close to her as possible, so we'll have to sort something out. Unfortunately, I can't see them returning to Boston until mid-June at the earliest."

"Oh, dear. You must ache to be back in the United States, Mr. Clifton."

The elderly man nodded. "The sooner the better. I cannot wait to see our house on Beacon Street again and to sleep in my own bed." He looked up at Maisie. "What news do you have for us?"

She sighed. "If you will bear with me, I believe I will have news for you in the next few days. I think it best to wait to give you my report at a time when I can recount my findings in such a way that all loose ends are tied—but rest assured, the person responsible for taking the life of you son will be brought to justice. You have my word."

Clifton nodded and leaned back on the pillows.

"I'd better leave now." Maisie looked at Hayden, who followed her as she left the room. He closed the door behind him.

"Do you really think you'll have an answer for the old man?"

"I do." She sighed. "Yes, I do."

They bid each other good-bye, and when Maisie stepped out into the spring sunshine, she thought about her response to Hayden's questions. *Yes, I do think I'll have an answer—and probably more than you would want to hear.*

Her next stop was the shoe department of Selfridges. Though it was rumored that the department store founded by the American Harry Selfridge might not survive the economic depression, she thought it was probably the best place to go to speak to a buyer in the shoe department. Buyers, she had discovered, understood much more about their suppliers than their suppliers had fathomed themselves; and they certainly knew more about those companies than they knew about the styles favored for the following season. Her visit to the store lasted only half an hour, with ten minutes spent winding her way through the different departments, and the remainder with a Mr. Buckingham, the shoe buyer. It was a fruitful encounter. Buckingham could not have known more about Clifton's Shoes had he founded it himself.

Maisie returned to Fitzroy Square, and hearing the telephone ringing in their first-floor office, she slammed the front door behind her and ran to answer the call.

"Miss!" Billy shouted before Maisie could announce the number.

"Is everything all right?"

"I've found her."

"You have? What's her name? Where is she?"

"Her name is Elizabeth Peterson, and she was about to do a runner—but I spoke to her first."

"Where are you?"

"Just off the Edgware Road. She's been living in a boardinghouse for spinster women, and she's about to leave."

"Oh, dear. Give me the address, then go back and stay with her. Tell her we'll look after her, and make sure you lock the doors until I get there."

"I didn't think it was that sort of case, Miss."

"Don't worry. I'm on my way."

Maisie started the MG and took back streets to the address provided by Billy. She parked the motor car outside a smoke-smudged building in need of some attention to peeling paint around the window frames. The dark maroon finish on the front door was curling back to reveal the blue and black of previous decades, and the brass knocker was encrusted with a green mold-like patina. She rapped at the door, then called through the letterbox, knowing that Billy would be listening for her.

She heard the *thump-thump-thump* of Billy's footfall on the stairs as he came to answer the door.

"Come on in, Miss. There's a Mrs. Blanchard who's the warden here, but apparently she goes to see her sister of a Monday afternoon, so we're all right. It's a bit of a strict place to live regarding visitors, to say that these girls are all getting on a bit."

"How old would you say is getting on?" Maisie followed Billy up the stairs to a landing with three doors.

"You know, about—oh, Miss, you're not going to get me like that. You know what I mean—they're all over twenty-one, and it's not as if they're in a convent, now is it?"

He knocked on the middle door and called out. "It's all right. Mr. Beale here, and I've got the lady I told you about—Miss Dobbs."

A chain rattled on the other side of the door, and it opened to reveal a petite woman of about thirty-five years of age. She was slender to the point of looking as if she could do with a good meal, and Maisie could see the woman was filled with fear. She locked the door behind them.

"I was so scared you'd come back with someone to hurt me."

Maisie introduced herself, and looked around the room. A kettle sat on top of a small single-ring gas stove in the corner, which in turn was set on top of a cupboard with a blue gingham curtain pulled to one side to reveal an assortment of crockery and two saucepans. Knives and forks were poking out of one of the saucepans.

"Would you mind if Mr. Beale puts the kettle on to boil for a cup of tea?" She did not wait for an answer, but instructed Billy, "Strong, with plenty of sugar in each cup." She motioned for Elizabeth Peterson to sit on the bed, and sat down next to her.

"You've had a horrible time of it, haven't you?" said Maisie.

The woman nodded, pulled a handkerchief out from the sleeve of her cardigan, and began to cry. Maisie put her arms around her and allowed her to weep until the heaving sobs abated, and the woman pulled back.

"I've been so scared, 'specially since Mr. Mullen didn't come again."

"You sound as if you didn't know him very well."

She shook her head. "No, I only met him a few months ago. He turned up one Saturday morning, saying he was an old friend of Michael Clifton's. I believed him."

"What did he want?" asked Maisie.

"He said he had always wondered about the woman his friend had fallen in love with, and he wanted to meet me, to tell me how much Michael had loved me too. Then he sort of kept coming round every now and again, and he started asking me whether I had anything of Michael's."

Maisie nodded. "Miss Peterson—Elizabeth—can we go back to the beginning?"

She rubbed her eyes with the handkerchief, and blew her nose. "But the beginning was in the war."

"Then let's go back to the war. What did you do in the war, Elizabeth?"

"I was a nurse. I was with Lady Casterman, she was the founder of The English Nursing Unit. Have you heard of us?"

Maisie nodded.

"Well, it all started when I met Lieutenant Clifton in Paris, when I was on leave."

Her eyes began to fill with tears, and before she could use her own soiled handkerchief, Maisie reached down into her shoulder bag and passed a clean linen square to the woman.

"I wasn't out to meet a boy, really I wasn't, but he was so kind, so charming, and he was alone in Paris—he didn't have family to go back to in Britain, and I only had a short time on leave, so I wasn't going back." She shivered, and gave a weak smile. "We had a lovely time, a really lovely time. We did all these things I'd never done before, and in Paris! We went to a show, we had coffee at these little cafés they have, and we just walked along the streets. And afterward we wrote to each other. But we had to be careful, because we were sending our letters back and forth with the ambulance drivers."

Maisie nodded again. She had done the same thing herself.

"That's why I had to think up another name, so I wasn't caught red-handed and sent home."

"Tennie."

"How do you know?"

"Later. Go on with your story. You saw each other again?"

"Once more. By that time we were in love. But I was very scared. I mean, he was an American. My friend said that he was probably just telling me all these things—about his land in America, his family's home in"—she faltered and shook her head—"Beacon Hill. I've kept his letters. She said he probably just wanted to, you know, have a bit of fun."

She looked at Maisie, who said nothing, but waited for her to continue.

"But I think my friend was wrong. And I don't know why I doubted him, but I started wondering why he told me he loved me, when there were so many girls out there. I began to have second thoughts."

Maisie looked at the woman and imagined how she might have been at twenty years of age, and thought she had probably looked like a ballerina, with her long dark hair drawn back into a bun, her delicate fingers and petite frame.

"And anyway, we had another leave together and . . . and we became very close. Very close, if you know what I mean. I loved him, really I did. Then we said good-bye, and it was very . . . it was very difficult, because I never knew if I'd see him again, and before I got back to the unit, I'd panicked. I was frightened. You see, I'd already lost my father and brother at Ypres, both of them at the same time, and I thought, 'What if I lose him too?' I didn't know what I'd do, so I wrote and told him that it was better if we didn't continue to write, didn't keep in touch. I thought that if we happened to see each other at the end of the war, then we'd know. I had the letter in my pocket for days afterward, and then I sent it off."

As the woman began to weep again, Billy pulled a chair across to use as a table, and set down two cups of tea.

"There you go—that'll do you good."

The woman stuttered her thanks, and Maisie smiled at Billy and whispered, "Thank you."

Billy sat down on another chair with a cup of tea in his hands, as Maisie asked another question.

"And you never heard from him again?"

She nodded. "Just one letter."

"Did you hear from anyone else?"

"Not for a couple of years, then I had a letter. It was from a man—I can't remember his name—asking if I knew Michael Clifton. He said he had known him in the army and wanted to find his friends so that his parents could find out about what he did in the war."

"Do you still have the letter?"

She shook her head.

"Did you answer it?"

"No. I didn't see the point. In any case, Michael had told me to be careful of anyone wanting to see me on his behalf."

Maisie inclined her head. "Why did he do that, do you think?"

The woman looked at Maisie and stared into her eyes for what seemed to be a long time, though Maisie held her gaze. Then she stood up, knelt down, and pulled back the threadbare carpet to reveal a small section of loose floorboard.

"I've done this in every place I've lived in since the war. I don't know why—it was just what Michael asked of me. To be careful."

She lifted the board and pulled out a parcel bound with rubbered cloth and string—the same type of cloth that had protected Michael

Clifton's letters and journal for years, while buried in the soil of a French battlefield.

"Do you know what's in here?" asked Maisie, taking the parcel.

Peterson shook her head. "No. It wasn't my property. I asked him if I should return his belongings when I sent that last letter, and received just the one letter back. He said he understood my sentiments, that the war had filled us all with fear and bravery both, and you never knew which would claim the best of you—that was what he said. And he asked me to keep the parcel safe, and that he would find me after the war. He said that if he didn't come, it meant he didn't need the things, or he was dead. And if he was dead, it wouldn't matter anyway." She began sobbing again. "And he said that if he found me again after the war, he'd whisk me off and take me to America as his wife. I suppose I never stopped hoping that he'd turn up one day. Stupid of me, really."

Maisie cast her eyes around the aching loneliness of the bed-sitting-room, a cocoon of solitary existence in a building of such rooms where women of a certain age—of her age—tried to fashion their lives to meet a circumstance never imagined in their earlier years.

"May I ask you a couple more questions?" asked Maisie.

"Yes, that's all right."

"Did you have more letters from the person who sent that first inquiry?"

"I might have," replied Peterson, "but I've had to move a few times, what with the rent going up and then losing my job."

"Where do you work now? Are you still a nurse?"

She shook her head. "I just couldn't bear it anymore, after seeing all those boys die. So after the war I went on a commercial course. That's what I do now. I'm in a typing pool, but I've been going to night school for my bookkeeping, and I'm up for promotion."

"And the next you heard was from Mr. Mullen?"

"Yes."

"Did he scare you?"

"No," said Peterson. "Not at first, anyway. He was all nice, friendly. Then he started getting, well, pushy. Kept asking me if Michael Clifton had given me anything for safekeeping. I was scared, so I said no. Then he came round with the advertisement, the one placed by Mr. and Mrs. Clifton. He kept on at me to reply to it, saying there could be money in it, because Michael was not only a rich man, but a rich man's son, and that we could all benefit from it. I didn't want to do it, then I thought they might want to meet me, to know someone who Michael knew, you know, the girl who sent him the letters. I thought about my brother and how my mother and I liked it when one of his pals came to see us after the war. It was only for a chat, but it meant the world to my mother."

"So you wrote to Michael Clifton's parents, and you went with Mullen to the Dorchester—is that right?"

"And we had a row, a nasty row. He started getting even pushier, and I knew I didn't want to see Mr. and Mrs. Clifton with him, I didn't want them to get that sort of impression of me. At first he seemed to be not such a bad sort, but then, when we were outside and that other man came up to us—"

"What man?"

"I don't know his name." She lifted the cup to her lips and sipped the piping hot tea. "He was quite tall, taller than Mr. Mullen, and I think he'd known him before."

"What did he look like—can you tell me anything else about him?"

"I didn't like to look at him, to tell you the truth. He didn't talk to me, but I knew he was Mr. Mullen's boss. He had that sort of look, you know . . ." Her voice trailed off as she searched for the right word. "Authoritarian. Yes, he looked like someone with a lot of power. I thought he looked as if he had it in him to be a bit cruel." She shrugged. "Mind you, I've never liked those cravat things on a man, makes them look as if they've got nothing to do all day, and that's not very attractive."

Maisie noticed that the woman was still shaking as she set the cup down on its saucer.

Peterson continued. "After he had a word with Mr. Mullen—I was standing to one side—off he went. Mr. Mullen took my elbow to steer me into the hotel, and because I didn't want to see Mr. and Mrs. Clifton, we started rowing again, and he was very angry with me. The doorman ended up telling us to leave, so I went off, but I'm sure Mr. Mullen went back to the hotel. He was dressed up a bit more than usual, so no one would've considered him out of place, and I'm sure the doorman thought I was the troublemaker. Mind you, Mr. Mullen probably knew another way in. He looked quite scared though."

"Are you afraid, Elizabeth?"

"I think that man had something to do with Mr. Mullen being dead. I saw it in the newspaper that he'd been found murdered." She rubbed her arms and shivered. "Yes, I am a bit scared."

"Is there anywhere you can go? Is your mother still alive?"

"She's in a home now, but I've an aunt and uncle in Shooters Hill."

"Would you be able to stay there?"

"Yes, I get on all right with them. I could go there."

Maisie looked at Billy. "Would you escort Miss Peterson to her uncle's house, Billy?"

"We can go as soon as you're ready to leave, Miss Peterson."

"I can pack my things in five minutes."

"Do you need to speak to your employer? If you like, I can make a telephone call on your behalf so your job is safe."

"No, it'll be all right, Miss Dobbs. Thank you very much. I've done a lot of overtime lately, so it won't hurt. I'll get in touch with them. They know I'm a good worker."

"Good. You pack your bag now, and Mr. Beale will leave with you. Take any valuables."

Elizabeth Peterson went to a chest of drawers and pushed a few items of clothing into a case she pulled from under the bed, while Maisie and Billy washed and dried the cup and saucers.

"Will you look after Michael's things?"

"Don't worry, everything is going to be all right. Either I or Mr. Beale will come to bring you home when it's safe to return."

"Will it be long?"

Maisie shook her head. "A day or two." She motioned for Billy to open the door and check the way out. "We'll leave by the back, if we can, Billy."

She watched as Billy steered Peterson along the alley at the back of the hostel, and did not turn to go back to her motor car until she saw him hail a taxi-cab. She looked both ways along the alley and went on her way. Before returning to her motor car, she went into a telephone kiosk to place a call.

"James?"

"Maisie—don't tell me, you can't meet me for supper."

"No, that's not it. James, does your office have a safe?"

"Do you mean the sort of safe behind a portrait of the Laughing Cavalier, moving eyes and all?"

"As long as it's a safe safe, James, and it's in your personal office, where only you have access to it, I don't mind if it's behind the Mona Lisa making eyes at you!"

"I have a safe, Maisie, a very good safe. It's next to my desk, and only I know how to get into it."

"I'll come to your office now. If you like, we can have supper in your neck of the woods, or stick to the original plan."

"Right you are. Does this mean I won't have the pleasure of driving you home afterward?"

"Not this time."

"Maisie—I can't wait to see you."

She held her breath for a second before answering. "Can't wait to see you, either."

EIGHTEEN

Maisie looked around what seemed to be an expanse of room. As soon as the secretary had closed the door, she could not help but make a comment. James Compton's office was enormous.

"You could fit my father's cottage in this room—to say nothing of my flat."

James laughed, and took Maisie in his arms.

"I've missed you."

"I've missed you too." She smiled at him, and realized she was telling the truth. She had missed him.

"So, you wish me to keep something safe for you?"

She nodded. "Yes. It's here." She took the wrapped parcel from a brown paper carrier bag.

"You need something a bit more, well, elegant—that bag looks a bit rough, if I may say so, Maisie."

"I had something more professional, but it was stolen, and when found, it was in no condition for me to use when I visit clients. I was very fond of that old case, and don't want to rush into replacing it. It seems disrespectful in some way."

"What's in the parcel?"

"I'm not exactly sure, but it was too important for me to stop and look on the way."

"I see. Dangerous important?"

"It would appear to be, when I think of the people who would like to get their hands on it."

"Do you want to open it? I can go out and leave you here for a few moments, if you like."

"Would you?"

He picked up a ledger from his desk, kissed her on the cheek, and left the office.

Maisie set the parcel on the desk and proceeded to untie the string and pull back the wrapping. The leather-bound sketchbook with silver-tipped ties that she held in her hands looked as if it had been used infrequently, perhaps for one set of notes. She loosened the leather ties and opened the book at the beginning. On the first page was a date in August 1914, followed by map coordinates for a place called the Santa Ynez Valley, in California. She turned the pages with care, aware that she was hardly breathing, so exquisite were the pen-and-ink drawings that followed. She had never been to such a place, yet in the simple sketches, she felt as if she could smell dried earth and the musky fragrance of a landscape so different from the lush greenness of Kent or Sussex. Following the sketches of broad swaths of land there was what she would call a close-up sketch of small bumps in the earth, of cracks where a narrow dark stream emerged, and of outcroppings of rock. There were paragraphs in technical language that made little sense to her, followed by delicate miniature maps, with notes to the effect that they were copies of larger versions.

She sat down on James' chair and looked out across the rooftops, the view almost jarring after being immersed in the sketches of a land so far away. The drawings, rendered with a nib so fine it was beyond belief that a person could wield the pen with such dexterity, were so beautiful that she could hardly bear to look at them. They had all been signed by Michael Clifton, who had been but twenty-three years old when he created this inventory of his land. She turned back to the notes and could see that he had clearly marked places where work must begin. It was the map to his wealth, to his legacy. It would show whoever had the map in his possession where to find the land's most valuable resource—oil.

According to the notes, penned in the fine, precise hand of an engineer, Union Oil and other companies had long surveyed most of the valley, but the farmer in this corner had refused to sell—until he met Michael Clifton. She gathered that even if those oil companies came close, they could not siphon off the oil from under his property. "It's been there for thousands of years," the farmer had said. "It'll be there until someone drills on my land, even if that person isn't me."

Maisie turned a few more pages until she came to the end of Michael Clifton's entries, which were all made in the days before he left for Southampton. It was clear from his notes that he thought he would be back in the United States by the end of 1914. As she closed the book, she noticed indentations on the back cover, so opened it again and found a pocket. She slipped a finger under the flap and pulled out a small key. Further investigation revealed a piece of paper bearing the words "The Central Bank of Santa Barbara," followed by details of two accounts held in the name of Michael Clifton. There was also information on a last will and testament in a safe deposit box, along with maps and documents of title pertaining to his land.

She heard James talking to his secretary outside the door, and replaced Michael Clifton's belongings as she had found them. The door opened.

"Had enough time?"

"Yes, thank you, James. It's ready to go into your safe now."

"Right you are, just a few clever flicks of the hand, and this will be as secure as the Bank of England."

James opened a cabinet set against the wall to reveal a small safe into which he placed the parcel. He spun the dial, then closed and locked the cabinet door.

"I will not touch this until you come to claim the parcel."

"Thank you."

As they left the office and walked to Maisie's motor car, James reached for her hand.

"James, do you know anything about land, inheritance, and such in America?"

"Oh, inheritance—that's a bit of a dark legal tunnel wherever you are."

"I wonder," said Maisie. "If someone died without family—or anyone else for that matter—knowing whether they had left a will, or indeed the deeds to their property, would it be difficult gaining access for those who might inherit?"

"There are laws of probate that might make it tricky, I do know that. These cases can carry on for years—and that's when you have proof that the deceased is actually no longer drawing breath."

"That's what I've been told." She was thoughtful as they approached the MG. When they had taken their seats and Maisie had started the engine, she turned to James. "And if someone else gained access—of sorts—to the deeds, would they have grounds for a claim?"

"They might, yes. Especially if they had a will." He turned to her. "I can see where your mind is going—and no, it might not take much to prove authenticity. The judges in such cases might just look at the paperwork and with a couple of thumps of the gavel let it go through. Or money could change hands somewhere along the line. I'm in the business of land, Maisie, and though we find that maintaining our ethics leads to less trouble in the long run, I have seen all sorts of bribery and other under-the-table goings-on in my time—and by people who are in positions made particularly vulnerable by such action. Comes down to greed. Pure greed." He shrugged. "And of course, there are other motivations, so you could go through several of the deadly sins. Sometimes people assume something is theirs by right simply because they deserve it. But I think it's the likes of you and Maurice who are the experts on that sort of thing, not a humble office boy like me."

Maisie looked at him and smiled, before slipping the MG into gear. "Thank you, James, I think that tells me everything I need to know."

It was late by the time Maisie and James left Bertorelli's.

"Do I have to wait long to see you again?" asked James.

"I think this case will be more or less wound up soon. I hope you can bear with me."

He pulled her to him and kissed her, then held her in his arms.

"I knew what I was letting myself in for, Maisie, so of course I don't mind waiting."

"Shall I run you back to your club?" offered Maisie.

He shook his head. "No, not to worry. I'll find a taxi-cab. You're tired, so go home." He kissed her again. "Sweet dreams, my darling."

Maisie took her seat in the MG, waved once more, and drove slowly down Charlotte Street. She did not have to turn to know that James Compton would watch her drive away until he could no longer see her crimson motor car.

She arrived back at her flat in Pimlico, took off her coat and hat, and put the kettle on for a cup of tea. Soon she was seated in front of the fireplace, and though the evening was not cold, she ignited a row of jets on the gas fire, to see and feel the comfort of warmth. She rubbed her neck as she considered the events of the day. The pieces were falling into place. She was almost ready to make her move.

After making a cup of tea, she took up Michael Clifton's journal again, and reread certain entries. He seemed unafraid to put his feelings down on paper, to share with no one but himself the emotions he experienced both on the battlefield and during the few short spells of leave he had in his two years in France. There were entries that made her laugh—observations of his new British friends, the way they spoke, their mannerisms; or impressions of the more senior officers. Yet his homesickness was palpable, and after a while it seemed to seep from between the lines, until his confession in the later pages:

It's cold here, a cold that goes right to your bones and eats away at them. It's not like the cold in Boston. Back home you can wrap yourself in warm clothing and fight it, and there was always a warm house to come back to—hot chocolate and marshmallows, coffee cake right out of the oven. But I want to go out west again, back to the valley. Every time I close my eyes, I see the valley. I want to feel that heat on my skin and the breeze that skims across your arms and feels like warm silk. I want to ride across the hills with the ocean in the distance. I guess I don't care about the oil anymore. I just want to build a cabin on my land and live there for as long as it takes to get this place, this mud and rain and terrible, terrible killing out of my system. I want to spend my days under one of those California oaks and know that I am far away from here. I want to go back to my beautiful valley.

Maisie could sense the ache in Michael's soul to be in a place that was his home. She thought that, young as he was, he knew that the valley had been the place where he belonged from his first view across its golden hills. And she thought that, though he had lost his life, he was blessed in such knowing—to have traveled far and found home.

At her desk the following morning, Maisie took a deep breath and picked up the telephone receiver to place a call to Chelstone Manor. It was answered by the butler, Mr. Carter, whom she had known since her first day of employ at 15 Ebury Place.

"Good morning, Mr. Carter, how are you?"

"Very well. Do I take it you would like to speak to Lady Rowan?"

"Lord Julian, actually."

"Right you are, Maisie." He cleared his throat.

"Is everything all right, Mr. Carter? You sound as if you have a sore throat."

"Fit as a fiddle." He coughed again. "I was going to say, though, we'll be calling you by another name soon, won't we?"

Maisie's stomach turned. "Might there be rumors going round about me, Mr. Carter?"

"No, not a rumor, Maisie, but—"

"I trust you know how to nip them in the bud, don't you?"

"I won't give credence to a word I hear spoken about—"

"I knew I could depend upon you. Now, may I speak to his lordship?"

"One moment. Very nice to talk to you, Maisie."

"You too, Mr. Carter. You too."

Maisie waited for a few moments, then heard the telephone receiver in the library being picked up, and the main receiver replaced.

"Maisie, how are you, my dear?"

My dear? Maisie was taken aback. Had Lord Julian ever called her "my dear" before? He was always cordial and more than helpful, but "my dear" was not an expected greeting.

"Very well, thank you, Lord Julian."

"What can I do for you?"

"I'm after information again, I'm afraid."

"Go on, I have a pen and paper at the ready."

"I'm interested in a Major Temple. He is currently at the School of Military Engineering in Chatham. I'd like to know who his commanding officer was during the war. I expect he was a first lieutenant then, or perhaps a captain. I believe he was in the artillery, but worked closely with a cartography unit, or perhaps working between several units—to tell you the truth, I am not sure, but I do want to know the chain of command above him."

"Right you are—I will see what I can do."

"Thank you, I am grateful for anything you can dig up for me."

"Anything else?"

"Um, yes. How is Maurice today?"

"Oh, dear, I was hoping you wouldn't ask, but I should have known you would want to remain apprised of his condition." He sighed. "He's not at all well. The doctor—that chap called Dene—has been to see him today, and he's comfortable. Maurice being Maurice, he's said he won't go back to the clinic, that he wants to remain at home for the time being. Of course, in my day, unless you were poor, you were treated at home, but now the doctors have more modern equipment at their disposal, don't they? So you have to go into hospital if you want that top-notch medical care with all the bells and whistles."

"Yes, you're right." Maisie thought Lord Julian was more loquacious than she had ever known him. "Would you please ensure that someone calls me if his condition deteriorates? If he gets worse, I want to be there."

Maisie could hear a voice in the background.

"Maisie, just a moment, Rowan would like a word with you."

Maisie blew out her cheeks. *I bet she would.*

"Maisie! How fortuitous that you've called to speak to Julian. I'm coming up to town with him tomorrow—a bit of shopping, and you know how I loathe shopping, but needs must—might you have time to join me for tea? Fortnum's, say, half past three?"

"Well, yes, that would be lovely. I'll see you there. Half past three."

"Excellent."

Though it was Lady Rowan who had first noticed her intellectual ability and love of learning, and later sponsored her education, Maisie remained somewhat intimidated by the thought of an invitation to tea the following day. She knew James had spoken to his parents and would have said something to the effect that they were walking out together—as her father might describe it—but she was sure that, underneath the warmth exuded in the telephone conversations, a dire warning was waiting for her. She had lived at Ebury Place as both a servant and, later, a guest with her own rooms, but this new development—now far from secret, as Carter's comment indicated—would test the Comptons' self-described socialist leanings.

Good morning, Billy. Did everything go smoothly when you delivered Miss Peterson into the care of her aunt and uncle?" Maisie looked up at Billy as he came into the office.

"Mornin', Miss." He rolled up his newspaper, pushed it into his jacket pocket, and sat down on the chair in front of Maisie's desk. "I told them I worked with her, and she'd been taken poorly at work, so I thought I'd better bring her back to family, being as she lived alone and didn't look like she should be on her own today, not with her being gray around the gills—which of course she was, with all the goings-on with that Mullen."

"You did well, Billy." She leaned back in her chair. "Tell me, I thought you'd already seen her once before, when you went through your list—she was in the second half of the alphabet. What made you go back?"

Billy ran his fingers through his hair, which always seemed to be in need of a comb, if not a cut. "I dunno, Miss. When I first went to see her, she didn't want to talk about it, said it was all a mistake, that her friends put her up to write a letter, and she'd never known any soldier in the war. Nigh on shut the door in my face, she did. But I did what you said I should do—I paid attention to how I felt in my middle—and I came away from that hostel feeling like I had a hive of bees in there, all buzzing around saying, 'That's the one, Billy. That's the one you're looking for.' I never said anything, just in case I was wrong, but after I'd gone through the others on your list, I went back to see her, and of course, it was the right moment for her to just spill it all out like milk from a dropped bottle. She was that scared, so she told me everything. Then I ran down the road to the telephone box to call you."

"You did very, very well, Billy." She regarded him as she spoke. "How are you feeling today?"

He nodded. "I'm all right, Miss." He looked at his hands. "What happens next with the Clifton case?"

"I'm waiting for some information from Lord Julian today—I daresay it will take him just one or two telephone calls to find what I'm looking for, and he'll have the details transcribed and sent to me in short order. I never have to wait long for intelligence from his sources."

Billy stood up. "I've got some work on those other cases to catch up with, Miss. Anything you want me to do on the Clifton case before I start?"

"Yes, there is one thing." Maisie leaned forward and scribbled a note on a piece of paper. "I'd like a birth date for this young man, if you don't mind. Shouldn't take long."

Billy took the note. "Must be, what? Sixteen by now?"

"Something like that. I'd like to know his exact date and place of birth—if you can get a look at his birth certificate or registration, so much the better. Take down as much information as you can."

"It's as good as done, Miss. I'll be back in a couple of hours."

"Thanks, Billy. I'll be out myself later, so just leave the details in an envelope on my desk."

Billy nodded, and left the office.

" 'I'm all right, Miss.' Who do you think you're kidding, Billy?" Maisie said the words aloud now that she was alone in the silence of her office. Alone but for the hive of bees.

Priscilla answered the telephone herself on the second ring.

"I'm so glad you telephoned, Maisie, I have been wondering what to say to Ben Sutton—you know he's interested, and I didn't know whether to say, 'Sorry, darling, she's spoken for.' Are you seeing that gorgeous James Compton, or not? The boys, by the way, will be crushed if he vanishes from their lives forever. All we've heard since you brought him here is Uncle James this, and Uncle James that. You see—it's Uncle now, because he came with Aunt Maisie. Douglas says that if it goes on much longer, he'll ask James to show the boys that he really can walk on water."

"Oh, dear."

"Maisie, don't tell me you've put the brakes on."

"No, well, not really—I just don't want to be pushed."

"If I'm any judge, my friend, you're going to fall anyway, so a bit of pushing won't hurt."

Maisie laughed. "I've got to hand it to you, Pris, you see the black and white in everything."

"And you see all that gray in the middle—that's why we get along.

Are you in my neck of the woods today? How about lunch? Or better still, if you're going to be out on the town with James Compton, how about something new to wear—my treat."

Maisie looked at her clothes. She was wearing her burgundy suit with black shoes and a cream blouse underneath. "I'm dressed appropriately for seeing my friends at Scotland Yard."

"Drab, I would imagine."

"'Suitable' is more the ticket." Maisie twisted the telephone cord around her finger as she spoke. "Pris, I wonder if I could ask you about your niece."

"Oh, Maisie, you should see her now, growing up into a lovely young woman—we'll have to keep an eye on her in Biarritz this summer, if I know anything about the Evernden women."

"She's coming for the summer?"

"Yes. We'll be going out from the middle of July until September. I cannot wait to see the villa again. You must come!"

"I might just do that. But in the meantime, I wonder, how is she, in terms of accommodating the news that she has a family she never knew a thing about?"

Priscilla sighed, and there was a moment of silence before she replied. "I know this is going to sound strange, but . . . well, I think she always knew. I mean, I don't think she knew consciously as in, 'I have an aunt, uncle, and three cousins somewhere.' I just think she had this . . . oh, what's that word you use sometimes?"

"Intuition?"

"Yes, that's it. I think she had that feeling you have when you just know something will happen one day, and though you're not exactly hanging around the gate waiting, there is that sense of anticipation."

"And do you think she has come to any harm as a result of the revelation? After all, her grandmother could easily have located you all before the discovery was made."

"No, I don't think she sees it like that. She was just so excited about having a family, and of course she loves her grandmother. I think it was me who felt shortchanged, not knowing that my brother had fathered a child in the war, a child I might have known since infancy, a child who might have helped fill the gap left by his loss. But I'm being selfish. Old granny Chantal did what she thought was best for Pascale. Of course, it doesn't work out that way for everyone—there were many children born out of wedlock in France during the war, and I am sure in England too. War and love—or perhaps I should say declarations of love—seem to go hand in hand, don't they?"

"Yes, I suppose you're right."

"And I have a feeling I'm to forget you ever asked me these questions, and never mention them again."

"It would be better."

"Lunch later in the week, then?"

"I'd love to. Oh, and Pris—I am so glad you're living in London."

"Me too, Maisie. After a troubled start getting us all settled, me too."

"I'll call tomorrow."

"Cheerio, Maisie."

"'Bye, Pris."

Maisie continued with her work for a while longer, but looked up when she heard the front door open and close, and a moment later, Billy returned to the office.

"That was quick."

"Didn't take long, Miss. And look, two birds with one stone—I was just opening the front door, and a messenger came along with an envelope for you. It's from the Compton Corporation." He held out the plain manila envelope with the company's insignia and address.

"Just what I was waiting for." She took the envelope and reached for her paper knife, nodding to Billy to take the chair in front of her desk. "What did you find out?"

"I thought I would have to go out to double-check against some parish records, but I found everything I needed at Somerset House. Here you are, all the particulars you asked for on Christopher Adam Giles Casterman. Born 1917."

Maisie put down the envelope and took the sheet of paper from Billy. "Hmmm."

"Something missing?"

She shook her head. "No, it's all here. It says he was born at the family's London home."

"His dad must have been right chuffed, you know, finally getting the son and heir, after having two daughters," said Billy.

"Yes, he must have been delighted."

"And it's really sad, when you think of it. That he didn't live to see his son grown up into a man."

Maisie nodded as she read. "Yes, it was."

They were interrupted by the doorbell.

"What, again? It's like Piccadilly Circus in here. I'll go and see who it is."

While Billy went downstairs, Maisie put the paper to one side, continued opening the envelope, and sat down to read through the notes sent by Lord Julian's contact. She was returning the pages to the envelope when Billy came into the room.

"Chap by the name of Roland came with this for you, from Henry Gilbert. Said Mr. Gilbert wanted you to have it straightaway. Nice bloke, told me all about how they had to get this done by bringing in another camera and—"

"Thank you, Billy. I've been waiting for this." Maisie reached for the envelope and took out the photograph. The image was blurred at the edges and still grainy, but as Gilbert explained in the accompanying note:

One of my contacts was able to do this for you. As you can see, the image being smaller than on the screen gives it more definition. I think you can see our raging ogre's face a little better.

She sat with the photograph in front of her, then set it down and went back over her notes and read for a while before picking up the telephone receiver. Upon connecting with the Scotland Yard exchange, she was put through to Detective Inspector Caldwell without delay.

"Miss Dobbs, what a nice surprise. I'm having a testing day, so I do hope you have some good news for me. If I have to see that embassy chap one more time, I will have to start singing the American national anthem."

"I have the information I've been waiting for." She looked up at the clock. "If you can be here later on this afternoon, I will go through my findings with you, and we should be ready to make our move."

"We should be ready to make our move?"

"Yes, Detective Inspector. I daresay you can break down the door without me, but you won't get anything else. I'll tell you what I know and what I think we should do. We can be at the home of the person at the heart of the attacks on Edward and Martha Clifton by lunchtime tomorrow and have the laundry washed and dried, so to speak, by mid-afternoon. I'll leave you to put it away, if I may, as I have an appointment at half past three, but I'll come to the Yard afterward for a debriefing, if that suits you."

"And what if I don't agree to this plan you've been cooking up in your head?"

"Do you know another way to get the embassy chap off your back by teatime tomorrow?"

"I'll see you later, then."

"I'll be here, Inspector. Oh, and Inspector, the person we're planning to bring in *is* a murderer, of that I am sure."

Maisie set the receiver on the hook, picked up the dossier from Lord

Julian's office, along with Billy's notes, and walked across the room to the case map. Billy joined her.

"Is it all falling into place, Miss?" asked Billy.

Maisie nodded, but said nothing.

"You all right, Miss?"

She swallowed back tears that could come all too easily if she allowed them to fall. "I was just thinking about Maurice, how we would always talk before a time such as this. He once said to me that it was my equivalent of going off into battle, you know, clambering out and into the no-man's-land where you don't know what might happen, what the outcome might be. You only know that you are marching off and trusting that it will all come right in the end."

Billy looked down, embarrassed by his employer's candor. "Don't mind me saying, Miss, but life's always a bit like that, ain't it? You never know what's going to happen. You just hope everything turns out for the best. And I reckon if Dr. Blanche were here, he'd just ask if you've taken all precautions to look after yourself. And he'd say to have a bit of time on your own today, you know, before the whistle blows." He turned away. "I'll go and put the kettle on, so you can have a quick five minutes to yourself. All right?"

She nodded. "Thank you, Billy."

When he had left the room, Maisie sat back in the armchair. She closed her eyes and tried to still her mind. But the vision that came to her was not one of nothingness, or even of an empty night sky. Instead the vision was that of a valley in a place far away, a fertile land rich with sycamores and oaks amid golden pastures, and earth kissed by the fragrance of blossom from plentiful orchards, and the salty warmth of air carried across mountains from the Pacific Ocean.

NINETEEN

Maisie's first task the following morning was to make the appointment she hoped would lead to an arrest. At noon she left the office in Fitzroy Square to meet Detective Inspector Caldwell, as arranged during their meeting the previous afternoon. Billy walked her to her motor car.

"You reckon you'll be all right, Miss?"

"I'll have a lorry-load of burly policemen at my back. In any case, don't worry about me."

"What do I say if Viscount Compton calls here for you?"

Maisie looked at her assistant, her head to one side. "What made you say that?"

Billy shrugged. "I dunno, Miss. It's just the sort of thing that might happen, ain't it? I mean, there's you going off into your no-man's-land, and it'll be just my luck that if anyone's bound to get on the old dog and bone and put me on the spot, it's him."

"Why him?"

"Well, Miss, it's obvious he's taken a shine to you, and he won't want to know you're putting yourself in danger, will he?"

"Let's assume my life is far from being in danger, and I am just going about my work. If he telephones, tell him I am out—which is exactly what I am—and that I'm having tea with Lady Rowan this afternoon at half past three." She took her keys from her shoulder bag. "That should give him plenty to think about."

"Take care, Miss."

"Don't worry, Billy, I will be perfectly safe. And I will telephone you as soon as I can after the police have completed the arrest—I won't keep you waiting for news."

Maisie arrived at the designated meeting place—at the end of a street of grand terraced homes in Hampstead—and waited for the black Invicta police vehicle to arrive. She envisioned the conversation that would soon take place with Peter Whitting, running back through her planned lines as if she were rehearsing a play, and hoping her words would draw him out. He was a man whose anger seemed parasitic, as if it were eating away at him from a place deep inside his being. She knew the only way to achieve the confession she needed was to goad him.

A tap on the window interrupted her thoughts, causing her to start.

"Detective Inspector—did you park around the corner?"

"Better to be out of sight."

"Yes, of course." She stepped from her MG. "Ready?"

"My men are getting into position, so let's go along to the house."

"And Major Temple?"

"Military police have been briefed, and he should have been taken for questioning half an hour ago."

"Thomas Libbert?"

Caldwell looked at his watch. "Should be being picked up about now by the Flying Squad boys. I spoke to your old friend Detective Chief Inspector Stratton, now of Special Branch. He has contacts where I need them—at the American embassy—and we'll be questioning Libbert in the presence of a consular representative who also happens to be a lawyer trained here in England. As you will appreciate, because the man is the citizen of another country, there are certain channels to be respected."

"Yes, of course. So, we're ready to go then?"

"When you are."

Maisie nodded. "Good. Let's get on with it."

"And hope we're right."

Maisie turned to Caldwell. "I'll accept full responsibility if you're unable to bring charges, and—"

"Yes, I know all that, Miss Dobbs. Against my better judgment, I am confident that we won't need to do anything of the sort. Shall we?" He paused. "And one final word before the balloon goes up: As much as I can't abide a screaming woman, I expect you to let us have it with both lungs if that man poses a threat to you at any time."

She laughed. "I've a confession—he can do that simply by looking at me. Come on, let's get this over and done with."

Maisie walked up the steps and pulled the bell handle. A wait of one minute seemed to take an hour, but soon the butler answered the door.

"Ah, Miss Dobbs, on time again—"

Caldwell stepped in front of Maisie, and held out a search warrant. "If you don't mind, Mr. Dawson, my men will accompany you into the kitchen, Miss Dobbs will find her way from here."

Two policemen flanked the butler, who was now florid of face and stuttering his complaints as they moved him towards the stairs that led to the kitchens. Two additional policemen preceded them to ensure the cook was prevented from leaving.

"All right?" asked Caldwell.

Maisie nodded.

Caldwell and his assistant followed her up the stairs towards Peter Whitting's room, the makeshift battlefield where all manner of conflagrations and skirmishes were fought and refought day after day. At the door between artists' renditions of the battles of Trafalgar and Marston Moor, Maisie made a fist with her hand and knocked.

"Come!"

She nodded to Caldwell, opened the door, and stepped into the room, taking care to leave the door ajar as she entered alone.

"Why, Miss Dobbs, isn't Dawson with you? I apologize for our lack of manners." Whitting looked up from the table, where a mock Flanders battlefield had been set up, with model houses, forests, and armies laid out and ready to be moved at any moment, dependent upon the outcome of Whitting's alternative opening salvos.

"He said he would bring tea and suggested that, as I know my way and you were expecting me, I should come straight up."

"He's probably had to check on the cook. She's turned out some less than palatable dishes in recent days."

"That might explain it." Maisie smiled. "Thank you for seeing me, Major Whitting."

He held out his hand towards one of the two chairs alongside the fireplace, and as soon as he sat down opposite Maisie, the calico cat stepped out from under the table and crawled up onto his lap.

"What can I do for you this time, Miss Dobbs?"

Maisie drew breath and began speaking, knowing she would have to inspire an eruption of anger in Whitting, who was now stroking his purring cat. She hoped his fuse was as short as she expected it to be.

"I am here in search of the truth."

"What on earth do you mean?"

"First of all, may we talk about Michael Clifton?"

"Is that the American you were asking about when you came here before?"

"Yes, and—"

"I told you, I don't bloody know him."

Maisie could see that Whitting's increased tension had provoked the calico into extending her claws and sinking them into the trouser fabric at his knee. Whitting did not lift the cat's paws as she turned towards Maisie, yawning to reveal needle-like teeth.

Maisie sighed. "The thing is, Major, I think you do know him. He is your cousin by birth, though he probably wasn't aware of the connection until the day you took his life. Is that not so?"

"Leave my house now, woman." Whitting did not shout, his temper as measured as his reaction to the cat's outstretched claws. "You are a pest, a nasty pest, and I don't have to—"

The cat made a low screeching growl as Whitting stood up, brushing her off his lap to the floor. She ran under the table. Maisie was already on her feet.

"I'll leave when you've told the truth. Michael Clifton *was* your cousin, wasn't he?"

"How the hell do you know?" Whitting snapped.

Maisie could not breathe with ease. He hadn't said enough yet. In temper he had revealed only part of the truth. She saw the throbbing vein at his right temple, and pressed her luck.

"It's what I do. I find things out, and I know your mother was Edward Clifton's sister, and her life was changed forever by his emigration to America."

"Emigration? Ha! Running away, more like. He was a yellow-bellied coward who took off to the other side of the world because he couldn't face his responsibilities. Changed forever, my eye! I was still a boy when it killed her."

"Is that why you took Michael's life?"

"What? Do you think I am going to stand here in my own home and take this from a bit of a girl playing with fire?"

"But you did, didn't you, Major? You heard that he had land, that the land was worth money, and you saw a chance to get something back from the Cliftons—your family had been left virtually penniless by the collapse of Clifton's Shoes."

"Get out of my house!"

Maisie remained calm. "Not yet, Major. I haven't finished yet. With Michael gone—and because he was a chatty sort, Lance Corporal Mullen had passed on information on the holdings owned by Michael and his wealth held in trust—you thought you could stake a claim on his property right under the noses of the Cliftons."

Color rushed to Whitting's face as anger enveloped him, and as he stood over Maisie, he held up his hand as if to strike. "And so bloody well what. So what? You can't make it stick, can you?" He brought his hand to his side, his fists still clenched. "Dear sweet Michael Clifton, brought up in the lap of luxury with a dozen silver spoons hanging out of his mouth. Big, kind Michael, who missed his family. Do you have any idea of the suffering—*suffering*—I saw in my family? My mother and father pained themselves trying to make a go of the business. And my mother worked. *Worked.* While that American woman probably did no more than go to her lunches and sit in her big house in Boston. And my mother kept her maiden name because 'a Clifton has to take care of Clifton's Shoes.' She was like an untrained captain on a sinking ship, and she didn't want me to go down with it."

Maisie felt Whitting's volatility, but knew she had to push him further. "So why did you kill Michael?"

He mumbled a response as sweat drenched his brow. She raised her voice in an attempt to press him again.

"I asked you a question. Why did you kill Michael Clifton?"

Whitting snapped. "I killed him because he wouldn't believe a word I said. Wouldn't have it that his father was a coward." He wiped a hand across his brow. "And because he was just so smug. I had watched him for weeks after I was put in charge of the area—and yes, I engineered the posting after seeing his name on a list of cartography units. From the moment I arrived in France, as far as I could, I kept my eyes on his every move, and when I couldn't stand it anymore, I went to see him down in the dugout. He pushed me, Miss Dobbs. Pushed me into it. He wouldn't accept his father's culpability in my parents' early deaths and in the ruination of my childhood. The army was the only place for me to go." He gasped for breath, as if all air had escaped his lungs. "But he wouldn't have it. Precious Michael Clifton wouldn't have any of it. He showed no respect for my position and just turned away from me. And to be frank with you, Miss Dobbs, I lost my temper with him."

"So that's when you hit him with an item of equipment—perhaps the theodolite."

"How do you know?"

"I read the postmortem report and saw the inconsistencies. His skull was smashed by something with the heft of a theodolite. You must have left shortly before the shelling began, shelling that took the lives of the other men in his unit."

"They were all resting, so I knew I had time before he was found."

"Time to give your friend, Major—then Lieutenant—Temple, orders to direct shellfire towards the location of the dugout, an action difficult to prove considering the melee, and given that the enemy was also sending over a good deal of ordnance."

"You think you're so damn clever, don't you? Well, I'm not sorry, you know. And you can't prove a thing."

"Oh, but she can, and so can I." Caldwell strode into the room, followed by his assistant and two uniformed policemen. He held the search warrant in his hand and stood in front of Whitting. "And when we get down to the Yard, you can tell us exactly how pally you and Major Temple really were and how you got Mullen—your little helper in this bloody mess—into so much trouble. I am charging you with the murder of Michael Clifton, and the attempted murder of Mr. and Mrs. Edward Clifton of Boston, the United States of America. You might as well confess to the killing of one Sydney Mullen, and you can also throw in attempted theft for good measure."

"You stupid little man. You and this woman here cannot prove a thing."

"Can't we? Major Temple is blowing his horn as if it's reveille down there in Chatham." He nodded to his assistant. "Read him the caution, if you don't mind. Oh," he said, turning back to Whitting, "and I think we might be able to add a certain young officer by the name of Jeremy Lockwood to the list of men who've stood in your way—he rumbled you, didn't he? Worked out what you were up to, so he had to go. Another death blamed on the enemy?"

Whitting's face distorted as he began to weep. "You just don't know what it was like, do you? She adored her brother, wouldn't have a word said against him. She said he had to make his way in the world, and if he didn't want to run the company, well, that was up to him. But I knew he was a coward. A soft, work-shy coward, that's what Edward Clifton was." He choked back tears and tried to garner some composure as he addressed Maisie while being handcuffed.

"It seems I underestimated you, Miss Dobbs."

"You should never underestimate the power of the moving picture, Major Whitting."

And as Whitting was led away by two police constables, and Caldwell and his assistant stood outside the door to discuss a search of the premises, Maisie sat down on the armchair; and in her mind's eye saw once again the image of Peter Whitting running towards Henry Gilbert's camera, his baton held high, his eyes filled with nothing but anger and hatred. She was only barely aware of the calico cat climbing onto her lap and extending its claws in delight as it kneaded the fabric of her skirt.

Billy?" Maisie used the telephone on Whitting's desk.

"Oh, Miss, I can breathe again. I don't know how many cups of tea I've knocked back, but I couldn't sit still for the waiting."

"We're almost there. Whitting confessed, and is in police custody. There will have to be a formal interrogation and signed confession for anything to really stick, but Caldwell thinks we're on solid ground."

"He was all right, then, Caldwell?"

"I'm sure we'll have our ups and downs when we cross paths again, but as we thought, he seems much easier to get along with now he's been promoted."

"What about the others?"

"Temple is in the custody of military police. Whitting had been his superior officer in the war, and it seemed he idolized him. He kept Whitting informed of everything Michael Clifton did, where he went—even on leave—and I think between them they made Michael's life a bit of a misery, nitpicking him for the slightest infraction. Of course, Whitting was at the HQ, but found plenty of excuses to go out to the units. And Temple was only too willing to cover for him—until today. I am sure Whitting called Temple to alert him to the fact that I would be in contact. And though Temple wasn't involved in the murders, he knew when to look after his commanding officer."

"And I suppose Whitting followed Michael to Paris, in the war."

"Yes, that's what happened, I'm sure." Maisie sighed.

"You all right, Miss?"

"I just wonder about the death of Michael Clifton. I have a feeling that, while Whitting considered Clifton's demise to be part of a plan, he might not have struck him had he not completely lost his temper. Whitting appeared to me to be a man who lived by a code of personal control, who had surmounted the grief of loss, but who was on the edge. Because of the degree of that control, the line separating it from personal anarchy was narrow. But after Michael was dead, it was easy to abandon the body—possibly rolling it into a blanket as if the dead man were asleep—and leave the dugout. There had been intermittent shelling, so all he had to do was use his chain of command to ensure the area where the dugout was situated came under intense fire. We must remember, though, that the dots may link up to reveal a different story, but one with the same outcome."

"No, I reckon you're right, Miss. But what about that other officer?"

"Jeremy Lockwood? I think that might be more troubling in terms of proof, but Whitting may help us there. Caldwell will no doubt exercise an element of brinkmanship and refer to evidence in order to obtain a signed confession. I suspect Lockwood was a naive but observant junior officer who realized that Whitting had ulterior motives in his interaction with Clifton and brought it up in one way or another. Death by sniper is easy camouflage."

"So now what?"

Maisie sighed again. "You may be swimming in tea, Billy, but I'm dying for a cup." She looked at the clock on Whitting's desk. "So I'm off to see Lady Rowan at Fortnum's.'

"Going from one extreme to the other, eh, Miss?"

"To tell you the truth, I think I might be going from a battle charge straight into the lion's den." She paused. "Were there any telephone calls for me?"

"One from Mrs. Partridge, and one from Viscount Compton."

"Oh, did he leave a message?"

"I said what you told me to—that you were out, but that you were having tea with Lady Rowan."

"What did he say?"

"Well, he didn't really. Sort of went all quiet, and then said, 'Thank you, very good,' and rang off."

"That's encouraging." Maisie spoke the words under her breath.

"Sorry, Miss, what did you say?"

"Nothing, Billy. Did Mrs. Partridge leave a message?"

"Just that you call her 'soonest,' as she doesn't quite know what to say to Mr. Sutton."

"That's nothing I want to sort out at the moment. Look, I'd better go or I'll be late for Lady Rowan."

"See you tomorrow, Miss."

"Um, Billy—be prepared to hold the fort tomorrow. I think I might pack my case and go down to Chelstone after tea. I need to see Maurice—I couldn't get him out of my mind all day. Even while I was with Whitting, I felt as if he were looking over my shoulder."

"Right you are, Miss. I've got plenty to get on with—but, Miss, is it all right if I come in a bit late tomorrow? I've got to go with Doreen to the hospital."

"Of course. Is it time for her checkup?"

"Yes. Yes, that's right."

"Oh, here comes Caldwell, I'd better go. 'Bye, Billy."

"'Bye, Miss."

I think we've got everything sewn up here. You're free to leave, Miss Dobbs." Caldwell extended his hand as Maisie stood up from the desk and collected her shoulder bag. "That was good police work, Miss Dobbs. I would've liked to have known earlier what you were up to, but on the other hand—though I hate to admit it—I can see why you wanted to get to the bottom of it all first. Stroke of luck, wasn't it, you seeing the cine film."

"We all need that serendipitous moment, don't we, Inspector?"

"Whatever you call it, I'm glad it happened. A couple of my men have been to see Henry Gilbert, and we now have the film in our possession so that we can prove association between Whitting and Clifton. The bloke wasn't very pleased, mind, said it was important to get it back for a—what did he call that thing? Oh yes, the *documentary* he was making. Personally, I'd rather see the likes of Louise Brooks at the cinema myself."

"Inspector, I think I will be driving to Kent later today. May I come to the Yard tomorrow afternoon to make my statement?"

"I'll make an exception for you."

"Thank you, I appreciate it." She smiled at Caldwell. "You sailed a bit close to the wind there, when you insinuated that Temple was 'singing like a canary.'"

"Well, it's true military police have him in for questioning, and one of my men is with them, but as you pointed out yesterday, Temple would probably be shocked to know the outcome of some of the orders he received from Whitting. And thankfully, he's talking about those orders, including Whitting's instructions to report even the most minor fault on Michael Clifton's part during the war. It won't do any harm to let Whitting think that Temple has more knowledge than he has, and for him to assume we are in possession of that information. I have no doubt we'll get the full confession we're after, sooner rather than later."

"And what about Libbert?"

"More or less as planned, though my opposite number in the Flying Squad is a bit put out at having to play by the rules because of the embassy. We want Libbert in connection with his relationship with Mullen, the Flying Squad want him because he was a player in Alfie

Mantle's game, and the Americans want him home where he can't embarrass them." He gave what Maisie now recognized to be his signature shrug and sigh. "In terms of the law, it could be said he was a victim first, but all the same, he might be encouraged to go back home as soon as we're all done with him and can get him onto a ship."

"Oh what a tangled web we weave, when first we practice to deceive."

Caldwell rolled his eyes, though he smiled at Maisie. "I'll be in touch."

Maisie spotted Lady Rowan Compton almost as soon as she walked into the tearoom at Fortnum and Mason. She was sitting at a table alongside the window, looking out at the street below. Maisie could see she was tense, sitting on the edge of her chair, her hands clasped around a warming cup of tea. As usual, she was dressed with understated elegance, wearing a pale beige skirt and light tweed jacket, set off by a flash of color in the cobalt blue silk blouse worn underneath her ensemble. It was a blue reflected in the feather set into the side of a navy blue hat pinned atop hair that had once been copper red, but was now toned with striking thick strands of gray.

Taking a deep breath, Maisie joined the woman who had discovered her reading in the library at two in the morning when she was thirteen years of age—a mistake on Maisie's part that would change the course of her life.

"Lady Rowan. I am so sorry to keep you. I was detained at an appointment."

Lady Rowan beamed a broad smile at Maisie and grasped her left hand in both her own. "I was about to get worried, my dear. I know what a stickler you are for punctuality—just like Maurice." She turned to summon a waitress, while Maisie seated herself in the facing chair.

Lady Rowan ordered another pot of tea, a plate of sandwiches, and scones with fresh clotted cream.

"You seem tired, Maisie. Was it a very troubling day?"

Maisie nodded. "A case was brought more or less to an end today, though I have yet to brief my client on my findings and the outcome—which will cause added grief to a very close family."

"They have each other, Maisie—that's a blessing when tragedy strikes." Lady Rowan looked out of the window again, then back at Maisie. She half laughed and went on. "That was a fortuitous turn of phrase, all things considered."

"Was it?"

"James told us that you know about our darling Emily."

"I am so sorry, Lady Rowan, I had no idea—"

Lady Rowan reached forward as if to take her hand again, then drew back. "But there was no reason why you should have known. Carter and Mrs. Crawford knew, but they were sworn never to talk about it to the staff. And the staff who were with us at the time all knew and were also charged with not gossiping about it, and to be perfectly honest, it seemed that, after the tears abated, no one wanted to discuss it again anyway. Though for us—Julian, James, and me—the challenge has never been greater." She shrugged, as if to shake off an untoward thought. "Losing Emily has made us all who we are."

Maisie sipped her tea, knowing that any words at all might sound trite.

Lady Rowan once more grasped her cup of piping hot tea in both hands. "I suppose I felt as if we all had to live two lives, one for ourselves, and one for dear Emily. She was such a lovely girl, you know."

"James told me. He adored her."

"Of course they could argue. I once saw their nanny take them each by the scruff of the neck and all but throw them into the garden. 'Sort yourselves out before you come in again!' she admonished them. So they set off down to the woods to play, and I daresay they forgot what the row was about in the first place."

"Lady Rowan, if you wanted to ensure my confidence, please be assured that I would never speak of Emily's passing. James entrusted me with his memories of her, and I will honor such trust."

"You, perhaps as much as his father and I, and of course, Maurice, know how much James has struggled since the war to—I don't know how to put it—'regain something of his old self' might fit the bill." Lady Rowan set down her cup. "I'm usually very good at getting straight to the point, but today all backbone seems to have abandoned me. Oh, blast, I'll just get on with it." She looked directly at Maisie. "James had a chat with Lord Julian and myself on Sunday evening. He told me that he has a great affection for you, and that you are, in effect, a courting couple."

Maisie nodded. The lump in her throat prevented her from speaking.

"Of course, I will make no bones about it, my mother-in-law, the Dowager Lady Jane Compton, would have had you both sent to islands as far apart as possible, but times have changed. Not much, but they have changed, and Lord Julian and I, having lost a daughter, do not intend to lose a son. I have my concerns, but you have our blessing."

Maisie felt her color become flushed. "And what are your concerns, Lady Rowan?"

The older woman shook her head. "Not what you think. You are not an Enid, and you are not sixteen—James *was* sent away in a bid to stop that affair. Now I have my voice, I will be frank. My reticence has nothing to do with one's station in life, or your father's situation as my employee—in fact, as we both know, he is more of a trusted friend to whom I can have a good old chat about my horses. So, no, that's not it."

"But—"

"Let me finish." She sighed. "Maisie, in the course of the next year or so your life could change in ways you might never have imagined—in fact, that's true of us all, really." Another sigh. "The truth is, I believe you are very good for my son. I have seen something of the old James in recent days. I lost part of him when Emily died, and I lost a lot more during the war. Do you know he put on a gramophone record and had me dancing with him on Sunday? He hasn't done that in years. I have my son back and I don't want to lose him again. And I fear I will if your courtship comes to an end at a time when you are both deeply invested in the outcome. You are, after all, a very independent young woman, Maisie. Such accomplishments are not easily relinquished, and the obvious conclusion to an affair of the heart always requires compromise. I should not admit this, but I found it difficult myself. I was a most headstrong young woman, but my mountains were never as steep as yours."

Maisie was silent as she looked out of the window, her eyes following the snaking lines of traffic moving in and out of Piccadilly.

"Lady Rowan, do I take it that you are asking me to end my relationship with James sooner rather than later?"

"That seems awfully brutal, doesn't it? But it is close to the truth. If you can see some longevity to the liaison, then you have our blessing. There will be talk, but we are all adults, and frankly, there's more to worry about in this world. When you have endured tragedy, the things that seemed so important to the maintenance of a way of life do not have the same significance. Maurice knew that, which is why he dragged me off to the East End to see his first clinic for the poor—and I have been a supporter of his clinics ever since. But if it is not to be, if you are just testing the water with James, then I ask you to draw back. Release him. We might lose him for a while, but we won't have to see our son drowning in despair."

"I understand, Lady Rowan. Do not worry, I will do what is right and good."

"I knew I could trust your integrity, Maisie." She smiled. "Now, tell me about that friend of yours—Priscilla. She sounds so much fun—how are her boys?"

The two women exchanged news for a while longer, and discussed the health of Maurice Blanche. Maisie informed Lady Rowan that she would be driving down to Chelstone that evening, and was invited to tea the following day, should she remain at her father's house. Soon they both declared that time was marching on, and they should be on their way.

"It was lovely to see you, my dear." Lady Rowan pressed her hand to Maisie's shoulder and smiled as they bid each other farewell. "Know that I remain your greatest supporter."

Maisie walked to the street where she had parked, wondering whether her fledgling courtship with James really did have the blessing of his parents—if it was good and true. And she supposed that, because her life had changed so much over the years, then more of the same might be expected, and Lady Rowan was fearful of the impact of such changes on Maisie and, ultimately, her son. Such thoughts occupied her as she opened the door of her motor car and took her seat. But as she drove away, she recalled a scene from her past when, while working as a maid at Ebury Place, she watched from the threshold of a door left ajar as James and Lady Rowan danced together. James had returned to the London mansion following his aviator's training, just before being sent to France. He was wearing the uniform of a junior officer in the Royal Flying Corps and was singing at the top of his voice as he steered his mother around the floor.

He'd fly through the air with the greatest of ease,
That daring young man on the flying trapeze.
His movements were graceful, all girls he could please,
And my love he purloined away.

TWENTY

Maisie packed a few items of clothing into her leather case, together with a flask of tea for the journey, and set off in the MG. She would doubtless be stuck in London traffic, but would use her knowledge of the back streets to negotiate her way through the rush. She stopped at the telephone kiosk along the road from her flat and placed a telephone call to the Dorchester, asking to be put through to Dr. Charles Hayden.

"Maisie, what's going on? I knew you would call, but Teddy is trying to find out where Tommy's been taken. The consular people aren't being very helpful."

"I have some news. There have been two arrests today, one directly in connection with the death of Michael Clifton, and the attack on his parents."

"And Tommy's involved?"

"No, but his association with a known criminal came to light as part of the investigation. He became the pawn of a man with quite a degree of personal power. Let me explain—hold on a minute." She pressed more coins into the slot. "Charles, are you still there?"

"Yes, I'm here."

"Here's what happened. A man named Sydney Mullen was a member of Michael's cartography unit in France. He thought a lot of Michael, and they formed something of a friendship, to the point where Michael had even offered Mullen a job if he went to California. Mullen was wounded; if it hadn't been for Michael, he would have lost his life. In England once again, Mullen took up the threads of his former occupation, as a self-appointed go-between, putting various people in touch with each other based upon mutual need or want. Suffice it to say, some of these people weren't exactly the sort you'd want to mix with. He was involved with the man accused of killing Michael, and it is more than likely he perpetrated the attack on Mr. and Mrs. Clifton—I'll be able to explain more when I see you.

"But to your question regarding Thomas, at some point it appears that Mullen went out of his way to make a connection with him. Given his previous relationship with Michael, he knew there was a fortune out there that was Michael's. He'd seen sketches and maps drawn by Michael, who had told him about the oil and the value of his land. In short, Mullen wanted to keep his dream alive. I suspect that, initially, he'd heard about Thomas from Michael; men share confidences in the trenches they might never allow to pass their lips at home. Mullen made contact, possibly to see if there was a gain to be made. Soon he discovered Thomas Libbert's problem with money, that it slipped through his fingers with ease, that he wasn't quite the businessman he fancied himself to be, and on top of that he gambled—and lost—a lot of money." Maisie sighed, fatigue scratching at her eyes. "Mullen saw an opportunity to increase his personal value to a certain Alfred Mantle, a very powerful man who operates all sorts of nefarious businesses, and who is quite a dangerous character. In short, once introduced to Mantle by

Mullen—and I should add that Mantle may be a crook, but he can pass for a gentleman, and he is of some considerable wealth—Thomas took advantage of Mantle's banking service; he was a loan shark, among other things. Thomas went from being a victim to an accessory to crime when he began referring other similarly compromised associates to Mantle, men he knew were in trouble following a loss of common sense at the card tables or the races. That's why he's of extreme interest to the Flying Squad, the Scotland Yard department responsible for gangs, armed robberies, and what you might call organized crime. Frankly, Thomas was naive, and didn't know that he'd opened a Pandora's box of problems for himself."

She paused. "I should add that Mullen was murdered, and in all likelihood by the man who took Michael's life, and not Mr. Mantle, though anyone who has dealings with that man is playing fast and loose with his own life. Mantle bears something of a resemblance to Michael's killer; not in looks, as such, but because Mantle observed men of a certain type, their bearing, the way they dressed, and so on, and then emulated them. With that presence, he broadened his base of acceptance, and power." She coughed, the air in the telephone kiosk catching in her throat. "And Mullen was like one of those performers at the circus, the ones who balance a series of plates on the end of bamboo sticks, then try to keep them spinning. But when you're in the service of much more powerful men, it's you who could end up in a hundred pieces—not the plate."

There was silence on the line.

"Charles, are you there?"

She could hear breathing, but no voice. Another couple of seconds passed before Charles Hayden responded.

"I'm shocked, Maisie. Absolutely shocked at this turn of events. Had I realized the danger I placed you in by recommending you to—"

"The truth always finds a way into the light. Sometimes it takes years, and sometimes it leads us on a path into danger. This is my work, Charles, though I'm glad the risk part is over."

"Will you be coming to see Edward? He's been released to a room here at the Dorchester. A nurse is with him, and I have taken responsibility for his care. I know he is anxious for word from you."

"This news will tell him almost all he needs to know. I have to go down to Kent on a matter of some personal urgency, but I expect to be back in later in the day tomorrow. Might I be able to see him in the evening?"

"As long as it's not too late."

"No, it won't be late, Charles. I have something to give to him, something very important."

"Maisie—thank you. If anyone could see through this mess, I knew it would be you."

"I'm not quite finished yet, Charles."

"Of course. Tomorrow then?"

"Indeed. Tomorrow."

Maisie ended the call and left the telephone kiosk. And as she started the MG and pulled away into traffic, she spoke aloud to herself. "No. No, I'm not quite finished yet."

She ran directly to The Dower House after greeting her father upon arrival at Chelstone. Andrew Dene came to her side as soon as Maurice's housekeeper announced her arrival.

"That was quick!"

Maisie half smiled. "What do you mean?"

"I only telephoned James Compton an hour ago. I knew he could pull strings, but he got you here pretty quickly."

"But I—I haven't heard from James. I was awake all last night, I kept thinking of Maurice and decided to come as soon as my work was finished today." She reached for his hand. "Andrew . . . Andrew, please—"

Dene reached for her and took her in his arms. "He's going, Maisie. I am so very sorry, I know—"

He led the way to the conservatory, which had been set up with all the necessary accoutrements of care for the acutely ill invalid. Maisie went to Maurice's bedside.

"Maurice, it's me, Maisie. I'm here."

She grasped his hand and felt his bony fingers clasp hers.

"I knew you would come."

"I should have been here earlier, I should have come this morning."

He turned towards her, his movements slow, deliberate. She could see the cracked skin around his lips, and eyes that still seemed all-seeing, despite being sunken in paper-thin gray skin.

"No, you shouldn't. You would just have been sitting in silence listening to a rattle in the chest of an old man."

"But you're not old, Maurice, you're only—"

He began to laugh, but coughed instead. Maisie reached for the glass of water at his bedside, and lifted his head to enable him to drink. He settled back on the pillow and began to speak again.

"It's a strange phenomenon, that we always think of people as being the same age as they were when we first met them. It has not always been easy for me to see the accomplished woman before me now, because I tend to see a young girl so thirsty for knowledge that she would risk her livelihood."

Maisie nodded, unable to speak.

"Will you tell me about today? It was today, wasn't it, that you brought your case to a close?"

"Almost," she whispered.

"Almost?" He paused, coughed once, then looked at her again. "Ah, yes, there is always that final speck of dust to be cleared, isn't there? And it can be so elusive."

"That's how I expect it to be."

"Then tell me about the case, the outcome."

"But, Maurice, you're not well. Surely—"

"Let us talk, Maisie, as if we were sitting by the fire, you and I. It would not be fair of you to keep the dénouement from me. Imagine me as well, and please, go on."

Maisie felt hardly able to breathe, but she set forth the events of the day as if she were once again reporting to him, as she had in the days of her apprenticeship. When she brought the story to a close, Maurice, who had listened with closed eyes, nodded.

"You could not have hoped for a better conclusion, though the death of the man Mullen is regrettable. He seemed to be a most unlikely player in Whitting's game."

"He was one of those people who managed to get himself in a tangle that he just couldn't unravel," said Maisie. "He was a small-time crook who had found some sense of himself in the army, and discovered a skill in cartography. But it was difficult for him to find work after the war, and he still had the dream of a new beginning, which had been seeded by Michael Clifton. He'd seen Michael's drawings, his maps, and he thought he could still get there even after Michael was listed as missing." Maisie paused, wondering whether to cease her account. Maurice raised his hand for her to continue.

"I suspect Mullen had uncovered Whitting's connection to the Clifton name, and realized that, if they were in league, and in possession of documents of title, a will in favor of Whitting could be forged. A story of long-lost cousins finding each other on the battlefield would have been quite compelling. Whitting and Mullen sought to find Michael's wartime love, rightly assuming she might know something about the papers they needed. As time went on, Mullen became desperate—I am sure Whitting was putting pressure on him—so when Mullen went to the hotel room to see what he could find and was disturbed by the Cliftons, he panicked. Once the attack had taken place, he was a liability to Whitting. As we know, the Mullens of this world are opportunists, speculators of a type. He would have kept his contacts separate, so there would have been no blurring of gains from association with Whitting and Libbert, for example."

"And Libbert himself?"

"I don't think of Libbert as evil, as conniving as Whitting. I think he's a weak man, a man who was trying to be every bit as clever, witty, and accomplished as the Cliftons. He was married to Anna, but wanted to have something of that Clifton ease with each other and life itself. Yet I suspect everything he tried turned to dust in his fingers—yes, he worked for the family corporation, but any power was due to his wife's name rather than his ability. Probably if he and Anna had lived at some distance from her family, he could have been his own man."

"People who do not have the resources of character to draw upon are easy prey for the trickster—and they become lesser tricksters themselves."

"The family are strong, they will recover," said Maisie.

Maurice nodded. "And that final speck of dust?"

Maisie was quiet for several moments, during which Maurice turned to look at her again.

"There is no completely satisfactory conclusion. I have wondered if I should leave well enough alone," said Maisie.

"That path is always available to you."

"I know."

Maurice coughed again, his frail body seemingly racked with pain at each convulsion in his lungs. Maisie held a bowl to his mouth as Dene came to his side and supported him. She drenched a cloth in cold water from a bowl set to one side, and pressed it to his brow and neck.

He struggled to breathe for another moment, then lay back against the pillows as the coughing finally subsided.

"I'm not finished yet. There is more to say." Maurice's voice was barely more than a whisper.

Dene held Maurice's wrist to take his pulse, then listened to his chest with a stethoscope. He looked at Maisie and shook his head.

"Maurice, you need to rest now," said Maisie. "Close your eyes, and I will remain here at your side."

Again she felt the force of his will as he took her hand.

"No. Stay and listen. Sit and talk. Until I am dead, I am alive."

Dene and Maisie exchanged glances, before he nodded and left the room.

"Good." Maurice's voice reflected pain in his throat. "I love Andrew, he is a fine doctor—he was born a doctor. To my advantage, he fortunately remains a little scared of me."

Maisie half laughed. "I think he's scared of me, too."

"I don't doubt he is."

Maurice tried to laugh with her, but coughed once more before speaking again.

"Maisie, I would like us to talk about you."

"Oh, Maurice, I—"

"But *I* want to." He reached for her hand. "And at this time in my life, I will claim the last word on everything. Now, let us speak of the past and the future." His chest lifted as he struggled to take a longer breath. "I was not going to speak of this, but I want to now. I have decided it is only right and fair. I prepared a letter for you that is currently in the hands of my solicitor. It speaks of my regard for you and deepest respect for your many talents. I do not have the energy to say more, but it sets out my intentions for your future. It was presumptuous, I know, but I was your teacher, so I am asserting my claim on your ear when I have something to say. I want you to know that you can always say no to any request, any offer that comes your way, even if that offer has been instigated by me. There have been developments in the more personal aspects of your life, and those might run counter to any future offers of employment. I counsel you to consider your responsibility to your heart before you consider honoring my memory."

"Maurice, I don't know what you mean."

"You will."

"Oh, I do wish people wouldn't talk in riddles. I feel as if I am constantly at work."

Maurice coughed again.

"You must rest, please, Maurice," urged Maisie.

"Life is a riddle, my dear. It is filled with clues along the way, with messages we struggle to understand. You've been working on the case of a cartographer; you should know that all maps are drawn in hindsight. And hindsight, if interpreted with care, is what brings us wisdom. I simply wanted to be assured that you know you have a choice. You must not do anything simply because I have said you have the ability to take on my work."

Maisie could see the deep fatigue in his body, could feel his spirit begin to flag. He had spoken to her with an energy that reminded her of a river bearing down strong across rocks before it diminishes to a trickle and then runs dry.

"Maurice."

"Yes?"

"I have loved you as if you were my father, though that has never stopped me loving my father."

"I know. And you are as my daughter."

She squeezed his hand, and felt the light pressure of his fingers in return.

"And I think you should know that I am seeing James Compton."

With his eyes closed, the corners of Maurice's mouth lifted into a smile.

"He's been there a long time. I'm glad you're finally seeing him."

Maisie remained with Maurice. Andrew Dene joined her vigil, then left to go home to his wife, who was nearing the end of her term. As day's light faded, she was joined by Lady Rowan and Lord Julian, and by James, all of whom stayed for just a while, knowing there was little time left, and the bond between teacher and pupil was so deep that Maisie would not leave. Only her father waited with her, sitting in a chair by the window and nodding off as the night wore on. He would be there, come morning.

As the sun began to filter a red-gold light between the trees and crows cawed the dawn chorus into life to welcome a new day, Maurice breathed his last; not with the deep rattle of death in his throat, but with the ease of one who is sleeping too long. Maisie, her head resting on a corner of the bed, did not look up into his open eyes, but felt her own hot tears flood across the cold, still hand she held to her cheek.

Maisie remained at Chelstone for several days. She broke word of Maurice's death to Billy, who could barely believe the news.

"I know he was getting on, Miss, but I always thought he would pull through."

"We all hoped against the odds that he would."

Maisie's head was heavy with grief, as Billy understood too well.

"Don't you worry, Miss, I'll hold the fort. I'll see you when I see you, and rest assured, there's plenty for me to be getting on with here."

Caldwell extended his condolences and said that Detective Chief Inspector Stratton would doubtless be in touch, as would others from the Yard.

"He was well liked, here, was Dr. Blanche. He was one of the best to have at a murder, in his day. Told you what you needed to know to get on with your job after just a quick gander at the body—and he did it with manners. That's what I liked about him."

"Thank you, Inspector Caldwell. I'm glad he's remembered."

"Never forgotten. In any case, you just come in when you're back in London. We've got the confessions we needed, and we've enough to get going on without your account of the events leading up to Whitting's arrest."

Andrew Dene had arrived soon after Maisie summoned him. He issued the death certificate and completed the formalities pertaining to Maurice's passing, and remained with Maisie as arrangements were made for the undertaker to come to the house. Frankie Dobbs waited in the conservatory.

"He was a good man, Maisie. No side to him, no looking down his nose at the likes of me—and he was an important man, was Maurice. So, if it's all the same to everyone, I'll just sit here until they've taken him."

Maisie nodded, and went about her business. Lord Julian had already assumed the task of making the formal announcements, and when there seemed to be little for her to do, Maisie walked through the house to Maurice's study. To her surprise, there was a fire in the grate, so she took her place in the wing chair at the side of the hearth where she would sit to talk with Maurice. How many times had they been together in this room, going through strands of evidence in a given case, or—as Maurice often liked to do—speaking of Maisie's future?

There was a soft knock at the door, and the housekeeper entered, pushing a trolley. "It's gone lunchtime, so I thought I'd bring you a little something."

"That's very thoughtful of you. Thank you, Mrs. Bromley. Did you light the fire?"

"Yes, Miss Dobbs. I knew you'd want to come to his study, and I didn't want it all cold in here for you." She rolled the trolley so that it was adjacent to Maisie's chair.

"Oh—" Maisie saw that on the trolley was a decanter of single-malt whiskey, and one of sherry. A wedge of Stilton cheese was flanked by a fan of plain biscuits, and two plates, table napkins, and knives were set to one side. It was Maurice's favorite late-evening repast.

Mrs. Bromley poured a glass of sherry for Maisie, then passed the malt whiskey decanter to her. She smiled and poured a good measure into Maurice's crystal glass.

"Won't you have one with me? A toast to him?"

"I think I will, Miss Dobbs." The housekeeper reached down to the second tier of the trolley, brought out another sherry glass, and smiled.

Maisie stood up and clinked her glass with the housekeeper's, then they both reached to touch Maurice's glass with their own.

"I'll miss you, Maurice," said Maisie.

Mrs. Bromley pressed her lips together and nodded. "Yes, sir, Dr. Blanche. You'll be missed."

Maisie spent only a short time with James at Chelstone. Lady Rowan had known Maurice since girlhood, and though she was taking his loss in her stride, she wanted to be in close proximity to her husband and son. For her part, Maisie felt her emotions too close to the surface to spend long hours with James. A deep sadness lay across her heart like a heavy gray blanket, and was weighted by memories of the conversation over tea with Lady Rowan, which had unsettled her. She knew she had to consider not only her own feelings, but the vulnerability of a man who had been, as Maurice observed, "in crisis."

Before returning to London, Maisie placed a telephone call to the home of Ella Casterman, and once again the lady of the house was the first to answer.

"Ah, Miss Dobbs—may I call you Maisie?" She did not wait for a reply. "Maisie, yes, I would be delighted to see you. Do come for morning coffee on Tuesday. See you then."

Maisie replaced the receiver and finished packing the small leather case that was a gift from Andrew Dene, who had once hoped to marry her. The small room in her father's house had cocooned her since Maurice's death, and now she wondered how she would ever walk out into the garden without looking up the hill towards The Dower House in all its grandeur, and the conservatory where Maurice would take breakfast looking across the land. She supposed the house would be sold, and new people would move in—how would she bear hearing voices other than his in the rose garden? And what if they removed his precious roses altogether? After all, not everyone liked roses.

James came to the Groom's Cottage to see her off on her journey back to London.

"James, may I come to your office tomorrow? I need to collect the parcel I left in your safe."

"Of course. I've been as good as my word—your belongings are as safe as houses." He ran his fingers through his hair.

Maisie smiled. "I've been so busy since Maurice—"

He put his arms around her. "It's all right, Maisie. I understand. More than you think."

She nodded. "Thank you—I'll see you tomorrow then, about three o'clock?"

He held her to him, kissed her once on the cheek, and then drew back. "I'd better be going back to the house; it's my turn to get ready to drive back to town. Take care."

Maisie watched James Compton walk along the lane towards the drive up to Chelstone Manor, hands in pockets, shoulders stooped. She wasn't the only one grieving the loss of Maurice Blanche.

Clad in her black day dress, black shoes, and black cloche, Maisie felt as if she was standing out in stark relief as she entered the bright, golden morning tones of Ella Casterman's mansion.

"Lady Casterman is in her rooms, but has asked me to show you into the library," said the butler.

Maisie had always felt at home in a library. She loved walking past rows of books, reading titles, taking down a book that piqued her interest, and opening the pages. She had seen libraries where the books were hardly touched, the spines of every text cracking with an unopened newness. And there were other libraries where each book seemed to have been read time and time again. Ella Casterman kept Maisie waiting for some moments, giving her an opportunity to peruse the shelves upon shelves of books. Books on philosophy and history might well have been the choice of an earlier reader, for although well-thumbed, the stiff pages did not yield easily, so must have not been read for many a year. Novels had been read and re-read, as Maisie could see by the frayed edges of cover and pages, and torn dust jackets. She suspected the Casterman girls had been lovers of romance—perhaps a reading preference shared with their mother.

A section of books on explorers, on travel, on distant lands appeared to have been used with some frequency. A series of new acquisitions had been added, and when she looked around at the oak table in the center of the room, a cluster of books on geographical subjects were open at various pages, and a notebook set alongside them. She smiled. The explorer was Christopher Casterman.

Close to the window, which looked out to a garden resplendent with the colors of spring, Maisie found another well-used collection, and thought she had found Ella Casterman's true literary love—poetry. Maisie took down book after book, each one well thumbed, each one with slips of paper here and there noting a favorite line, a verse that touched the heart. It was when she found a shelf of books by Elizabeth Barrett Browning that she stopped. She ran her fingers along the spines of the books until she found the collection she was looking for. It came as no surprise that, as she took the book in her hands, it fell open to one page in particular.

THE BEST THING IN THE WORLD

What's the best thing in the world?
June-rose, by May-dew impearled;
Sweet south-wind, that means no rain;
Truth, not cruel to a friend;
Pleasure, not in haste to end . . .

"Ah, there you are. I am so sorry to keep you, but I was speaking with my daughter. All being well, I will be a grandmother before the week's end."

"Congratulations, Lady Casterman."

"Ella, please. Do call me Ella." She turned as the butler entered, carrying a tray with a coffeepot, hot milk jug, two cups, and some arrowroot biscuits. "Ah, just the ticket. Let's sit down, Maisie."

A few moments later the women were seated, each with a cup of coffee. Maisie had already placed the book of poetry on the table in front of her.

"I see you are a fellow reader. What have you found?" Ella Casterman set her cup on the low table and reached for the book. "I knew you would love Elizabeth—I have adored her poetry since I was a girl and feel that we are on Christian name terms."

"Yes, I can see that—you have quite a collection there," said Maisie.

"Here, let me read you one of my favorites." She turned the pages.

"Oh, I think I know which one it is." Maisie reached for the book. "May I?"

The poem was easy to find. Maisie held the book open as she faced Ella Casterman, and recited the verse.

"Ah, you were already familiar with her work." The woman blushed.

Maisie shook her head. "No, and—in truth—I think you know why I know this poem, Ella. I first discovered it written on a scrap of paper and tucked into the back of Michael Clifton's journal."

"I—I don't know what you're talking about. Do explain. Michael Clifton?"

Maisie set the book on the table, once more, then reached out and took her hostess' hand. "Please, Ella. I know. I know about your affair with Michael Clifton."

"I don't know what you're talking about." Ella Casterman stood up and began to pace. "This is really . . . really . . ." At once she bent over from the waist as if in pain, and the tears came so quickly that Maisie thought she might collapse and went to her aid.

"Come, please sit down," said Maisie, her voice soft.

The woman continued to weep for some moments, then sat back on the chesterfield.

"I thought you might find out the truth. As soon as I met you—it's your eyes, Maisie, they seem to just go right through a person."

"Ella, you've harbored this secret—and the fear that goes with it—for so long. Would you like to tell me about it?"

"Do I have your word that it will not go beyond these walls and this conversation?"

"I keep many secrets, Ella. It's part of my job."

She nodded, reached for her now-cool coffee, and took a few sips before placing the cup back on the tray.

"How did you meet Michael Clifton?" asked Maisie.

"I—I first saw him in Paris with one of my nurses. They seemed to be having so much fun together, so much joy. There wasn't much that was uplifting in the hospital, though of course everyone did their best to put on a sunny face for the wounded. But it seemed there was this frenetic desire among the young people, when they were away from it all, to just get out there and enjoy life for what it was—fleeting, at best. I did as much as I could for my nurses, you know, and I thought they should have some lightness when they were on leave. And as I told you before, I tried to ensure they didn't get themselves into any difficult situations."

Maisie nodded. "Of course."

"But . . ." She looked down at the handkerchief bundled in her hands. "I also harbored some envy. Oh, dear, I know that sounds just dreadful, and I really wasn't myself. You see, I was married when I was quite young, and my husband, my dear, precious husband, was so much older than I. It seemed of no concern for such a long time, and we had two beautiful daughters to whom we were both devoted. But time marched on, and we went through a troublesome interlude—or perhaps I should say that *I* went through the troublesome interlude."

Once again, Maisie did not offer any interruption, but leaned forward to pour more coffee for herself and Ella Casterman, who sighed, then went on.

"I was only thirty-six or so. I was as fit as a fiddle, had more energy than I knew what to do with, and I was married to a man who suddenly seemed so much older. He no longer wanted to be in company and seemed to retreat to his library or to his club on many occasions. My love for him had not waned, rather it had become . . . it's hard to explain, but it wanted for fresh air. *I* wanted a breath of fresh air."

As if to underline her words, she walked to the windows and opened them wide, returning to continue her story only when she had taken several deep breaths.

"I was very active with charitable work, and of course you know about my nursing unit. You could say my husband, not wanting for wealth, indulged me, though my work was always with the best of intentions. I went across to France as often as I could. I wanted to play as big a part as possible in the day-to-day running of the hospital, and I made a commitment to personally support my staff." She looked at Maisie as if to underline that she would not draw back from telling her story.

"It was by chance that I saw them. I had accompanied a small group to Paris on leave and stopped for a cup of coffee in one of those lovely cafés they have there—have you been to Paris, Miss Dobbs?"

Maisie nodded. "Yes. I love the city, it's quite beautiful."

"Then you know it has its own intoxicating qualities. I watched them, the young couple, and—oh, dear, I know this sounds quite awful—but I was at once envious. I wanted to know that young love, that . . . effervescence of the heart. You see, though I had been in love with my husband when we married, because he was much older, his love was more measured, not youthful. In truth, he wanted an heir, and I was of an age, but of course we had two girls." She reached for her coffee, sipped, and placed the cup on the tray. "Later I heard, through the unit's grapevine, that the girl—Elizabeth Peterson—had brought an end to the affair. Youthful exuberance followed by a fear of what might come around the corner. Very sad."

"Yes, I suppose it is."

Ella Casterman looked at Maisie, her head to one side. "Ah, you know."

"Yes, I know."

"I'd better finish my story, before I lose courage. When I returned to Paris, I made a point of staying in the same area. I went to the same cafés as I had before, and though I would not admit it to myself in the looking glass, I was hoping to bump into that young American. I imagined us sitting together over coffee with hot milk, dipping our croissants and laughing over shared jokes. It did not occur to me what I might do if the imaginings became real. But they did. I was at the café, the one where I had seen him with my young nurse, and there he was. But there was no joy in his face; in fact, he was absently stirring his coffee and staring at the cup. I went over, introduced myself, and sat at his table. He seemed happy to have company—he was clearly homesick. We talked and talked, and soon he confided that he had recently seen his brother-in-law, who had frequently caused him much concern over his financial dealings. I suggested I should treat him to supper that evening, to take his mind off unpalatable matters before he returned to his unit, and I to mine. Suffice it to say, I remained in Paris for several days, until it was time for him to leave. We were inseparable, and it was as if the years just melted away—friends had often said that I looked like my daughters' older sister, not their mother, and for once I felt like it. And my heart was lifted out of the mire of age that I was stuck in at home, and the terrible sadness of the war. We both knew it could not go on forever, though perhaps I knew that more than Michael; but there were intimacies shared that I would never have wanted my husband to know about."

Ella Casterman spoke with a calm forcefulness, as if to bolster her resolve and not draw back from the truth.

"Michael Clifton and I were lovers. I was some twelve years older than him and I was a married woman, but for four short days we knew love and we experienced the joys that come with a new deep attachment."

"Then?"

"When I was expecting my daughters, on both occasions I knew the very moment I was with child. The very moment. Shortly after leaving Michael I felt those same sensations within my whole body—and indeed, before more proof was needed, the usual indisposition followed. In short, I was as sick as a dog. As soon as I could, I returned home and assumed relations with my husband. Almost nine months later our son was born."

"Michael's son."

"Yes. Michael's son. Of that I have no doubt."

"And your husband never knew?"

"If he suspected, he never said."

"So the secret remains with you."

"As it will with you, Miss Dobbs."

Maisie nodded. "Michael's parents are in London. Let me tell you what has happened to them, and to their family since they last saw their son." She recounted the story of Michael Clifton's death and the subsequent events since discovery of his remains by a farmer in France.

"I had no idea he came from such wealth. And I never connected Clifton's Shoes with Michael Clifton. I mean, he spoke of his property in a valley in America, but I imagined a smallholding, a farm, that sort of thing."

"He loved land, loved exploring. Rather like Christopher, if that collection of books is anything to go by."

"Will you keep the secret, Maisie? I have much to protect. I have a son who is still more boy than man, and there is also the question of his inheritance."

"I will not reveal any details of our conversation; however, I do hope that one day Christopher might know more about the man who was his true father. I think Michael deserves such respect." Maisie reached into her bag. "Here you are—the address of Edward and Martha Clifton in Boston. They are getting on, especially Edward, and I think their years are numbered, especially following the attack. You must do what you feel is right."

The woman who had been Michael Clifton's lover took the piece of paper, folded it and placed it within the pages of Elizabeth Barrett Browning's poems. She turned to Maisie.

"Truth, not cruel to a friend."

TWENTY-ONE

It was Maurice who had taught Maisie that, following the closure of a case, it was important to ensure that she was at peace with her work, and that she had done all in her power to bring a conclusion to the assignment in a way that was just and kind. This process, known as her "final accounting," would also help to wipe clean the slate, so that lingering doubts might not hamper work on the next case.

With Maurice's funeral just one week away, Maisie wanted to complete her final accounting sooner rather than later. It was not only with regard to the case that she sought to bring peace to her heart, but to the most recent weeks in her life. So, following a visit to Scotland Yard, and the time spent making a statement in the presence of Detective Inspector Caldwell, her first stop was to see Edward Clifton in his room at The Dorchester Hotel.

Charles Hayden greeted Maisie in the foyer of the grand hotel.

"Maisie, how are you? I was so sorry to hear of Dr. Blanche's death—I never met the man, but from your letters, I knew of your affection for him."

"Thank you, Charles. It's been a very sad time for everyone who knew Maurice. I miss him so much already." She shook her head, as if to dislodge the painful thoughts that gathered at the mention of Maurice's name. "Anyway, I came to see Mr. Clifton—how is he?"

"Anxious to see you. I gave him as full an account of events as I could following your telephone call. He is so grateful to you, Maisie—as am I. I never thought you would find the man responsible for Michael's death, though I knew you'd find the woman who loved him. Anyway, Edward is waiting for us, and Teddy is with him."

She put her hand on his arm. "Before we go up—how is Mrs. Clifton?"

Hayden nodded. "Now that she's out of the woods, she's making progress every day. It will be slow—I'm trying to sort out a suitable place for her continued convalescence. Of course, she wants only to go home, but I am loath to give my blessing to the passage until she is completely well again."

"There are some lovely convalescent homes out in the countryside. I could have my assistant look into it for you."

"Would you?"

"Consider it done. Shall we go up now?"

Edward Clifton had insisted upon getting up from his bed, and now sat alongside a window in pajamas and dressing gown. He wore a dark blue cravat at this neck, and Maisie could not help but smile, for he reminded her of a certain type of English gentleman depicted in American films. His son, Teddy, sat in a chair opposite, and was dressed casually in gray trousers, shirt, and pullover. The table in front of them was set for coffee, and a selection of pastries had been served.

"Miss Dobbs. We've been anxious to see you." Teddy Clifton rose from his chair to greet Maisie, shaking her hand before steering her to his chair. He and Charles Hayden then pulled up chairs and the four were seated together.

"Charles tells me you're doing well, and that Mrs. Clifton is making good progress."

"According to Teddy, she complained when he visited her yesterday, so I consider that a good sign. Slowly but surely she's on the mend."

"I'm glad." Maisie looked at Teddy.

"Miss Dobbs, Charles gave us as many details as he could, but we'd like to hear the whole story, start to finish—frankly, I didn't even know I had a cousin called Peter Whitting. And needless to say, the whole family is shocked at what has happened to Tommy. Fortunately, my sister Meg is with Anna now—it's a boon we all live so close to each other."

"Even close families can grow apart, so it's not surprising that distance and time played a part in the fact that you had no knowledge of your cousin. Your home is a great distance from your father's place of birth."

"I blame myself. I was little more than a boy when I left, and I let them all go. When I arrived in the States, I wrote a few letters, but they were returned. Time passed, and with it any connection to my former life. My new family was all that mattered to me. Perhaps I should have tried harder."

"Do not blame yourself, Mr. Clifton. Many families have been divided by the distance of emigration, and it is usually left to subsequent generations to renew the blood ties, if at all."

"Miss Dobbs is right, Dad. You can't take all this on because you wanted something different from the life your father had dictated for you." Teddy turned to Maisie. "Please, tell us the whole story, from the time you began work on my parents' behalf."

Once again, Maisie recounted each milestone in her investigation, annotating here, cutting a detail there. She told them about the attack by Mullen, about viewing the cine films at a house in Notting Hill, and about her visits to Whitting, Temple, and Thomas Libbert. She described the help given by Priscilla, the fortuitous meeting with Ben Sutton, and gave only the briefest account of her visit to the home of Lady Ella Casterman. Finally, she told them about her meeting with Michael's young nurse, and Whitting's arrest. Then, opening her shoulder bag, she brought out the parcel that had been kept safe by James Compton.

"I think you will find everything here to lift the legal stalemate regarding Michael's property. There's a key and details of a bank, and as you will see from his notes, you will also be able to locate his original maps and the documents of title—we call them deeds—to the land he owned in the Santa Ynez Valley. His last will and testament are also mentioned with notes as to his final wishes, which are in favor of Anna's children. All papers are dated August 1914."

And as she passed the package to Edward Clifton and watched as his liver-spotted hands fingered the wrapping, she felt tears prickle the corners of her eyes, for at the mention of that place so far away she could see Michael's simple drawings in her mind's eye, and on a rainy day in London, could almost feel a breeze from the Pacific Ocean ripple across the hills and kiss her skin.

Edward Clifton sat with the package held tight in his hands and bowed his head. His eldest son reached forward, placing an arm around his shoulder.

"Dad," said Teddy. "It's Michael, come home to us."

Maisie cleared her throat. "Michael's relationship with the young woman came to an end before he was killed. I managed to open pages in both the letters and his journal that were fused, and it was clear they had considered war to be an inauspicious time to continue a courtship. She kept his belongings, which he had given to her for safekeeping, all these years in the hope that one day she might know how to find his family. She is not a worldly woman."

"We must write to thank her, Teddy," said Edward Clifton, before turning back to Maisie. He shrugged his shoulders. "Martha will be a bit disappointed. She had an idea in her head—I didn't say anything to you when we first met—but she had a notion that there might have been a child. It was a real bee in her bonnet, and it started in France. She said it had happened a lot, in the war, that war does things to people, makes them mad for each other when reason would suggest they exercise caution in their personal lives. You don't know her, she can be a terrier where family are concerned. I have to rein her in. As much as we agreed that our children have to find their way in the world and do as their hearts decree, she would have the whole tribe living in adjoining houses on Beacon Hill." He held the book to his chest, as if to touch his heart. "She kept saying that she just knew, so I'd better tell her that this time, she just didn't know. We have wonderful children and grandchildren, Miss Dobbs, and Teddy's boy is the image of Michael—isn't he, Teddy?"

"Right down to talking nonstop about the places he'll go when he leaves Harvard," said Teddy Clifton.

Maisie smiled. "What's his name?"

"Christopher—Chris to the family. Suits him—he's becoming a real Columbus!"

Maisie's next visit was to Elizabeth Peterson, who had remained at the home of her aunt and uncle, though Maisie assured her it was safe to return to her bed-sitting-room. The comfort of family and attendant companionship proved difficult to leave. The police had already taken a statement, and she was able to provide much-needed evidence with which to bring charges against Peter Whitting.

After each visit, Maisie fought the need to give in to the deep exhaustion that accompanied her sadness. There were only a few days until the funeral, and if she was to complete the final accounting before Maurice was laid to rest, there was much to accomplish. As each item was completed, she drew a line through the name and place listed on a sheet of paper, and went on to the next.

At the home and studio of Henry Gilbert, she assured him that his cine films would be returned, and committed to keeping in touch until they were once again in his possession. She almost ran into Ben Sutton as she left the house, and was relieved that he did not press her to accept an invitation to supper or the theater.

She visited the British Museum, where she did not ask to see books of poetry, but instead inquired if there were books that included photographs of California, in the United States. Several books were brought to her, and she read for an hour from *Under the Sky in California* by Charles Francis Saunders, imagining Michael Clifton poring over such a book before embarking upon his journey westward. She knew some words would remain with her for days.

> *Sauntering over these open mountains through miles and miles of chaparral—that sun-scorched tangle of sumac and manzanita, adestoma, islay and wild lilac, rarely above a man's head . . .*

Maisie waved to Mrs. Hancock and left the museum, bound for Selfridges, where she completed the simple task of walking through the shoe department.

Martha Clifton was asleep when Maisie called at the hospital, but she left flowers for her client, along with good wishes for her recovery and a timely return to her home in Boston. A letter of thanks was dispatched to Lady Ella Casterman, in which Maisie enclosed the small sheet of paper bearing the verse of Elizabeth Barrett Browning she'd given to a young American man with whom she had fallen in love. Tucked inside was the lock of her hair he had cherished enough to keep.

When her visits were complete, Maisie compiled her written report for Michael Clifton's parents, which she placed in a box along with a final statement of her charges and Michael's belongings previously entrusted to her. Before packing the journal, she lifted the leather cover once again and began to read.

I'm finally on the high seas bound for jolly old England. Dad wrote to me in New York to say I was out of my mind, that I didn't know what I was doing. He said war was something that old men get us into and young men rush into, and that if I had any sense at all I'd come home. Then he wired me to say that he and Mother loved me very much, that they were proud of me. He told me I was under orders to remember everything that happened to me so I'll have some good stories to tell around the tree at Christmas. So, here I go! Michael Clifton's Grand Adventure Over There, Part One . . .

She closed the journal and set it in the box to be delivered to Mr. and Mrs. Edward Clifton at The Dorchester Hotel.

There, I think it's all done now, Billy."

"Can we fold the map and put it away in the file then?"

"Yes. Seeing that table bare is always a bit of a dubious pleasure," said Maisie. "There's the joy of knowing the work's done, and the worry that another big case will never come in."

"We're always all right, though, aren't we, Miss?'

"A sizable job seems to present itself in the nick of time, and while we wait, there are always these little bits and pieces to be getting on with."

Billy walked across to the table by the window, where he unpinned the Clifton case map, folded it with care, and put it away. Maisie sighed and leaned back, wondering whether this was the right time to talk to Billy. She still could not put her finger on her reason for thinking that something was amiss, that there was a change about him, but she also knew that she was rarely wrong in her suspicions.

"How's Doreen, Billy? Did she get on all right at her checkup?"

"Fit as a fiddle. Dr. Masters is very pleased." He did not turn to reply to her question.

"Good. Yes, that's good news."

Still holding a folder in his hand, he came to Maisie's desk and stood before her.

"Why don't you sit down, Billy." She held out her hand to the empty chair and waited for him to speak.

"I can't keep a secret from you, Miss, never could. It's written all over my face, I know it."

"And I've known you for a while, so perhaps I see things that others mightn't."

"It's Doreen."

"Yes."

"She's in the family way."

"Oh, Billy! Billy—what lovely news. Congratulations!"

Billy pursed his lips, then broke into a smile. "I was worried, to tell you the truth, Miss, but I'm dead chuffed—we're both as pleased as punch. It's a bit of light for us, though as I said to Doreen, we've still got to get ourselves out of here, get over there to Canada. We've got a new nipper to think about as well as our boys, and we want the best for them." Billy's words seemed to tumble out as he spoke of his plans, thoughts, and concerns. "I mean, Doreen went off the idea of Canada, to tell you the truth. She didn't want to leave our little Lizzie cold in the ground without us around the corner, but now, with the new baby on the way, she wants the best, doesn't want to lose another one."

"Billy, how far along is she? When's the baby due?" Maisie tried not to convey her own concerns: Doreen's health was still so fragile, carrying the baby brought with it a risk of miscarriage or stillbirth.

"Reckon it'll be an October baby—she's about three months gone now." He blushed. "The doctor said we had to be careful, and I know she's not very happy about it, but it's not like we meant it to happen, and Doreen—"

Maisie reached out and placed her hand on his arm. "I am sure everything will be all right, Billy."

"I reckon so. Doreen's really perked up, though she's a bit off-color of a morning." He smiled again. "Well, this won't do, will it? I'd better get on with some work today. Cuppa tea?"

"I'd love one, Billy."

As he left the room with the tea tray, Maisie walked to the window to look out across Fitzroy Square. Daffodils nodded their golden heads in a light breeze, reminding Maisie of a column of excited schoolchildren in yellow uniforms. A few clouds scudded across the sky, and she thought there might be some rain before the day's end. Her heart was full with Billy's news, and with all that had happened in the past weeks. Maurice's funeral was just two days away and, in truth, she dreaded the moment when she would have to say a final good-bye.

The day of the funeral was bright but not too warm. Once again Maisie dressed in her black day dress, a black cloche, and black shoes, and longed for the day to be over. When they arrived at Chelstone village church, she could barely believe the number of people who had come to pay their respects. Among those she knew—Lord Julian, Lady Rowan, James Compton, Maurice's housekeeper, Billy Beale, Andrew Dene—were several men whom she recognized to be government ministers. Richard Stratton and Robert MacFarlane from Special Branch were there, wearing black armbands to signify they were mourners. She was somewhat surprised to see the famous pathologist Sir Bernard Spilsbury, along with various men and women of letters, some of whom she had met years ago, when she was Maurice's eager student.

As she moved towards the church with her arm linked through her father's, she felt a hand on her shoulder. It was Brian Huntley, whom she had met through Maurice almost two years before. He was with the Secret Service.

"Miss Dobbs. Allow me to express my condolences. He will be greatly missed."

"Yes, he will, Mr. Huntley. It was good of you to come today."

"He was a most trusted servant. I learned much from working for him." He cleared his throat, and lowered his voice to a whisper. "I am sure we will meet again soon, Miss Dobbs."

"I'm sorry, Mr. Huntley, I—"

Huntley gave a brief smile, and turned to enter the church.

"All right, love?" asked Frankie.

"Yes, Dad. Don't worry. It's time now—we'd better go in." She increased her hold on her father's arm as they followed the snake of black-clad mourners.

The service was simple and without ostentation, according to Maurice's last wishes, and following the round of prayers and hymns, he was laid to rest under the boughs of an oak tree in a far corner of the ancient churchyard. Maisie joined James and his parents to shake the hands of mourners, and was surprised when Lady Rowan insisted Maisie be first in line.

"He had no family, Maisie—I am sure he would have wanted you to stand for him."

She stood as instructed by Lady Rowan, and when her ankles and back began to ache, wanted nothing more than to go back to her father's house to rest in a comfortable armchair with her feet up. There would be no opportunity for such repose until after a reception with light fare for invited guests at The Dower House. For his part, Frankie Dobbs preferred to return home, and had already informed Maisie, "I'd rather sit in my kitchen and pay my respects to the old boy with my memories, if it's all the same to you."

She had been at the reception about an hour when guests began to depart, and she thought it would not seem too soon for her to take her leave. Part of her wanted to walk through The Dower House, for she had known the property intimately, having been but a girl when she lived there as companion to the old dowager in the months before she passed away. It was after her death that Maurice had purchased The Dower House, along with a substantial acreage of land that had belonged to the property when it was first built several centuries earlier. But it was too late to take that final look now. Maurice had gone and, like her father, she wanted to honor him with her memories. She bid farewell to several guests, and informed James Compton of her leaving. They'd had precious little time to speak in recent days, and Maisie was still smarting from her conversation with Lady Rowan.

"Would you let your mother and father know that I've left? I'd rather like to sneak out, if I may—I need some fresh air."

He took her hand. "May I see you tomorrow, before you leave?"

"Yes, of course. A walk across the fields would clear the cobwebs a bit."

"I couldn't tempt you onto a horse, could I?"

"Another time, James. I'd prefer to be on firm ground at the moment."

"All right. I'll telephone in the morning."

"See you then."

As Maisie turned away, a man dressed in a black pinstripe suit stopped her and held out his hand in greeting.

"Miss Dobbs? We haven't met. My name is Bernard Klein, and I am Dr. Maurice Blanche's solicitor. I do hope you weren't planning to leave."

"Actually, yes, I was. Is something wrong?"

"I have already spoken to Lord Julian and Lady Rowan, and to Dr.

Andrew Dene, as well as Dr. Blanche's housekeeper—I require your attendance at a short meeting to discuss Maurice's last will and testament."

"Oh well—it never occurred to me. Am I to be a witness to something?"

"No, not quite. Well, in a way, yes." He consulted his watch. "I have suggested we meet in about a quarter of an hour, in the dining room. There's a large table there for me to spread out some papers. I have two clerks waiting for us, and I've asked for tea to be served."

"Thank you, Mr. Klein—I know I could do with a cup." Maisie looked around the room. The last few guests were departing, so for a short time she feigned interest in a conversation between James and Andrew Dene about the latest motor cars on the market.

All too soon the house was quiet once more, and a small group comprising the Compton family, Andrew Dene, Mrs. Bromley, and Maisie filed into the dining room, where Bernard Klein stood at the head of the table, reading through a clutch of papers. He looked up over his half-moon spectacles and held out his hand towards the chairs set around a deep mahogany table. He did not speak until they were all seated.

"Ladies and gentlemen, thank you for convening here today at a time of great sadness. Maurice Blanche was a close friend to everyone around this table, including myself, so it is with heavy heart that I am now tasked with conveying the details of his last will and testament."

Maisie looked down at her lap. She supposed that Maurice might have left her a small bequest, and perhaps some books. It occurred to her that she had never even thought about such things. She had been so caught up with a desire for his recovery that all thoughts of his passing focused on how much she would miss him. Now she was sitting here at this table with his solicitor, she thought he might he have left her his papers—perhaps that was why Huntley wanted to see her.

The senior clerk handed one set of documents to Klein, and he studied them, pushing his spectacles higher on his nose. She suspected he knew the contents by heart, but needed to consider how he should frame his words to those who loved Maurice.

"First, I will deal with the issue of Dr. Blanche's clinics. It was his wish that the work continue as long as there is a need for such medical services. If that need should diminish—as you know, he believed that it is a weak country that does not take care of its own, and he hoped for developments in that regard—he has outlined plans for the closure of the clinics, with any funds remaining to form bequests to a series of charitable concerns listed in his instructions, which form a codicil to the will." He nodded to the junior clerk, who handed out a clutch of pinned papers to each person present. "As you will see, Dr. Andrew Dene is to be brought onto the Board of Governors, which will now be set on a firmer footing. Miss Dobbs will also join Lord Julian and Lady Rowan Compton and Viscount James Compton as members of the board. I will not go into the necessary details at this point, but suggest a board meeting within the week so that all parties can peruse my notes, and discussion can be embarked upon at a time when we are refreshed by time and rest. However, there is a bequest to Dr. Dene of two thousand pounds, in addition to an annual stipend in recognition of his work on behalf of the clinics—an amount of two hundred pounds per annum."

Maisie watched as Dene struggled to keep his composure, rubbing his jaw back and forth. He had come to Maurice's clinic as a boy with his very ill mother, who had subsequently died. Maurice had given him work, and when he realized the boy's innate talent for medicine, sponsored his education and his training in medical school. He was now an admired orthopedic surgeon.

"Dr. Dene, I am sure you have questions; however, at this juncture, you are free to leave. Thank you."

Dene bade his farewells and left the room.

Klein smiled at the housekeeper and explained that Maurice had provided excellent references, and she would be welcome to remain at The Dower House until the new owner took possession of the property, though he felt sure she could expect her service to continue. In addition, she would receive an annual pension which, if she wished, could take the form of a single bequest. He pointed out that the pension was a most generous one.

Mrs. Bromley was soon racked with sobs, so Maisie leaned across to soothe her. When she was given notice that she could leave, Maisie stood along with her to accompany her to the door.

"Miss Dobbs, I require your presence here. My clerk will see that the lady is looked after."

The junior clerk placed an arm around the housekeeper's shoulders and escorted her from the room, though her keening could still be heard through the closed door some moments later.

"Now then, almost there."

Maisie looked at the Compton family and hoped she would be free to leave soon. The air in the room seemed to press down on her, and she wanted nothing more than for the day to be over. If Maurice had left her a bequest in connection with the curatorship of his papers, hopefully Klein would get to it next, and she would be released from the meeting—she could hardly breathe.

"Finally, the estate." He again turned towards the senior clerk, who distributed several sheets of paper. "Miss Dobbs—Lord Julian and Lady Rowan will remain, as they are coexecutors of Maurice's last will and testament, and Viscount James Compton will have a future interest in decisions made regarding The Dower House, per Maurice's instructions. The following will serve to clarify."

Maisie at once felt as if she were on ground that was less than solid, yielding to her weight in a way she could not fathom.

"Now, you each have a listing of key assets, which form a not-inconsiderable estate. Dr. Blanche had no brothers or sisters, and was the son of parents who in turn had no siblings. Thus he had in earlier years inherited properties in France from his father, and significant wealth on his mother's side—she was, as you may know, the only daughter of Frederick MacLean, the shipbuilder."

Maisie's eyes widened as she realized how little she knew of Maurice's own parentage. Though Lady Rowan had known him from early years and had talked about her brother bringing his friend, Maurice, home from boarding school, Maisie could not imagine him as a boy.

"There are several properties in France, including a house in Paris under long-term lease to the British government—Maurice retained the upper apartments for use during his visits to the city. The land belonging to Item B on page two—a large château-type property in the Dordogne region currently leased to a diplomat—is worked by a local family of farmers. My firm liaises with Maurice's Paris lawyers to see that all monies collected from leases and agricultural profits contribute to the upkeep of those properties and residue used to support the clinics—I should add that there is also one in a poor area of Paris. Now, moving down the page, the property in Glasgow—it was his grandfather's home—is on indefinite loan to the university at no charge and is used to accommodate academic staff visiting from abroad. There are tax advantages to such an arrangement."

Klein reached for a glass of water and, over his spectacles, seemed to use the moment to take the measure of those seated before continuing.

"On the next page, you will see a complete inventory of the property known as The Dower House, including the house and gardens, plus two farms with long-standing tenant farmers, Mr. Arthur Lodge and Mr. Cecil Button. The acreage is given, along with terms etc., etc. Dr.

Blanche's instructions are as follows." Again he peered over his glasses at the listeners in turn, but focused his attention upon Maisie as he went on, barely consulting his notes.

"All properties in France, Scotland, and England, together with monies held in investment and bank accounts, I leave to Miss Maisie Dobbs, my daughter in kind, if not in name. Should Miss Dobbs see fit to sell The Dower House, the property should first be offered to Lord Julian Compton, and if he predeceases such divestment, to Viscount James Compton, so that, if desired, it may once again become part of the Chelstone Manor Estate."

He smiled at Maisie. "I should add that there are no mortgages attached to any of the properties listed, which were owned in their entirety by Dr. Blanche. I am sure you would like clarification on multiple points; however, before you and I continue speaking alone, is there anything regarding the foregoing that you wish to discuss in the company of Lord Julian and Lady Rowan, specifically, Maurice's stipulation pertaining to a future possible sale of The Dower House?"

Maisie stood up, only vaguely aware that her knees were shaking. "If you don't mind, I think I might need some fresh air."

James Compton was already standing, and caught her as she collapsed.

When Maisie opened her eyes, her first thought was that she was in her room at her father's cottage. She closed them again when she realized that she was still in The Dower House, resting in the guest room she'd occupied long ago when she first came to live in the house. Mrs. Bromley was by her side, and leaned over to press a cold, damp cloth to her forehead.

"How are you feeling, mu'um?"

Maisie shook her head. “Please don’t call me that, Mrs. Bromley. You’ve always called me Miss Dobbs—don’t change now.”

“You took quite a turn there. The viscount carried you up the stairs—he’s down in the drawing room. Lady Rowan was very worried, and will want to know you’ve come around.”

“I—I think I’ve been imagining things.”

The housekeeper shook her head. “No, you haven’t, Miss Dobbs. Dr. Blanche was a dark horse—you of all people knew that. But he loved you as if you were his own, and I know he told you as much. So he left you what he would leave to a daughter—and he’s done right by you.”

Maisie sat up on the bed and took the glass of water offered. “I’d better go downstairs and show my face. I’m so embarrassed at having fainted.”

Mrs. Bromley took an envelope from her pocket. “Mr. Klein gave me strict instructions to give this to you straightaway, as soon as you were well enough. He said he would telephone tomorrow to make an appointment to come to the house again—he said there’s a lot of things to talk about.”

“It’s a letter from Maurice.”

Mrs. Bromley stood up and opened the door to leave. “You take your time, Miss Dobbs. I’ll make tea for everyone downstairs. I baked some Eccles cakes for you this morning—I know they’re your favorites.”

Maisie smiled and expressed thanks at such thoughtfulness, and when the door closed and she was on her own, she slipped her finger under the flap of the envelope, and removed Maurice’s letter. It was a letter she would read time and again in the weeks and months that followed.

EPILOGUE

Maisie sat on the floor in The Dower House conservatory with sun streaming through the glass panes. She was surrounded by a series of boxes, each clearly marked in Maurice's flowing script, with the year cataloged and a description of the contents, be it letters, reports, or case files. Several weeks had passed since the funeral, weeks in which she had felt as if she might flounder. It was clear to her, now, why Lady Rowan had shown such concern, and why she had intimated that Maisie's life would change, though Maisie herself was pleased with the many ways it had not changed, thus far.

Knowing she needed time to absorb all that had come to pass, she had taken a week of leave from work and instructed Billy to come into the office only to gather the post and be in touch with potential new clients, though otherwise he should consider the time his own. She did not bring him into her confidence regarding the bequest from Maurice, for she considered the matter to be one that required utmost privacy on her part, at least until she had assimilated all that it meant to her life. She had yet to spend a night at The Dower House, preferring to sleep in her father's cottage, or if there were meetings with Maurice's solicitors—who now acted on her behalf—she welcomed the spartan surroundings of her own flat. In any case, The Dower House was being prepared for the arrival of Edward and Martha Clifton, who would spend four or five weeks at the country home so that Mrs. Clifton might convalesce before returning to Boston.

She had begun to read, again, the letter written by Maurice and lodged with his solicitors before he died. He wrote of his recollections of their early days together as teacher and pupil, days when she supped eagerly from the table of learning he laid out before her. He spoke of his pride at her acceptance to Girton, and his deep respect for her when she gave up her studies to enlist for nursing service in the war. He confided that he had always known she would become his assistant, that they would work together, for he could think of no other student who would best take on the legacy of his life's calling. His reflections became more serious when he looked to the future.

> *We have spoken on many an occasion, you and I, of the darkness I fear will envelop Europe once again. You will find in my archive of papers much that will help you in the years to come, for you will be called to service as I was prior to and during the last war. My work in this realm continued until recent months, as you learned when we were in Paris together not two years ago. I believe you are ready and suited to any challenges that come your way, and I predict that they will be the making of you. I have observed your work in recent years and, in my estimation, it does not claim the full measure of your skill or intellect. In time there will be a new path for you to follow. It will not be an easy one, but one for which you are supremely suited. I will say no more on this subject, save that you have received my highest commendations and I have great faith in your ability to assume challenges that stand between you and the quest for what is right and true.*

The letter continued with advice regarding her communications with Bernard Klein, and his recollections of each of his properties and their individual significance in his life.

I leave my estate in your good hands, Maisie, not only because I know you will comport yourself with excellence in the face of such a change in circumstance, but because you deserve all that I have to leave to you.

Now, having come to the end of the letter, Maisie folded the pages and placed the envelope in her cardigan pocket. She remembered Maurice's words regarding his letter, that if her personal situation should change, she must not feel beholden to follow his hopes for her to their conclusion. Now at least part of the riddle had been made clear, and in going through each box with care, she was slowly but surely preparing herself for what might come.

She stood up and walked to the windows to look out across the land. Her land. Though she had visited Maurice many times over the years, she realized that she had never really spent time looking out of the conservatory windows—her attention had always been on Maurice, on his counsel, his opinions, news, and ideas. Now she could see why he loved the room so much, for as he had described to her, from this vantage point he could see for miles. To the right the carriage sweep snaked past the boundary of The Dower House gardens, and she could follow it with her eyes along to the main entrance of Chelstone Manor. The lane that branched off to her father's cottage was in clear view, as was the cottage itself and gardens to the rear, which adjoined the bottom edge of Maurice's rose garden. She could see—as Maurice could in his day—the gate that led from her father's garden up towards the conservatory, and another gate at the bottom of her father's garden opening out into one of several fields that surrounded both their homes. Her gaze followed the path down to the woods, and across to the land rising up on the other side, where sheep were grazing in the late morning light.

And as she closed her eyes, allowing the warmth of sunshine on glass to envelop her, she thought of Michael Clifton and how he yearned to return to his land, how he ached to rid himself of dark, cold days on the battlefields of France, so far from home. She realized that, in his letters over the years, in his teachings, and in the many pages she would read in the days, weeks, months, and years to come, Maurice would continue to be her guide as she negotiated new terrain. He would not be lost to her forever, and in his own way he had left her with a compass, octant, waywiser, and theodolite, the tools she would need to face a new horizon.

A cawing of rooks giving chase to a predatory kestrel caused Maisie to open her eyes. She smiled as a whole parliament of the black crows rose up from the trees and gave chase, and as she followed them, her attention was drawn to James Compton, making his way across the field towards the Groom's Cottage. She watched as he came through the gate at the end of the garden, where he stopped to talk to Frankie, who was tending his vegetables. Frankie turned and pointed to The Dower House, and they exchanged a few more words before James walked on, up the path towards the conservatory. He saw Maisie watching him and raised his hand. She waved in return.

Love, when, so, you're loved again.

ACKNOWLEDGMENTS

Thanks must go to Holly Rose for once again being my trusted first reader—what would I do without your highlighter, Hol?

Maureen Murdock kindly allowed me to use the term "wound agape" from her wonderful book *The Heroine's Journey*. Thank you so much, Maureen.

For the term "artillery's astrologers," I must acknowledge Peter Chasseaud's definitive book on the subject of cartographers in the Great War, *Artillery's Astrologers: A History of British Survey and Mapping on the Western Front, 1914–1918*. The book represents extraordinary scholarship in a field crucial to understanding the war, and greatly increased my knowledge of the work of the cartography units.

The California Oil Museum, based in the original headquarters of the Union Oil Company in Santa Paula, California, proved to be a wonderful resource in my research into early exploitation of the state's black gold.

Deepest gratitude to my editor, Jennifer Barth at HarperCollins. Thank you, Jennifer, working with you is such a joy. You always manage to raise the bar while trusting the author's judgment—it's a gift.

To my agent, Amy Rennert—thank you, as always, Amy, for your sound counsel, your integrity, and your support. Most of all, thank you so much for these years of friendship.

And to John Morell—thanks for putting up with me, and those books and maps all over the floor.

Insights,
Interviews
& More . . .

Alexander McCall Smith Talks with Jacqueline Winspear

This interview was conducted by Alexander McCall Smith and originally appeared on Amazon.com.

Alexander McCall Smith: *Characters, once created, have a way of staying on. Maisie is an attractive character—when did she say to you: "I want a series"?*

Jacqueline Winspear: As I was writing the first novel in the series, *Maisie Dobbs*, I realized that scenes and ideas were coming to me that were not part of the book. I started keeping notes on those other scenes, passages of dialogue and so on, and when I had finished *Maisie Dobbs*, I went through those notes and realized I had rough plans for another five or six books. Indeed, as I was writing the second book in the series, *Birds of a Feather*, I really had to push any thoughts of the intended third novel from my mind, so strong were the images for *Pardonable Lies* that kept popping into my mind's eye. I had to be very disciplined not to be distracted by those images—it was rather like being nagged by one's own characters.

Smith: *Maisie Dobbs is firmly placed in the past. Would you be comfortable writing about contemporary Britain?*

Winspear: That's a very good question, and indeed, I have a more contemporary novel on the proverbial back burner. However, although I visit my parents in Sussex several times each year, for me there is a certain detachment from everyday life in the UK. I am not as familiar with various aspects of life there, so it might be difficult to get that ring of authenticity. On the other hand, one could argue that the lack of transparency could act in my favor, because I now take notice of so many things that might have passed me by. I believe one of the reasons I am so comfortable writing about the past is that when I was a child we lived in a small hamlet with very few children, so it was a world of adults, many of them elderly, and all of them ready to tell a story of their own youth.

I have always been drawn to the past through family history, a curiosity that has its roots in my grandfather's experience in the Great War—he was wounded and shell-shocked at the Battle of the Somme in 1916. Even as a very young child I understood the extent of his suffering and struggled to fathom how something so terrible could happen to a beloved grandparent. And I am sure my interest in the women of that generation—the first generation of women to go to war in modern times—is rooted in memories of the ladies of a certain age who lived in our neighborhood as I was growing up. They were typical of that generation, very independent women who had remained single due to circumstance, for the men they might have married had been lost to war.

So, to the question of writing about contemporary Britain—I think I'll find out more about my level of comfort with modern times when I pull that contemporary novel off the back burner. In the meantime, there's so much that I want to explore from the past, though when I immerse myself in the preparatory research for my books, I am always reminded of the old adage: "History repeats itself."

"When I immerse myself in the preparatory research for my books, I am always reminded of the old adage: 'History repeats itself.'"

Smith: *You and I both started as novelists rather later than is perhaps usual. Is that a good thing or a bad thing?*

Winspear: When I was sixteen I rather precociously announced that I would write my first novel by the time I was thirty—it seemed such a formidable age of adulthood, ▶

Alexander McCall Smith Talks with Jacqueline Winspear *(continued)*

I suppose. Of course, thirty came and went with no novel to show for it, and in the meantime I was becoming more and more interested in nonfiction writing. I was in my late thirties by the time I made a real commitment to getting my work published, and I concentrated more on essays, articles, and other creative nonfiction. I believe my writing at that time represented something of an apprenticeship in that I was really working at the craft of writing, of building my understanding of framing a scene, of bringing the reader along with metaphor, and with developing scenes that were something like the literary equivalent of a zoom lens on the camera; I was trying to find out what worked in terms of drawing the reader in and placing them at the center of the action. Though I had no plans to write a novel until the idea for Maisie Dobbs actually came to me, upon reflection it seems as if I had been preparing for the task with my literary cross-training in the same way that an athlete prepares for the big event.

I believe the journey to becoming a writer is one that is very personal to the individual and is neither good or bad—it's just what it is. There are times when I think it would have been so much more fun to have started writing fiction earlier, but had that happened, the stars might not have aligned to bring the character of Maisie Dobbs into my life. And I think that in embarking upon being novelists in our middle years, we've probably both brought something to our work that we might not have been able to offer in younger days, either due to other responsibilities, or simply who we were at the time (though having said that, I am sure your readers wish the wonderful Precious Ramotswe had been created many years before you decided to write *The No. 1 Ladies' Detective Agency*!).

“In embarking upon being novelists in our middle years, we've probably both brought something to our work that we might not have been able to offer in younger days.”

Smith: *Have you written anything about Maisie that you would like to unwrite?*

Winspear: No, not at all, although I should add that I have never gone back and reread any of my books, a prospect I find rather daunting. Of course, I dip back into the books to check a point here and there, but I have never read the books from beginning to end—if I had done so, I might have a whole list of things that cause me to shudder.

Smith: *Do you think that transplanting oneself—in your case from the UK to California—helps one as a writer?*

Winspear: Another very good question! Many years ago, during a visit to New York, I went along to an exhibit at the main branch of the New York Public Library on Fifth Avenue—it was called "Writers in Exile." The focus was on writers who lived in a place other than the land of their birth, "by will, or by compunction." I spent ages going around the exhibit taking copious notes, and remember it left me with a real sense of the power of being transplanted, whether by one's own choice or by circumstance, and I have to say, I often think of it when people ask me if being here in California contributes to my work as a writer—and it does. To give an example, I can immerse myself in the time and place about which I write—Britain from the Great War on up to the 1930s—and I am not distracted by British life as it is today. Yes, of course, there is contemporary life here in California, but it is different (the way people speak, interact, shop, travel, work, etc.) so I can draw a firm line between life here and the world about which I write.

I should confess that one of my recent challenges came when I started writing *The* ▶

" I have never gone back and reread any of my books, a prospect I find rather daunting. "

Alexander McCall Smith Talks with Jacqueline Winspear ***(continued)***

Mapping of Love and Death. The opening is set in California in 1914, so I had to ensure that my knowledge of that region today did not seep into the story. To that end I immersed myself in old books about the region, and managed to procure some vintage photographs to pin on the wall so that the past was very much with me as I wrote.

When I write, the time and place of my imagination becomes very distilled, very sharp in my mind's eye. In terms of the series featuring Maisie Dobbs, it has definitely helped to be living here; when I sit down at my desk to write, I step from my world into her world, and I'm aware of nothing else until I stop writing. And when I drag myself back from a morning spent in the smog-enveloped London of the 1930s, it's not bad to be able to walk outside into the garden and warm my bones in the California sun for a while.

The Story Behind *The Mapping of Love and Death*

VISITING THE WORLD WAR I battlefields of the Somme and Ypres is a very moving experience. The landscape still bears the scars of the miles upon miles of trenches from which hundreds of thousands of men went "over the top" into no man's land—and, for many, certain death. I have visited many cemeteries in this region of France, reading the names on the markers and stopping often to wonder about those young men who were buried with no name, soldiers unidentified in the aftermath of battle. For them the marker reads, "A Soldier of the Great War, Known Unto God." At the same time, I have read the endless lists of the missing at the Menin Gate in Ypres, at Vimy, and at Thiepval. Where did they fall, these young men who were never found? I knew that one day I would write about the Great War's missing, but until 2005 I wasn't quite sure how I might shape that story and incorporate it into the series featuring Maisie Dobbs.

It was in 2005 that I saw a letter published in the *Santa Barbara Independent* newspaper that intrigued me. The writer, David Bartlett, is a British man and an expert on the region who is also deeply involved in identifying the remains of British soldiers. He had been called in to help identify the recently discovered remains of a young man who had been serving with a British regiment. Among his possessions were a collection of rather expensive colored pens and a wallet with the name of a bank embossed into the leather—it was the Central Bank of Santa Barbara. Now, of course, the man could have been given the wallet, could have won it playing cards or obtained it by other means—but there was always the chance that he had been in California ▸

"I knew that one day I would write about the Great War's missing, but until 2005 I wasn't quite sure how I might shape that story and incorporate it into the series featuring Maisie Dobbs."

The Story Behind *The Mapping of Love and Death* *(continued)*

before the war. Was he an Englishman who had followed his dream to come to America? Might he have been an American who had, perhaps, lied to enlist in the British army?

I thought long and hard about the young man and suspected he might have been a cartographer—those pens must have been used for something. He might have been a journalist, or an artist. The story led me to create Michael Clifton, a young American who, in August 1914, goes to the land of his father to fight for the old country in her hour of need. Of course, he expects to be home by Christmas, for surely the war would have been brought to an end by then. But the war doesn't end, and Michael will never see America again.

An Excerpt from the Next Maisie Dobbs Mystery

Read on for an excerpt from A Lesson in Secrets *by Jacqueline Winspear. Available in hardcover in April 2011 from HarperCollins Publishers.*

Prologue

Maisie Dobbs had been aware of the motor car following her for some time. She contemplated the vehicle, the way in which the driver remained far enough away to avoid detection—or so he thought—and yet close enough not to lose her. Occasionally another motor car would slip between them, but the driver of the black saloon would allow no more than one other car to narrow his view of her crimson MG 14/40. She had noticed the vehicle even before she left the village of Chelstone, but to be fair, almost without conscious thought, she was looking out for it. She had been followed—either on foot, on the underground railway, or by motor vehicle—for over a week now and was waiting for some move to be made by the occupants. This morning, though, as she drove back to London, her mood was not as settled as she might have liked, and the cause of her frustration—indeed, irritation—was not the men who followed her but her father.

Maisie was now a woman with a good measure of financial independence, having inherited wealth in the form of a considerable property portfolio as well as investments and cash from her late mentor, Dr. Maurice Blanche. To the outside observer, the windfall had not changed her character, or her attachment to her work; but those who knew her best could see that it had bestowed upon her a newfound confidence, along with a responsibility she felt to Blanche's memory. Dust was settling on the events of his death, ▸

“To the outside observer, the windfall had not changed her character, or her attachment to her work; but those who knew [Maisie] best could see that it had bestowed upon her a newfound confidence.”

An Excerpt from the Next Maisie Dobbs Mystery ***(continued)***

and as she moved through the grief of his passing to acceptance of her loss in the process of going through Blanche's personal papers, Maisie wanted—possibly more than anything—to see her father retired, resting, and living at the Dower House. She had not been prepared for her plans to be at odds with his own, and this morning's conversation, over tea at the kitchen table in the Groom's Cottage, capped several months of similar exchanges.

"Dad, you've worked hard all your life, you deserve something better. Come and live at the Dower House. Look, I'm away throughout the week in London, so it's not as if we'll get under each other's feet. I don't see how we could do that anyway—it's a big enough house."

"Maisie, we've always rubbed along well together, you and me. We could be in this cottage and live happily enough. You're my own flesh and blood. But this is *my* home—Her Ladyship has always said as much, that this house is mine until the day I die. And I'm not ready to hang up my boots to sit in an armchair and wait for that day to come."

Frankie Dobbs was now in his early seventies, and though he had suffered a debilitating fall several years earlier, he was in good health once again, if perhaps not quite as light on his feet. His role as Head Groom—a job that came with the tied cottage—now chiefly comprised advising Lady Rowan Compton on purchases to expand her string of racehorses, along with overseeing the stable of hunters at Chelstone, the Comptons' country seat.

"Well, what about not giving up work and just moving into the Dower House? Mrs. Bromley will take care of you—she's such a good cook, every bit as good as—"

Frankie set down his mug with a thump that made Maisie start. "I can do for myself, Maisie." He sighed. "Look, I'm happy for you, love, really I am. The old boy did well by you, and you deserve all that came to you. But I want to stay in my home, and I want to do my work, and I want to go on like I've been going on without any Mrs. Bromley putting food on the table for me. Now then . . ."

Maisie stood up and walked to the kitchen sink. She rinsed her mug while looking out of the window and across the garden. "Dad, I hate to say this, but you're being stubborn."

"Well then, all I can say is that you know where you get it from, don't you?"

They had parted on good enough terms, with Frankie giving his usual warnings for her to mind how she drove that motor car and Maisie reminding him to take care. But as she replayed the conversation in her mind—along with those other conversations that had come to nought—she felt her heels dig in when she looked at the vehicle on her tail. She was damned if she would put up with some amateur following her for much longer.

She wound down the window and gave a hand signal to indicate that she was pulling over to the side of the road, thus allowing an Austin Seven behind to pass, followed by the motor car that had been shadowing her for at least half an hour. As soon as they passed, she turned back onto the road again and began to drive as close to the vehicle in front as safety would allow.

"Now you know I know. Let's see what you do with it."

She noted that there was no number plate on the black motor car, and no other distinguishing marks. Both driver and passenger were wearing hats, and as their silhouettes moved, she could see the passenger looking back every so often. When they turned left, she turned left, and when they turned right, she followed. Soon they were back on the main road again, traveling up River Hill ▸

“'Dad, I hate to say this, but you're being stubborn,' 'Well, then, all I can say is that you know where you get it from, don't you?'”

An Excerpt from the Next Maisie Dobbs Mystery ***(continued)***

towards Sevenoaks. At the top, the Royal Automobile Club had stationed two men with water cans, ready to help motorists having trouble with overheated vehicles. It was a long hill, and on a hot day in August, many a steaming motor car lurched and rumbled its way to the brow, with the driver as glad to see men from the RAC as a thirsty traveler might reach out toward an oasis in the desert. Allowing the black motor car to continue—she thought it was an Armstrong Siddeley—Maisie pulled in alongside the RAC motorbike and sidecar.

"Having a bit of trouble, love?"

"Not yet, but I thought I might get the water checked. It's a hot day."

The man glanced down to the radiator grille and nodded when he saw the distinctive silver RAC badge with the Union Jack below the King's Crown.

"Right you are, miss. Don't want to risk burning up a nice little runner like this, do you?"

Maisie smiled while keeping an eye on the road. Soon the Armstrong Siddeley approached the hill again, this time from the opposite direction, and as it passed, both driver and passenger made a point of looking straight ahead. *Police*, thought Maisie, sure of her assessment. *I'm being followed by the police.*

"She didn't need much, but just as well you stopped," said the RAC man. "Can't be too careful, not with this weather."

"Thank you, sir." She reached into her shoulder bag for her purse and took out a few coins. "I wonder, could you do me a favor? A black Armstrong Siddeley will presently be coming back up the hill; he's probably turning around at this moment. Could you pull it over for me?"

The man frowned, then smiled as he took the coins and looked in the direction

"*Police*, thought Maisie, sure of her assessment. *I'm being followed by the police.*"

Maisie indicated. "Is this the one, coming along now?"

"Yes, that's it."

Maisie thought the man looked quite the authority as he stepped forward into the middle of the road in his blue uniform and peaked cap. He held up his hand as if he were a guard at a border crossing. The Armstrong Siddeley came to a halt, and Maisie stepped forward and tapped on the window. After a second or two, the driver wound down the window, and Maisie leaned forward just enough to appear friendly, smiling as she affected a cut-glass aristocratic tone.

"Gentlemen, how lovely of you to stop when you must be so terribly busy." Her smile broadened. "Would it be too boring of me to ask why you've been following me? I think it might save on petrol and your time to explain your actions. After all, it's been over a week now, hasn't it?"

The men exchanged glances, and the driver cleared his throat as he moved his hand toward his jacket pocket. Maisie reached forward and put her forefinger on his wrist. "Oh, please, don't ruin a perfectly cordial conversation. Allow me."

She reached into the man's jacket, took out his wallet and smiled again. "Can't be too careful, can we?" The man blushed as she opened the wallet and removed a warrant card. "Charles Wickham. Ah, I see. So you must be working for Robert MacFarlane. Oh dear, I think you're going to get into horrible trouble when he finds out I've seen you." She tapped the wallet against the fingers of her left hand before offering it to its owner. "Tell you what. Inform Detective Chief Superintendent MacFarlane that I'll be at the Yard this afternoon at—let me see—about three o'clock. He can tell me then what this is all about. All right?" ▶

“She reached into the man's jacket, took out his wallet and smiled again. 'Can't be too careful, can we?' The man blushed as she opened the wallet and removed a warrant card.”

An Excerpt from the Next Maisie Dobbs Mystery *(continued)*

The driver nodded as he reclaimed his wallet. To her surprise, neither man had spoken, though there was little they could say. There would be plenty for them to talk about when they were summoned to explain themselves to Robert MacFarlane.

Maisie and the RAC man watched as the black motor car went on its way towards Sevenoaks and London.

"Funny pair, them."

"They'll be even funnier when their boss hears about this."

Maisie waved to the man as she pulled out onto the road again. She was deep in thought for much of the time, to the extent that, when she reached the outskirts of the capital, she could barely remember passing landmarks along the way. Though she had kept the exchange light, she had cause for concern given that the men were reporting to Detective Chief Superintendent Robert MacFarlane of Special Branch. She had worked alongside him at the turn of the year on a case involving a man who had threatened death on a scale of some magnitude. At the close of the case, she hoped never to have to encounter such terror again. But now she suspected that MacFarlane had deliberately sent a pair of neophytes to follow her, and therefore subsequently expected her call. She shook her head. She was not in the mood for Robert MacFarlane's games. After all, Maisie Dobbs was her father's daughter, and any sort of manipulation did not sit well with her.

Don't miss the next book by your favorite author. Sign up now for AuthorTracker by visiting www.AuthorTracker.com.